FIERCE
DREAMER

ALSO BY LINDA LAFFERTY

The Bloodletter's Daughter

The Drowning Guard

House of Bathory

The Shepherdess of Siena

The Girl Who Fought Napoleon

Light in the Shadows (with Andy Stone)

FIERCE DREAMER

A NOVEL

LINDA LAFFERTY

LAKE UNION
PUBLISHING

Text copyright © 2020 by Linda Lafferty
All rights reserved.

Published by Lake Union Publishing, Seattle

www.apub.com

Amazon, the Amazon logo, and Lake Union Publishing are trademarks of Amazon.com, Inc., or its affiliates.

ISBN-13: 9781542017626

ISBN-10: 1542017629

Cover design by Faceout Studio, Jeff Miller

Printed in the United States of America

Dedicated to my father,
Commander Frederick Reid Lafferty, Jr., with love.
Writing this novel has made me appreciate the complex
relationship between a father and daughter.

Prologue
VIA PAOLINA
ROME, CAMPO MARZIO
1596

Orazio Gentileschi dabbed the tip of his brush into the umber flesh tone on his palette while still staring at the painting on his easel.

He worked surrounded by a clutter of half-finished paintings, clay pots of paints, trays of pigments. Scattered about were a burnished lute, a crimson velvet drape, woolen shawls, and baskets woven of river reed. A sword lay unsheathed atop an unvarnished table, its blade gleaming in the late-afternoon light. In the shadowed corner of the room lurked an enormous pair of feathered wings, dark and menacing.

Before him—the subject of his painting—was his beautiful young wife and their firstborn child, Artemisia.

The fumes of turpentine scorched the three-year-old's eyes, flooding them with tears. She turned away, suckling hard at Prudenzia's breast, blinking up at her lovely face turned in profile.

"Open a window, Orazio. The turpentine—"

"*Stai ferma,*" said Orazio. "Hold still. Don't look at the child. It will double your chin and cast a shadow."

Signora Gentileschi pressed her lips together, her eyes fixed with worry on her child.

The orb of the mother's breast without her maternal smile beaming down was insufficient for Artemisia. She felt eclipsed from the sun. Outraged at her neglect, the child thudded her little hands at her mother's body, begging for her attention.

"Shh! Shh, Artemisia. Your papa is painting us." Without moving her head, Signora Gentileschi jostled Artemisia higher in her arms so she could see her father's head darting sideways from behind the easel.

"Guarda!" she whispered. "Look at him and his pretty colors, *tesoro.*"

As Artemisia turned her gaze away from her mother's nipple, the turpentine stung her eyes again.

Signora Gentileschi heard her daughter whimper and said nothing. She wasn't prepared to evoke her husband's rage.

Artemisia stared at the white birch palette clutched in her father's hand, his thumb sticking up through the hole like a worm curling out of an apple. The spots of bright crimson, the muted ochres and browns played hide-and-seek as his hand extended and retreated behind the easel. The paints swayed, angling toward Artemisia and away again as her father dipped his brush in the small pools of pigment.

"She likes the paints," Signora Gentileschi murmured. "Look how she stares at them! Artemisia cocks her head just like you do, Orazio."

Orazio smirked, making his pointed beard jump. It was as close as he came to a smile. "Babies like colors," he said, shrugging.

"No, Orazio. I think she wants to paint like her *babbo.*"

Orazio set down his paintbrush and palette. His bushy brows rose and fell above his eyes. How he wished his firstborn was a son. A son who could paint.

He sighed, rubbing his hand with a rag. "She's a girl."

Signora Gentileschi's smile vanished. She would not tolerate criticism of her beloved Artemisia. "Look at her, Orazio," she insisted. "She is fascinated by your colors, your movement . . . your brush. She's your daughter, your blood."

Orazio stared hard at his wife, then at Artemisia.

Is she?

The sun's warmth faded from the little girl's cheek, a chill creeping into the room.

Orazio picked up another brush, colored with a muted yellow ochre, and waved it in the air. He followed Artemisia's eyes as they tracked it. He set down the brush and the little girl turned back to her mother's breast.

"Artemisia is too old to breastfeed," he said.

"What difference does it make? I make milk for her," Prudenzia said, looking down at her daughter. "I love her at my breast. And it saves money."

Orazio approached and took Artemisia in his arms. She protested, holding her hands out to her mother.

"Mama!"

"You are all right, Artemisia," said Orazio. *"Tranquilla."* Calm down.

Artemisia's father smelled of paint and oil, his hands were rough. She twisted in his arms and reached up to grasp his beard. He jerked his chin away, evading her grab.

"My paintings are selling," he said, carrying the child toward the easel. "The battle of light and dark. Caravaggio's *chiaroscuro* has brought us fortune, *bella.*"

"And he will land you in jail one day, the scoundrel," Signora Gentileschi retorted.

"My paintings are selling," he repeated. "We have enough to feed another mouth. And more babies . . . sons, artists!"

Signora Gentileschi blushed, buttoning up her blouse. She was pregnant again but hadn't told her husband.

"Look, Artemisia," Orazio said, setting her down in front of the canvas. "Who do you see there, eh?"

The toddler stared at her likeness, not recognizing it. But she did see the perfect replica of her mother, her breast. And a strange child nursing there.

Artemisia's hand reached out to seize at the image of her mother and knock the other child away.

Orazio caught his daughter's wrist before she smudged the painting.

"Oh, you sassy one. You think you know that pretty woman, don't you? A better compliment I could not ask for." He laughed. He released her wrist with a flourish.

Artemisia looked at him solemnly and then stared at his paint-splotched hands. The paint, the paintbrush, the canvas. The holy trinity of art. In her young mind Artemisia recognized that somehow her father had replicated her mother with his hands and a paintbrush.

Magic.

She grabbed his paintbrush, clutching it tight.

"Oh, no, you don't!" he said, trying to pull back the brush, amazed at her tenacious grasp as they played tug-of-war.

He pried it from between her little fingers. Artemisia let out a bellowing scream.

"Take her, Prudenzia," said Orazio. "I have work to do."

❧

Artemisia cried inconsolably for hours into the night, beating her hands against the wooden slats of her bed. Long after midnight her father appeared above her, his face illuminated in candlelight.

He placed a small paintbrush in her tiny hand. She ceased squalling and held it tight in her fist.

He looked down at her, his eyes glittering. "You are my child," he whispered to her. "My child and no other's! I will prove this to the world. To God himself!"

Chapter 1
ROME, 1599

"Where are we going now, Papa?"

"To show you a miracle."

Artemisia's little hand folded like a toy inside her father's, her fingers warm and sticky from sugared almonds bought in Piazza Navona. She felt the coarseness of Orazio's skin, roughened from solvents he used in painting, his calluses from stretching canvas, grinding pigments, and making frames for his art.

The late-afternoon sky painted Rome in golden tones, coaxing warmth from the stones of Piazza Navona. The slanting light brought out a richness in the rocks, coloring them a luminous ochre.

Orazio led his daughter through the warren of streets beyond the piazza, which were cloaked in the shadows of the setting sun. Stray cats ran ahead of them, frightened by Orazio's long, confident stride. He dragged little Artemisia along, her skinny legs churning to keep up with him.

The narrow streets were strewn with rotting garbage and slick with the slop of chamber pots. Orazio swung the little girl up in his arms when he saw sordid puddles her little stride couldn't avoid. Artemisia covered her nose at the acrid stench.

Her father smelled of the cheap wine that, with a plate of greasy fried sardines, had been his afternoon meal. He had supped in a tavern while meeting with an art procurer for the House of Farnese. The offer was too low for Orazio to accept, but the businessman paid for the wine and sardines, so the meeting wasn't a complete loss.

At last father and daughter broke out into the sunlight at the edge of the city.

"The Rome of the ancients stretched beyond our current limits," he told her. "The city has shrunk . . . but behold!"

The sunset colored the tumbled ruins of the Colosseum. The great blocks of rock both absorbed and reflected the light, throbbing golden-rose.

"Look at the glow. See what a superb painter the sun is."

Artemisia took in the massive structure. Flocks of white sheep ripped at the tall grass in the rubble of the ruins.

"Come on. I'll show you the gladiators' cells. They were kept as prisoners who only survived by fighting and vanquishing their opponents."

In the dusky light Orazio led Artemisia through the maze of massive limestone blocks that littered the interior of the Colosseum. She stood gaping at the destruction, the towering piles of rock.

"It looks like a giant kicked his boot through the walls, Papa."

"Many earthquakes over the centuries have done their work. You have to use your imagination. You see the grass growing there, that patch? All this area was covered in turf—sometimes in water to imitate the sea. Imagine the powers of emperors! And all to watch one man best another. It is a game, Artemisia. To win. Or die."

He gripped his daughter's shoulders fiercely, turning her to face him.

"Life hasn't changed. Daughter, are you listening?"

As they picked their way over the slabs, he told her stories of lions, and bears, and one man against another, on land and on sea. He made her imagine the crimson blood staining the ground, the roar of the crowds, the emperor who would give his nod and spare a life. Or just as easily see one sacrificed.

Moment by moment the sun deepened its descent. The shadows grew longer and Artemisia marveled at the golden glow fading as Rome plunged toward night. The stones lost their luster, their magic. The warm rose gold faded away, leaving behind ugly gray rocks, formidable and hostile.

"Come," Orazio said to his daughter. "We'll sit on the hill."

They made their way out of the darkening interior of the Colosseum to a grassy hill. A shepherd's hut stood in the near distance, smoke rising just outside, where the shepherds had built a fire and were warming themselves as they ate a simple meal of olives and cheese.

One by one the stars appeared over the archways of the Colosseum. Soon they were too many to count . . . hundreds, thousands in the dome of the sky.

As the sky darkened to pitch, Orazio stretched out on his back, his hands clasped behind his neck. Artemisia wrapped herself tight in her woolen shawl.

"What did the gladiators win, Papa? When they defeated the other man?"

The wind rustled the grass around them.

"They won their life, Artemisia. To live another day. To fight again." Orazio looked at his daughter, his eyes shining in the dark. "That is the lesson I want you to learn. Engrave it on your heart."

❧

By the time Artemisia's brothers were born, she was already sketching with black lead in her papa's *bottega*. Francesco had been born in 1597, four years her junior. When he was two, he was given a stick of chalk to scrawl with. By then Artemisia had graduated to simple paints.

"Look, *figlio*," said Orazio to Francesco, pointing to Artemisia's studies for paintings. "Your sister has the knack for drawing, doesn't she? The Accademia delle Arti del Disegno in Florence would marvel at her ability."

Orazio himself was not adept at sketching and relied entirely on his vision as a painter. He held the miracle in his head until it was executed directly in oils on the canvas, with minimum hatch marks as blocking for his subjects.

He frowned at his son, who was entranced by a fat fly crawling on the floor. The chalk lay cast off, forgotten on the floor.

The artist threw his hands in the air.

"You, my son, show no aptitude whatsoever. Doubtless you'll grow up to be a worthless thug."

"Papa! Francesco is only two," Artemisia protested, kissing her little brother's cheek.

"He can't even grasp the chalk correctly."

Artemisia fumbled with her brother's chubby fingers, trying to help him hold the stub so he could scribble. He threw it down and went back to chasing the fly.

"He is my son," said her papa, sternly. "He will be a painter. He should learn criticism early on, as you did." He turned to his son and roared, "Francesco! Draw!"

Francesco looked at his father with terror and began to cry. Artemisia scooped him up into her arms and held the chalk for him. He grasped her hand and felt the flowing movement as she sketched an apple resting on a plate. Under his sister's hand the fruit took shape. Francesco shrieked with joy at the image they created together.

"You'll spoil him, Artemisia," said Orazio. He studied the apple carefully.

He looked at his daughter and then toward the window, listening to the sound of the street.

"Artemisia, you and I are going to the Ponte Sant'Angelo tomorrow. Bring your sketch pad and black lead."

Chapter 2
ROME, 1599

Maddalena, the Gentileschis' servant, served Artemisia a slice of bread rubbed with fresh tomato, oil, and salt. It was early morning, the first pinkish rays of dawn tinting the kitchen walls.

The tomato colored the bread as scarlet as the sunrise. The grains of salt stood out like fading stars, melting into the red blaze. Artemisia pushed it one way and then another on her plate, angling her repast in the morning shaft of sunlight that sliced through the kitchen window.

"Artemisia! Don't just look at it . . . eat it, *amore*," coaxed Maddalena.

Artemisia reluctantly bit into the sunrise. Words floated down the stairwell as her parents argued in their bedroom.

"She is too young!" said Prudenzia. "She is still a child, Orazio! I forbid it."

"*Cara!* Artemisia is a special child," he answered. "You don't know how special. She must know the truth of life. And death. How to interpret raw emotion. There will be plenty at an execution."

"*Che morbido!*" How morbid!

"The great Leonardo himself instructed artists to attend executions, autopsies. The power of emotion, the human body under duress—and today, three nobles! This is a historic moment. She must be there."

"That poor Beatrice. Raped by her own father. I would have murdered him myself!" said Prudenzia. "So innocent!"

Artemisia looked up at Maddalena.

Why is Mama so upset? What is rape?

∽

Orazio, as always, got his way. Artemisia would accompany him to witness the public execution of Beatrice Cenci and her family. They walked together toward the Ponte Sant'Angelo on the bank of the Tiber. A scarlet streak bled across the horizon, the late summer sun an angry ball of crimson rising to make Rome sizzle and writhe with heat.

Thousands of Romans spilled out into the dusty streets, fighting to hold their own amid the carts and wagons jostling wheel against wheel along the roads leading to the Ponte Sant'Angelo, where the scaffold was erected high on the bridge over the Tiber so everyone could see the execution.

Orazio pulled his daughter through the throng, fighting his way to a spot where they could see the young noblewoman, Beatrice Cenci, who pressed her white-turbaned head against the bars of the cage as the wagon rocked over the cobblestones toward the scaffold. Strands of her hair, wet with perspiration, clung to her elegant neck. Her stepmother, Lucrezia Petroni, moaned in prayer on her knees next to her, her gold brocade gown torn and filthy.

Artemisia stared at Beatrice, committing her face to memory. She saw no fear in the noblewoman's eyes, only a dogged resignation.

What could bring such a beautiful young woman so low?

Artemisia didn't know the sad details of Beatrice Cenci's life. Her father, Francesco Cenci, was one of the wealthiest men in Rome. He had been accused several times of raping women and even murdering one who had not succumbed to his advances. He locked his second wife, Lucrezia, and Beatrice in a crumbling castle outside Rome. There he raped his daughter repeatedly—and was rumored to have done so to her younger brother too. Beatrice had taken her destiny in her own hands, plotting her father's murder with the knowledge and help of her brothers, stepmother, and two servants—a burly blacksmith and Olimpio Calvetti, the caretaker of the castle.

Lucrezia slipped her husband a sleeping potion in his wine. After he fell into a deep sleep, the two male servants entered the bedchamber, armed with a hammer and a chisel. Francesco woke, struggling against his murderers, but they killed him quickly with a deep blow to his head. They carried his body to the top story of the castle and dumped him off a wooden balcony, breaking the wood to make it look like an accident. The body fell to a rubbish heap below.

Suspicion arose when he was discovered the next day, his body rigid and cold. The wounds on his head made it clear this was no accident.

Suspicion swirled and the Cenci family was arrested.

The pope, eager to confiscate all of Cenci's vast wealth, had Beatrice and her family tortured until they confessed their crime. The pope condemned the family to death and the Church inherited the entire Cenci estate, a great fortune for the Vatican coffers.

The pleas of the Roman people—both nobles and commoners—for mercy had fallen on deaf ears. Pope Clemente VIII showed no sympathy for the accused children and stepmother. Rebellion in the noble order—especially patricide—would not go unpunished. The only family member spared by the pope from execution was the youngest boy, twelve-year-old Bernardo, who was sentenced to watch every moment of the torture and death of his family.

And now Rome was gathered to watch along with him.

"Take a look at Orazio Gentileschi's girl. See how she stares," said a woman. "How odd!"

"She's an artist, that one," said a man. "Like her father."

"Don't be silly," said a bearded drunk next to him. "Impossible. She's a girl!"

Artemisia stumbled ahead as her father pressed through the mob. She heard the remarks.

Impossible. A girl.

"Look at Signorina Cenci. So innocent a face," said a bald man to his wife. "What father commits such crimes against a young maiden?"

"*Sì,*" said the woman. She dabbed at her eye with her fingertip. "Poor soul. I'd have killed the bastard myself. *Stuprare la propria figlia!*"

Artemisia thought, *Mama said she, too, would have killed him. And again that word "rape." Stupro.*

"And the son too," said the husband. "May Francesco Cenci rot in hell! Serves him right they murdered the *stronzo!*"

Sex with the son? With his own daughter? Is that what rape is?

"Are you paying attention, Artemisia?" said her father. "I will ask you to prepare a composition and a list of paints. Look now! Choose!"

Artemisia's eyes shot to her father.

Why did he bring me here?

She imagined the girl naked, her father mounting her, like the stray dogs did in the streets. She felt sick, fighting an urge to vomit.

"Papa!" she said, gagging.

"Shh, Artemisia," he said, his hand smoothing her hair. "*Tranquilla,* calm down. Just observe. Beatrice's situation is too difficult for you to comprehend. Only focus on the art, *cara.* That is why we are here."

There was a scream like the shriek of a dying rabbit. Artemisia's eyes searched for the source and focused where Beatrice's older brother, Giacomo, writhed in agony as he was tortured with red-hot pincers. His sister cocked her head, straining to hear the last syllables from his mouth before he died. Lines of anguish crumpled her brow. She extended her filthy arms through the bars toward the sound like a beggar pleading for alms.

"Canvas preparation," whispered Artemisia's father, more gently. "What priming would you use?"

Artemisia stared at Beatrice Cenci, feeling the condemned girl's anguish soaking into her own body.

"What priming, Artemisia?" her father repeated.

"A dark undercoat."

"More specific."

"Maybe red—the iron?"

"Red ochre," said Orazio.

A wail hung in the air, from Beatrice's little brother.

"He's fainted again," said a woman in a dirty kerchief. *"Poverino!"*

Artemisia watched the guards douse the boy with a pail of water, bringing him to consciousness. They picked him up by his arms and made him watch.

"Did you see how the boy's muscles went slack?" said Orazio. "Sketch him."

Artemisia hunched over her sketch pad, trying to capture the unconscious body, the limp muscles, the slight parting of his lips showing his muddy teeth.

"Did you capture that spasm of muscle?" said her papa. "The roll of the eye?"

"Credo di sì, Papa." *I think so.*

"Bene, Artemisia. Now, red iron as a primer—what would your primary background be?"

A mewing sound as the boy staggered to his feet, the guards' hands under his armpits.

"Sketch him now. Hurry. His expression is changing."

"Umber," she said, her pencil scratching at the parchment. She looked from her sketch pad to the boy and back again. "Dark umber," she corrected, still sketching.

"Why?"

"To make the ochre and the white stand out like you do. I would paint Beatrice's dress in ochre tones. It's beautiful fabric, even if it is torn and dirty."

"Specifically?"

"I don't know yet, Papa!" she spat back at him, annoyed at his questions. "A blend of ochres—I would have to see the pigment before I blended. But rich and golden."

"And, Artemisia: skin tones?"

"A loaded brush, thick," she said. "Like you do, Papa."

"Impasto. The term is impasto."

"Of white lead. Umber for the dirty streaks."

"While still wet?"

"Yes, I'd draw it in finely. With a gloss of amber varnish over it all . . ."

"What kind of questions are those to ask the girl?" said the woman in the dirty kerchief. She craned her neck, looking at Artemisia's sketch of the wretched Cenci brother. "Let her watch the execution in peace."

"Signora," said Orazio, sneering at her. "My daughter is a genius, an artist of great potential. It is not for you to comment."

The woman put her hands on her hips, giving Orazio the evil eye. "A woman is about to die here, and you are discussing paints? It has the kiss of the devil to me. Making art of such evil things." She crossed herself.

People around them began murmuring. They pointed at Artemisia's sketch pad.

"Guarda!" said the woman to the others. "Look what she has drawn. The very likeness of the boy."

"The terror in his eyes," said the beggar next to her. "Just as he is, the very image."

"See him turn away, the guards forcing him to look!" said a man who stunk of dog dung and piss, a leather tanner taking the day off from the vats to watch the execution along with all of Rome.

"This girl is an artist," said a voice in a hushed tone. The others nodded, staring at Artemisia.

Warmth rushed up Artemisia's spine and colored her face, fed by the observers' attention. She knew she had captured Bernardo Cenci's agony well because she had felt the emotion in her gut. Her hand had transformed what she saw and felt into truth on the paper.

She basked in the onlookers' compliments. Other than her papa and mama, no one outside the Gentileschi household had recognized Artemisia as an artist before.

For the rest of Artemisia's life she would savor that recognition, her appetite piqued. After that day, she would crave praise as a form of addiction.

"Runs more to witchcraft, to my thinking," grumbled the first woman. "A girl that young who can make such images—"

"Come along, Artemisia," said Orazio. "I see Caravaggio there ahead, right by the scaffold."

They pushed their way through the crowd.

"I knew I'd see you here, Michele," said Orazio, as he clasped Caravaggio's shoulder.

Caravaggio turned to see his old friend and his daughter. "You brought Artemisia to witness this debacle?"

"She insisted," lied Orazio. He pulled out his own small notebook and began sketching. "Look how the little brother Cenci suffers."

"Bastards!" said Caravaggio. "Filthy fucking *bastardi*."

Artemisia stared at Caravaggio—his swarthy face, mop of tangled black hair, and stocky build. But it was his keen black eyes that entranced her, eyes as sharp as a crow's. She had seen the master on a number of occasions at Orazio's bottega. He had borrowed props from her papa—the set of dark angel wings that had terrified her as a toddler and a Capuchin monk's habit. But Maestro Caravaggio had ignored the girl, preferring to talk about art, brawling, and whores with her father.

Caravaggio felt her eyes studying him and turned to her, a curious look on his face.

Artemisia shifted her focus to the executions, her pencil moving again.

"I heard the father began raping her from a young age, the *pezzo di stronzo!*" whispered a grizzled man to his companion. He pinched savagely at a large wart on his face. "The piece of shit! What justice is this?"

Artemisia tugged on her papa's tunic. She had to confirm her suspicions. "What is 'rape,' *Babbo*?" she asked. "Is it what dogs do in the street?"

"I'm sketching, daughter," said her father, gruffly. "I will explain later. Leave me in peace."

Artemisia puffed out her cheeks and then exhaled noisily in frustration. She looked at his page and saw poorly drawn figures. She shook her head. Her father was a gifted painter but she knew her own sketches were already better than his.

Artemisia pushed Caravaggio aside so she could better see the scaffold where Beatrice Cenci stood. The great painter swore, annoyed that a girl would dare touch him—move him!—when he noticed the intense look on her face.

"Is the girl all right?" Caravaggio asked her father. "Look at her, Orazio."

"She is a sensitive child," Orazio said, still stabbing at his sketch. "With more heart and conscience than our pope and clergy, the disgusting swine."

"Perhaps you should take her home," said Caravaggio, his eyes pinned on Artemisia. "She looks . . . haunted."

Orazio shrugged, exasperated. "Of course she does. She is a painter too. She'll remember this day for the rest of her life."

Caravaggio didn't answer. He nodded at Artemisia as she looked up from her sketch pad at last. "May I see?" he asked.

"Certo," she said, showing him her sketches.

Caravaggio narrowed his eyes, examining her work. "You have the Tuscan blood in you," he said. "You captured the emotion. Impressive."

"Grazie, Maestro," she said, still trying to draw the ever-changing scene. She craned her neck, annoyed at having to look around him.

"I never sketch before I paint," he said. "Your drawings are good. More than good, Artemisia. *Brava.*"

"Grazie, Maestro," she said again, though she wished he'd leave her alone to draw.

He said nothing more, though his dark eyes darted now and then at her sketch pad.

The September sun baked the stones of the piazza, reflecting the merciless heat. The people pressed closer to the scaffold, their body odors mingling in sour wafts.

No one could look away.

"Are you thirsty, child?" said a kind woman next to Artemisia. She extended a gourd of cool water.

Water beads had formed on the bumpy orange surface, smudged where the woman's fingertips had gripped it. The image mesmerized Artemisia.

"Ragazza, drink. Don't just stare at it." She tipped the gourd gently against Artemisia's lips.

She drank greedily. She had had no idea how thirsty she was.

"Poor child," whispered another woman next to her. "Her father should tend to her."

Caravaggio glanced at Artemisia, hearing this. Artemisia blinked, saying nothing. She turned back to watch Beatrice Cenci, pencil in her hand.

After the death of her brother, Beatrice betrayed no fear, no human sentiment, facing her imminent death. She walked to the executioner like a martyr, dignity in her bearing. Without struggle, she bared her neck.

"Innocent souls!" wailed an old woman. Other voices in the crowd shouted, *"Certo! Gli innocenti!"*

"Innocent lamb!" cried a fishmonger. "What justice is this?" He waved his arms wide, supplicating to the heavens.

"Shut up! You will be next, you fool," said the man's wife. "Stick to fish. What do you know of lambs?"

"Poor girl!" moaned a gray-haired woman in a ragged kerchief. "Spare that one's life at least!"

The crowd hummed with dissention as the sun broiled overhead.

"Spare the girl! Spare the girl!" shouted Roman voices in unison.

Artemisia stopped sketching. She cocked her head, studying the young woman on the scaffold.

"Spare the girl! Spare the girl!" she cried along with all of Rome.

Beatrice Cenci lifted her head only enough to gaze out to her defenders, the mob who had gathered to witness her death.

Then she looked directly at Artemisia.

The sword lifted.

Artemisia screamed, her pencil and sketches tumbling to the ground.

The executioner's blade sliced through Beatrice's neck as the Romans gasped. A spurt of blood stained the swordsman's tunic.

He looked down at his work and swore silently. Part of the noblewoman's neck remained intact, her head still attached. The executioner withdrew a dagger from a sheath behind his back.

Artemisia's eyes were riveted on the executioner now, not the victim. The swordsman's face showed the concentration a butcher would, the practical task of severing the remaining bone and muscle from a piece of meat.

The girl's head rolled a half revolution on the stones and came to an abrupt stop.

A hand nudged Artemisia. She turned, still paralyzed with emotion. Caravaggio handed her the pencil that had dropped along with the sketch pages. "Are you all right, Artemisia?"

She nodded, saying nothing. The images of the execution had seared her vision.

Long after the sword had parted Beatrice's head from her shoulders, the people stood stunned. Even the *sbirri* with their swinging cudgels and curses could not disperse the people of Rome.

As the sun sank mercifully into the west, its surrender bathed the city in crimson light, coloring the stucco of the buildings a golden-rose.

Mourners brought candles, costly to the poor, to line the biers of the dead, lit against the blackening night. Women, men, and children wept in the darkness.

The flickering candles lit the savage gash where Beatrice Cenci's head had been replaced upon her marble-white neck. Children brought crowns of flowers to adorn Beatrice's head, her bloody turban long discarded as the street sweepers rinsed clean the cobblestones. Mothers combed out the dead woman's hair using their fingers.

Orazio put his arm around his daughter's shoulders and they walked toward home in silence.

But that night, sitting by the fire, trying to make sense of what she had seen, what she had drawn, Artemisia insisted that her father tell her why they had killed that beautiful young woman.

And he explained how Beatrice, raped repeatedly by her father, had taken revenge at last, abetted by her family.

"And Beatrice was beheaded for that?"

"The power of the Church, the power of men," said her mother, knitting quietly in the corner. "A hard lesson for you at such a tender age, *figlia mia*." *My daughter.*

And so a girl of six learned for the first time what the word "rape" meant. And that a young woman had been executed because she dared to seek revenge.

Chapter 3
ROME, 1603

After the Cenci execution, Orazio Gentileschi began taking Artemisia all around Rome to see paintings and altarpieces. By the age of ten she knew most of the prominent artists of Rome and had visited their bottegas. Those same artists visited the Gentileschi bottega in turn, though Artemisia was strictly forbidden to talk to them without her father's permission.

"You tend to your painting," he told her.

Artemisia, who wanted no part of the men's conversations, was content to focus on her work.

Orazio also took Artemisia to the cheap taverns where he discussed art with other artists. She listened to their rough language and talk of whores, the price of lapis lazuli, and the cutthroat politics of art patronage.

"Giovanni Baglione has procured another commission," said the round-faced Mario Minniti, spearing a fried sardine with his fork. Artemisia watched how the artist relished his food and drink—such gusto!

"Piss on Baglione," said her father. "His art is shit."

"I agree," Minniti answered, munching on the fish. "But the cardinals like it. He and Caravaggio are neck and neck in competition."

Artemisia pulled her father's sleeve. "Maestro Caravaggio painted this man!" she whispered. "He was the wine god—*vero?*"

"*Sì,*" said Orazio. "He painted Maestro Minniti as Bacchus."

"Ah!" said Mario, taking a swig of wine. Bloodred drops stained his linen tunic. He wiped his lips, his teeth purple. "You recognize me, eh, Artemisia?" He turned to her father. "She's got a good memory and eye for art, this *ragazzina!*"

Orazio grunted. "You have no idea, Mario. Her work will excel beyond yours in another year."

Mario laughed and went back to spearing his sardines.

∽⑤

"Tomorrow," Orazio announced, "Artemisia and I are going to visit Caravaggio's studio."

Prudenzia Gentileschi was not keen on the plan.

"She's so young," she objected. "Tuzia says she'll grow up corrupted, spending so much time with artists, exposed to their debauchery—"

"Tuzia is ignorant," said Orazio. "Our neighbor knows nothing of art. You could fit her wits in a child's marble bag."

"Orazio!"

"Tuzia is stupid, Prudenzia. She doesn't realize the genius our daughter has. Artemisia deserves to be in the presence of the great master of Rome and learn from him.

"And she is twenty-one scudi late with her rent to us," he went on. "Where is her good-for-nothing husband?"

"You know he travels. Tuzia has to feed the children and has nothing—"

"*Basta!*"

Prudenzia didn't argue further. The next day, Orazio and Artemisia set out from Via Paolina toward Piazza Navona. Under his arm he carried her first oil painting, executed in his studio under his careful tutelage.

Father and daughter walked across Piazza Navona and into the little warren of streets surrounding it. They stopped at 19 Vicolo dei Santi Cecilia e Biagio. A boy—good-looking but shy—greeted them at the door. His skin was moist and flawless like a girl's; his eyes shone wet. He was only a handful of years older than Artemisia.

"*Buongiorno*, Cecco. We've come to see the maestro," said Orazio. "I've brought my daughter to see his paintings."

"Is that you, Orazio?" shouted a gruff voice from the second floor. "Come in. Bring your *ragazzina* upstairs."

Artemisia wrinkled her nose. The house smelled of rancid food, turpentine, and sour wine. The boy Cecco watched her as he followed them, a smile blossoming on his lips.

"I know," he whispered, touching her shoulder. "It takes some getting used to. These men are old and their nostrils have been scarred with turpentine."

He pinched his nose, making a face. Artemisia laughed. She studied his long eyelashes, the bloom of red on his cheeks. Cecco was beautiful.

As they topped the stairs, a blast of cool air struck Artemisia's face. In the daylight cast by an enormous hole in the ceiling stood the disheveled, fierce artist, stocky and black-bearded.

"Ah! Little Artemisia!" said Caravaggio. "I haven't seen her since the execution." He bent near her, studying her as if she were a statue rather than a child. Artemisia stared back at his dark eyes, remembering how he had watched her draw.

"She's grown. She's going to be a beauty," he said. "You'll have to keep your wits about you, Orazio. The Roman boys—"

"She's a painter," snapped her father. "It's the beauty she will create on canvas that will stun the world."

Caravaggio eyed Artemisia like an eagle would eye its prey.

Instead of becoming uncomfortable, Artemisia stared back at him, wondering how she could capture his dark, darting eyes in paint.

Such an intensity! What pigment would I use? A bit of white lead to show the depth, the gleam of his eye.

Orazio scowled at Caravaggio. "You don't believe me, eh? She has supreme talent. I'll show you what we've brought."

He unrolled the canvas. It was a painting of Artemisia's mother breastfeeding her little brother Giulio. Her right hand cradled him; her left hand lifted her breast and nipple to his lips. Artemisia remembered how hard she had worked to capture the love in her mother's gaze, the soft flesh of her exposed breast.

The painting was far from masterful—a painting by a ten-year-old—but something in it made the great Caravaggio lose his smile. "You painted this," he said, turning to his friend. "*You*, Orazio! It is in your style. Lyrical, the composition. Your signature shade of ochre—"

"I did not, Michele," said Orazio, making a sharp, slicing gesture with his hand. "I've told you. She has genius."

Caravaggio stared at the painting. Artemisia heard a rustle behind her. It was the boy.

"Cecco!" Caravaggio said. "Look at what this girl's hand created."

Cecco approached, staring at the mother's face, her skin, her breast. He scoured every detail, each brushstroke, as if it were a map to buried treasure. Artemisia watched his face intently, his eyes widening. Then she saw the change.

His lips pulled down, thin and mean. "She has the perspective wrong," he said, his face reddening. "The hand—"

"Damn it, Cecco!" said Caravaggio. "She is much younger than you! A baby almost. How old is she? Nine, ten? She doesn't yet understand perspective."

Cecco sank his head deep against his throat like a turtle ducking into his shell.

Artemisia didn't like the change. The nice boy now stared at her with hatred.

Orazio watched the two children, saying nothing.

"Show me your work!" Artemisia said to Cecco, jutting out her chin. "Let me see your perspective, if you think mine's so bad!"

Cecco shook his head violently.

"I showed you mine," Artemisia said. "Now show me yours, *ragazzo!*" Boy.

"No!" he shouted back at her.

Artemisia screwed up her face, shaking her finger at him. "You criticize me and you don't have the *palle*—the balls!—to let me see your art! Shut up then about mine, you coward."

Caravaggio burst out a terrifying roar of a laugh. "Where did she learn to talk like that?"

"In the taverns and bottegas with me," said Orazio, rubbing his chin. "But she was born with that attitude."

Cecco's face had colored deep crimson, but he said nothing.

Caravaggio watched him, a stormy look in his eyes. "*Basta!* Let me show Artemisia some of my work. Another time we'll share Cecco's paintings."

Cecco receded into the shadows.

The maestro took Artemisia by the hand and walked to where the shaft of light struck an easel. He grasped her skinny shoulders, steering her around. She felt a hot power emanating from those hands—they were firm, commanding.

She was not frightened.

"There, Artemisia. *Guarda*," said Caravaggio. "Look. This is my *Calling of St. Matthew.*"

It was a copy of the great masterpiece he had painted in situ at the San Luigi dei Francesi church. In a dim room, four men and a boy sat around a table, counting coins. A shaft of light pierced the darkness, brushing past two other figures: the Lord Jesus Christ and a disciple.

Jesus pointed to a man who looked incredulously at the Messiah. The man in turn pointed to himself. "Me?" he seemed to say.

Me?

With his hands on her shoulders, Caravaggio felt Artemisia's reaction, the awe that the painting inspired in her. The quick pulse of her blood.

"You understand, Artemisia," he said quietly. "I can feel it. Which man is Matthew?"

"The one who is pointing at himself, questioning."

"What do you think of him?"

"He doesn't seem . . . nice," she said. "He's not a nice man. *Non è molto gentile.*"

Artemisia felt a change in the air as Caravaggio lifted his hands from her shoulders. She turned to look up at the maestro's face. His features had hardened, his nostrils flaring. *"Nice?"* His voice was cutting.

The girl drew back. "*Cosa, Maestro?* What did I say wrong?"

"'Nice'! What a waste of a word. I could stab that word through the heart and bury 'nice' for good!"

Artemisia blinked back at him. "He looks rough. For a saint he doesn't look—"

"He isn't a saint," said Caravaggio. "He is still a sinner. Just a man."

His black eyes connected with hers, holding her gaze. He was seething, like a madman. Never had Artemisia seen anyone more mercurial, not even her temperamental father.

But unlike most adults, he didn't dismiss her as a child. He cared what she thought. As if she were a man, and an artist.

"Sinners are vastly more interesting than saints," he said. "They show the truth. You find them in the alleys, the brothels, the slaughterhouse, not fluttering like pigeons in the heavens—"

"Michele," said Orazio, laying a hand on Caravaggio's shoulder, "Artemisia is still learning. She's but a child."

"Artemisia is an artist in a child's body," said Caravaggio, waving his finger at her. "One day she will remember!"

Perhaps a normal child would have cowered and backed away, cried or run from the room. But Artemisia was not a normal child.

She walked closer to the painting, cocking her head to study it again. She was drawn to the shadows and the nebulous shaft of light. She put her face close to the painting to look at the brushstrokes. She backed up again. Then approached once more, marveling at the magic Caravaggio had created.

"What a strange girl," said Cecco. "See, Maestro. She has already forgotten you."

"Be quiet," said Caravaggio. "Let her be."

Caravaggio understood. His art mesmerized the young girl. She was attracted like a moth to Caravaggio's light—and darkness. She moved back and forth, side to side, studying how he had created the miracle of light and shadow.

"Artemisia dances with your art," whispered Orazio.

Caravaggio stepped back to speak to him. "You are right, Orazio," he said, his voice calmer. "She has the calling. She is bewitched with potential.

"But fucking *never* let her paint something 'nice.'"

❦

The Gentileschis walked home toward Via Paolina, cutting across the carriageway that surrounded Piazza Navona. The *via* was chock-full of farmers' carts and nobles' carriages.

"Did you enjoy our visit with my friend?" asked Orazio as they stepped onto the dirt track.

"He is a strange man," Artemisia said. "But his paintings are magical."

"You see! He is an artist like no other."

"What did he mean, your 'signature ochre'?"

"He thinks I overuse the color. Gold."

"Maestro Caravaggio uses it too," she noted. "The spinning dust in *The Calling of St. Matthew*. In the fabrics of his subjects, I saw it there too."

Orazio beamed at his daughter. "You do have a good eye, Artemisia. But what he means is that my patrons are especially attracted to the color I achieve by adding a drop of lute varnish. My colors glow rich because of it. The gold above all. He's begged me to share my secret."

"But you won't tell him?"

"Of course not. It is our secret. Gentileschi gold!"

Artemisia bit her lip in wonderment. "Ah! *Fantastico*, Papa! We have a secret color, a technique even the great Maestro Caravaggio covets . . . Gentileschi gold!"

Orazio maneuvered through the traffic on the *strada*. The horses' hooves churned up dust that coated their clothes, hair, and eyelashes. The late-afternoon sun fell on each swirling mote, filling the space with a golden haze.

Father and daughter stopped in the road, enchanted.

"It's just like Caravaggio's shaft of light!" said Artemisia.

"*Attenti!* Watch out!" shouted a coach driver from his box. "*Via!* Get out of the fucking way, you idiots!"

Orazio lunged out of the way, pulling his daughter to safety. "That was close! But you saw the light, didn't you?"

"*Sì, sì! Magnifico!* But look." She pointed back to the place they had stood just seconds earlier. "It's already fading."

"Artists have to look hard and fast. Everything vanishes in an instant. Those instants are the magical vision."

"Like the instant Christ called Matthew while they counted coins on the table. Just as the light hit his face."

"Exactly. In any other instant, the drama—the art—would have been lost."

"Papa," she said, squeezing his hand, "why did the boy Cecco not show us his paintings?"

He tousled her hair, playing with the auburn curls. "I think he was embarrassed."

"Embarrassed? Why?"

"He was embarrassed because he saw your talent. At ten years old. A girl!" crowed Orazio. "My daughter. My very own daughter."

Artemisia chewed on her lip. "I didn't like how he looked at me. He was so funny and kind before he saw my painting. Then he stopped. He changed. He became ugly."

"You'd better get used to it."

Orazio stopped in Piazza Navona, next to the Fontana dei Calderai, the Fountain of the Foundries. Nearby in the neighborhood, hammers pounded against metal, the sweating tinkers and blacksmiths hard at work. The wind whipped up a fine spray from the fountain, misting daughter and father. The water drops formed a partial rainbow just in front of them.

Artemisia stood transfixed.

Orazio lifted his daughter's chin with the crook of his finger and placed his thumb in the dimple of her chin. "Artemisia. Boys will be jealous of you for the rest of your life. You have a gift they would kill for. Yes, you have the promise of physical beauty, but there are plenty of pretty girls in Rome. You possess something much more rare. You have God-given talent. You will be a great painter. And many will hate you for your art."

"But why?" she protested. "The boy was so nice—"

"Nice!" scoffed her father, looking up at the blue sky above them. "Remember what Maestro Caravaggio said about 'nice.' It's poison."

Artemisia hung her head down, scuffing the toe of her shoe on the stones. She silently vowed to strike "nice" from her vocabulary.

"Shall I tell you the truth, Artemisia? Or would you prefer to live the lie?"

"Truth, Papa," she said reluctantly. He had always demanded truth.

"That 'nice' boy Cecco is Caravaggio's *amante*."

"His . . . lover?"

"Caravaggio does the same things with him as I do in love with your mother. They share the same bed."

"But—" she said, shocked. "But he was funny. And kind—"

"And he, too, is talented. I've seen some of his work. What I am saying is that Cecco has a passionate love for his master. He could not stand to see a mere girl outshine him, even for an instant."

Artemisia swallowed hard. She felt as if she had been slapped. A boy, sharing Caravaggio's bed. A boy who hated her for her art.

"This is your first lesson in how jealousy coils its tentacles into even the most tender hearts. A boy who would love you for your beauty but hate you as a rival. And how do you respond, Artemisia?"

She shook her head. She looked at the fountain water splashing from the copper pipe in the center of the pool. Flecks of soot colored the white marble basin. She fixated on the color contrast, forgetting her father.

"Look at me and remember," said her father, turning her face toward him with his hand. "You respond by ignoring their hatred and by improving your art. Seize the emotion and thrive!"

"Thrive?" she said. "When I'm spit upon, Papa?"

"*Sì*, daughter. Each time you see that glint in their eyes, that hunger to possess your talent—to possess you!—*you* feed on it. Do not let them touch your heart. Your art is sacred. You must guard it with the same devotion as Cerberus guarding the underworld."

"They will hate me? The boys?"

"*Sì, figlia,*" he said. "Some will worship you, but others will hate you. They may even seek to destroy you, to stamp out your fire. But it will make you stronger, a better artist. *Capisci?*"

Artemisia nodded, turning to examine the soot embedded in the stone. She knelt down, running her fingers over the smooth marble. "I understand, Papa. But I don't like it."

"That does not matter, Artemisia." Her papa stood tall, surveying the Piazza Navona. "The only thing that matters is art."

Chapter 4
ROME, 1604

Orazio demanded Artemisia's attention in the studio, but her mother insisted she needed her only daughter's help with chores in the house. Artemisia shelled beans, scrubbed pots, hung laundry out the window to dry until it was hard and stiff and scented with the cooking odors that wafted across Via Paolina. Her work was never done.

Artemisia hated every second of it. Every moment away from the studio tortured her and she made that very clear.

Her mother, in turn, admonished the girl for her extravagant sighs as she dragged her feet from one chore to the next. Artemisia's gaze always lifted up to the studio above and she cocked her ear to hear snippets of visiting artists' discussions with her father.

"Artemisia. You know you will have to do these things for your husband," her mother said, looking up from the new baby, Marco—she had had a baby at her breast for as long as Artemisia could remember. "You need to learn how to run a household."

Artemisia drew in a breath and planted her feet, hands on hips. "I will not! I'm going to be a great artist."

Instead of slapping her daughter across the face, Prudenzia smiled at her obstinacy. "*Forse.* Perhaps," she said, "but, my *Signorina Grande Artista*, your father is a great artist and still does not earn enough for us to have but a part-time woman to cook and clean. All our money goes to buying pigments and canvas. There are rarely enough scudi in art to support a household in the style you aspire to. Will you expect your husband to do the housework and cooking?"

"If need be," she sputtered. "Why shouldn't he? I certainly—"

At that moment Orazio burst into the kitchen. "Artemisia! I need that canvas prepared. Now!"

She took a deep breath, her eyes closing in delight.

"And grind more dark umber," he said, beckoning her from the stairs. "What I have won't last but an hour more."

"Think about what I said," called her mother as Artemisia followed her father to the second floor—and she couldn't scramble up the stairs fast enough.

The bottega was a cluttered room, but heaven to her. The smells of paints, resins, walnut oil, and solvents held an intoxicating power. From the windows she could hang her head out and see a bright slice of the Piazza del Popolo at the end of the street. There was life and light out there. Life she wanted to live. Light she wanted to capture.

Prostitutes and artists lived in their neighborhood, Campo Marzio. Artemisia breathed in the lively, scented air of Rome—the garlic frying in olive oil, the fish cooking, even the sewer smells intrigued her, foul and pungent. She knew they carried the "truth" that Caravaggio spoke about, the earthiness of sin and filth, the smell of humanity, of Rome: spicy and sharp like the language of the taverns and artists' bottegas.

"*Buongiorno!*" called the knife sharpener pushing his cart in the street below. "Signorina Gentileschi, does your mama need her cutlery filed?"

"I don't think so. Our cook cut herself last night on the blade you sharpened last week. She cursed you to hell and back, *Signor Affilacoltelli!*"

"I do fine work." He chuckled, doffing his hat in respect to the unfortunate Maddalena. "My apologies to the signora . . . that knife was sharper than Perseus's sword!"

"Artemisia! Stop chatting and get to work," said her father. "The canvas! And I need both tones of umber *subito!*" *Immediately!*

"*Sì,* Papa."

Artemisia hurried away from the window, still smiling as she took the earth-colored nuggets of pigment from their jars and set to work with mortar and pestle. The Roman sun streamed in from the three windows facing the street, flooding the studio with light. A fat pigeon lit on the windowsill, cooing and strutting until Orazio threw a rag at it.

"Damned bird is ruining my concentration!" he roared, gripping his paintbrush.

Artemisia stifled a laugh.

From the street below came the whistles of the Roman boys pestering the prostitutes and the women's saucy retorts.

"*Che bella,*" said a squeaky boy's voice. "Your breasts are like sweet ripe melons, tempting me."

"You grow a few more years, Lorenzo, then we'll talk," said one of the women.

"You'll have to grow in more ways than one," called another woman, laughing. "And have coins jingling in your pocket, *ragazzino!*" *Little boy.*

Orazio and Artemisia exchanged a quick look. Artemisia burst out laughing.

Her father frowned, running his hand through his graying hair, making it stick up in wild tufts. "You shouldn't laugh at such things," he said. "It isn't right."

"But it's funny," she said.

"You are a girl."

"It's still funny, Papa. Maybe funnier *because* I'm a girl."

He shook his head, regarding her. "No, it's wrong! You are becoming too independent. It will get you in trouble one day."

"Shouldn't artists be independent?" she said. "You've always said a great artist is uncompromising."

He sighed and walked over to the window. He looked down on their neighbors, the prostitutes. "The world is a cruel place," he said. "Especially for women."

He turned back to the studio and worked next to her, preparing his paints for the day. From a silver flask he measured two drops of Venetian amber varnish onto his palette, his secret to the luminosity of his skin tones.

"A few more drops of varnish and I will have finished the flask. I will send you to the lute maker this afternoon to fetch more." Staring at his canvas, his hair uncombed and savage, his eyes rheumy with the fumes of turpentine, he looked like a madman.

"*Sì*, Papa," she said. Artemisia loved running errands like this, negotiating the busy streets of Rome.

"Have you finished applying the first coat of glue to the big canvas?"

"No, Papa. Mama had chores—"

"Damn those chores!" he said, thrusting his hands in the air. "We have work to do. I want to prime that canvas day after tomorrow or I'll be behind schedule. The glue has to dry completely before the red and gray-white layers. Otherwise—"

"Otherwise it will bleed into the glue. I know, Papa."

"Artemisia. You leave your mama to me. I forbid you to work more than four hours a day on household chores. Art comes first!"

"*Sì*, Papa! *O sì!*"

Art would always come first.

∞

Artemisia loved her mother. They had tender moments together. But her father embodied art—her passion, her lifeblood. How could she not wish to spend every waking minute with him in the studio? Her mother was a pretty but pale bird next to his brilliant plumage, his dashing Tuscan manners. And his talent! He could coax living figures out of paint and canvas.

Artemisia wanted to be just like him.

Her childhood was focused entirely on art. She didn't care about boys or ribbons in her hair. Or even learning to read and write. And her father was more than glad to have it that way. She would deeply regret this later, but as a child she couldn't see his selfishness in not providing her an education beyond art.

And right then, any knowledge other than art would have been wasted on her. Artemisia lived and breathed only for painting.

She would have slept every night in the studio if her mother had allowed it. Often she would creep upstairs to stand in the darkness, touching the blank canvases with her fingertips, pretending she was painting. Prudenzia would find her in the morning curled up in the wipe rags, her chestnut hair tangled with resin and dried paint. Prudenzia scolded her, but Orazio refused to punish her for a sin he secretly condoned.

One night when Artemisia was in the studio, sound asleep, she was awaked by a harsh shriek from down below. Prudenzia's wailing filled the air as Artemisia scrambled out of the nest of paint rags and ran to her, her bare feet skidding down the stone stairs.

"Mama! Mama!" she cried, bursting into her parents' bedroom. Her mother held her baby brother, pressed tight to her breast. The infant was still, silent, and pale.

"Stay with her, Artemisia," said Orazio, throwing on his cloak. "I'll fetch the priest."

"The priest?" Artemisia cried. "No! The doctor first!"

Her father grabbed her by the shoulders and shook her hard. "The baby is dead," he whispered. "Look at him. Look at him, Artemisia."

She stifled a scream. It seemed sacrilege to add her lament to her mother's.

"No! Giovanni is dead?"

"Go to your mama," he whispered. "Comfort her. But look hard at the baby. His skin. The color. How the orbits of his eyes have sunk, the folds in his skin."

Her eyes widened with horror but his held steady.

Art first.

Artemisia nodded. She silently approached her grieving mother and put her arm around her shoulders. Helpless with grief, Prudenzia turned her swollen eyes to her daughter.

Artemisia stared down at the still—so still!—body. She saw the pale skin, the glaze beginning to set in the baby's eyes.

Poor baby! This was the second Giovanni who had died as a babe.

Lead white, whispered a voice inside Artemisia's head.

"My son!" cried her mother in a hushed voice. "My baby!" Her mouth opened in a silent, gaping sob. Then she choked for breath, her grief consuming her.

"Oh, Mama," Artemisia said, pressing her body against her mother's in an embrace. "Please stop crying! Your poor heart will break—"

Bluish cast to lips. The thinnest cast of lapis lazuli? No, too costly and too intense. But paled out with the white paint—

"Oh, daughter!" cried Prudenzia, holding her tight. "Artemisia! You loved him so, your baby brother. Only you know how my heart is shattered."

Artemisia's heart paused a beat. She felt God looking into her mind, enraged at her hypocrisy. Her thoughts weren't of comfort. They were of painting.

"Mama!" she said. "The priest will be here soon. Our little one will go straight to heaven. Please don't cry," she said through her own hot tears that suddenly flowed.

"Artemisia," her mother sobbed over the little body sprawled now on her lap. "You are my angel. Only a daughter can understand these things. Men don't feel like we do."

Lead white. Definitely. With no hint of umber, no warm lute varnish, no tone of life. Ashen.

But the focus of the composition was her mother herself. The mourner and her grief. Artemisia turned to study her contorted face, the way her skin puckered and the narrow, angled slits that were her eyes. Her body wracked with paralyzing sorrow. Artemisia would sketch them both within the hour before the priest arrived.

A pietà.

I'll go to hell for thinking these thoughts. But I'll go as an artist.

Chapter 5
ROME, 1604

Above the Gentileschis' home on Via Paolina rose the Pincian Hill. It was encompassed by the old Roman wall, its bricks tumbling down under the canopy of the oak and linden trees.

Because it was so close to the house and a wild, open space, Orazio would take Artemisia there to run and play. She loved gathering acorns and rooting around the ancient ruins now reduced to rubble—far more tumbled-down and decayed than the Colosseum or even the scattered stones of the Forum.

After Mass on Sundays, Artemisia was allowed to play among the stones, building the outlines of fortresses where she would stage battles, withstand sieges, and set out on her imaginary stallion to conquer kingdoms beyond Rome.

Orazio would often sketch his daughter as she galloped her horse around the decaying foundations or bent down to gather flowers. One day he took her by the hand, leading her to a particularly large heap of masonry, a crumbled wall.

"I'm going to send you on an adventure, Artemisia," he said.

She squinted up at him, a pocket of sunlight piercing the branches above them. "Me? Alone?"

"Not alone," he said. "I'll be right here. I was told that there is a treasure in these ruins." He pointed to the pile of rubble. "A man I know saw it when he was a boy, but like me, he is too big to enter now. But you . . . you are still little enough."

They gazed at the tumbled rubble, exposed bricks made many centuries ago. A thick tangle of ivy looped around the collapsed structure, obscuring a dark hole.

"You've learned so many biblical scenes in my art, but I will show you something just as powerful," he said. "I only wish I was small enough to accompany you and see for myself."

Artemisia wiped the sweat from her brow and cocked her head.

"Come, Artemisia. Today I will teach you about the Minotaur." He sat on a rock and focused on her with his fierce gaze.

"There once was a King Minos who ruled over the great kingdom of Crete. He was married to a goddess, Pasiphae, whom he loved very much. He was given a beautiful white bull to sacrifice to Poseidon in gratitude, but the bull was so beautiful he spared its life and sacrificed another one instead.

"When Poseidon learned that the white bull had been spared and replaced by an inferior one, he became enraged. The angry god caused Pasiphae to fall in love with the white bull. She had Daedalus, a cunning engineer and sculptor, design a hollow cow made of wood, an invention so perfect the white bull fell in love with the replica. Pasiphae crawled inside and the white bull made love to her.

"The result was that Pasiphae gave birth to a half man, half bull."

"Half bull?" Artemisia said. "Which half?"

"You will tell me, daughter," he said, leading her closer to the rubble and the dark entry within.

Orazio stomped his feet.

"That's to warn the vipers back in their holes," he said. He produced a candle from his pouch and lit it, the flame almost invisible on the sun-soaked Roman day. He knelt and pulled the vines away from the entrance. "Go on, Artemisia. Crawl in. This is your journey. It is a secret—I was told there are frescoes from the ancient Roman Empire. Tell me what you see."

Artemisia swallowed hard, wondering if her father had done enough to warn the snakes.

"Are you frightened?" Orazio examined her face.

"No," she said, shaking her head. And once she said it, all fear fell away. She crawled in, tucking her skirt hem around her waist so that she could move. The rocks cut her knees and she winced.

"When you get in farther I will hand you the candle," he said.

It was dark, impossibly black. The recesses of the hole opened up. Artemisia stuck her hand back out of the hole for the candle.

"Shelter the flame, Artemisia."

She cupped her hand about the flickering light. She could stand up and walk by just lowering her head a little. A whole room was visible to her now.

Red! Cinnabar red, a jolt of color.

"What do you see?" His voice was fainter now.

"A room, Papa."

The walls were covered with frescoes and mosaics. The frescoes were water-damaged and blurred, the once-bright colors smeared from centuries of damp. Artemisia was astonished at the vermilion of the borders, the blue of the women's drapery, the green of the laurels. She could make out urns and water being poured but little else.

Then she saw it.

In the corner, at eye level, there was a mosaic. It was the image of a monster—the shaggy head of a black bull and the body of a man. His genitals were prominent, his penis erect, and his *palle* as big as a man's fists. She shuddered and gasped.

The flame blew out.

"Papa!" she screamed. "The candle is out!"

She heard his voice at the entry. "Come to me, Artemisia!" he called.

She whirled toward the sound, but it echoed in the stone chamber. Where was he? She couldn't see. She was lost. Her breath rasped in her throat. She choked in her panic. She was blind! She fought back the wave of fear. Her father's voice was still calling, but in the echoing space it was useless. Another deep breath. No, she wasn't blind. And in the dark she could sense a far shore where the drowning sea of tar black was tinged lighter brown. It was not so much light as it was the color that Orazio had taught her to use in highlights on black. Afraid she would trip, she dropped to her knees and crawled toward the brownish tone. She could hear his worried, hoarse breath.

"Artemisia!" he called. "Artemisia!"

She felt the brush of his fingers, reaching out for her. She grasped his hand. He pulled her out of the hole, her face grazing against the rough stone.

"You are bleeding!" he said, pressing his shirt to her cheek. "Are you all right?"

"*Sì*, Papa," she said, though she was still shaking. From what, she couldn't say. From the enveloping dark? From the image she had seen?

Papa held her tight. "Forgive me, daughter," he said. "I wanted to see through your eyes what I could not see myself."

"It's all right, Papa," she said, though terror still coursed through her body. *How could he have sent me into that black void?*

"It's all right," she repeated.

A minute passed in silence. He released her and looked away, ashamed of himself. And then, as she knew he would, he came back to her, hunting like a wolf.

He gave her a sly look, hungry for knowledge.

I cannot trust you, Papa. I know that now.

"What did you see?" he whispered. "Tell me, Artemisia."

She looked into her father's eyes, brilliant with desire. In that moment Artemisia knew him and hated him. Art would always come first, even before his own daughter.

"Nothing, Papa," she lied. "Nothing at all."

Chapter 6
ROME, 1604

Life in Campo Marzio was never peaceful. Almost any time of day or night there were bawdy songs, drunken voices, and brawling. The Piazza del Popolo was teeming with traders, their tents set up to ward against the hot sun, peddling food and drink to the vast and constant river of pilgrims who coursed through the main artery of Rome.

Artemisia often walked the few blocks to the piazza and—Francesco at her side—joined the crowd lined up to see Caravaggio's *Conversion of St. Paul* in the church of Santa Maria del Popolo. Unlike any painting she'd ever seen, this one made her feel the presence of God. Saint Paul lies blind, struck down off his horse, his hand waving in religious fervor. The perspective is jarring: Saint Paul's head reaches the limit of the frame and the horse's rear end appears enormous.

The painting was both a colossal joke and a miracle.

Artemisia stood rooted in front of Saint Paul despite the rough jostling of the pilgrims swarming beside her, pushing close for a better look. The exhausted masses, who pressed into the church for the art, for the communion, and for the cool air after Rome's scorching sun, stood awestruck, some even genuflecting before Caravaggio's canvas.

"Can this miracle have been painted by a mortal man?" whispered a gap-toothed woman standing next to her.

"It was indeed. The great Caravaggio."

"God has sent an angel to Earth," she said, crossing herself.

Artemisia stifled a laugh. Maestro Caravaggio was a thug and a lecher, just as likely to be in jail or drunk in a tavern as to be painting a masterpiece. He was no saint.

And oh how their mother hated him! "He'll die early, that one," she said. "I pray to the Madonna each night that he doesn't drag your papa into prison—or the grave—with him! Tuzia agrees—"

"What do I care what Tuzia says?" Artemisia said.

"She knows the way of the street better than we do," snapped her mother.

Probably because she is a slut herself. Artemisia stopped herself from taking the argument any further. But she saw how Tuzia slid her eyes to Orazio, pouting her lips when she thought Prudenzia wasn't looking. She always colored her mouth and cheeks with beetroot before she knocked on their door. And Artemisia knew she didn't do that for Prudenzia's sake.

But in the end, Tuzia was not wrong.

Late one night when her mother was fast asleep, Artemisia crept into her papa's studio, blindly painting masterpieces in the blackness with her imaginary paintbrush. She heard a great commotion in the streets, raucous laughter and bawdy songs. Among the loudest voices were Caravaggio's and her father's. The others she recognized were Onorio Longhi and Mario Minniti.

"We'll skewer that bastard with a poem! Rome will scorn him," said Longhi, slurring his words.

"Teach Baglione a lesson," said her father.

"*Vaffanculo!*" laughed Minniti. *Fuck him!*

"His canvases aren't good enough to wipe my ass," said Caravaggio. "Give me the quill."

They wrote poetry—and the dirtiest words Artemisia had ever heard. They scribbled and bellowed until the cocks crowed, and then staggered off to bed.

∞

The finished poem began to circulate throughout Rome. Artist friends of Caravaggio distributed copies from studio to studio. All Rome's artists were eager to procure one.

It was quoted in Campo Marzio taverns by loud and strident voices, fueled by drink and grudges. Artists who hated Baglione recited the verses by heart, even sang them at full lung in the streets after midnight. Artemisia learned the poem by heart and quietly recited it along with the drunken louts as she lay on her pallet at night.

It was then that Artemisia set her heart on learning to read and write. Her father had pulled her away from the convent school when she had just begun to learn her letters and sign her name.

"What more do you need as an artist?" he growled. "You are a girl. To sign your name is enough."

But it wasn't!

The power and politics of the written word. Artemisia's father and his artist friends had shown it to her that night.

Caravaggio's art staggered Rome. But this poem—vulgar and crude—set Rome ablaze.

Artemisia feared it would not end well.

Chapter 7
ROME, 1604

"I told you Caravaggio was poison!" said her mother, her eyes red and swollen from sobbing. "He brings nothing but bad luck."

Artemisia bit her lip. Her father was in jail because of that poem. So, yes, Caravaggio was poison. Strong and bitter, a viper's bite. And *intoxicating*. There was nothing as powerful in the world of art.

A rap on the door.

Tuzia stood outside. Her face was a map of distress. She had a baby boy on her hip, playing with her long blond braid.

"How is your mother faring?" she asked Artemisia. "Your father is in the Tor di Nona! I told her that Caravaggio was dangerous—"

"Mama is distraught. We don't know how we'll manage without Papa."

"I'll help," she said.

"Tuzia!" Artemisia said. "How can you help? Your husband is so rarely here and you have your own children to care for."

"I'll help," she said stubbornly. "*Per favore.* Let me in so I may sit with her."

Artemisia moved aside, holding open the door. She wrinkled her nose at the waft of the baby's dirty diaper as they slid by her.

Maybe she can give Mama comfort. But I don't like her!

Artemisia's mission on this day was to comfort her papa in Tor di Nona prison. Francesco accompanied her there. Orazio shared his cell with other prisoners, though none of his accomplices in poetry were there. They kept the men separate so they couldn't discuss their alibis.

She brought her papa salami and bread, soup, and fresh cheese wrapped in a moist cloth. The prison guard inspected everything thoroughly, taking a bite or two of what the girl brought. *Soon he will be taking half,* Artemisia thought. *I will have to double the portions so that my father will have enough to eat.*

Drunks and cutthroats, the dirty trash of Rome's streets, lurked in the shadows of the cell, awaiting their trials. The guard stood close to her. Artemisia knew he was trying to hear what they said, but just the same the girl was glad for his protection as she felt dangerous eyes slide her way from the corners of the room.

"How is your mother?" asked Orazio.

"Sad and worried. But the boys and I are taking care of her."

"And your art?"

"I'm finishing some still lifes. And working on studies for *Susanna and the Elders.*"

"Ambitious," said Orazio, around a mouthful of salami. "Are you using the triangular composition from my painting?"

"*Sì,*" she said, looking away. "But different, Papa. I see something different . . ."

"You are an artist," he said. "But you need guidance, Artemisia. Pay attention to how I painted that scene. You are far too young to even attempt a composition so ambitious on your own."

Artemisia's shoulders lifted in an angry shrug.

My Susanna *will shine. You'll see.*

"Mama thinks Caravaggio is venom," she whispered to him.

"She always has," he said. "But his venom fires his art. You understand that, don't you?"

She nodded. She'd had a sip of Caravaggio's poison. She thirsted for more.

As Artemisia and Francesco left the prison of Tor di Nona, the slanting sun colored the stone honey-gold. She stopped to study the light and noticed a lanky boy wandering around the perimeter.

"Cecco!" she called. *"Aspetta!"*

Francesco grabbed his sister's arm. "You are not to speak to strangers."

"He's not a stranger," she said, slapping his hand. "I know him. He's Caravaggio's assistant!"

"Caravaggio's boy!" muttered her brother, spitting on the ground.

"Stop it, Francesco," she said. "Stop it this instant or I'll tell Mama how you paid the whore in the street to give you pleasure with her hands. I heard you bragging to your friends."

Francesco blushed beet-red. "You wouldn't!"

"Try me," she muttered defiantly as Cecco approached.

"Signorina Gentileschi," he said, doffing his cap.

"May I present my brother Francesco," she said. Francesco gave a curt nod but did not extend his hand.

"This poem business with your father," said Cecco. "I'm so sorry."

Artemisia nodded, accepting his sympathy.

"They will be convicted," Cecco said. "There is too much evidence."

Artemisia frowned. What would happen to her father? What would happen to the Gentileschi household, with no income?

What would happen to her art?

"But my master is beseeching Cardinal del Monte to intervene," Cecco went on. "The cardinale has gotten him out of worse scrapes than this one. Your father will be released too."

Francesco and Artemisia both heaved sighs of relief. Francesco now extended his hand to Cecco. "Tell your master *grazie*."

Cecco took his hand. He smiled shyly. "You are an artist, too, Francesco?"

"*Sì.* Everyone in our family is."

"Come to our studio. There is something there I think you'd appreciate. Will you follow me?"

"*Volentieri,*" said Francesco.

They wound their way through the streets toward Piazza Navona and then to 19 Vicolo dei Santi Cecilia e Biagio. The bad smell inside had faded as the wind blew through the hole in the roof, carrying fresh cool air.

Cecco led them to a painting covered in a damask cloth. He carefully uncovered it.

A bald man with a gray beard holds a squirming boy's head under the flat of his hand. In his right hand is a knife. The boy writhes in terror, but an angel seizes the man's knife hand, saving the boy's life.

The boy is Cecco.

"*The Sacrifice of Isaac,*" said Cecco.

"It is magnificent," Artemisia said. "Pure power—and terrifying."

Francesco nodded, unable to speak. He stared unblinking at the canvas.

"That is the way I often feel with my master," said Cecco. "It was not hard for me to pose that way for him. The panic in my eyes, the horror of him wielding a knife. I live on the edge every day."

Cecco's face was a mask of tension. Artemisia put her hand on his shoulder.

"This time my maestro will escape punishment," said Cecco. "Maybe just pay a fine. I don't know. But every day I wonder if he won't be killed in the streets, brawling. Or murder someone himself."

Francesco and Artemisia nodded. They spent long minutes approaching and retreating from the canvas, inspecting the brushstrokes, parsing the paint colors, undercoat, and varnish. They exchanged looks of awe and bewilderment.

At last Francesco told Cecco they needed to return home.

"It was good to have you back in the studio, Signorina Artemisia," said Cecco. "I think I was rude last time we met. Forgive me. I was astonished at your ability."

Artemisia smiled at him. He was a beautiful boy. She could see how Caravaggio had fallen in love with him. "You are gracious, Cecco. Thank you."

"It is a comfort to have you here. You both are artists. Without my master it is a lonely place."

As they left, heading home, Artemisia thought, *Aren't all artists lonely?*

Chapter 8
ROME, 1604

While Orazio was locked in Tor di Nona, Artemisia made up her mind to learn how to read and write. She knew once her father was released he would not give her time away from art for her education. They would have to make up for lost time in the bottega.

Her father was literate and interested in the world around him. He had several books on shelves, including an ancient prayer book. Armed with that precious heirloom, Artemisia made her way to Santa Maria del Popolo, ready to beg the priest to teach her to read.

"Signorina Gentileschi!" he said, seeing her unaccompanied. "Does your father know you are here?"

"My father is locked in a cell in Tor di Nona."

"*Sì,*" said the priest, crossing himself. "I'm ashamed a member of our congregation has gone so far astray."

"I want to learn the word of God," Artemisia said slyly. "And not repeat the sins of my father. Teach me to read the Bible, Signore."

That should do it.

The priest took her well-worn prayer book, its pages tattered, its spine broken open. "Signorina Gentileschi, I haven't time to tutor you. If you truly want to read the word of God, the best way would be to enter a convent and learn there."

Artemisia recoiled. "No! That would not work. I have my work—my art."

"Like your father?" sniffed the priest. "As you wish. But if you are too busy to enter the convent, I would suggest you come each day to Mass, memorize the litany—then go back to the pages of the prayer book and read it again."

"In Latin?"

"Certo!" admonished the priest. "If you learn to read in Latin, Italian will be simple!"

Artemisia had a sharp memory, and in the weeks to come, she worked hard to learn the prayers by heart. She spoke the words aloud, moving her finger slowly under the letters.

Her lettering and cursive handwriting were pieced together—excruciatingly slowly—by copying out Orazio's contracts and personal correspondence, especially the raucous, filthy poem he had been imprisoned for. Bored by the daily litany, she soon realized she could turn to the poetry created by a drunken handful of Rome's most outstanding artists as her daily lesson.

That lurid poem was by far her favorite primer as she taught herself to read.

∞

Once Orazio was released from prison, he was even more fervent in expanding Artemisia's education in art. There was no mention of literacy.

In addition to Caravaggio's studio, Orazio saw that she visited other Roman artists' bottegas. The Gentileschis made the rounds to the churches to see every painting they could. Many were high up, either as looming altarpieces or ceiling frescoes. Her neck ached from casting her eyes heavenward as her father lectured about composition, color, technique, and perspective. Orazio never skimped on the mythology or storytelling, so that Artemisia knew all the important references in the Old Testament and a good deal about Greek mythology.

She only wished that he would teach her to read and write so she could learn more on her own.

One bottega the Gentileschis visited was Guido Reni's. Reni was a Bolognese artist who was part of Annibale Carracci's studio. He was a likable soul and had painted an exquisite canvas featuring Beatrice Cenci.

"I like his fierce colors," Artemisia said.

"If only he were as brave as his palette," muttered her father.

Still, Signor Reni, like Caravaggio, took time to speak to young Artemisia when so many others wouldn't. She was usually dismissed as a child, her father's shadow.

When Artemisia entered Reni's bottega, she heard whisperings among his apprentices.

"Maestro Gentileschi thinks his daughter will be a painter," said one.

"I hear she already is," said another. "With great talent, Ottavio. More than you."

"And you are a dirty bastard, Jacopo."

Artemisia suppressed a smile, looking straight ahead.

Her father had brought her to the studio to see Reni's painting of Beatrice Cenci. She stared at the painting, remembering the day of the girl's death.

"It is beautiful, Maestro Reni," she said. "Every detail—the turban, her face. I could imagine she once smiled this way."

It was only conjecture, because the Beatrice that Artemisia had seen was witnessing the torture of her brother—and facing her own imminent execution. But already Artemisia had acquired the artist's way of looking at a face, its muscular composition and tension, and knowing how that face might smile, laugh, or cry.

"You saw her die?" asked Maestro Reni.

"*Sì,*" she said. "I was there."

"Along with all of Rome," said Orazio. "We were there with Maestro Caravaggio."

"Ah, Caravaggio," sniffed Maestro Reni, clearly not fond of the master.

"I like your painting very much," Artemisia said. She was careful what she said to him and how she approached him. She had been warned that he was "funny" around women. Perhaps she was young enough not to alarm him.

"Grazie," he said. "Your father says you like my colors."

"I do. I love their passion, their bravado. And the enameled look of the varnish on all of them."

Orazio crossed his arms. "Enough, Artemisia. You will make Maestro Reni's head explode with pride."

"Ah! It is your father who has the touch with finishes," the maestro said, nodding. "Rumor is that he uses lute varnish."

"Ridiculous!" thundered Orazio. "Come along, Artemisia. We've got to go to the apothecary for some herbs for your mother's cough."

"I'll accompany you," said Maestro Reni. "I need fresh air and time away from the smell of paint and varnish." He gathered up his velvet cloak and walking stick. Artemisia thought it was curious that Maestro Reni had an aversion to women when he seemed so much like one himself. He reminded her of a well-groomed countess.

Orazio with his eagle-nosed, noble face and aloof demeanor made a suitable companion for the elegant Reni. Artemisia tagged along behind them, proud to be an artist walking the streets of Rome.

It was market day and the Piazza Navona was chock-full. They passed a dark tavern exuding a sour smell of cheap wine, the shrill laughs of prostitutes. Artemisia could hear the rattle and spill of dice.

She saw Maestro Reni hesitate.

Orazio shook his head, pulling him along. "I hear they load their dice in that one. And the *sbirri* are bound to bust them soon."

Maestro Reni groaned. "I've lost too much in there already."

As the trio emerged from the shadows into the dazzling light of the piazza, people began to point at them and whisper.

"They recognize you, Maestro Gentileschi," said Maestro Reni.

"No, my friend. It's you they recognize," said Orazio. "Gird your loins, *amico mio*."

A knot of merchants gathered, looking and gesturing. The vendors looked up from their wares and a buzz erupted across the piazza.

"It's him!" shouted a voice. "Guido Reni!"

"Maestro Reni!" said another.

"Oh!" cried a fishmonger's wife, throwing down the catch she was gutting. "Let me kiss those magical hands!" She wiped fish guts on her apron and ran toward Reni.

Maestro Reni snatched up his hands, holding them high in the air, terrified.

"Kiss my hands?" he cried. "Do you think I don't see through you? Back away, you sorceress!"

"Sorceress?" said the befuddled woman. "I'm no sorceress. I worship God Almighty, Lord Jesus, the Virgin, and all the saints. Your hands brought our blessed Saint Peter to life."

"Back away!" shrieked Maestro Reni. "I won't fall for your witchcraft! Don't think I'm not wise to you."

"What's he talking about, Papa?" Artemisia whispered.

"Come along," he said, catching his daughter's elbow and steering her across the piazza. "We don't need to be involved in this."

∞

Artemisia didn't speak of the Guido Reni incident for a few days. Her father was an impatient man and tended not to dwell on matters when they did not affect him. He focused only on art. But the moment in

Piazza Navona haunted her. She could not erase the image of the fishmonger idolizing a painter—and that painter calling her a witch.

"Papa," she said as she ground pigment, "why did Maestro Reni make such a scene in the piazza the other day? The fishwife was devoutly religious and she was merely admiring him for his painting of Saint Peter."

"He has terrors, *figlia*," said her father, his paintbrush rasping on the weave of the canvas. "He doesn't trust women. He believes in the *Malleus Maleficarum*, that women are witches—and that the blessing she was giving him was really a curse."

"A curse? The *Malleus Maleficarum*?"

"The *Malleus Maleficarum* states that women are weak vessels—devoid of brains, promiscuous—more open to the devil. Seductresses of evil."

"That's absurd!"

"Ah, so you say, Signorina!" said her father, drawing back from the canvas to inspect his perspective.

"But it's wrong of him to assume all women are stupid, weak, or sorceresses."

Orazio's fingernail dug at the end of his paintbrush. "Why, Artemisia? Most men do."

"You don't, do you, Papa?" she said, aghast. "Would you believe Mama to be a sorceress?"

It took him too long to answer. Far too long for Artemisia's liking.

"She has her secrets and her powers," he said, dabbing at his paint. "I suppose all women do."

Artemisia looked at him, horrified. "What? What do you mean?"

"With her beauty, she is a temptress."

"Mama? A temptress?"

"You are a child," he said, shaking his head. "You don't understand women the way I do."

Artemisia sucked in her breath in fury. She hated him when he dismissed her this way. He did the same in his criticism of her art, her taste for color, and her predilection for shadow and drama.

"You make me angry!" she said, throwing down her pestle. She glared at him, her hands on her hips and her chest heaving with rage.

"Harness that emotion and use it in your art, daughter," he said, going back to his canvas. "We'll see where your passion takes you."

Chapter 9
ROME, 1605

Francesco and his two brothers hunched over their bowls, shoveling soup into their mouths.

"Finish up your lentils, Francesco," said Maddalena, looking up from her chopping board. "Your papa is sending Artemisia to buy pigment. You must accompany her."

"Varnish, Maddalena," Artemisia said. "Not pigment today."

"What difference is there and why should I care?" said the cook, dicing carrots at a staccato pace. "Francesco! Make sure no men approach her. Our Artemisia is becoming a signorina."

"Maddalena," she said. "I'm only twelve."

"You've started your monthlies," she whispered to the girl. "You could take a husband within a year or two. You are a lady now. Enjoy your freedom to walk in the streets. Soon your father will forbid it."

Artemisia looked at her in horror. "Why would he not let me out of the house?"

"Rome is a dangerous place for young maidens. Hurry along, Francesco."

Francesco tipped his bowl up, sucking at the last drop. "*Sì*, Maddalena. I will uphold the family honor."

Artemisia made a face of disgust. How she would love to wander the streets of Rome on her own. But Maddalena was right. Rome was a brutal, dangerous city, despite its alluring pleasures. A woman—even a young girl—could be snatched from the streets and raped or even sold into slavery by the foreign mercenaries within the city's walls. The Roman streets were men's terrain. Women were cloistered in homes or in shops alongside their husbands.

Francesco—though younger than she—represented a male witness and protector. She was lucky that she could leave the house, even with his escort.

Her father was indeed becoming stricter about her outings.

"I've heard in Florence, women are permitted to walk alone . . . or at least in pairs," Artemisia said, licking plum jam from her fingers.

Maddalena snorted. "And what red-blooded Roman would want to live in Florence? Of course the women are safe," she said, savagely attacking carrots with her blade. "The men of Florence have no *palle!*"

"No balls!" laughed Francesco. "*Brava*, Maddalena. *Brava!*"

"You take care of your sister," said Maddalena, shaking the tip of her knife at Francesco. "Or you'll end up a Florentine boy, *ragazzo!*"

Francesco winced.

"Come along!" Artemisia said, throwing her shawl over her shoulders. "I will wait for you downstairs."

She drew in a greedy breath of the city as she descended into the teeming streets of Rome.

As they walked, she realized that Maddalena was right. She was becoming a signorina. Although she wore a shawl and her most modest dress, men leered at her, muttering.

"What gorgeous chestnut hair you possess, *cara!*"

"Your skin is as delicate as a calla lily."

"You have the amber eyes of a tigress. Let me tame you!"

Francesco scowled at them like a tethered bulldog, his hand pressed tight against his sister's back.

"I'd like to hit them with a rock," Artemisia said. "Why should they stare at me?"

"You're a girl. Of course they will look at you that way."

"I shall look back at them. I will stare right at their *palle*." *Their balls.*

"Don't you dare! You bring dishonor to our family."

"*Vaffanculo!*" *Fuck you!*

The next passerby was a middle-aged man with brutish features and thick, stubby fingers. When her brother wasn't looking, he rubbed his groin, leering at Artemisia.

Instead of looking away as was expected, she narrowed her eyes and stared hard between his legs. She lifted her hand and stuck out her pointer and middle finger, imitating a witch's hex.

The man's fleshy eyelids flew open in horror.

"Stop it this minute, Artemisia," hissed her brother, who had turned around and seen her gesture.

"Why should I?" she said, not taking her eyes off the man she was attempting to hex. "You have no idea what it is to be a girl, Francesco! I want to be free."

Artemisia bit her index finger in the gesture that meant bloody revenge . . . and castration. The man hurried away, looking over his shoulder.

"Rome and Roman brutes. I want to go to Florence—"

"You can't really believe girls can walk in Florence without being accosted."

"They do, Francesco! In groups. I've heard so. Haven't you ever wanted to visit our Uncle Aurelio and see his bottega?" she said as they walked along the Via di Ripetta, bordering the Tiber River. Artemisia looked down into the swirling green-brown water.

"No," said Francesco, spitting on the ground in disgust. "I'm Roman. Florence? The Medici. Fucking faggots."

Artemisia stopped midstride. "Oh, *merda*!"

"Cosa?" What?

"Look. There is that disgusting friend of Father's, Cosimo Quorli. Quick! Let's cross the street before he sees us."

As they dodged through the maze of traffic, clattering carts, carriages, and wagons, a voice called out.

"Aspettate!" Wait.

Quorli, a prosperous, well-fed papal steward, panted hard as he chased after the two Gentileschis, his cloak and jowls fluttering.

"Wait, I say!"

Artemisia and Francesco reached the other side of Via di Ripetta. Artemisia grabbed Francesco's hand and ran, her long skirt flying. She had only gone a few strides when she tripped on her hem, falling to her knees.

Before she could scramble to her feet, a hand grasped Artemisia's shoulder, hot, meaty breath in her ear. "Is this how you treat a friend of the family?" Cosimo Quorli demanded, panting like a dog. "And a patron of your father?"

"Take your hands off her," said Francesco.

"Oh, the little signore," said Quorli, his lip curling up. "Defending the honor of your beautiful sister!" He dismissed Francesco as he would a bothersome gnat and turned toward Artemisia.

"I haven't seen you in a few years, *bella*," he said in a guttural whisper. "My, how you've grown. Soon you'll be ready to pluck, little flower. A couple of years—"

"Forgive me, Signor Quorli," Artemisia said, gathering her skirt and composure. "We are on an errand for my father. You will excuse us, but we are pressed for time."

"Why the hurry? On a beautiful sunny day in the streets of Rome, made for sauntering . . . why, you must be overjoyed to be let loose from your cage, my little bird."

"Come, Artemisia," said Francesco in a loud voice. "You are not permitted to speak to strangers."

"Ah, but I am no stranger to you," said Quorli, gesturing wide with upturned palms, as white as pig lard. Artemisia stared hard at them. *How could anyone have hands as ugly as his?*

He saw Artemisia staring in disgust. "No stranger, but a family friend!" he said, hiding his hands in the folds of his cloak. "To your father . . . and especially to your beautiful mother. You look so much like she did at your age, so innocent—"

Francesco turned on the papal steward, his face maroon in anger. "Do not speak of my mother," he shouted. "Do not speak to my sister! *Buongiorno, Signore!*"

Quorli was taken aback at the boy's anger and the volume of his voice. Several gawkers had gathered, standing witness to Francesco's loud protests.

A butcher wiped his bloody hand on his apron and left his meat tent to shake a finger at Quorli. "Lecherous old man. Leave the girl alone."

Quorli made a sour face, waving him away. He was a *nobile*, the butcher was nothing. But still, Quorli turned and walked away.

∽⊚

"Finish up shelling the beans, Artemisia," her mother said, breastfeeding her baby, Marco. "Maddalena will be here shortly and will need them." She sighed, shifting the baby in her arms.

"*Che succede?*" Artemisia said. "What's the matter, Mama?"

"Ah, *figlia mia*. It seems you have no time for your mama anymore."

Artemisia hung her head, feeling hot shame. Her father did demand more of her time, working with painting and taking her to visit other bottegas. And she cherished every moment, greedy for art. He had told her when she reached the age of thirteen, she would be his full-time apprentice.

Artemisia reached for her mother's hand, stroking it, at the same time caressing Marco's soft skin.

Already Mama's belly is rounded with another baby, she thought.

"I can find more time after sundown before bed, when the light has vanished," Artemisia said.

"It's not the work." There were tears in her mother's eyes. "It's that you are my only daughter. I want you by my side, to laugh and cry together, to see your beautiful face, your smile, your eyes. We are girls. You are my little *figlia*."

"You know I love you, Mama."

Girls shell beans, scrub pots, empty night soil from stinking pots, and gossip. They marry, feed their family, get pregnant, grow old, and die.

"*Sì,* I know you love me. But your papa holds you hostage up in the studio. *Cara,* I'm jealous of him, his time with you. Tuzia says a girl's place is beside her mother—"

"Tuzia! Why should I care what that vicious woman says?"

"Artemisia! She's my friend."

"No, she's not," Artemisia said, throwing down a bean pod in disgust. She thought of Tuzia's rouged lips. "Why is her husband never around?"

"He works outside Rome—"

"I despise that woman!"

Her mother's face crumpled. She didn't have many friends—she was too busy trying to keep up the household for her husband and his band of unruly child artists.

"Oh, Mama," Artemisia murmured. "I'm sorry."

"Forget Tuzia, *mia cara*," she said. "I'm talking about how much I love you. But you are growing up before your papa's eyes, not mine. You hurry through your work so you can go running to him and your paints."

Artemisia shoved away her pile of bean pods, making them rustle. She stood up and kissed her mother's cheek. "Oh, Mama. Forgive me."

"My daughter," Prudenzia said, raising her chin. Suddenly Artemisia saw a solemn look in her eyes. "I want to tell you things you should know. Important things you should know before . . ."

"Before what?"

"Before you hear dirty lies from someone else," Prudenzia said, turning away. When she turned around again her face was pale and pinched. "Francesco told me you saw Cosimo Quorli on Via di Ripetta today."

"Oh, Mama! How I loathe that man! He gives me *la pelle d'oca.*" *Gooseflesh.*

Her mother bit her lip, looking like she was about to cry. "That's why I must tell you, while there is time—"

"Artemisia!" Orazio's voice interrupted her. "Come up immediately and prepare that canvas!"

"*Sì*, Papa! *Subito!*" She turned to her mother, squeezing her hand. "There's time!" Artemisia laughed. "I'm not going anywhere, Mama."

A shiver shook her mother's spine. The tremor disturbed the baby from her nipple. He looked up and wailed.

"Say a prayer, Artemisia," whispered Prudenzia. "Someone just walked over my grave."

Chapter 10
ROME, 1605

By the time Artemisia was twelve she was able to paint well enough to sell her work, especially with Orazio's dash of salesmanship. He played up the fact that the artist was a girl who had great talent. An anomaly. *What an investment these paintings are! Now pleasing canvases to decorate a wall—but someday, this girl will be famous!*

As Artemisia painted she thought of Caravaggio's advice. These were indeed pretty pictures—flowers and fruit—and she was excited to see them sell, one by one. But she yearned to produce a painting—a work of true art—that was not "nice." Artemisia dreamed of Caravaggio's images. Stunning canvases that plunged into wells of darkness, resurfacing in pools of light. The power, the drama of his composition. Human beings caught in the frenzy of life. His was the exquisite skill that seized her soul.

Flowers and fruit . . . Bah! She hated them.

Beatrice Cenci's execution haunted her. Her bare neck, the executioner's botched attempt with his sword . . . blood, the life force draining from her veins.

"Finish painting that damned pear, Artemisia!" said Orazio over his shoulder. He had grappa on his breath. She knew that he had spent the afternoon drinking in Piazza Navona with Caravaggio, Mario Minniti, and others who added up to trouble. "And don't put a rotten spot on the fruit."

"Maestro Caravaggio does so. Windfall apples, wormholes, and brown blemishes."

"You are not Caravaggio. You are a twelve-year-old girl who is still learning to paint. We need to cultivate patrons. No one wants bruised fruit from a novice!"

She seethed, chewing the inside of her mouth. "Caravaggio said I was not to paint 'nice' things. He said—"

"Maestro Caravaggio isn't paying our rent. Damn him! I cannot even get him to pay for a jug of wine. And today he hurled a plate of artichokes at the waiter because he served them with oil, not butter!"

"Did he really?" she said, sucking in her breath with pleasure.

"He's a madman. He'll land the whole lot of us in prison again. Or in the galleys, rowing in chains for the rest of our lives."

Artemisia dabbed her brush in the madder lake, deepening the red on her blemish-free apple. She smiled, thinking of Maestro Caravaggio hurling artichokes.

∽

Artemisia's mother's *pancione* was rounded, huge with child. She was still young but each pregnancy had taken its toll. Artemisia sketched her in her mind: the lines of her ashen skin, her eyes sunken into the orbits of her skull. Her graceful stature crumpled under the hunch of her shoulder and her breasts were drooping, withered. The babies had consumed the bloom in her cheeks, extinguished the sparkle from her eyes.

In total there had been six Gentileschis born, but now only four remained: the three brothers—Francesco, Giulio, Marco—and Artemisia. Each one had drained the lifeblood from their mama. Artemisia bit her lip with guilt.

And one by one, each of us disappeared behind an easel in the studio, leaving her downstairs, alone.

As her mother grew more tired by the day, Artemisia asked her father for more time to help her with the housework, especially with a new baby on the way.

"She'll manage," said her father. "You focus on your art, Artemisia."

"But Papa. She is so tired—"

"And I'm tired of your mistakes! Look at the hand you painted on your Madonna! It is wildly out of perspective—it looks like a lion's paw. Scrape it off and try again."

The insult stung her, a hot flush climbing her neck and pulsing in her cheeks.

Papa is so cross with me these days. I can't do anything right.

Francesco and Giulio snickered from behind their easels.

Artemisia returned to her work.

Papa was right. My sense of perspective was all wrong.

As she set to work, she forgot all about her mother, wrestling instead with the Madonna's hand.

<hr>

Once a week on market day, Maddalena took the boys and Artemisia with her to the Campo de' Fiori. The boys carried big baskets and burlap bags to fill with their purchases. Next to visiting the pigment shop there was no errand that Artemisia loved more, especially on a crisp fall day when the apples were brought in, the mushrooms were copious, and the nuts had been harvested. In the autumn the scent of delicious food and woodsmoke carried far in the cool, brisk air.

The Roman marketplace was a palette of color, a festival of aromas. The bright vegetables and fruits—verdant lettuces and artichokes, scarlet peppers and tomatoes, orange pumpkins and Sicilian oranges. A brace of teal-toned pheasants hung in the butcher's tent alongside an open-mouthed hog's head, brown prosciutto, red fat-beaded salamis. The olive vendor dipped a wooden ladle deep into barrels of brine, drawing out his shining jewels in shades of bright green and glossy ebony. The intoxicating aromas of cheeses, roasting meats, and fresh-baked bread called from every direction. Stray cats yowled for trimmings and tidbits, weaving between the vendors' legs.

And the flowers! Lavender, tender violets, yellow-eyed daisies, and lacy wild carrot blooms were stacked in tarred buckets filled with cool water. Bouquets of purple lilacs attracted bees from every corner of the city, the market alive with buzzing.

The boys hurried off to buy themselves cones of honeyed almonds and roasted chestnuts. Maddalena and Artemisia inspected mushrooms from the forager's stand. The proprietor was in the mountains gathering and had left his elderly mother, Chiara, in charge. She was a one-eyed woman—her good eye startlingly blue, like a chip of the sky. Artemisia pored over the wood-colored porcini, separating the young, tender buttons from the more showy umbrella-shaped adults. Her hands flashed out of their own accord, arranging them in what seemed a haphazard pile, gracefully spilling like a cornucopia of bounty. She stepped back, letting the morning light bathe her composition.

She felt the blue eye studying her.

"You are an artist," Chiara said, pointing to the stack of mushrooms.

It wasn't a question, but Artemisia answered anyway. "Yes. I study under my father, Signor Orazio Gentileschi."

"I've heard tell of you. Your father is talented . . . they say you may be more so. I see that gift in you."

Artemisia blushed. "They? Who are they?"

The woman waved her hand, swooping the air. "*La gente, i Romani.* The people, the Romans. I hear things. People think because I am afflicted with blindness in one eye, I must not have good ears either."

Artemisia laughed.

"You must be very careful, Signorina," Chiara whispered, moving close to her ear. "There are bad people in the world. Very bad."

The girl studied the old woman's face, mapped with concern. The dark pupil of her eye constricted in worry.

Is this woman a witch?

Artemisia pointed to the porcini she had selected, her head cocked, studying the perfect still life they formed before the vendor's hand destroyed it. The woman plucked them gently from the pile, one by one, her fingernails rimmed with filth.

"Why are you staring at my hands, Signorina?" she asked.

Artemisia looked up at her sharp blue eye. "I admire them and want to remember. I'd like to paint them someday."

The old woman's face ruptured into a smile.

Maddalena called Chiara over to a pile of wood mushrooms—the ear-shaped *orecchione*—and orange chanterelles from the mountains. Before she left Artemisia, the old woman bowed. The blue eye blinked. "Heed my words, *cara*." *Dear one.*

Artemisia wandered away from Maddalena to inspect some buffalo mozzarella in the dairywoman's vat. The vendor drew out two pieces Artemisia indicated and laid them on a linen cloth—creamy balls, beaded with moisture.

"Two good ones," said a guttural voice next to her. "Round and firm."

Artemisia snapped her head around to find Signor Cosimo Quorli leering at her. She smelled his rancid breath, a front tooth black with rot.

"Every time I see you, Artemisia, you are more beautiful."

She backed away. The dairywoman saw her customer was threatened, or at the very least she feared she was going to lose a purchase. "See here, Signore!" she said. "Leave the girl in peace."

She said it loud enough that the melon vendor adjacent lifted his head. He whispered something to his son, who took off running.

Signor Quorli turned his back on the woman, moving closer to Artemisia.

"Providence must provide these fortunate encounters," he said, rolling his eyes up at the blue heavens. His lower lids were flaccid and rimmed in red like bloody meat. "Here I am to see the tooth puller and you appear. Your beauty takes away the pain."

Artemisia felt a flood of bright rage flowing in her veins.

Why should I have to have my little brother defend me or a man rush to my side?

She loved Campo de' Fiori and would stand her ground.

Her shoulders and back straightened as her anger blossomed. "Signor Quorli," she said with disdain. "I am charged with marketing for the week. Forgive me if I don't have time to speak to you." She turned back to the dairywoman. "Yes, I will take those two. And one more, even bigger than the pair together!"

The dairywoman laughed, covering her broken teeth with her hand. Her laugh and Artemisia's dismissive tone enraged Signor Quorli.

"How dare you talk to me in that way, Signorina," he said. "What are you, all of twelve? A girl, no less!"

She ignored him, saying nothing as the woman wrapped up the mozzarella in damp cloth. She gave coins to the vendor, then faced Quorli, her chin held high.

"Didn't you say I had grown?" she said, looking him straight in the eye. "Well, I've grown enough not to be afraid of you, Signor Quorli."

He glowered, rage seizing him. "Artemisia! Look at my face," he hissed, pointing to himself. "Don't you see a resemblance?"

A resemblance?

As she looked at him in shock, a hand pulled hard at her elbow. Maddalena pushed her charge behind her, defending the girl like a lioness. The melon boy stood panting beside her.

"Signor Quorli!" said Maddalena. "You know better than to talk to this girl unescorted!"

Signor Quorli snorted. "Bah! She's the daughter of my friends. Why shouldn't I?"

A growl began, low and mean, in Maddalena's throat. "Tend to your own business, Signore. You are never to approach her. *Ha capito?*" *Do you understand?*

Quorli's face hardened, the leer long gone but a dangerous expression taking its place. His narrow nose pulled up in haughtiness, his eyes narrowed to slits. "You forget your place, woman," he said. "How dare you address me in that tone! You are a servant."

"I am servant to Signor Orazio Gentileschi," she said, "and the signora. I know for a fact that I represent *her* wishes. Good day!"

❧

Walking home through the twisting cobblestone streets, Artemisia asked Maddalena, "How does that vile man know Mama? He told me once he knew her as a girl my age."

Maddalena gave her a hard look. "Rome is vast, but Rome is *piccola*—small as a teacup. He was a family friend when your mama was a girl."

They stopped on Via del Pellegrino and waited for the boys to catch up with them, the brothers burdened with the heavy load of groceries. As a noble's carriage rolled by, Maddalena looked at Artemisia.

"Signor Quorli is a wealthy patron and your father behaves courteously with him. He is not without influence. But do not speak of him to your mama."

"Why not?"

"Don't pester me with questions, Artemisia!"

"I have to know why he badgers me so," she insisted.

"Don't be selfish. You know your mother is weak now. The baby could come at any moment, though she's not due until Christmas. You mustn't say anything that will upset her."

"But Maddalena! He told me I resembled him."

Maddalena's mouth dropped open. "That evil monster!" she said, aghast. "Forget what he said! You are a beautiful girl—you look just like the signora! You paint like your father, but you have the face of an angel. Not of the devil!"

"But why would he say—"

"Because he is an evil demon who loved your mother, the lecher! She can't stand the sight of that man!" said Maddalena. "Stay away from him. He will bring your family nothing but dishonor."

The boys had caught up with them. Francesco glanced at Maddalena's angry face and then his sister's.

He knew better than to say anything.

Chapter 11
ROME, 1605

Artemisia fumed during her walk home from the Campo de' Fiori.

That wretched animal hunts me like prey. I shall never let that monster touch me!

She thought hard how she could seek revenge. Somehow. She looked down at her chipped nails, colored a nasty yellow. A sickly skin tone. An evil one.

Of course! She almost laughed. *I shall have my revenge, by God!*

By December Artemisia had finished over thirty still lifes—fruit or flowers. She assisted in the preparation and background work of five of her father's new canvases.

Her fingers were deeply stained with mottled color, her fingernails cracked like eggshells from the caustic turpentine. She worked and reworked studies for her *Susanna and the Elders*, trying hard to avoid her father's criticism. She knew she did not have the honed craft to complete the painting . . . not yet. But someday.

In the Bible story, Susanna, a married woman, is relaxing in the waters, bathing in her walled garden. The maid, her chaperone, leaves her for a few moments to fetch soap. Then the two village elders, powerful men and lechers, peek over the wall, watching the young nude woman at her bath. They call to her: "Let us lie with you—each one of us taking his turn—or we shall report that we have witnessed you making love to a young man."

"I am a virtuous wife!" cries Susanna, clutching a cloth to cover her nude body.

"No matter," they sneer. "You must choose. Lie with us or be stoned for adultery."

And now, as Artemisia pictured the scene, she saw one figure emerge, the face of an elder, rich and portly. Lecherous.

Cosimo Quorli!

She smiled triumphantly.

The other face, the second elder, she could not see.

Yet.

As soon as they arrived home after Christmas Mass, Artemisia ran into the house to find her mother without taking time to hang up her shawl or cloak. She had decided she would demand that her mother tell her about her past with Cosimo Quorli.

She could not wait another minute. She wanted to empty her heart to her mother on that Christmas Eve.

But as she put her foot on the first step of the stairs, something deep inside gnawed like a rodent, chewing at her gut.

Something was wrong.

"Mama! Mama!" she cried, flying up the stairs.

What Artemisia heard in response was a low moan that paralyzed her.

Her mother lay in her room, the shutters closed tight. Her father sat beside her, his face twisted with worry.

"The baby?" Artemisia said.

"It's—it's not going right," said her father. "I have seen her in labor many times before. Go! Find Francesco and send him to fetch the midwife."

Artemisia burst out of the room and ran through the corridor, nearly knocking down Maddalena, who was putting the food into the larder.

"Mama's not well!" Artemisia cried. "Francesco's to fetch the midwife, *subito*!"

"Santa Maria!" Maddalena whispered.

Francesco heard his sister's voice and appeared at the threshold of the kitchen.

"Run for the midwife, brother! Mama's having a hard time."

He was gone before she could finish the sentence.

The afternoon faded into evening. Maddalena left out prosciutto, bread, and cheese for the family on the table, but it lay untouched.

Artemisia stayed by her mother's side, bathing her forehead and temples in cool water. She coaxed her to drink, a cup at her lips.

"No, *figlia*," her mother said, her hand pushing the cup away.

"But Mama," she said. "You need refreshment. The baby's coming."

Her mother rocked her head feebly from side to side on the pillow, her dark hair fanned out on the bed linen. "This baby will not come. He and I will both die."

"Oh, Mama!" Artemisia clasped her mother's hand tight. "Say a prayer at once."

"You pray for me. Paint me someday. That would please God."

Artemisia shook her head, mute with fear.

Paint you? I've been secretly painting you since I was six years old!

Artemisia did not say that her mother's beauty had vanished and the ghost of death possessed her features now. There was no blood in her face, her lips were blue. Her belly was bloated and still.

Only her eyes were alive, but just barely.

"Let her rest," said a kind but authoritative voice. It was the midwife, whom Francesco had finally tracked down at the market in Campo de' Fiori. "Eat some food now. Rest. I am here with your mama."

Francesco hung back in the doorway, his hands clasped on the frame as if he would faint. Artemisia embraced him as she left the room.

"Will she die?" he asked, his brown eyes terrified.

"I don't know."

The midwife stood up and murmured into Orazio's ear.

"Fetch the priest, *figlio*," he said to Francesco. "Run as fast as you can."

Then they all knew.

⁓

Hours later, long after midnight, Prudenzia called for her daughter. Maddalena ushered her into the darkened room, fetid with rancid sweat and blood. Artemisia drew her hem up over her nose to cover it, but Maddalena gently pulled her hand away.

"You'll get used to it," she said, her face illuminated by the flickering candle.

Get used to it? I can hardly breathe!

"Let me see my daughter . . . alone," croaked Prudenzia.

"*Sì*, Signora," said Maddalena, bowing her head. She turned, closing the door soundlessly.

Prudenzia sought her daughter's hand. Her grip was cold, her fingers like ice.

"I want to warn you," Prudenzia said. "Artemisia! There are such dangers in the world. And lies."

"What danger? What lies?"

"Men. Men lie."

"What, Mama? Who lied to you?"

"That man you hate. Cosimo Quorli. You are right to hate him."

"He's an awful man, Mama! How do you know him?"

She groaned and closed her eyes. Tears spilled down her cheeks. "He took me as a young girl, as a husband takes a wife, but against my will. My reputation was ruined. Your father married me. An artist doesn't care. Doesn't care . . ."

She began to cough, her tears choking her.

"Your papa loved me, no matter what Rome thought. But he always doubted . . ."

"Doubted what?"

"Whether you were really his child."

"Cosa?" What?

"You *are*, Artemisia! You are his flesh and blood. Never doubt it."

Artemisia couldn't speak.

"Men can rob you, Artemisia. They take everything. Your reputation, your respect. Don't let them, *cara*. Promise me you won't let them."

Artemisia looked into her mother's eyes, faded with pain and fatigue. She squeezed her hand harder than she should have, and saw her mother wince. "No man shall hurt me like Signor Quorli has hurt you. I shall hate him for all my life, in your honor, Mama."

"Don't speak of this with your papa," Prudenzia gasped. "The doubt destroys him. He pushes you so . . . hard with your art. He wants to prove . . ."

She broke off, stabbed by a twisting pain that stole away her breath.

"Don't talk any more, Mama," Artemisia said. "Hush and rest. I'm with you. I promise."

She crawled into the narrow bed next to her mother, stroking her face until Prudenzia closed her eyes. She never opened them again, but Artemisia felt the wetness of her mother's tears long after the warmth left her body.

Maddalena was right. Artemisia grew accustomed to the air.

Her mama was gone. All the tenderness Artemisia had known vanished with her.

The thought of Cosimo Quorli enraged her. She swore she would never trust what he said. Or any man. Ever.

What sacrifices Mama made for her husband, for us. Her beauty and strength faded with each birth, but her love never weakened.

Artemisia stared, numb, from the doorway at the dead body, lit by beeswax candles. She had lain that way as Artemisia had crawled away from her last embrace.

The word that Orazio Gentileschi's wife had died was carried from one mouth to another. A steady stream of friends, patrons, and neighbors arrived to pay their respects, bring candles, and offer prayers. They pressed into the room, filling it with the warm scent of the living.

Her sons gathered around her bed, their faces contorted in sorrow. The unborn baby was left in her womb, her bloated belly his burial mound.

"Come," said Tuzia, the neighbor. "Sit next to your mama, Artemisia. Keep vigil."

"That's not my mama," Artemisia said, too stunned at the transformation to cry. "My mama is gone."

Tuzia clasped Artemisia's hand and led the girl over to the chair where the midwife had sat. "Your papa is making burial arrangements," she whispered. "It's your place to be at your mama's side."

But that's not Mama! Artemisia wanted to scream.

Through a gap in the curtains, the afternoon light streamed over Prudenzia's once beautiful face. The golden rays illuminated her waxen skin.

A sob rocked Artemisia's body and she bent over, crying into her hands. She felt the warmth of the sun kiss the top of her shoulders and neck, where her blouse and pinafore left her skin bare.

"It is good for her to cry," pronounced Tuzia to the crowd of mourners.

"Is it?" said a man's voice.

Artemisia recognized that voice. It was Caravaggio.

By the time she had wiped the tears from her eyes, he had vanished.

Chapter 12
ROME, 1605-06

After her mother's funeral Artemisia threw herself into painting. She slept in the studio every night, begging for more candles and oil to illuminate her work.

Orazio obliged her. Perhaps it was to feed her passion and progress. Or perhaps he was simply happy that his sorrow-stricken daughter was upstairs and out of the way. Shortly after Prudenzia's death, Tuzia began sharing Orazio's bed.

Tuzia's husband was rarely home and didn't pay the rent. Artemisia supposed her father accepted Tuzia's body in exchange for the twenty-one scudi they still owed for the upstairs rooms.

Even from the studio, Artemisia could certainly hear her father's grunts and Tuzia's moans and coaxing from below. Bitter tears spotted her smock as she painted on through the night. Tuzia had been her mother's best friend. She hated Tuzia for lying in her dead mama's bed so soon after her death. And she hated her father for his weakness, yielding to Tuzia's flesh.

Never had Artemisia felt so lonely. Moreover, after Prudenzia's death, Orazio forbade his daughter to leave the house.

"You are a whore to want to walk the streets," he accused her one night while finishing off a flask of wine.

"A whore!" she screamed at him. "Because I want to breathe fresh air, to see the faces and life of Rome?"

"Work on your still lifes."

"I want to paint people, Papa! Like you do, like Caravaggio does!" She threw the bread plate, smashing it to bits on the tile floor. He grabbed her hair, yanking her into her room. He pushed her roughly onto her bed and stood in the doorway, panting.

"You are no better than your mother!" he bellowed.

Artemisia sat up in bed and stared at him. "What are you talking about?" she shouted. "My mother was a saint! A saint to put up with you!"

Orazio slammed the bedroom door, locking it. She pounded her fists against the wood until her hands came away bloody. No one let her out until Maddalena turned the key the next morning.

"He calls me a whore, Maddalena!" she cried. "I've not so much as kissed a man! I'm not yet thirteen years old."

Maddalena comforted her, pulling the girl tight to her breast.

"You father is mad with grief . . . and doubt," she said. "Cosimo Quorli's long, ugly shadow haunts him. He is tormented."

Artemisia thought about Maddalena's words. As much as Orazio hated Quorli, they were business partners. Quorli convinced rich Roman nobles to purchase Orazio's paintings.

Cosimo Quorli and Orazio Gentileschi were inextricably bound.

❧

The still lifes Artemisia painted brought in money. She had an eye for detail, form, and color that translated into a pleasing product. Noble families bought them to decorate their villas.

Still lifes! I hate every one of them.

One day she was painting a bowl of pears. A fly crept across the blemished skin of one piece of fruit. She painted what she saw, freezing the insect forever on the bruised flesh.

She felt her father's presence behind her shoulder.

"Scrape that off," he grumbled.

"Why should I?" she said, whirling around to face him. "It's the truth! You can't force me to paint these lifeless canvases for the rest of my life!"

"When you are more accomplished you can paint with more ambition. These paintings are selling well."

"I don't care whether they sell or don't! I despise them."

Orazio's face turned stony. She prepared herself for a slap across the face.

"Get your cloak and shawl."

"Papa?" she said. "We are going out?"

"Do as I say."

❧

It had been weeks since Artemisia had been allowed out of the bottega. They walked along the Via del Corso, Orazio exchanging morning greetings with the passersby.

"Buongiorno, Maestro Gentileschi," ran the greetings.

"Such a *bellissima* day! Ah, and your daughter! She, too, is *bellissima.*"

"Grazie," he said, guiding her along by the elbow.

"Do not smile so much, Artemisia," he muttered. "You attract attention."

They reached an oak-plank door studded with iron spikes. Orazio raised the metal door knocker, letting it fall and resonate against the wood. A boy answered the door, his linen shirt spotted with resin and paint.

"Please tell Maestro Gaia that Orazio Gentileschi and his daughter, Artemisia, are here to see him."

The boy nodded, opening the door wide. *"Certo, Maestro Gentileschi,"* he said, bowing. "Please wait here."

The boy had barely mounted the stairs when Maestro Pietro Gaia, a fine-boned, pale man, came down, wiping his hands on a cloth. "Orazio!" he said, his wan face splitting into a smile. "To what do I owe this great honor?"

Maestro Gaia spotted Artemisia, and bowed.

"This is my daughter, Artemisia," said Orazio. "I would like her to meet your niece, Giovanna Garzoni. I understand she paints in your bottega. I have seen her work in the market. Remarkable talent."

"Piacere," said Maestro Gaia, kissing Artemisia's hand. *A pleasure.* *"Certo.* She is upstairs working now."

Artemisia smiled at the gallant man. She recognized his accent as Venetian.

The Gentileschis were ushered up the stairs. The maestro had four apprentices working in his studio that morning. Among them was a pale, blond girl not more than six years old, dressed in a blue smock. She stood in front of an easel, painting a plate of fava beans.

Artemisia felt a shiver of astonishment—and a quick stab of jealousy—at the little girl's skill with watercolors, a notoriously difficult medium.

"May I introduce you to my niece, Giovanna Garzoni," said Maestro Gaia.

The little girl looked at Artemisia reluctantly. Artemisia recognized the annoyance—even pain—of an artist being dragged away from her work.

"Giovanna. This is Maestro Gentileschi and his daughter, Signorina Artemisia."

Her mouth opened in delight, forming a perfect O. *"Piacere,"* she said. "I have heard much about you, Signorina Gentileschi. How I have hoped to meet you!"

"You have remarkable talent for such a young age," Artemisia sniffed. She was only thirteen herself and thought she was the only girl in Rome who painted skillfully.

"We have come to show Artemisia your graceful—and stunning—still lifes, Signorina Garzoni," said Orazio.

"You are very kind," said her uncle. "Giovanna is of course only learning to paint. But I am quite pleased with her progress. We sell these pieces in the Campo de' Fiori now, but she will have her own patrons in a few years if she continues to work hard at her art."

Artemisia looked at the girl's hands, as pale as snow. She could see tracings of blue veins through her delicate skin. *How can this little bird of a girl possess such talent?*

"I hear that you paint figures," said Giovanna to Artemisia. "Dramatic scenes of passion! My uncle has seen them in your father's bottega."

"Only as practice," said Orazio. "Right now she has a lucrative practice painting still lifes. I wanted her to see your talent. Your success!"

"I paint still lifes because I admire the tranquility," said Giovanna. "To paint the passionate scenes of history—ah, how I should love to see your work, Signorina Gentileschi."

Orazio jutted out his lip, frowning. Artemisia smiled.

Ha! This meeting is not going as he planned!

She seized on the moment. "I should love you to see my work. May I call you Giovanna?"

"Certo!" the girl said, smiling.

Artemisia kissed her cheek. "You must call me Artemisia. Please show me all your paintings."

Although she saw the flaws in Giovanna's work, Artemisia also saw the stunning potential. They chattered about the challenges of tempera versus oil paint, the decisions of light and shading, the delight in finding blemishes and flaws in a subject—bugs, rot, speckles, and irregular forms.

Artemisia had never had a close girlfriend, and though this girl was seven years her junior, they forged a bond that day.

As they walked home, Orazio fumed.

"You see the talent that girl has!" he said. "Her paintings will someday grace the most prestigious households of Europe. Wait a few years and mark my words. The Medici will catch wind of her—"

"Giovanna is most talented," Artemisia said. "She was born to paint . . . still lifes!"

"What is wrong with still lifes? They sell!"

"They don't . . . call to me, Papa. You know that. You don't paint still lifes."

"I'm a man."

"What difference does that make?"

"Still lifes . . . even portraits. They are a lesser art. Softer, more feminine—"

"You see! I'm no different than you. The human form—the drama of life!" Artemisia stopped walking and stood in the Via del Corso. She pinched her fingers to her thumb, shaking them in his face. "Papa! You taught me this! You! How can I settle for still life?"

She saw a wave of recognition drift over his face, striking a bright spark of pride in his eyes. "You are indeed my daughter," he said, embracing her. "I only meant to protect you from the world of men."

"It is too late for that," she said, breathing in his scent. "I am an artist."

◦◦◦

One day, seven months after Prudenzia's funeral, there was a knock on the door. Maddalena answered and Artemisia heard a familiar voice float up from the entryway.

"May I speak to Signor Gentileschi?"

Cecco!

Artemisia gathered her skirts above her ankles and ran down the stairs at breakneck speed. Maddalena, who had not seen her so animated in months, stared at her in shock.

"Come in, Cecco!" Artemisia said. "Come in."

Escorted by Maddalena, she led Cecco into the small sitting room off the kitchen.

"Tell me. How is your art progressing? Has your master completed any new works?" She was bursting with questions.

Cecco bowed his head. "He sends his respects to you and your father. He did not attend the funeral, but would like to invite you— all the Gentileschis—to the unveiling of his newest painting. It shall be three days hence in Trastevere at the Carmelite Church of Santa Maria della Scala, in the midmorning hour when the light strikes bright from the east. He says it is most important that you be in attendance, Signorina Gentileschi."

"We shall be honored to attend. Thank him for the honor of his invitation."

She felt Maddalena's eyes on her. The older woman smiled and nodded at Cecco. This was to be only Artemisia's second outing since the death of her mother.

Orazio, Francesco, Giulio, Marco, and Artemisia crossed the Tiber River early on an August morning to attend the installation of the painting. They hired a coach to take them to Santa Maria della Scala. The sun was already a round, mean patch of fire rising in the east, promising a searing heat by midday.

The cream-colored Santa Maria della Scala, with its simple facade, was unimposing.

"The Carmelites are strict, hawkish in their observance of the scriptures and the Holy Catholic Church," said Orazio.

Artemisia squinted in the sunlight. "Caravaggio—his art—"

"*Sì.* It does not bode well for our friend Michele . . . I can't understand why he was given this commission."

They heard the murmurs even before they entered the church. Milling about were brown-robed friars, their sandals slapping against the marble floor.

"How dare he?" sputtered a Carmelite monk. "Our blessed Holy Mother, sprawled like a common whore across the bed."

"The bloated belly!" said his companion, rubbing his head. "Blasphemous!"

Artemisia swallowed hard and looked up at her father. He closed his eyes for a second and then nodded that they should proceed forward.

The church was mobbed by the clergy of Rome, every major artist in the city, and nobility. The commoners kept their distance in the pews, silently kneeling, peeking through their hands folded in prayer.

More than ten feet tall and eight feet wide, *Death of the Virgin* was visible from the entry. Artemisia stood paralyzed. Her middle brother, Giulio, bumped into her from behind. "Move ahead, Artemisia!" he whispered hoarsely. "You're blocking everyone."

As she moved closer, she saw Caravaggio at the foot of the painting, engaged in a fierce argument with three monks. He made an angry gesture with his hand, dismissing a remark. His face was tense, colored red with rage.

Then he saw that the Gentileschis had entered the church.

As Artemisia looked up to study the painting, she felt his eyes watching her.

Caravaggio's Mary sprawled across a bed, her head turned toward the viewer. Her right hand was stretched over her bloated abdomen, her left hand inert, bent at the wrist, hanging off the pillow and bed.

The bloated abdomen. Could she be . . . ?

Mary's dead face was bathed in dazzling light against a dark background of mourners, the disciples of Jesus.

Beside Mary was a girl, dressed in an ochre-colored pinafore.

My pinafore!

The girl held her head in her hands, weeping. The sunlight that illuminated Mary's lifeless face also struck the grieving girl's bare neck.

My shoulders. My grief!

Artemisia covered her mouth in awe, her eyes wide, taking in every detail. Caravaggio looked at her. He nodded solemnly.

Then he returned to his argument with the monks, with renewed energy.

Chapter 13
ROME, 1606–08

Tuzia spent more and more time in the Gentileschi household. Artemisia heard her grunts and squeals night after night in her father's bed—her mother's bed, damn them! She knew her suspicions had always been correct.

The next morning Tuzia always appeared in the kitchen, bustling about as if she were the lady of the house.

"I hear that Caravaggio's latest catastrophe has been removed from Santa Maria della Scala," she said one morning, counting the iron cutlery adorned with bone handles.

"Why are you counting the knives and forks?" Artemisia wanted to slap her hands. *These things belonged to my mother!*

"You never know, with the help," sniffed Tuzia.

"What are you implying? Maddalena? Maddalena was my mother's maid when she was a girl. She raised me and all my brothers. There is no one more trustworthy."

"One cannot be too cautious," said Tuzia, her eyebrow raised. Her beefy, low-class hands that fondled Artemisia's father's body now touched all her mother's possessions as if she had inherited them.

"So," Tuzia said. "I hear that Caravaggio's painting was taken down almost immediately."

"And sold to the Gonzaga family, dukes of Mantua. They recognize great art."

"Nonetheless. He's a hateful man. They say this last rejection has driven him mad. Serves him right."

Artemisia closed her eyes tight, trying to erase Tuzia's words, her proximity—everything about her—from her mind. "His painting *Death of the Virgin* was exquisite."

Tuzia stared at her, aghast. "The Madonna is dead, sprawled across the bed! I heard he used a prostitute as a model. Do you think God wants the image of the Holy Mother to be a whore?"

All Rome thought the model was a prostitute. Artemisia knew better. Perhaps the face, yes. But Caravaggio had been in their house the night her mother died.

"His talent is he can make a prostitute into the Holy Mary," said Artemisia. "God aside, that is his genius."

"Shameful is what it is! Why can't he paint pretty pictures like Maestro Carracci and Maestro Baglione? Your father can do that, too, when he's inspired to do so. Maybe I can convince him to soften his tone, to paint something nice . . . even if your mother couldn't."

Her words punched Artemisia hard in the gut.

"You don't understand," she said in disgust. She picked up her skirt and marched up the stairs to the studio. "You'll certainly never influence my father's art. You couldn't possibly."

∽◌

Her father told her Caravaggio had fled Rome.

"Perché?" Why?

"He murdered a man, Artemisia," said Papa. "He killed a pimp in a duel. Some say it was a bet unpaid. I know better . . . it was a woman."

Artemisia thought of Cecco. What would become of him?

"Serves that damned Caravaggio right," said her father. "Rome is well rid of him, as are we."

"What are you saying?" she cried. "He was your best friend—"

"He landed me in prison in Tor di Nona. Your mother hated him—" Orazio's face crumpled and he began to cry.

Artemisia watched him, astonished. She studied her father's face. Her father was changing before her eyes. He was becoming a bitter old man. And the great master Caravaggio had left his life.

And her life as well.

Artemisia had seen *Death of the Virgin* and exchanged looks with the great master embroiled in a heated argument with the Carmelite monks.

Did Papa even realize Caravaggio painted my dead mother—only putting another woman's face on her body?

Did he realize that weeping girl—her face covered by her hands— was me?

She watched her father sob, a broken wreck of a man. She would never mention it.

"Will he ever return?"

"Only dead or in chains to row in the galleys," said Orazio, wiping his eyes with his wrist. "The pope has a price on his head. We will never see him again."

That night the two artists—father and daughter—mourned Caravaggio, though it would be several years before the news reached them of his tragic death along a desolate shore north of Naples.

Artemisia looked out the window, stunned. Rome spread out below her, noisy and alive, unaware that its great master was gone forever.

Every day—and every night, by candlelight—Artemisia examined her body. Her breasts had developed, round and full. She loved the curving softness of them, the delicate pink of the nipples. Her hips were wider now, her pubic hair dark, and she was getting her monthlies, as was normal.

As she matured, she realized: her body was art.

Orazio gave her a handheld looking glass for her fifteenth birthday. It was small but costly. She threw her arms around him.

"*Auguri*, Artemisia," he said. "Best wishes. You are a woman now."

She gasped with joy, gazing at her own face. Then she caught the sunlight from the window in the mirror, sending a medallion of gold bouncing off the walls. She laughed, playing with the light as her youngest brother, Marco, ran wildly around the room, chasing the reflection and never catching it.

Tuzia frowned. "A looking glass?" she said. "Orazio, such an expensive gift. Are you trying to teach the girl to be vain?"

Orazio looked at Tuzia as if she were an imbecile. "I'm teaching the girl about herself, Tuzia," he said sharply. "A girl so beautiful must know and respect her body. She is a work of art."

"Well. Perhaps she'll learn to comb her hair and wash the paint and charcoals from her face. She is an untidy mess."

With the mirror, Artemisia examined every inch of her body, painting study after study until she mastered the techniques required to capture the young flesh, muscles, and undulations of her developing physique. She lay on her bed with her sketch paper, twisting this way and that, perfecting her execution of the female form.

She studied her face, something she had never been able to do before in private, without fear of being caught gazing at herself and accused of vanity. Her tumble of auburn hair, its thick waves . . . a range of ochres with burnt earth umber would do, playing with lighter highlights and shadowy browns according to the thickness and how the light caught the red. Her luminous brown eyes. Yet they were not just "brown," were they? A touch of golden softness muted with earth tones, a hint of moss-colored green. Her mouth was sensuous, lips full and curving, her neck and shoulders womanly.

Her flesh—white from confinement and plump with youth—almost a baby's. How had she not realized the sweet vulnerability of her skin? Ah, the looking glass revealed secrets about herself she was only beginning to discover.

And with each discovery came a valuable lesson in the painting of a woman's form.

∾

After her mother's death, her father grieved through his art for years. He painted an exquisite series of beatific Madonnas, with the Lord as a baby suckling at her breast. But Artemisia gasped at his inept rendering of Mary's breast. It was as if he had no knowledge at all of a woman's bosom and how it swelled and retreated, meeting the armpit.

She spent weeks studying herself and especially her breasts, employing her looking glass to see the shadows and angles of anatomy.

How could my father make such a colossal mistake?

She came to understand the depth of her father's grief through his art. Though the presence of Tuzia in their household disgusted her, she gradually realized Orazio took only physical comfort with the woman. Tuzia was no more than another whore in his bed, a warm release for his carnal desires.

Tuzia would never take her mother's place. And she would never be his muse.

With time, Artemisia came to see Tuzia as another servant, though not beloved like Maddalena, who had raised her mother and who had assisted in the births of all of the Gentileschi children. Nevertheless, in Tuzia's efforts to take over her mother's role, she cleaned, scrubbed, shopped, and cooked alongside Maddalena, though constantly sparring with her. Artemisia never shelled another bean and never was called away from her art. Thanks to Tuzia, she did not step into her mother's role as housewife but spent every hour painting in the upstairs studio.

With Tuzia as her matronly—and shrewish—escort, Artemisia was able to walk the streets of Rome again. No one would cross Tuzia. She became a chaperone, though she was more interested in swapping gossip with the other women they met in the streets and markets.

Artemisia wondered what Tuzia thought as her father's paintings of breastfeeding Madonnas multiplied. Was she jealous? Or could she even see her mother's resemblance in the paintings? Tuzia was as stupid as a block of wood. When she looked at Orazio's art, it was as if a cat had been set in front of the canvas. She saw nothing, could feel nothing.

∞

News of Caravaggio in Naples reached them in Rome. He had painted *The Seven Acts of Mercy* for the Pio Monte della Misericordia church. Copies by other artists trickled into Rome. The artists of the Campo Marzio gathered in a bottega off the Piazza Navona, discussing the composition.

The whirling vortex of drama was unlike anything Caravaggio had ever painted. Seven acts of mercy, among them succor to the poor, the ailing, the destitute. Artemisia's eyes fastened on a young woman baring her breast to suckle an old man.

"What is she doing?" she asked her father, pointing at the image.

"It is the classical story of Pero, the daughter, giving nourishment to her incarcerated father, Cimon," he said.

"His daughter gave him her breast?"

"He was sentenced to death by starvation. His daughter's milk kept him alive until she was found out by the jailer. The officials so admired the selfless deed that Cimon was released."

"No purer example of a devoted daughter," said the artist Annibale Carracci, listening to their conversation. He put his hand on Artemisia's shoulder.

She recalled the warm weight of Caravaggio's hand on her years ago when she had viewed *The Calling of St. Matthew*.

Two masters of Rome have touched my shoulders.

"I only wish I could see the original," Carracci said. "I may have to make a trip to Napoli to see it in person."

Artemisia swore to herself that she, too, would one day see Caravaggio's work in Naples.

༄

The next day when Orazio applied the varnish to yet another misshapen Madonna, Artemisia frowned at his work.

"What's the matter?" he asked peevishly. "You look like you just swallowed a lemon."

"Papa. It's all wrong . . . Can't you see that her bosom is suspended in the air like a child's ball? No woman has a breast like that!"

Orazio's hands tightened into hard fists. His face turned white, then purple with anger. "How dare you criticize my work! You . . . you vicious slut!"

Her father had always doted on Artemisia as his protégée, but she had felt the gradual winds of change in the air since her mother's death. The storm was only worsening.

"Slut? Slut! You call your own daughter a slut because I dare say what is obvious? Any fishwife would laugh at your clumsiness, knowing her own body."

Orazio trembled with anger. "Get out! Get out of the studio! You—whore!"

Artemisia threw up her hands in anger and walked to the door. She turned back to him from the doorway. "You raised me to be an artist. I see what I see . . . and I tell you the truth, Papa. It's all wrong!"

As she pulled the latch closed she began to think. She had always admired her father's work—none of it quite approached Caravaggio's vision or execution, but his art inspired her, nurtured her.

Is it his fault that he has no model to pose nude for him?

The Vatican had forbidden women from posing nude. Yes, there were *delle puttane* who would work for the right price, but they were expensive and capricious, and the risk—especially as Orazio received more and more commissions from the Church and clergy—was not worth it.

You'd think a man who frequented whorehouses and had women in his bed would know something about how to paint their bodies!

Orazio's voracious lust for the act of sex rendered him blind to a woman's physical aspects while he was in the throes of animal passion. Then he left the bed or retreated into sleep.

What a wasted opportunity!

Artemisia lingered outside the studio, realizing how difficult it must be for Papa. These Madonnas, his art, were all he had left now that Mama was dead.

And he had made them imperfect.

"Papa," Artemisia said gently as she reentered the bottega.

"Go away!" he sniveled, collapsed on the floor. "Get out of—"

"I want to help you, Papa," she said. She dared to touch his cheek— wet with tears. He pulled his face away from her as if she had scorched him. "Let me pose for you. You'll see. You will capture—"

"What?" he gasped.

"Papa. For art. For your art."

"My daughter!" he said, straightening up. His mouth dropped, aghast. "I could never ask such a thing of you—"

"You have not asked," Artemisia said, unlacing the tie of her blouse. She pulled the linen garment over her head.

Her father stared at her breasts, swallowing hard.

"It is my gift to you. Art is what is most important. Now pick up your brush. And get it right this time, Papa."

Chapter 14
ROME, 1608

Cecco had disappeared. It was rumored that he had accompanied his master to Naples.

Artemisia hoped she would see him again—that she would see both of them. Every time she went to Piazza Navona, she surveyed the area, looking for Cecco's face among the dense crowd. Though she never saw him, she did see the beautiful prostitute who was the model for many of Maestro Caravaggio's paintings, including the face in *Death of the Virgin*. She always stood in front of the church of San Giacomo degli Spagnoli.

While Tuzia was busy gossiping with a knot of her friends, Artemisia stepped a few paces away to where the woman stood, her back against the wall of the church, waiting for business. Her head was lowered, her gaze not meeting the eyes of the decent women in the piazza.

"*Scusa,*" Artemisia said. "I know you from Maestro Caravaggio's work. You were the model for *Madonna di Loreto*, weren't you? And *Death of the Virgin?*"

The beautiful woman unfurled her head like a violet blooming. Her face lit up, radiating happiness. Then she looked around dubiously.

"Signorina!" she said, meeting Artemisia's eyes. "Aren't you afraid of what your chaperone will say?" She nodded toward Tuzia, still busily exchanging news with her friends.

"I don't care what she says or anyone else. Your beauty astounds me. I can see why Maestro Caravaggio was so taken by you."

The smile that spread across her face was beatific. Artemisia understood why Caravaggio had fallen in love with her.

"The baby Jesus in his painting *Madonna di Loreto* is my own son," she said shyly.

"Your son? He is magnificent as well! Is it his little foot treading on the snake in the *Madonna and Child with St. Anne*? How did you ever get the boy to hold still for so long? None of our young models will do that."

"Oh! You are an artist!" gasped the woman, covering her mouth and less-than-perfect teeth.

"I am."

"My name is Lena Antognetti," the woman said, bobbing a curtsy as if Artemisia were nobility.

Artemisia stepped forward and gave her a kiss on both cheeks. Lena flushed, her hand hovering over her left cheek in astonishment.

"I am Artemisia Gentileschi, daughter of Orazio, a good friend of Caravaggio."

"I know your father," Lena said, lowering her eyes.

Artemisia wondered if Lena knew her father intimately. Perhaps he was a regular customer. She had no idea where he took his pleasure. She only knew that some mornings when Orazio took his place behind his easel he reeked of sex, even when Tuzia had not shared his bed.

"May I?" Artemisia said. She gently lifted the woman's chin, drinking in her perfect bone structure. She turned Lena's head slightly in profile to see the sun glance off her cheekbones.

Artemisia continued studying Lena's skin, wondering what paints she could prepare to capture her luminous complexion.

"You look at me the way Michele did," Lena whispered, her chin still balanced in Artemisia's hand. "As an artist. But . . . you are a girl."

How would I capture the vulnerability in her eyes, how could I harness her spirit?

The humility. The shame.

Yes . . . the Penitent Magdalene!

"Signorina Artemisia. People are staring at you," said Lena, gently pulling the artist's hand away from her chin. "They think your behavior strange."

"Hmm . . ." Artemisia said, still studying her. "I'm used to that."

When Artemisia finally looked away, she caught sight of a white-kerchiefed woman whispering in Tuzia's ear. Tuzia's head snapped around, searching for her.

"Have you seen Maestro Caravaggio lately?" Artemisia asked Lena, her words tumbling out now. Tuzia would be there in no time. "Or Cecco?"

"I spoke to Cecco only briefly," said Lena. "He is living in Naples, though his master is to depart for Malta. I suppose the boy will return to Rome soon."

"Malta? Caravaggio is sailing to Malta?"

"He will be safe from the pope there. Who knows? Perhaps he will become a Knight of Malta." She laughed, which provoked a convulsion of coughing. She pulled a blood-speckled handkerchief from her cleavage. "Forgive me," she sputtered.

"There you are!" said Tuzia, snatching at Artemisia's arm. "Come away from this whore! Can't you see she carries disease?"

Artemisia swatted hard at Tuzia's hand, releasing her clutch.

"Lena," she said. "Caravaggio has made you immortal. What a supreme honor it is to have met you. I hope we will meet again soon."

Lena gave her a wan smile. Then she looked down at the paving stones again under Tuzia's accusing glare.

Artemisia bowed to Lena as if she were a contessa and strode away, leaving Tuzia blinking and mortified in front of the woman she had called a "whore."

∞

"Your daughter is strange," hissed Tuzia that night in Orazio's bedroom. Artemisia heard her voice float up to the studio, where she slept among the half-finished canvases and drying paint. "She touched a whore with her hand, holding up her chin. Admiring her, Orazio!"

"So?"

"Orazio! She's shameless! Everyone in the Piazza Navona saw her."

"Hmm . . . which prostitute?"

"A dark-haired whore who stands next to the San Giacomo degli Spagnoli church—"

"Ah, Lena Antognetti! A beautiful woman. *Bellissima!*"

"Orazio! She's *una puttana*! Have you no sense of decency?" sputtered Tuzia. "I tell you that your daughter touches a whore's face in public, admiring her . . . and you have no intention of punishing her?"

"Punishing her?" Orazio was incredulous. "For what, woman? For admiring beauty? Artemisia is an artist. That is her vocation. Now take off your clothes and shut your mouth. *Basta!*"

Artemisia laughed in her hand. Tuzia would never possess her papa. And she certainly would never understand artists.

Chapter 15
ROME, 1610

"You are sixteen years old," said Tuzia, chopping carrots for a soup. "You pay no attention to your looks, Artemisia."

Artemisia sat at the table eating buttered toast. Crumbs sprayed out of her mouth with every bite. She watched them fly, randomly alighting on the tablecloth. She traced the tiny bits of toast with her fingertip, drawing patterns.

"Look how you eat! Stop playing with the crumbs."

"Why? They are pretty. Look—"

"This is precisely what I am talking about. You pay no attention to your appearance. Look at your hair! Your clothes!"

Artemisia reached for her thick tangle of waves. "What's wrong with my hair?"

"What's wrong? You walk around Rome disheveled, your hair uncombed, tumbling down around your face—like a prostitute!"

Artemisia ran her hands through her hair, her fingers sticky with butter. "People compliment my hair," she protested. "I think it is my best feature."

"And you push your dress sleeves up above the elbow. I cannot iron them flat anymore. They have tears and permanent wrinkles. You look like you've been scrubbing floors in them."

"I can't paint with my sleeves dangling down, Tuzia. Perhaps we should cut off the sleeves above the elbows."

"Artemisia!" she screeched. "It's time you found a husband. Both of my older daughters are married and they are younger than you."

"Hmm . . . are they happy, your daughters?"

"What kind of question is that? Of course they are! They are married, did you not hear me?"

Artemisia said nothing but went back to tracing patterns in the bread crumbs.

"You are impossible! What kind of man would be tempted to enter matrimony with a woman like you?"

She wants me married and out of the house.

"Why should I marry?" Artemisia shrugged. "Unless it would help my art."

Tuzia stared at her, incomprehension on her face. "All decent women marry! You should start your own family."

"Ah," Artemisia said, nodding. She took another bite of toast. "There is an advantage. I could start my own studio with my daughters and sons working with me. Like Papa does. Maybe Papa would move in with us," she said, teasing.

How I love needling this woman.

"Don't you . . ." began Tuzia, trying another tack. "Don't you see yourself wanting a man in your bed? To know the secrets of lovemaking?"

"Like you?" Artemisia said, looking directly into her eyes. "With Papa?"

Tuzia glowered. The fact that she slept with Orazio when her own husband was gone was never mentioned. Artemisia had broken an unspoken rule.

Tuzia hissed, as low and mean as a snake. "Do you not have the stirring of passion in your loins? Aren't you curious what lies beyond virginity, what happens in the bedroom between a man and a woman? The passion, the heat?"

Artemisia stared at her.

Of course I have feelings. But I would not share them with you!

"You call yourself an artist," Tuzia said. "You study your own body with a looking glass. But what do you know about a man's lust and lovemaking? What happens to that flesh when your lover touches it."

Artemisia had nothing to say. She looked down at the scattered bread crumbs and brushed them away. She heard footsteps descending the stairs while Tuzia continued her tirade.

"You need a man to have his way with you. A husband—"

"I think this conversation has gone on too long!" said Orazio, storming into the kitchen. "Tuzia. Mind your own business! Leave Artemisia alone," he raged, raising his hand and slapping Tuzia hard.

Tuzia raised a hand to her cheek where his handprint remained emblazoned on her skin.

Yet Artemisia knew his hand was impotent against Tuzia. He would reach for her body night after night.

The older woman raised her chin defiantly. Her eyes glinted at Artemisia as if she could read the girl's thoughts.

∞

Orazio stared at Artemisia's studies for *Susanna and the Elders*.

"Where is the second elder?" he said, pointing to the empty space next to the one lecherous man leering over the stone wall.

"He hasn't come to me yet," Artemisia said, flipping her fingers to dismiss his question. "I will fill him in later."

"How curious . . . he is a central figure. Paint him! Do you have any preliminary sketches?"

"No, I have nothing."

Artemisia held her breath, waiting to see if Orazio saw any likeness of Cosimo Quorli in the one elder. He did not seem to notice. Perhaps she was not yet as accomplished as she thought.

"It's flat, Artemisia," he said. "You haven't captured the depth of the wall separating the elders and Susanna."

"I'm trying, Papa. I didn't say I was finished."

"I will help you," he said. "But you need lessons in perspective." He stroked his neat, short beard with his fingers. "Let me speak to Agostino Tassi. Perhaps he could give me some techniques to teach you."

Tassi? That name echoed from the past. Then she remembered, and frowned.

"The fresco painter, your drinking companion? What does Signor Tassi know about painting on canvas?"

"He paints canvases as well. He's quite good—and executes uncanny perspective."

Perspective had always been a sore point for Artemisia.

"Cosimo Quorli has assigned him to work with me on Pope Paul's frescoes in the Quirinale."

Artemisia's nostrils flared as if she had caught a whiff of rotten meat. *Cosimo Quorli!*

She knew better than to protest. Orazio's future as a painter depended on the papal steward. The Quirinale frescoes were a great coup for him.

"Will I accompany you to the Quirinale?" she asked. "I so want to see your work. The frescoes—"

Papa shook his head. "No. I don't want you there. There are too many unsavory characters—hordes of workmen. They would gawk at you. Or worse! No, no."

"But Papa!"

"No! I think Agostino should come here. Tuzia can chaperone."

"I don't know that I would like that. To have Tuzia breathing over my shoulder."

Orazio shrugged. "Well. He is probably too busy right now to tutor. We have much work in the Sala Regia at the Quirinale to complete."

Artemisia drew a deep breath. "Work at the Quirinale." What a magnificent world of artists! "What is he like, Agostino Tassi?"

Orazio rubbed his beard. "He's not very tall. Dresses well for an artist. Reddish-brown hair and a trace of a beard. Some women have said he's quite attractive. And to listen to him you'd almost believe it."

Artemisia laughed.

"He is a braggart," said Papa. "He's quite fond of himself. We call him *lo smargiasso*—the show-off.

"But he's quite skillful at what he does. He paints frames for my frescoes, sets them off with borders to enhance the illusion of depth. Perhaps I should bring him into our bottega as a partner. Then he will teach you—"

"No, Papa. I want to be your apprentice—and only yours. I don't want anyone else working in our bottega."

He smiled, curling a tendril of her hair around his finger. *"Mia figlia,"* he said. *My daughter.*

Artemisia watched her papa set off for work at the Quirinale. How he walked confidently down Via Paolina, nodding to the neighbors, the merchants, and giving an appreciative eye to the prostitutes.

What freedom he had!

As a woman, Artemisia was as caged as a goldfinch. While she sang full-throated in front of her easel, working, the second she put down her brush, she was a prisoner, with only the church bells' tolling to remind her of life's passing. Rome's sounds drifted in the window, but she could only look down into the street, locked in her tower.

And so she painted herself as reflected in her looking glass.

∽

About this time, Orazio took on an assistant to help all five of the Gentileschi artists. His name was Niccolo Bedino. He was a sulky young man about Artemisia's age—perhaps sixteen or seventeen. He had served as assistant to Agostino Tassi, cleaning his house as well as preparing his paints.

The Gentileschis needed the help. Things had begun to fall apart when Maddalena realized that Tuzia was Orazio's lover—she refused to set foot in the Gentileschi house from that moment on. Then Tuzia caught a fever. She was several months convalescing, and during that time, her long-absent husband came home. And all of a sudden, the Gentileschis were on their own. Though a neighbor, Caterina, helped them occasionally, taking care of five full-time artists was more than she had bargained for.

But Niccolo was certainly most unimpressive when he arrived at their door.

Artemisia showed the boy in, noticing his narrowed eyes and hunched posture. He had a spray of acne over his chin and forehead. He looked around and dropped the small bag he carried.

"I am Signorina Gentileschi," she said.

"*Sì*, I know who you are," he said, giving her a cold fish eye. "My master, Agostino Tassi, told me there was a signorina in the house."

He studied her curiously.

"What are you looking at?"

"Nothing. Is your father here?" he asked, his gaze shifting about. He sniffed the air, wrinkling his nose.

"No. I shall show you what to do."

"*You?* But I am to be an apprentice to your father." From his bag he produced a parchment with a seal. It was a contract. "Here. Read what it says. I am apprentice to your father."

Artemisia shook her head. "I can't read very well."

He smiled, showing wolfish teeth. "Pity. But of course, you are a girl."

Artemisia glared at him, her nostrils flaring. "My father contracted you to work for us. That includes cleaning the house. Let me show you what to do."

The boy scowled. "What need does your father have for a house-maid if you are here?"

She arched her right eyebrow. "You are to learn art from my broth-ers, and my father . . . and me. First let us see if you can clean the kitchen and make the beds properly."

"Make the beds? Wash the pots and pans? That is women's work."

"Not if you are our apprentice. I certainly do not have time to housekeep," Artemisia snapped, losing patience. "When you have fin-ished the housework we will talk of grinding pigments, stretching and priming canvases."

Niccolo drew up his lip, his eyes glaring with contempt. She stared him down and he dropped his focus to the floor. He scuffed his toe against the tile and brought up a bit of ground carrot smashed into the terra-cotta.

"The boys' chamber pot is in the corner of their bedroom," she said, showing him to the tiny room strewn with unwashed clothes and filthy linens on unmade pallets. In the corner stood a tarred wooden box with a lid like that on a sea chest, watertight.

"That is my father's room," she said, pointing to the next space. "He keeps his chamber pot under the bed. He is very tidy, mind you. Take special care with his room."

Niccolo nodded, constricting his nostrils in distaste. "*Va bene, Signorina.* Now can you please show me to the studio?"

"One more room, just here." She pushed open the door to her bedchamber and walked past the little oak bed to her washing area. "And this is mine," she said, removing the delicate terra-cotta bowl with handles from its place between the white basin and the pitcher of water. It contained only a little urine from early morning. "Be careful with it, *per favore.* It belonged to my mother."

"Your chamber pot?" said Niccolo, horror in his eyes. "*Your* cham-ber pot—"

"Needs emptying. Make sure to sluice it out with lots of water, so that it is fresh and clean."

Niccolo stared at the chamber pot as if it were a viper. "You are a girl! You must empty your own chamber pot!"

"Why should I? I am very busy in the studio, night and day. We have hired you to work for us. What did you expect?"

"Not this. Not emptying a woman's—"

"You must empty Maestro Tassi's chamber pot every day. Why should my urine be different?"

Niccolo looked aghast. He shook his head like a wet dog. "The house is very dirty," he said. "Slatternly."

She drew in a breath. The word "slattern" not only was used for bad housekeeping but equated disorderliness with loose morals in a woman. *I know what you are implying, you son of a whore!*

"So clean it up, apprentice," she said, putting the chamber pot in his hands, its contents sloshing. "That's your job, boy!"

He dropped his eyes, studying the unswept floor.

"And never use the word 'slattern' again in my presence!"

Cᴘᴏᴄᴏᴘᴏᴄ

Niccolo did not stay long with the Gentileschis.

The big explosion came one day when Artemisia was applying a coat of varnish on one of her father's paintings, *Young Woman Playing a Violin*. Orazio had ordered Niccolo to grind a nugget of lapis lazuli, easily the most costly pigment in their bottega.

Niccolo paid little attention to the task. He presented Orazio with a small dish of pigment, ground much less finely than it should have been. Worse yet, he had presumed beyond his skill, adding walnut oil and turpentine to raw color without asking permission.

"I know your precise proportions, Maestro Gentileschi," said the apprentice. "I have prepared the paint myself—"

"I've told you twice now about the consistency I expect of the lapis lazuli!" Orazio roared. "Do you see how badly ground this powder is? Can you imagine what will happen if I apply this costly pigment in a brushstroke and have this"—he plucked out a speck of coarse-ground blue between his thumb and pointer finger—"*this* on my brushstroke?"

"I am sorry, Maestro," said Niccolo, ducking his head. "Your mortar and pestle are different than Maestro Tassi's."

"You always have an excuse, Niccolo!" snapped Orazio. "What difference should that make? You know what the end result should look like. Keep grinding until you've reached it!"

"*Sì*, Maestro," said Niccolo, sulking.

"Now salvage every precious grain of that pigment. You'll have to let it dry and regrind it." Orazio poked his finger at the ruined paint. "Artemisia! Show him what to do. We can't afford to lose this lapis lazuli. It is worth its weight in gold!"

Niccolo's eyes narrowed as Artemisia's name was mentioned.

"Come on," she said, tapping her paintbrush. "Let's take it outside to dry in the shade so the color doesn't diminish. I'll show you how to grind—"

"I can do it!" he snapped, brushing her hand away. "I'm not an idiot."

"Well, you made a mess of it, didn't you?"

"Mess!" he snarled. "Signorina, what about the mess you leave me every day in the house?"

"That's *your* work, Niccolo," she said. "To clean it up."

"No," he said. "You are the woman. That's *your* job."

"How dare you speak to my daughter that way!" shouted Orazio. "I'll—"

Artemisia shoved her father away, taking Niccolo on herself.

"You listen to me, apprentice," she said, a brush gripped in her hand like a dagger. "My profession is to become a master painter. That is the only job this girl has, you insolent *bastardo!*"

Orazio sent Niccolo packing. He had proved himself worthless as an apprentice in all ways. If he had stayed another day, the Gentileschi brothers would have beaten him to a pulp.

Agostino Tassi took him back as an apprentice. And Artemisia found her chamber pot, the heirloom left by her mother, shattered and ground to bits of dust.

Chapter 16
ROME, 1611

Maddalena was right. As Artemisia matured, her outings became few and short. Eventually she was forbidden even to sit near the light of the window.

"Whores show themselves in the window, Artemisia," snapped Orazio. "You show your face there, you are begging for trouble."

"I want to see the world! Can I not even sit on the second floor window and look at the street?"

"*No!*"

Artemisia was locked in the house, a caged bird. Her only outings were to go to the well behind the house to draw pails of water for the household.

She watched bitterly as her brothers accompanied Orazio to work on frescoes at the papal palaces of the Quirinale.

"I watch Papa strut down the street like a bantam cock," Artemisia confided to Tuzia. "He paints in the papal palaces, he communes with men of intelligence! How I would love the chance to paint and converse with the elite of Rome."

Tuzia watched her carefully. "I may be able to help. My husband has an acquaintance who very much wants your father to paint his portrait. He is a man of some means, a cleric at the Vatican. But I fear he cannot pay Signor Gentileschi's asking price. But you . . ."

"What do you mean?"

"If you were to paint his portrait I doubt the price would be as dear."

"Who is this man?"

"I told you. A friend of my husband's. A priest. His name is Father Artigenio. Will you do it? I will sit in the bottega all the while he is posing."

Artemisia thought. A commission! Her first. And a man of some means. At least he would pay her a few scudi. She so desperately wanted to paint the human figure—on her own terms, not her father's.

"Tell him to come tomorrow. We will start immediately."

Artigenio—he told her to address him as such—was a stocky man with a double chin. Artemisia observed he must have excellent fare at Vatican repasts. He had an impressive wart on the left side of his nose from which sprouted three black hairs. It was orbited by a much smaller red wart.

He was indeed a Vatican cleric, one of hundreds. Despite his vows of chastity he was besotted with a signorina and wanted his portrait painted as a gift to her.

"You will make me look . . . attractive, will you not, Signorina Gentileschi?"

Artemisia frowned, looking at Tuzia.

Tuzia answered, moving closer to Artigenio. "But of course she will!" she said, patting his hand. "You are such a handsome man it will simply show your likeness. Signorina Gentileschi will see to it, I assure you."

Artemisia closed her eyes behind her canvas. She had hoped to have an erudite conversation with this man. To speak of Rome, of the collections of art that the pope and his nephew Cardinal Scipione Borghese possessed.

Anything but the mundane.

The only subject Artigenio was willing to elaborate on was how beautiful and tender was his true love. Oh, how angelic her face, how white her skin! Her voice! Her kindness and fine demeanor.

How he longed to marry her but alas! He was a cleric, beholden to God and the pope. But perhaps she would agree to become his mistress.

Artemisia rolled her eyes, her face hidden behind the canvas.

Merda, this randy priest! The sooner I finish this portrait the better. I will pack it off to him and collect my payment in record time.

And that she did. Warts and all.

∞

Soon after turning seventeen, Artemisia finally met Agostino Tassi.

Through Cosimo Quorli's connections, Orazio was contracted to paint more frescoes at the Sala del Concistoro in the Palazzo Quirinale, along with Maestro Tassi, now renowned for his beautiful landscapes and his geometric acumen in perspective—a skill Gentileschi did not possess.

One night Orazio came home jubilant. He and Agostino Tassi had been awarded the honor of painting the frescoes for Cardinal Scipione Borghese's Casino delle Muse. The cardinal, favorite nephew of the pope, was a great appreciator of art and owned a large collection of Caravaggio's work.

Amid the congratulations and flowing wine, Orazio shared news that made Artemisia's blood run cold.

"It is all Cosimo Quorli's doing!" said Papa, drinking a toast to his benefactor. "Cardinal Borghese admired the frescoes in the Palazzo Quirinale. Cosimo sang our praises. There is no end to what Signor Quorli's influence can achieve!"

"I'm happy for you, Papa," Artemisia said. "You deserve to be recognized."

He gave her a curt nod.

A temporary truce, she thought.

By this time Tuzia's husband had resumed his travels, and she had regained her health, returned to Orazio's bed, and installed herself once again in the household. Her two children ran from their neighboring rooms to the Gentileschi house unchecked, always underfoot.

More now than ever Artemisia felt the urge to escape the house, into the streets of Rome.

"Papa. I want to see your frescoes in Palazzo Quirinale."

Her father grunted. "I do not like the idea of the workmen gawking at my daughter. They are the worst sort, randy as goats."

"Papa! Do you think I care a fig what workmen think of me? I want to see your frescoes. You must let me see them at least once. And I could bring you a hot meal, fresh from the stove."

Orazio regarded her, seeing how her once-bright face had faded. He took her chin in his hand and turned her toward him. "You are pale."

"I only go out on Sundays to Mass! Of course I am pale, Papa!"

Artemisia could feel he was relenting. Her health, her beauty were guarded ferociously by her father. Perhaps he considered how his artist colleagues would regard her as they paid visits to his bottega. A sickly daughter, an infirm protégée, would not do!

And Orazio remembered Prudenzia's early death.

"*Per favore*, Papa! Think of it—a hot lunch! Home cooking—"

"I would prefer that to cheese and olives." He smiled. "And I've painted the study I did of you last week. I put it in the scene of *Concerto Musicale di Apollo e le Muse*."

"Oh! I must see it, Papa. *Per favore!* I need to breathe fresh air."

Francesco, working on a still life of fruit, could not resist. "Artemisia is pale. She's becoming ugly."

"Shut up, Francesco!" she shouted.

"*È vero!*" he said. *It's true.* "Look at you. Your hair looks like a haystack after a windstorm. You have paint on your earlobes!"

Orazio studied his daughter. "*Sì*, Artemisia. An outing would do you good. But Tuzia must attend to your grooming. I want you to look your best—as you do in my fresco."

"*Grazie*, Papa! I shall see if you achieved my likeness accurately. I hope you have done me justice."

Papa rubbed his lip. "How strange. Cosimo Quorli just mentioned the same concern today. Whether I had painted your exact likeness."

"Oh! That despicable man!"

"Artemisia," he said, holding up his hand. "Don't talk that way. He is a great patron."

"I told you how I hate him. How he spoke to me! An old man making overtures to a young girl."

"He was merely complimenting your beauty. It's the Roman way!"

"He was not complimenting me, Papa! He said I was almost ripe for plucking." She was shouting now. "I was only twelve!"

Francesco put down his paintbrush. "It's true, Papa. He is a bad man."

Orazio's face showed bright red above his beard. He sucked in his breath.

The temporary truce was broken.

"'Ripe for plucking'? Is that all he said? Artemisia, he was only throwing you flowers. He was a family friend of your mother's."

"What? Mama despised him. She told me—"

Orazio's face turned stony in an instant, losing all color. "She talked to you about him?"

"She said he was a very bad man. She—"

She snapped her mouth shut. She had said too much. She had broken the deathbed promise she had made to her mother.

Orazio looked away from her. His hand covered his face.

"We will not discuss Signor Cosimo any further," he said. After a moment, he dropped his hand and went on. "Mind your manners if you encounter him tomorrow. He often looks in on our work. I need—*we* need!—his patronage. I have mouths to feed and rent to pay! We would be doomed without him."

Both Francesco and Artemisia remained silent. The Gentileschis all returned to work.

The rasp of paintbrushes against canvas was the only sound in the room.

∞

The next day Artemisia and Tuzia left for the Quirinale palazzo with a basket of hot bread from the baker and a pot of rabbit stew. Francesco escorted the women. He and his brothers worked at the site as Orazio's assistants, and he was not keen on his talented sister invading his domain.

"Papa and I work well together," he boasted. "We get on—the two of you only fight."

"Don't flatter yourself, Francesco," Artemisia said. "When Papa needs a skilled hand, he turns to me."

Francesco flinched. "Not in fresco. You'll never be on the scaffolds, Artemisia—"

"Stop it, the two of you," said Tuzia. "Francesco, tell me about Agostino Tassi. I hear he is handsome—and a rake."

Francesco threw her a disgusted look. "Agostino Tassi is a loud-mouthed braggart. He tells tales of his escapades with *le puttane*. As if any of us are impressed by a man who pays for women night after night."

"Caravaggio didn't have to pay," Artemisia said. "He painted them and they fell in love with him."

"No more about Caravaggio!" snapped Tuzia. "He's burning in hell where he belongs after those repugnant paintings."

Both Gentileschis turned on her.

"What do you mean, repugnant?" Artemisia demanded.

"He was the master!" said Francesco. "Everyone in Rome tries to imitate him. Even Papa."

"Enough!" said Tuzia. "Ah, there is Cardinal Borghese's carriage, in front of the palazzo."

"He owns Caravaggio's last canvases," Artemisia said. "Perhaps he would—"

"*Basta!*" said Tuzia, sweeping up her skirts in her hand as she mounted the steps of the palazzo.

The marble floors were blanketed in oiled cloth, protecting them from the wooden platforms and the drips of paint. Young men scurried about, moving towering scaffolds, pots of paint, buckets of wet plaster and trowels. A boy with a runny nose stood stock-still, staring at Artemisia, and another tripped, spilling part of his plaster.

"You there," said Tuzia, pointing to a red-haired boy with two trowels in his hand. "Show us to Maestro Gentileschi."

"*Sì, Signora,*" squeaked the boy, pointing. "He's up there on the top, painting the balcony scene."

Artemisia looked up and saw Orazio working on the image of a black-skinned man staring at a woman who stood with one hand on her hip, the other holding a fan.

Artemisia's mouth dropped open in astonishment.

It's me!

"You have him all wrong," said a voice, calling from above. "The slave's eyes must be more focused on the woman's neck and shoulders, Orazio. Take a direct line . . ."

Artemisia whirled around, searching for the voice.

Who would dare to criticize my father's work!

Standing at a lower level of the scaffolding was a man of medium height, hands on his hips. He had remarkable coloring—soft brown eyes and hair and a rosy blush to his cheeks like a schoolboy. His lips were full and sensuous.

Artemisia imagined painting him. She found him devilishly handsome, even though he was criticizing her father.

". . . a straight line of focus," he said. "You have his eyes merely scanning her hair, perhaps even looking at the woman beyond the column—you must lower the focal point of the gaze."

"Signor Gentileschi!" called Tuzia. "We have your meal. Please come eat it while it's hot."

"Tuzia!" Artemisia said. "He can't possibly come down now. The plaster is drying. He must apply the paints!"

Both men looked down at her.

"Santa Maria!" gasped Orazio's critic, staring at Artemisia. "I thought the woman your papa painted was beautiful," he said, his voice reverberating around the vast hall, "but not as *bellissima* as his daughter is in real life. He does not do you justice, Signorina."

"I do her justice enough," answered Orazio. "She's my daughter! This is exactly as she looks."

"Signorina Gentileschi," said the other artist, ignoring him. "It is a supreme pleasure to meet such a beauty in person."

Artemisia was used to Roman men whispering compliments in the crowded streets, but not in front of her father. She raised her face up toward the painter.

"It is not wise to criticize my father's work, Signor Tassi. It is Signor Tassi, isn't it?"

"At your command, Signorina," he said, one hand grasping the scaffold post as he bowed deeply from the heights. His eyes fastened to her with a rakish gleam.

"Leave the food there, Tuzia," growled Orazio. "Artemisia is right. I must finish this work while the plaster is still wet."

"Are you not going to introduce me to your partner?" said Tuzia, her face hardening in offense.

"This is a workplace, not a ballroom!" said Orazio, turning back to his work. "I don't make formal introductions."

Tassi held up his hand in protest. "Signora, it is a great pleasure to make your acquaintance. Signor Gentileschi has sung your praises, day after day."

Orazio made a disgusted sound in his throat as he wiped his brush. Artemisia stifled a laugh. *Agostino Tassi is a flatterer . . . and a liar.*

Tuzia giggled, curtsying to the artist.

Artemisia stepped back to take in the full scene of the elaborate fresco. It was a triumph of perspective: A crowded balcony of gothic arches and Roman geometric decoration showed the skilled perspective of Agostino Tassi. Orazio had populated the balcony with at least eighteen figures—well enough executed—conversing above the banister, playing musical instruments, and the woman—Artemisia's likeness—fanning herself and looking off into the distance.

"What do you think, Artemisia?" Orazio called, frowning as Agostino climbed down from the scaffold.

"It is exquisite," she called up to him. "But Signor Tassi is right. The blackamoor's eyes are focused more on the woman beyond my likeness."

Agostino bowed again to Tuzia but approached Artemisia, his eyes devouring her every feature. She felt her skin on fire.

"It's too late for me to tamper with it now," said Orazio, gruffly. "Fresco is unforgiving. I would only smear my work. It is finished!"

"I am relieved the slave does not gaze at you," whispered Maestro Tassi, his warm breath touching her ear. "If he did, I would burst into flames of jealousy!"

Artemisia felt a flush of heat on her cheeks and the fine hairs on her neck prickled.

He bowed and turned away.

⚬⚬

"What do you think of Signor Tassi?" Tuzia asked her as they walked home. She turned around to see Francesco strolling several paces behind them. His eyes were riveted on two *puttane* leaning against a stucco wall along the Via del Corso. His hand cupped his groin as he ogled at them.

My brother is as coarse as a ditchdigger.

Francesco had adopted the ways of the street since their mother's death. *She would be so ashamed.*

"Well . . . what do you think of him?" repeated Tuzia.

"Maestro Tassi? His sense of perspective is good. I thought his colors a bit muddy—"

"No, silly girl!" said Tuzia, pinching her. "Not his art. *Come uomo!*" *As a man!*

"I don't know what you mean. All I know about him is his art. We barely conversed."

"Don't lie to me, Artemisia. You saw how his gorgeous brown eyes followed you everywhere. Did you not find him attractive?"

"I did not consider him. I was more interested in his art." Artemisia was not about to admit that she had seen how handsome he was—certainly not to Tuzia. "He has clever ways to denote perspective. How he has recessed the balcony scene—"

"Nonsense! Perspective! You silly girl. What a catch he would be as a husband! He's not rough and brutal like that Caravaggio you adore. He has a Florentine flair, debonair and cultured." She was almost swooning with lust. "So much like your father."

Artemisia shrugged. Tuzia was right. Artemisia loved the civility and culture of Florence. But those qualities now seemed lost in her father. He had grown boorish and demanding, more Roman than Florentine. He called her vulgar names . . . whore, slut. He was not the man she knew when her mother was alive. His fine manners had died with her.

Now, outside at last, Artemisia realized how desperately she wished to be free of him. He had denied her an education, insisting every second of her waking hours be spent in the bottega, painting. When she was young, all she ever wanted was to paint. Now she wanted more. She wanted everything the world had to offer, to savor it and smack her lips in pleasure. To become cultured. To be at home in Florence. Home of Michelangelo, Donatello, Leonardo!

Agostino Tassi.

"Signor Tassi has a knack for perspective and trompe l'oeil," she repeated. "Nothing more. He is not nearly as talented as Papa."

∾

As she grew older, Artemisia's fights with Orazio grew fiercer. She suspected that he realized her skill was approaching his own, that she would someday challenge him.

She was his daughter, but he treated her more as a sibling, criticizing her work as a jealous brother might. In many ways he was worse than Francesco, who openly resented her talent.

Chapter 17
ROME, 1611

Finally Orazio insisted Artemisia was ready to execute a finished version of *Susanna and the Elders*. She was seventeen and her education in art would be tested . . . and ultimately debuted. Papa was eager to introduce her to the art world as his protégée.

But first she had to finish *Susanna and the Elders* to his approval—no easy task. She had been trying for years to achieve that goal. She wanted to paint the pain, the searing shame and innocence of the victim.

She had never forgotten the execution of Beatrice Cenci, and she was burning to illustrate the torment of that violated girl, who was sacrificed by the Church, by the pope, for defending herself from her loathsome father. She had been raped over and over again by her father. All this was exposed to Rome, to her shame. And still she had been put to death. For his sins.

Wasn't it the same with Susanna? The patriarchal elders, punishing the victim yet again. And fleetingly Artemisia would think of her mother—and the thought of the ogre Cosimo Quorli touching her mama as a girl made her ill.

Through her mother's painfully whispered secret, Artemisia felt in her heart and bones the crippling shame and fear that must have gripped Susanna, having not one but two lechers menacing her. She could either surrender to their grasping hands or be shamed, ostracized forever by their lies.

Men have all the power. Unjust, cruel, and unlimited.

She had still not identified the model for the second elder. In his place she tried half a dozen faces—composites of men she saw from the studio window, even her father himself. Each time she had to scrape the face away. It wasn't ever right.

"When will you paint the second elder's face?" said Orazio. "If you could ever get this painting finished, I'd send it to my brother in Florence."

"Would you?" Artemisia said, her eyes flashing wide in wonderment. "To Uncle Aurelio?"

"I might do better than that. I might send it directly to Cristina di Lorena de' Medici as a gift."

"Oh, Papa!"

Artemisia's art studies had evolved over the years. Now, with her looking glass, she continued examining her own body, comparing her attempts to capture the feminine form with the reality she saw in the little mirror.

She knew she had captured Susanna's body to perfection.

Orazio drew her attention to his own painting *Susanna and the Elders*. She secretly hated his version.

"Look how I've centered Susanna between the two elders."

"Lechers, you mean," she said. "Vile lechers."

"Susanna is the center of focus. In your work you have her off to the left side."

"It's her against them, Papa! Not a tug-of-war with Susanna in the center. That's why I have them on the right, her on the left. There is a distinct divide, two forces—good and evil."

Orazio shook his head, his jaw clenching tight. "You see how my Susanna gazes up to heaven, beseeching God? Your Susanna curls away, a passive motion."

"Passive?" she said, turning on him. "She's humiliated! She's in agony. She has to have sex with these lecherous men or die of stoning for a lie they invent!"

"Still. She does not look up to God."

"No, she doesn't!" Artemisia shouted back. "It is the moment she recoils in agony, trapped. God has no place here. Where was he when they blackmailed her?"

"It is a biblical story! The patrons you seek will want to see Susanna beseeching our Lord to help her."

"No," Artemisia said. "Not *my* Susanna. I want to show her torment, the injustice of these filthy men, their power. You cannot understand how a woman feels being violated, Papa!"

Her hand brushed her cheek. She was shocked to feel it wet.

Orazio looked away, out the window. He did not speak for a very long time.

"Look at your Susanna's arms, her hands," he said at last. "It's not an appropriate response."

"It is emotion!" she screamed at him. "Anguish! What do you know about a woman's anguish? Her arms reject them and their vile proposition—her honor or her life!"

"It's all wrong—"

"No! It is exactly right!" She seized her paintbrush and jabbed it in the air. "I pronounce it finished. I shall sign it this minute!"

She scrawled her name across the bottom with a flourish of finality.

"You cannot sign the painting! You haven't painted a face for the second elder!"

"It's done, Papa. *Susanna* is mine."

135

In the spring, the Gentileschis moved from Via Paolina to a house on Via del Corso, still within the Campo Marzio and only blocks way. The house was a little more spacious but, to Artemisia's great regret, Tuzia—and occasionally her frequently absent husband—and her brood moved with them. In this house a connecting door from the studio gave way to Tuzia's apartment, in addition to Tuzia's principal door in the foyer.

Santo Dio! As if I needed to see this woman more often, Artemisia thought.

Orazio brought Agostino Tassi to their house one afternoon when Artemisia was painting the finishing details of a nude in the sweet light of a sunset. The two men stomped up the stairs, their clothes speckled with plaster.

"Artemisia," said Orazio. "You have met Signor Tassi, I believe."

She nodded, irritated at being disturbed.

"May I see what you are painting, Signorina Gentileschi?" said Tassi.

She felt a rush of blood scald her face. "Why not?" she said, more boldly than she felt. "I'm rectifying a few errors."

Tassi gave a little gasp that made her look at him. The corners of his lips turned up in a smile. "She is exquisite," he said. "Who is she?"

"Not a prostitute." Artemisia arched an eyebrow. "She is a woman from the neighborhood."

"Magnificent," he said. "She actually looks quite like you."

Artemisia felt her father's eyes on the two of them. "Artemisia," he said. "I have persuaded Maestro Tassi to give you lessons in perspective."

Her eyes flashed to her father and then to Tassi.

"Without consulting me?"

"Artemisia! We've talked many times about your weakness in this area. Maestro Tassi is an expert in perspective."

Tassi approached her painting, examining it again. He crossed his arms, regarding the nude. "You are very talented, Signorina," he said. "But I believe I can sharpen your skill."

She glared at him. "Well, the two of you seem to have made up your minds."

"You don't listen to me—" began Orazio.

"Why should I? Your sense of perspective is—"

"*Basta!*" said Orazio. "Tomorrow we will begin at the Quirinale by noon, but you and Maestro Tassi will have the morning light for your lesson."

"So I have no say." She looked at Maestro Tassi. He was smiling. "I'm a terrible student," she said defiantly. She jerked her chin at Orazio. "Just ask my father."

The maestro studied the nude and then shifted his gaze to her. "I think it will be a challenge and a pleasure to teach you, Signorina," he said. "You have tremendous potential."

She looked at him coldly. "I have tremendous skill, Maestro Tassi."

Agostino Tassi arrived early the next day.

Artemisia was leaning out the window, shaking crumbs from the tablecloth, and she saw his confident stride far up the street as he mixed with the crowd of pedestrians. He tipped his head toward a gaggle of the neighborhood's housemaids. She could see by the way they lowered their gazes he was complimenting them or perhaps speaking lewd words of proposition. As he came close enough to touch them, they scattered like frightened pigeons.

She shook her head in disgust.

His brown velvet cap was tilted rakishly off his head to the right. The early sun glinted off his hair, showing the red highlights in the deep brown.

Agostino Tassi was the youngest of all her father's friends—perhaps only fifteen years older than Artemisia.

The linen collar of his shirt was open under his tunic, baring his skin to the morning freshness. She could see his throat move as he gulped in the cool air, the dark hairs of his chest curling up where he had untied his shirt.

He spotted her, tablecloth in hand.

"Buongiorno, Signorina Gentileschi!" he called.

She flapped the cloth hard, shaking off the last of the crumbs. "I will have Tuzia descend to greet you," she said, slamming the window.

Tuzia had reapplied beetroot to her lips after Orazio had left the house to buy pigment. She accompanied Tassi up the stairs to the bottega, chattering like an African parrot.

"We are so honored to have you in the Gentileschi household."

As if she's the matron of the house, thought Artemisia. She clenched her teeth and returned to work on her canvas.

"Ah! Here is your pupil now, practicing," said Tuzia, opening the door and gesturing toward Artemisia.

"I am not practicing," Artemisia snapped. "I am painting."

"May I see, Signorina?" asked Tassi.

"I can't very well hide it. The paint is still wet," she said. *"Avanti!"*

He approached the easel. She was working on the dirty nails of an elder in her *Susanna.*

"This is magnificent," he said. Artemisia could tell by his hushed tones that his admiration was sincere. His eyes hovered over each inch of the composition. He moved closer, inspecting her brushstrokes. He shook his head, incredulous at the shape and form of the nude Susanna.

"I've heard your father say it is nearly finished. But there is no face on the second elder."

Tuzia, who was never more than a few steps away, interjected, "That painting!" She turned her palms up in exasperation. "Signor Gentileschi and the signorina are at each other's throats over this one!"

"I return to it now and again," Artemisia said, ignoring Tuzia. "It is 'finished and signed' as far as my father is concerned. He constantly meddles with my work, despite my protests. I wanted his hands off."

Tassi moved closer. "Your perspective is excellent here," he said, pointing to a space between Susanna's outstretched arm and the carved stone wall.

"Grazie," she said, annoyed that she enjoyed his praise.

"But . . . to the left of Susanna's head, I think there is room for improvement. If you showed the elder's cuff—the white sleeve of his shirt—sticking out here," he said, pointing to the horizontal plane of Susanna's head, "then you could show the depth between her, the wall, and the elders."

His finger lingered above the lecher's hand.

He's right.

She nodded, her eyes studying the sleeve.

Sì! That would work.

"Now, Signorina," he said. "Shall we begin?"

Tuzia settled down in a chair by the window, mending a basket of clothes.

"Begin with a straight line," said Tassi. "Horizontal. Across the center of the page."

From that simple beginning, he guided her in a series of small steps: dots, squares, rectangles, more lines converging to a vanishing point.

Eventually, Artemisia threw down the black lead she had been using to draw.

"This is a child's game. I want to improve my paintings, not waste my time playing. I am more—"

"We start at the beginning so that I can see what you know. If you know everything, there will be nothing to teach you. But I suspect that is not the case, Signorina."

With a grudging sigh, she picked up the black lead again, and they spent the rest of the morning drawing cubes and rectangles.

The next morning they moved outside, standing in the street in front of the house with Artemisia's sketch pad on an easel. Tuzia sat on a stool nearby, stopping each passerby she knew for a word of gossip.

People stared at them, a man and a young woman with an easel—and a gossipy chaperone—the only figures not moving in the busy street.

"I feel foolish with a sketch pad on an easel. It's awkward."

Agostino waved her objections away. "You need to be vertical, not hunched over a sketch pad on your knees." He stood straight upright himself, as if to demonstrate. He pointed imperiously down the street. "Now look beyond the buildings, where the space opens for the piazza. What do you see?"

"Light spilling left to right where there are no buildings to block it."

"Exactly." He drew a horizontal line through the air with his finger. "That's your eye level. Now draw the buildings along the street as they appear below and above that line."

She smiled. The buildings were sets of cubes and rectangles receding into the distance.

"Vanishing lines," she murmured. The sun came out from behind a cloud, a brilliant shaft of light warming her face and scalp.

He nodded. "Yes, vanishing lines." She felt him looking at her hair. Her scalp tingled under his gaze.

"You have the most magnificent copper mane," he said. "A most unusual color."

Her hand reached up to touch her hair. She snatched it down again, irritated. She turned back to her work, blushing.

∞

They moved on to study her paintings, all the while chaperoned by Tuzia in the bottega. They critically examined her works one by one, and then her father's. She sketched the compositions on parchment using vanishing lines to pinpoint her perspective to compare it to the execution on canvas.

Tuzia grew bored. She crossed her elbows and leaned out the window, calling to the neighbors in the streets.

"You there! Silvia! Where are you going with the children?"

She leaned farther out the window and began to chat.

"Can you see the difference in your sketches?" said Tassi over Artemisia's shoulder.

"Very subtle," she said.

"Subtle but distinctive. It's not that you and your father don't understand perspective intuitively," he said, hovering closer to her. She could smell his breath, the tang of wine. "You are both gifted artists. It comes naturally—you perceive it. But this practice will hone your skill."

Tuzia's head and torso were still inclined out the window, her large bottom acting as ballast.

"Let me know if you find good melons at the market," she called to a neighbor in the street. "And I need a fish head for soup. Bring me one and I'll pay you back—"

Tassi lingered over Artemisia's left shoulder. She could feel the heat emanating from him.

He turned his head away from the sketch and looked at her, his eyes turning soft. He moved his lips close to her ear and whispered, "And my charge is to sharpen your skills." His hand reached out and touched a tendril of her hair, curling it around his finger.

She pulled back.

"That will be all for today," he said, turning to leave. "Good afternoon, Signora Tuzia."

"*A domani!*" Tuzia called. *Until tomorrow.*

"*Arrivederci, Signorina Gentileschi,*" he said, touching his velvet cap.

She caught the wisp of a smile on his face as he disappeared out the door.

Chapter 18
ROME, 1611

That night as Artemisia ate her bowl of lentils and carrots, Tuzia came into the kitchen with her two youngest children, a pair of boys, aged four and seven.

"These rascals are driving me mad!" she said, plopping her ample body down on a stool. "I promised them they could play marbles."

"Please, Artemisia!" they begged. "Could we please play with your marbles?"

She heaved a sigh, wishing Tuzia and her brood would leave her alone. But Tuzia's husband was home so rarely that Artemisia took pity on the children.

She reached up on the shelf for the bag of marbles, chipped and rough from years of play.

"*Grazie, Signorina Artemisia! Grazie!*" they screamed. The seven-year-old boy kissed her hand like a gentleman and the littlest one beamed, sticking his fingers in his mouth with joy.

The children crouched over the terra-cotta tiles on the kitchen floor—scattered now with bright balls of glass. Tuzia reached across the table and tore off a hunk of bread from the loaf, stuffing it into her mouth.

"What do you think of Maestro Tassi?" she asked through a mouthful of bread.

Artemisia blew on her spoonful of hot lentils.

"I'm learning some subtleties of perspective," she said.

"I bet he could teach you far more," Tuzia said, arching her eyebrow.

Artemisia threw down her spoon, making a sharp clink against the bowl.

"What do you mean by that?" she demanded.

"I see how he looks at you," Tuzia said. "I saw him touch your hair—"

"You did? Then you should have reprimanded him at once. You are my chaperone."

"Don't be cross," she said, slyly. She pressed her fingers to the tablecloth, collecting bread crumbs she popped in her mouth. "Agostino Tassi is delicious. A perfect suitor and an artist! You could do no better than—"

"What do you mean I could do no better? Maestro Tassi is here to teach me perspective. That is all!"

"You are high and mighty, aren't you, Signorina Gentileschi." Tuzia sat back to regard her. "What's wrong with a gentleman finding you attractive? And I haven't seen your father line up any suitors. Other than Signor Tassi—"

"He is my tutor! I'm not interested in suitors." Artemisia went back to her meal, arranging the carrots in neat rows. "I'm improving as an artist. Papa doesn't want to marry me off until I have made my debut in Rome."

"What?" scoffed Tuzia. "With that half-finished painting?"

"*Susanna and the Elders?* It is almost finished. I just haven't found the right model for the face of the second elder."

"I don't understand . . . just paint some old man's face on the body and be done with it."

Artemisia waved her words away. "You are right. You don't understand. I have to *see* that man's face, feel it in my gut. The man who causes Susanna such revulsion, such a life-threatening choice. It can't be anyone's face."

"Susanna!" Tuzia threw up her hands. "I never could sympathize with her. She could have just slept with the two elders and saved face . . . and her life."

The lentils and carrots roiled in Artemisia's stomach.

Of course Tuzia would not understand Susanna's dilemma, her anguish and shame.

"Have the *bambini* pick up the marbles when they are finished playing," she said, leaving her dirty bowl in the stone sink. "I'm going back up to the studio."

∞

Some days while Artemisia drew or painted her exercises, Agostino would hold forth about the beauty of Florence. She wondered if he had any idea how she dreamed of seeing that city.

"The Arno's waters are green as a cat's eyes," he said. "The Duomo caps the red-tiled city with splendor—Brunelleschi's miracle! And the Basilica of Santa Croce that houses the bones of Michelangelo is a triumph. Oh, the beauty of Florence is a siren to my soul."

"You talk of Florence as if she were your mistress," she laughed. "Why did you ever leave her for Rome?"

Agostino rubbed his upper lip. She watched him hesitate. *Was there some reason he had to leave Florence?*

"I wanted more commissions . . . to be part of Rome, the heartbeat of the world. What master does not?"

"But the Florence you describe is so beautiful. Brimming with art and grace."

"*Sì.* Florence has a graceful refinement, but Rome has a brutal edge, like a sharpened dagger."

Artemisia closed her eyes, dreaming of Florence, its art and culture. Its freedom.

"I could take you there, Signorina," he said quietly. "And show you the marvels of Tuscany."

Artemisia sat upright. Her eyes darted to Tuzia who, as usual, leaned out the window, gossiping with a neighbor across the street. Her linen blouse stretched tight across her back as she gestured emphatically with her arms.

"Show me perspective," Artemisia said. "That is what my father contracted you to do."

"As you wish, Signorina Gentileschi," he said. "But there are many sweet secrets I long to share with you beyond your father's limited wishes."

"That is your misfortune, Maestro."

One day Artemisia came back from the pigment seller—a rare outing—with her basket full of wrapped nuggets of color. Francesco had tarried, exchanging greetings with his tough new friends in the streets. She scowled at them as they shot dirty glances at her. Her brother was taking a bad turn in life, seeking out dangerous scum as companions.

Artemisia unlocked the door and stepped into the coolness of the house. Upstairs she heard Tuzia's voice sing out, a taunting, amused tone. "You are bold, Signore," she laughed.

Agostino Tassi.

Artemisia hurried upstairs and found them in Orazio's bedroom. Tassi had his hand on Tuzia's neck, his fingertips under her double chin.

Artemisia gasped. "What are you doing in my father's bedroom?"

Tuzia pulled back as if lightning had struck her. Her hands flew to her face. "I—we—" she stuttered.

"I asked to see your father's painting of Judith and Holofernes," said Agostino, pointing to a picture of a violent beheading.

"Without my father's permission? In my father's bedchamber?"

"He just asked for a peek at it," said Tuzia, recovering her tongue. "I didn't think it would hurt to let him take a look."

Artemisia stared at them in disgust.

"I think we will cancel today's lesson," she said. "I feel quite sick to my stomach."

She turned and walked up the steps to the studio, slamming the door behind her.

∞

Artemisia kept thinking about *Susanna and the Elders*. Who was the other lecher, the younger one? Why could her mind not let it go? Surely there were hundreds of faces in the streets of Rome that would do. Ugly faces leering at every corner. Old men fondling their genitals as women walked by. How many men had she told to put their pecker away? She had mortified her brothers, who wanted her to just ignore the old goats.

Artemisia stared at the still-faceless elder who had tried to blackmail the innocent Susanna. "I'll find you," she murmured. "Soon enough."

She sniffed the air. There was a delicious aroma of frying garlic mixed with the richness of olive oil. Her stomach growled. Tuzia was cooking.

She couldn't face seeing Tuzia in the kitchen. She must have been preparing Orazio a special dinner, especially if she suspected Artemisia would tell him that she and Agostino were snooping around his bedroom.

About half an hour later there was a timid knock on the door.

"I'm painting," Artemisia said. "Leave me in peace."

"Please let me in," said Tuzia. "I've brought up a tray with your favorite foods . . . artichokes *alla giudia*."

The heartless she-dog! Tuzia knew Artemisia was helpless when confronted with *carciofi alla giudia*.

Artemisia unlatched the door.

Tuzia stood holding a wooden tray brimming with flattened artichokes, crispy and hot.

"May I please come in?"

Artemisia stared at the artichokes and made an exasperated gesture, ushering Tuzia into the bottega.

Tuzia set the plate down and filled a cup from the terra-cotta jug of wine they kept on the shelf. She handed it to Artemisia. Already Artemisia's fingers were shiny with olive oil, her mouth full.

"Artemisia," she said. "I only let him in to see the painting. He said Signor Quorli—"

"Cosimo Quorli!" Artemisia exclaimed through a half-chewed artichoke.

"Signor Quorli would pay your papa many scudi for that painting."

Artemisia swallowed the artichoke, washing it down with red wine. She wiped her mouth on the back of her wrist. "Papa would never sell it. At least not to him!"

"Why not? Your papa needs the money. He has debt with everyone around the city. The butcher, the winemaker, the cobbler."

"The parchment merchant and the pigment seller," Artemisia couldn't help adding. She had not been able to buy madder red last week, or even walnut oil, because the Gentileschi account was in arrears.

"A woman who has just hacked off a man's head in bed," said Tuzia with a shudder. "His head in a wicker basket like soiled laundry. That painting is a horror. I hate it."

"That painting is marvelous. That is why Signor Quorli wants it."

"Soon I will not be able to show my face at the shops and market. Everyone knows we live on credit. It won't last forever."

Artemisia took another lusty bite of artichoke. She tugged the tender ends of the leaves over her bottom teeth, skinning the savory flesh from the petal.

Tuzia was right. But then she remembered.

"I saw Agostino touching you," she said, stabbing her three-tined fork into the heart of the *carciofi*. "His finger was under your chin."

Tuzia looked away. "It was nothing," she said. "I'm a married woman with children. It's you he wants."

"I couldn't care less what he wants! He was touching you. You should have forbidden him."

"I was about to. He did not harm me."

"In Papa's bedroom. That's disgraceful."

Mama's bedroom. Oh, if Mama had known. Better she be dead than to know what a treacherous friend she had.

Tuzia dragged her seat nearer, the stool's legs clattering on the floor. "Listen to me, Artemisia. He is madly in love with you. He has hinted he wants to marry you."

"What?" Artemisia shoved away her plate, staring at Tuzia. "That is madness! I've never encouraged him in the least. Papa would never agree."

Tuzia gave her a sly look. "Why not? He is a successful—"

"Artist! He is an artist! Papa wants me to marry above our social class. That's why he keeps me locked up like a goldfinch. If it weren't for my skill in selecting pigment, I would never leave this wretched house again—"

"Agostino is already procuring commissions from the pope's nephew. His work is admired. He could provide well for you."

"Papa would strike you across the face for saying that! He's got his eyes set on nobility."

"Nobility?"

"As soon as I finish *Susanna*, he is going to send it to Uncle Aurelio Lomi to present to the Granduchessa Cristina de' Medici."

Tuzia made an exasperated sound, a noisy puff of air blowing from her lips. "And then?"

"And then I could be presented at court. Perhaps I would meet a courtier, a noble who would love me for my art. And take me as his wife. Then I could paint, and procure—"

"Nonsense!" said Tuzia. "I don't think your father believes that for a moment!"

"He has told me since I was a little girl he would take me to Florence when I could paint well enough—"

"Ah! When you were a little girl. Papas indulge little girls, not grown women. That was just a pretty fairy tale he told you. He knows a man loves a woman for the comfort he finds between her thighs, not the pretty paint she applies to a canvas. Nobility marry nobility. You'd do as a mistress, but never a wife!"

She might as well have struck Artemisia across the face. Mistress? A whore?

The same as you are to Papa!

Artemisia turned away and looked at her painting of Susanna. She suddenly felt a profound sadness and longing for her mother. There was no decency in the world since her death. The world around Prudenzia's daughter had cheapened and turned bitter.

Chapter 19
ROME, 1611

The next day, Artemisia and Agostino worked on another perspective exercise, on the steps of the Piazza Trinita dei Montei. They set up the easel on the midpoint of the limestone steps.

"Focus on the buildings across the piazza." Agostino indicated them with a wave of his hand. "I want you to block out a form both of the horizontal—the building in front of us—and the corner building. Mark the center of the two buildings . . ."

And so the morning passed. Lines of view and vanishing points. Light and shadow. There were occasional triumphs and words of praise. But more often it was "There. You see how your eye was mistaken. That misperception will throw off your entire painting. Start again."

Absorbed in her drawing, Artemisia forgot about her fury at finding Maestro Tassi and Tuzia alone in her father's room. She didn't think about seeing her tutor's finger under Tuzia's chin.

The work was demanding, and her mind could not wander elsewhere.

When the sun reached the top of the sky and the shadows disappeared, it was time for the midday meal and the end of the day's lesson. And Artemisia's mind was free to think of other things. As they packed up their supplies, she waited until Tuzia was deep in conversation with the roasted chestnut vendor and then she turned to her tutor.

"Why were you in my father's bedchamber?" she demanded.

"I thought I told you. I was admiring his painting of Judith. It is quite remarkable."

"You had no business in there—"

"You are quite right, Signorina. But to gaze upon such a magnificent painting is a powerful temptation. Forgive me."

If he had answered any other way, Artemisia might have attacked. But for him to argue it was the pull of a painting—this she could understand and forgive.

"You know I painted at least a quarter of it," she said. "Papa signed it, of course, but much of the work is mine."

Agostino regarded her, his eyes wide with admiration. "Would your papa ever part with it?"

"With *Judith*? Not unless it was for scores of scudi. It's one of his best and he knows it. That is why it is in his bedchamber."

"Pity. I know someone who would kill to possess it."

"Who is that?"

He gave a sidelong glance. "Signor Quorli."

"Cosimo Quorli! That filthy swine!"

He narrowed his eyes, a flicker of anger. "I beg you, do not speak of him so. You know he is my patron, do you not?"

"That is your misfortune, Signor Tassi. I know him for what he is. A detestable man!"

"His contacts and influence have helped not only me but also your father. Significantly, Signorina."

"I don't care."

"Perhaps you should. I hear your father's spending exceeds his earnings. He hasn't paid me for these lessons in weeks."

Artemisia turned to him, mortified. He had been tutoring her for free?

"Listen to me," he said. "As a papal quartermaster and steward, Signor Quorli commissions many of the Vatican paintings and frescoes—he has the pope's ear. He helped to procure the work your father and I have now at Casino delle Muse, where your face now graces the ceiling."

"He is a horrible man," she spat. "I don't care how influential he is."

Tuzia waddled toward them, swinging her ample hips. The fat pigeons reluctantly fluttered up out of her way, plopping down just a few feet in her wake. She stopped at the bottom of the limestone steps.

"It is time for the *colazione*," she called. "Signor Tassi, will you not join us for the meal? Signor Gentileschi will be arriving soon. I have some wonderful sardines in garlic and parsley."

"*Certo!* Of course, *grazie!*" He whispered to Artemisia, his lips brushing her ear, "Anything to spend more time with you, Signorina Gentileschi."

Artemisia rolled her eyes.

∞

That night Orazio went out in the streets of Rome with Agostino. From the glint in her father's eye and the amount of red wine they'd had at lunch, Artemisia figured the two were setting out for a night of whoring in Campo Marzio.

She was left at home with Tuzia and her two children. While Tuzia sat by the fire mending Orazio's trousers, Artemisia wandered to her father's bedroom to stare at Judith.

Both Tassi and Quorli find this painting magnificent. I find it awkward and ill-conceived. The women's cocked heads look like hunting dogs hearing whistles in the dark from different directions.

There might be much to compliment—the execution of the fabric, the drape and fluency. But if I were to paint it, I would not use such a rigid composition, nor would I have the looks on the women be so insipid, as if they were almost bored to be holding a freshly severed head in their grasp. I would—

"Artemisia?"

She turned to find Tuzia at her elbow.

"I wish your father would rid his bedroom of this obscenity," Tuzia said. "It's not right to have such a horrible image where he lays his head."

Where you lay your head, lying naked beside him, Artemisia thought.

She said nothing. They could hear the whistles and lurid howls on the street.

Finally Tuzia spoke: "Signor Quorli covets it. I wish your papa would give it to him."

"Give it to him!" Artemisia said. "Never! It is Papa's treasure. He'll only part with it for a purse full of scudi."

"It's an ugly mess," said Tuzia. Her littlest boy let out a bawl from the kitchen.

"Non è culpa mia, Mama!" protested the older brother. *It's not my fault!*

"These *ragazzini* will drive me insane!" Tuzia said. "The sooner that painting goes, the better . . . Either it goes or I do!"

Artemisia made a face at her back as Tuzia headed down to the kitchen.

One more reason for keeping the painting right where it is. If only it truly had the power to drive Tuzia away!

❧

Agostino did not smell of wine and whores the next morning. His face was clean and bright as a schoolboy's. Clearly he had washed away the night's sin, for he smelled of soap.

His eyes shone as Tuzia led him into the bottega. Artemisia glanced up at him and grunted a greeting, though she was secretly pleased he brought no odors as souvenirs of the night's carousing.

Men!

She was working on her father's painting of Saint Jerome. Her task was to paint the book resting by the human skull.

"You must be careful with the shadowing of the saint's little finger and the book cover," Agostino said, putting his hand between her brush and canvas. "The adjacent angle requires skillful shading."

"Do you think I am a fool?" she snapped at him. "My father would beat me if I didn't execute this correctly!" He pulled back, alarmed.

Tuzia grimaced at the outburst. *"Scusa,"* she said, twisting her apron hem in her hand. "I must put on the fava beans. I won't be but a minute." She disappeared, lumbering down the stairs.

"I beg your pardon, Signorina Gentileschi," Agostino said. "I did not mean to offend you. I only made the observation as your tutor."

Artemisia shook her head, still fuming.

His eyes grew softer as he gazed at her. "You are an angel. A fine artist and a beatific beauty. Would your father really beat you?"

"Of course! Were I to destroy the perfection of his work, I suppose I would merit a thrashing."

He dragged a stool next to her. "My blood boils to think of Signor Orazio striking you!"

She shifted her gaze to him. Between her brothers and her father, she was not used to compassion. It was a curious experience.

"Do you have any idea how I admire you, Artemisia?" he said softly. She cocked her head at his use of her first name.

"A woman who not only is the most striking beauty in Rome but possesses a soul that lives and breathes art. You are priceless."

She began to protest. He pressed his finger to his lips to silence her and then slowly moved the same finger to her lips.

"No, listen to me. It is so rare to have a chance to express my feelings for you. I've encountered no other woman in my life with your sensibilities, your raw passion—your talent! You will soon put all of us Roman artists to shame."

"I hardly—"

He grasped her fingers tight, then took her right hand in his, cradling it like a baby bird. "You have divinity in this hand, Artemisia." He pressed his lips to her palm, kissing it passionately.

His mouth was warm and moist. She felt a shock of pleasure at his touch, a wave of warmth that coursed through her veins.

Hearing Tuzia's labored breath as she mounted the stairs, Artemisia snatched her hand away from him and stood abruptly, upsetting the stool with a clatter.

∞

That night Artemisia dreamed of her mother. She did not come to her in kindness as she usually did, her sweet face pulling up in a warm smile, her eyes lighting up upon seeing her beloved daughter.

Instead, Artemisia saw a look she had never seen on her mother's face. Terror. She was running through the dark streets of Rome in a drenching rain, from one guttering oil lantern to another, each lantern illuminating an image of the Virgin.

Her face was pale, her eyes beseeching. The leather soles of her shoes slapped against the wet cobblestones, the only sound in the night.

And then another sound. Heavy boots, pursuing her. Suddenly Artemisia took her mother's place. It was the daughter who was being chased.

She began to cough as her mother had in the weeks before she died. The thudding boots came closer and closer.

She crumpled to the ground in a spasm of coughs in front of La Madonna Addolorata, the Virgin of Pain.

A hooded figure approached her. Artemisia could not see his face. He reached for her breast. His body covered her.

The marble Madonna looked on, tormented, her quartz teardrops sparkling in the lamplight.

Chapter 20
ROME, 1611

"I want to stop my lessons with Maestro Tassi," Artemisia said to her father.

He paused midstroke in his work on the skull that Saint Jerome contemplated.

"Stop? Whatever for? You are learning. I see improvement in your work, daughter," he said. "We shall profit from it."

"I don't think I need any further instruction." She set her jaw tight. "That's all."

"Humph! You are far too proud, Signorina. Did it ever occur to you that you could improve your skill? You are so rock-headed—"

"Papa!"

"No! You shall continue with Maestro Tassi until I decide you have made sufficient progress. I have several commissions I hope to obtain. I need a more professional hand than you possess now to help me finish them. Perspective is essential!"

He paused before he added, "And Agostino Tassi is my friend and closest colleague."

Artemisia clamped her mouth shut. Any more protests would launch his open hand across her cheek.

She was her father's protégée . . . but she realized she was his slave as well.

⌒∽◎

That night she heard an awful row between Tuzia and Orazio. At first their voices were indistinct, the usual murmurs overheard in the night. Then Tuzia hissed something Artemisia couldn't understand, and Orazio responded in a bellow.

"She is my daughter. Don't you dare instruct me how to raise her!"

"Shh! She will hear you."

"Then shut up! And take off your clothes, woman."

"You are drunk, Orazio. You drink too much when you are out with Signor Quorli and Maestro Tassi."

"Who are you to complain, you slut?"

"See. You are drunk!" Now Tuzia was shouting too. "Artemisia should have suitors. She's seventeen years old, Orazio!"

He grumbled something unintelligible.

"No, you listen to me!" she screeched. "What are you going to do with her? Keep her locked up in your bottega for the rest of her life? Find her a husband!"

"Tuzia, shut up!" he roared. "Stop filling her head with talk of marriage."

"Why should I?"

"I'm not giving her up. Together with the boys, our studio can grow. We can—"

"Will you have her be a *zitella* for the rest of her life? A maiden, then a spinster? Will you let her beauty wilt with age so no man will have her?"

"Shut up! Shut up! No man shall have her! Ever!"

"What are you saying?"

"Stop talking to her about suitors. Talk to her about the convent instead."

Artemisia sat bolt upright in bed.

The convent?

She curled her fingers tight around her bedsheet. She stared hard at the holy crucifix hanging on the wall.

What about Florence? Joining my Uncle Aurelio's bottega, vying for a position in the Accademia delle Arti del Disegno? Were all these nothing but pretty fairy tales, just as Tuzia said?

Orazio must have reached for Tuzia in lust for she heard only murmurs after that. The argument had cooled, extinguished in guttural sounds of sex. Perhaps Tuzia was content with the idea of having her out of the house, one way or another.

As a nun?

Artemisia coiled her long braid around her hand and cried into her hair.

∞

A most unwanted man entered the Gentileschi house the next day, accompanied by Agostino Tassi. Tuzia led both guests up into the bottega.

"Signor Quorli!" Artemisia gasped, swiveling around on her stool, her paintbrush wet with paint.

"Ah!" said Quorli, sweeping off his velvet cap and bowing low. She stared at his balding, fat head, greasy with oil. When he straightened, he turned to his companion. "Indeed you are right, Agostino," he said. "Signorina Gentileschi's beauty exceeds all expectations. I have not laid eyes on her for quite a time."

Agostino's face darkened. Artemisia sensed a dangerous shift in the air.

Quorli offered his hand so he could grasp hers and kiss it. Artemisia suddenly bent down to the floor and scraped paint off the floorboards with her fingernails.

Quorli stiffened at the slight.

"Leave us, Agostino," he said, looking down at her. "I want to speak to Signorina Gentileschi in private."

"Tuzia!" Artemisia shouted. "You stay here with me!"

But Tuzia only bowed, ushering Agostino out the studio door.

Cosimo Quorli leered at Artemisia, the flesh around his eyes crinkling.

Artemisia's eyes flew to Tuzia, who still hesitated in the doorway. "I cannot believe you let this man in unannounced!" she said to her. "How dare you!"

"Your father told me he would be visiting." Tuzia looked at the floor. "He has come to inspect your work. With your father's permission."

"All right. He may see my work. But you are to stay here, Tuzia!"

Tuzia said nothing but moved two paces forward into the bottega, silently closing the door behind her. She stood as a reluctant sentinel.

"*Sì, Signorina Gentileschi,*" Quorli purred. "Your father begged me to cast a judicious eye on your paintings."

He made a show of walking from one canvas to another. Artemisia was relieved that *Susanna and the Elders* was in the corner of the room, not easily visible to this intruder's eyes.

She folded her hands together, her paint-stained fingers fidgeting as he considered one painting after the next.

"Hmm . . . most impressive, Signorina. Remarkable. Your style is not only like your father's, but quite reminiscent of Caravaggio's."

She said nothing.

"Too much so," he said, his nostrils pinching in disgust.

"What do you mean?"

"Caravaggio was a brute. He brought the filth of the street into his paintings instead of the purity of the divine."

"His paintings are pure genius!"

Quorli shook his head, dismissing the notion. "Your father said that it was your brush that painted the severed head of Holofernes."

"I have a hand in most of my father's work. I am his apprentice."

"It is unbefitting a woman," he said. "Vulgar and brutal for the fair sex to paint so savagely. What do you know of knives, blood, and swords?"

"I've helped the midwife deliver four of my brothers. My hands were drowned in blood. I cut the youngest's umbilical cord. I—"

"Enough!" said Quorli, disgusted. He approached her and took a deep breath. "Your art is impressive, I'll give you that. I would like to procure the *Judith* your hand has painted."

"You should discuss that with my father, Signor Quorli."

He whispered low so that Tuzia could not hear from the doorway. "I should like to gaze upon your *Judith*, knowing your hand caressed the canvas." His breath smelled of wine, tooth rot, and briny sardines. She held hers, turning away. "But you—you! Signorina Gentileschi. It is you I've come to see."

She backed up a step, but he grabbed her arm.

He bent down, hissing in her ear. "I have a proposition to make . . . It would profit you personally and fill your father's coffers. But it has nothing to do with your art. *Capisce?*"

She understood. She understood too well.

She stared at him, enraged. Her nostrils clenched tight against his breath and his sour, old-man smell. "Does my father know about this?"

"Of course not!" he said, his face hardening. He darted a look at Tuzia. "*Ascolta, Signorina.* Listen! If you dare tell him that I visited you other than to inspect your work, he will be outraged. That would lead to unpleasantness. Severe unpleasantness. He would lose his position painting at the Quirinale. He would be jailed—"

Blackmail!

"Get out of this house!" she screamed. "Get out of this house this minute!"

"Signorina Gentileschi. You don't know what you are saying." His face turned stony. He no longer cared if Tuzia heard his words. "You should not dismiss my offer so quickly. You would have a luxurious life. You would have your own house and servants."

"I am a painter!"

"Not for long, Artemisia," he said, his face sour. "The word in Rome is you are destined for the convent."

Papa has talked to others about his plan!

"If you do not accept my generous proposal," he said, his reptile eyes staring coldly, "I will see that you are slandered throughout Rome, you cunt. You will have the most disgusting reputation. As will your dead mother."

"Get out! Get out!" she screamed. "I shall call out the windows! I shall shout for the *sbirri* to remove you." When he made no move to leave she sprang forward, shoving him with both hands. The nails of her right hand gouged a bit of skin from his flabby throat. He stumbled back two steps and then regained his balance, his hand flying to his scratched neck.

"I warned you, Signorina!" he said. "Now it begins!"

Cosimo Quorli stormed past Tuzia and out the studio door.

"*Larva disgustosa!*" Artemisia shouted—disgusting maggot!—digging furiously under her paint-spotted nails to dislodge his flap of skin.

"*Stai bene?*" asked Tuzia, hurrying to her. "Are you all right? Oh, what a horrible man!"

Agostino shouted Artemisia's name from below.

"Tuzia!" she said, choking back hot tears. "Tell him I cannot possibly have a lesson today. Tell him—"

Then she heard his voice again, urgent—almost a growl: "What did he say? Tell me!"

Artemisia looked up to see her tutor standing in the open door. He stormed in, his eyes riveted on her. "What did he say, Signorina?" His eyes were orbits of rage.

"I—I'm sorry. I'm not at liberty to tell. You must excuse me. I have a throbbing headache."

"No!" he said, stepping closer to her. "No, you must tell me. Did he threaten you?"

"How could you have brought that monster into this house?"

"He—he is my patron, Signorina. I was asked to escort him here with your father's permission. It was your father's request."

"You know how I despise him! I've told you."

"You never told me why!"

She turned away from him. "I don't want to discuss it. Just please leave."

Agostino tried to take her hands in his. She snatched them back, holding them against her heart.

"Please don't send me away," he pleaded. "Please! I can see you are upset. Forgive me, Signorina!"

Artemisia looked up at him. He suddenly seemed gaunt, hollow-eyed. He was only fifteen years her senior but now appeared her father's age. Haggard and bloodless, like a starving man from a battlefield.

Tuzia put her hand on his arm. "*Per favore, Maestro.* It will be better if you go."

He pulled away in fury.

"You don't understand, Signorina," he said to Artemisia, throwing himself to his knees before her. "You—you have cast a spell on me. A wicked enchantment that leaves me unable to sleep or eat. I can think of nothing but you!"

"That is your misfortune, Maestro Tassi."

"Be not cruel with me, I beg you!"

"Please, *go!*" she shouted. "I cannot abide you."

Tuzia pulled him away successfully this time. Artemisia heard their footsteps as they descended the stairs.

∽

Artemisia was still upstairs painting when Orazio arrived home from the Quirinale. Bits of plaster stuck to his tunic and a smear of malachite green sliced across his left cheekbone.

"What did Signor Quorli think of your work?" asked her father. "Was he impressed?"

She turned to him, her eyes still swollen with fury, her face an ugly mask. "How could you have sent that man into our house without telling me!"

He sniffed in annoyance. "How could I? Because I knew you would not admit him if I had told you. What's more important is what he thinks of your work. Tell me."

"Papa!"

"You are a grown woman now, Artemisia. It is time you began to act like one. Signor Quorli is a most powerful man. I put food in your bowl because of him!"

"He is a monster!"

Orazio did not answer. In that moment, Artemisia realized that her father did not ask why she thought Quorli was a monster.

Did he have any idea that Quorli would make advances toward me?
She sat back, stunned.

"What did he say about your paintings?" Orazio repeated.

"Nothing! Nothing of value. He purred some compliments but he offered to purchase nothing."

Except me.

"Damn it! Did you show him *Susanna*?"

"No, Papa!" she said. "Never. She's for you to send to the Medici Court. When I finish—"

"The Medici!" he scoffed. "We need money *now*, Artemisia! And we can't afford to offend this man."

"Keep him away from me, Papa!"

Orazio fumed. "He is my friend and patron. He and Maestro Tassi are my closest friends."

"Papa! Listen to me—"

"You! You are a vain and foolish girl!"

She thought hard about describing Signor Quorli's proposal. But if Orazio understood Quorli's intentions, he would probably kill him.

Or so she thought. So she hoped.

Artemisia stood up from the easel and fled the room. She hadn't mentioned Quorli's interest in the painting of Judith.

❧

The next morning, Maestro Tassi arrived early.

"We didn't expect you quite yet," Artemisia heard Tuzia say as she opened the door. "The signorina is still finishing her breakfast."

Artemisia stuffed a piece of bread in her mouth and hurried upstairs to the bottega. She had to compose herself before facing him.

"Ah! She must have finished," Tuzia said below, in the kitchen. "*Per favore*, go on up. I shall be there momentarily."

How lax Tuzia had become about her chaperoning duties. *What is she thinking?*

"Signorina Gentileschi," Agostino said as he entered the bottega, bowing low, cap in hand. "I trust you feel better this morning."

"*Sì, grazie,*" she said, sorting through various canvases.

"Look at me, Signorina, I beg of you."

She turned and regarded him. He was gaunt—it had not been her imagination the day before. There were dark pouches under his eyes, like a hound's. He had a haunted look.

"I have come to confess my love for you, Artemisia—"

"*Cosa?* What are you saying? Please—"

He strode toward her, taking her hand in his. "No, don't put me off," he said. "Look at me. I cannot eat or sleep, Artemisia. I walk the streets and end up outside your window. Have you not seen me after midnight, staring up at your bedroom window?"

"No. No!" she said. "Why would I—"

"Confess you have the same feelings for me, Artemisia—"

He pulled her close, kissing her neck. His scent was intoxicating. She felt she was sinking, her body unmoored.

This is the pleasure Tuzia told me about.

She pushed him away. "Tuzia!" she shouted. "Tuzia, come up here this minute!"

"Artemisia!" he said. "*Ascolta!* Listen . . . come away with me!" He shook her, his hands clamped tightly over her shoulders. "I will take you to Florence, introduce you to the Medici Court. We could display your work there . . . present you to the Accademia delle Arti del Disegno. We'll take your *Susanna!* You must finish it. That painting will enchant the *granduca*."

She stared at him. It was as if he were privy to her dreams.

"We'll walk along the Arno at night. I will buy you the finest paints—lapis lazuli, cochineal, malachite. I will set you up in your own studio, *amore mio!* Oh, *cuore mio!*"

He embraced her again, covering her face and throat with passionate kisses. She smelled wine on his breath, felt his warm tongue on her flesh, in her mouth.

An urge twisted in her gut. *All of this is forbidden!* Her father—

"The two of us alone," he said. "In Florence! Think of it, Artemisia—"

And she did think of it. *Florence! The home of Leonardo and Michelangelo! Of Donatello and . . .*

They heard the slow, labored steps of Tuzia climbing the stairs. Instead of releasing her, Agostino held her tighter.

Freedom! Art, culture—

"I knew you loved me," he whispered into her ear. "I knew you wouldn't accept Cosimo Quorli as a lover. No matter how much he offered."

He knew about Quorli?

The bastard . . . he knew!

From the corner of her eye she spied her painting of Susanna leaning on the wall near the doorway. The arc of her naked body and the panic in her eyes.

Tuzia crossed the threshold and saw the two of them in an embrace. A smile spread across her face and she gave them a knowing look.

Artemisia's eyes shot back to her painting of Susanna, the fingers of the girl's left hand spread in defense against the two lechers.

She broke away from Tassi's grasp. She pushed him away, hard. He fell to the floor with a crash, toppling her easel.

She stood over him, heaving with fury. Strands of her hair had pulled loose from her combs. She pushed them angrily from her eyes and shouted down at him, "Get away from me!"

"My angel!" he cried. "I love you! You are a prisoner here. I could take you away, free you from your—"

"If you wish to take me away," she said, extending her hand in front of his face, "marry me and put a wedding ring on this finger." She took a step away from him. "Until then, you will remember your place as my tutor . . . and nothing more."

Artemisia threw the dirtiest scowl she could muster at Tuzia. "You!" she said, shaking a finger in Tuzia's face. "You *ruffiana!*" *Pimp!*

She stormed past Tuzia down the stairs and out the door, her black rage frightening three masons who were working on repairing the entrance to the house.

She walked out into the busy Via del Corso, unescorted. Her wrath burned away men's whispers, the lewd propositions, even the packs of little boys who might taunt a girl walking alone as if she were helpless prey. She could have killed them all!

Chapter 21
ROME, 1611

Fleeing Agostino Tassi, Artemisia raced down the street without a chaperone, without her brothers at her side. She kept walking down the Via del Corso leading to the Piazza del Popolo. There she mixed in with the crowd of pilgrims entering that major northern gate of Rome.

Water vendors with enormous jugs on their backs sold dippers of water to the parched pilgrims. The piazza smelled of smoke from the chestnut seller's fire. A grubby, bearded man held a fistful of cords tied to inflated animal bladders colored red, yellow, and green.

"Mama! I want a balloon!" cried a child not more than five.

"We are here to worship our Lord and the Holy Mary," scolded his mother, who was wearing a tattered scarf. "We haven't the money for trifles, *figlio!*"

Artemisia merged into the crowd pushing their way into Chiesa Santa Maria del Popolo. In that struggling mass she felt safe. The pilgrims had walked for days, even months to reach the Holy City. The Chiesa Santa Maria del Popolo was their first holy site in the city of the pope.

They were asking the Virgin Mary to bless their souls. Ah, but how their bodies stank! The sweat, the odor of unwashed skin and dirty clothes. The stinking breath and shit-stained trousers, the women whose menses had soaked their underclothes. The enveloping miasma took away her breath.

She pulled the hem of her painter's smock up to cover her nose, marching along with them.

As the crowd shuffled over the cobblestones toward the entrance, she looked up at the travertine limestone steps and the facade rising above the portals. She remembered the day of her mother's funeral. Prudenzia was buried under the floor of Santa Maria del Popolo.

But Artemisia was not here today to visit her mother's grave.

The wave of pilgrims broke against the limestone and stalled, the walkers standing helpless, waiting for the chance to enter the sacred church through the single doorway.

"They say the emperor Nero was buried here," a shawled woman said, lisping through gapped teeth. "And with his evil soul, this place was haunted."

"I know the story!" said a youth with a dirty red rag tied around his neck. It was clearly a tale he had recounted before on the long journey to Rome.

"Nero—the worst tyrant Rome has ever seen!" he began. "*Sì*, his remains were buried here and his spirit haunted the place. None of the Romans would come near. Only the unknowing pilgrims passed through the gate."

"Is it haunted now, boy?" demanded an old man, stabbing his stick in the air in agitation.

"*Aspetta*, old man!" said the youth. *Wait.*

"Let him tell his story, cobbler," said a red-nosed man, a hard-muscled laborer.

The boy continued, "But the earth despised him and his sepulcher was buried under a landslide. From the rubble a walnut tree grew, larger than any Rome had ever seen. And a host of demons roosted in the branches and fornicated at the foot of the tree. The demons preyed like wolves on the arriving pilgrims coming to pay homage to Christ. They beat, tortured, and strangled the flock, humble pilgrims just as we are standing here today."

"God save us!" wailed a woman.

The gap-toothed old woman sucked in her breath, making a whistling sound through her missing teeth.

The boy continued his tale, encouraged by how many ears were cocked his way. The crowd lurched forward and the pilgrims started again making their painfully slow way toward the church doors.

"But the good Pope Paschal II fasted for three days, praying to our merciful God and our Lord Jesus Christ—"

"And of course the blessed Mary!" added a man in tattered rags, lifting his clouded eyes up to the heavens.

"I'm getting to that!" said the boy, testily. "He prayed to the Virgin to guide his purge of the demons."

"Go on, boy," said the gap-toothed woman. "Finish up. We are almost to the steps."

Ahead Artemisia saw the white limestone and the dirty heels of pilgrims slapping their worn sandals and bare feet up the steps toward the doors.

Black crows cawed above them, circling in lazy loops.

"There are the demons!" said the boy, pointing up at the birds. "They take the form of crows."

The man next to Artemisia shuddered.

The boy went on, "The Virgin Mary gave the pope a vision to free the city of the scourge. The third Thursday after Lent, he led the faithful of Rome up to the walnut tree, holding a gold crucifix high above his head. When the crowd of the faithful reached the walnut tree, the pope performed a powerful exorcism. Then the Holy Father took an axe, blessed it, and struck a mighty blow to the tree."

"And then?"

The pilgrims' progress halted as the priest shut the door of the *chiesa*, forcing them to wait until other pilgrims had left to make room

173

for their entry. The pilgrims groaned. Their faces were shrunken with hunger and thirst, their skin weather-beaten, bronzed, and as tough as leather from the heartless sun.

"Hundreds of demons flew out of the tree, screaming and howling. Like bats from the bowels of hell they flew, writhing in fire!" said the boy. "When they were gone, the pope ordered the body of Emperor Nero dug out of the ground. His bones were thrown into the Tiber, and his pestilence was carried away with the flood."

Artemisia found herself thinking not of Nero, but of Cosimo Quorli. She imagined his head submerged, his flabby shoulders bobbing in the current, disappearing toward Ostia and the sea.

The boy's voice continued, "Pope Paschal II blessed the church in the name of the Virgin, consecrating the holy ground."

The priest appeared again, opening his arms wide like Moses parting the waters. "The doors of blessed Santa Maria del Popolo are open to you now," he called as two pages flung open the doors to expel one crowd of pilgrims and accept more. "Behold the House of Our Lord!"

Carried forward with the mob, Artemisia realized she knew the priest, Padre Simonello. She tried to duck behind the gap-toothed woman, but the priest spotted her. He caught her arm and took her into the pews, a section roped off from the dirty horde.

"This is not the hour of Mass, Signorina Gentileschi." He craned his neck, searching for her brothers or chaperone. "What on earth are you doing here mixed in among pilgrims? Are you alone?" His brow furrowed. "With a crowd of strangers?"

"I felt safe with them," she said. "I have come to pray."

This satisfied him, at least temporarily. "My child. I will see someone accompanies you home. Look for me after your prayers. I must go now and control the flow of pilgrims."

As he moved off, Artemisia knelt. She peeked through her clasped fingers to the left of the altar, where Caravaggio's masterpiece, *The Crucifixion of St. Peter*, hung in the Cerasi Chapel.

She knew she should be praying to the Virgin. Carracci's *Assumption of the Virgin* was next to Caravaggio's great work. But Carracci's Virgin was rising into the clouds like a sparrow in the wind. She was perfect. And Artemisia had no time for pretty Madonnas and fluttering doves. She understood Caravaggio and he understood her. Caravaggio was a colossal sinner—at home with darkness, striking back with brilliant light and insult. His Saint Peter looked as dazed and confused as she felt as she made her way to the painting.

"Why is the good Saint Peter upside down on the cross?" asked a woman.

"He did not want to imitate our Lord Christ," said a man next to her with a clump of hair sprouting from the bridge of his nose. "He considered it blasphemous."

"I would think he would get dizzy. Upside down like that."

"Good God, woman," said the hairy-nosed man. "He is about to die!"

They moved on along the roped-off path the priest had set. Artemisia pushed her way closer to the painting.

Dizzy.

Artemisia felt that way. She looked at the men straining to lift the cross—and Saint Peter, his face filled with despair and utter confusion, upside down on the cross.

I feel upside down now.

A man swears he loves me. Oh, treacherous beast. He and his friend plot to steal my virtue. Betray me! Without my virtue, what other currency do I have to buy my freedom?

She studied the painting.

Caravaggio's sorcery with light transfixed her: the blackness of the night, the torchlight striking the buttocks of the man crouching beneath the heavy weight of Saint Peter and the cross, pushing upward, his dirty feet mirroring the dirty feet of the dying saint, as two other men pulled to haul the cross upright.

Buttocks, filthy feet. A saint in fear and doubt and pain. Caravaggio found miracles in the mundane.

Unexpected laughter burst from her. The strange sound made the silent pilgrims turn and stare.

"God heal her pain," said a woman, making the sign of the cross.

Artemisia felt warm tears on her fingers. Her laugh had turned to sobs.

∞

That night she lay atop her linen sheets, which were stiff and scratchy from drying in the afternoon sun. She clenched and unclenched her fists.

What can I do? Papa must hear my story.

At last she heard the bolt slide in the door, her father returning from another late night in Rome's taverns and brothels.

She lit a taper and stole down the stairs to meet him. A gigantic silhouette flickered on the stucco wall, the oil sconce casting light as her father ascended the stairs.

His eyes were bloodshot and ominous.

"Papa!" she said, pulling her nightdress close around her neck. "I must speak to you."

Seeing her candle, he turned and snuffed out the oil lamp in the entry. The weak moonlight lit the travertine steps an eerie white.

"Wait 'til morning." His words were slurred. "I'm going to bed."

"It can't wait until morning!"

He pushed past her, nearly knocking the candle from her hand. *"Basta, ragazza!" Enough, girl!*

"No!" She snatched at his arm. *"Ascoltami,* Papa!" *Listen to me!*

He reached the top of the stairs. Artemisia was a step below.

"Maestro Tassi tried to make love to me! And Signor Quorli propositioned me to be his mistress."

Orazio stopped and looked over his shoulder at her, his face contorted with wrath.

"You and your vanity!" He wheeled and lashed out, striking her hard across the face, sending the candle spinning down the stairs. Its flame died against the stones. "You think my best friends would betray me? You are full of ugly fantasies that would turn me against Agostino . . . and Cosimo Quorli. Without their help I would be ruined—"

"Papa!"

"Get out of my sight! Your whorish ways would blind me to the truth. You will destroy everything! You are no better than your mother!"

Her eyes adjusted to the pale moonlight entering the windows of the first floor. From his perch a step above her, he turned and staggered into his room, slamming the door.

She walked down the stairs and heard footsteps shuffling from the floor above. She looked up the staircase and saw Tuzia lean her head over the banister, a lamp in her hand. Her night braids hung over her shoulders. "He won't ever believe you," she whispered. "Men!"

Artemisia put her hand to her cheek, which was aching from the blow her father had struck.

"Best to get Agostino to marry you," Tuzia said, descending the stairs. "It is the only way you'll ever earn your father's blessing. Agostino will set you free."

When did she begin calling him by his Christian name?

"Free? He takes his liberties with me!"

"You've captured his heart, Artemisia."

"It is not his heart that I fear. Never leave me alone with him!"

"I will . . . try. But he frightens me. His passion for you—"

"If he should compromise me, all is lost!" said Artemisia, falling to her knees on the travertine stairs. "I will be defined as a *puttana*. No man will marry me. Rome will cast me and everything I touch in the gutter. My art included! The only resort is a convent for those women who have fallen."

Tuzia descended the stairs and knelt beside the anguished girl. She stroked Artemisia's hair.

"Tuzia!" she pleaded. "You could tell Papa! Tell him how I did not encourage the maestro's advances, how he took advantage—"

"He would not listen to me either." She shook her head so that her braids swung side to side. She went back up the stairs, suddenly furious. "For a great artist, you are a fool!"

She disappeared from the stairwell and the flicker of lamplight vanished, leaving Artemisia in the faint moonlight.

Chapter 22

ROME, 1611

Agostino did not come the next day, or the next. Artemisia began to wonder if maybe her father had reconsidered her words and at last believed her and had banished him. Still she avoided Orazio and did not speak to him.

The third day, Cosimo Quorli entered the Gentileschi house. The masons were still at work on the entrance and paid no attention as he walked in.

"You! You she-dog!" he said, finding Artemisia working on one of her father's paintings. "What spell have you cast on my friend?"

"Leave this house!" Artemisia said, rising. "Tuzia! Tuzia!"

"He cannot eat or sleep. He walks like a demon has possessed his soul. All for the lust of you."

"Tuzia!" she screamed.

"Give him what he wants, you slut. You give it to so many others around Rome, why not him?"

She turned to him, horrified. "You son of a whore!" she said. "What do you mean? I am a *zitella*!" *A virgin!*

"That's not what Rome says," he sneered. "I know someone who can list your lovers, you slut: Niccolo Bedino!"

Artemisia cocked her head, looking at the portly Quorli smirking at her.

"Niccolo Bedino? The failed apprentice?"

"He told me he hardly slept at night with you sending messengers with love letters all over Rome to arrange rendezvous with your lovers."

"Liar!"

"Give some of what you share all over Rome to Agostino. He has the fever for you. Give it to me!"

"*Tuzia!*"

Tuzia came panting in with her two youngest children in tow. "Signor Quorli!" she said. "Forgive me, Signore, I did not hear you knock at the door."

"Because he didn't knock!" Artemisia shouted. "The masons left the door open—anyone can come in. Even this maggot!"

Tuzia looked alarmed. She shot Artemisia a quick look, then turned to Quorli. "Please forgive me," she repeated. "May I escort you downstairs? Or offer you a cup of wine in the dining room?"

"I'll see myself out," Quorli said, dismissing her and turning back to Artemisia. "You think long and hard about what I said. I need an artist who can paint, not pine for some promiscuous slut!"

Tuzia ducked her head, saying nothing.

"Get out of this house at once!" Artemisia cried. She picked up a jar of turpentine and hurled it at his head. It missed but shattered against the wall just beyond him.

"You'll regret that," he snarled, wincing as the fumes stung his eyes. "You'll see, Artemisia Gentileschi!"

Artemisia was unable to eat the midday meal. Signor Quorli's insults and threats raced through her mind.

Niccolo, that useless apprentice? Has he really told Quorli and others that I had lovers all over Rome? Who else heard this lie? Will it reach my father's ears?

Her abdomen cramped, the first twinge. Her menstruation had started.

Her body was oblivious to what transpired beyond it. Like the full moon rising every month, her period announced itself punctually.

"Artemisia."

She started.

It was Tuzia. "Forgive me, Artemisia. That man Cosimo Quorli—I had no idea how wicked he is. I saw him as your father's benefactor."

"I tried telling you. Why does no one believe me?"

"Forgive me, *cara*," she said. "Your papa instructed me to be courteous to him. He is not at all like Maestro Tassi, who loves you!"

Artemisia glared at her. "Don't speak of love! I am desperate to finish these paintings for my father and to finish *Susanna*. I can't bear to talk of suitors. What do I care for their love? I have not asked for it. Why can I not be left alone to work?"

There was a long silence. Artemisia struggled to keep from sobbing.

"You need to get away from this house," said Tuzia eventually. "You have been trapped in here far too long. A stroll in the vineyards of Basilica di San Giovanni. I shall suggest it to your father. After Mass, why could we not have a family outing?"

Artemisia sighed, thinking of the sun on her face, the birds singing in the trees. When she was a young girl, her father took them often to the vineyards near San Giovanni, where she and her brothers would run up and down the rows of grapes, scaring away the birds who pecked at the ripening fruit.

"I would like that, Tuzia. *Grazie.*"

A strong menstrual cramp seized her. She buckled over in pain.

"What's the matter, Artemisia? Is it your monthly?"

"*Sì,*" she said, wincing until the spasm stopped.

"Oh, dear one. Let me make you some chamomile tea."

Tuzia's two boys appeared, entering the studio cautiously. The fumes from the crock of turpentine Artemisia had hurled against the wall that morning were still strong, wafting across the room and into her bedroom. She left her room's window open in an attempt to air the studio before her father returned from work.

"You work too hard, Artemisia," said Tuzia, petting her youngest son's head.

Artemisia gazed at Tuzia. As much as she had detested Tuzia, she had to admit that Tuzia was a simple creature. She loved her children, she loved Orazio. She even loved Artemisia. Her outlook on life was much like a street dog's. She fought to survive. Her husband was rarely home, did not pay the rent. What was it to share Orazio's bed? She was lonely, as was he. She cleaned the house and made sure there was food on the table. Who was Artemisia to judge her?

Tuzia was a survivor.

"Let me paint your portrait, Tuzia," she said.

"*Cosa?* What? Really—you want to paint me?"

"You and your two boys. Yes." Artemisia moved a chair close to her easel. "Sit here and have Simone stand next to you, his arm draped around your shoulders. Put Gregorio in your lap."

With a little coaching the family was brought together in a perfect tableau.

"There!" Artemisia said.

"Signorina Artemisia!" Tuzia said, dabbing at her eyes with a kerchief tucked under her sleeve. "I am so honored."

Artemisia began with a preliminary sketch. She wanted to capture the sweetness of the youngest boy, Gregorio, the sun glancing off his golden hair, the tender nature of his gaze. The older boy, Simone, looked protective of his mother, his arm embracing her shoulders. Artemisia wondered if the shouting with Signor Quorli had frightened him, or if he had been ready to fight to protect Artemisia from the advances of the stranger.

Minutes passed and Artemisia did not notice. She had to bark at the children to hold their poses, and Tuzia had to shift Gregorio's weight on her leg. She groaned but repositioned herself, content she had been asked to pose.

It was going to be a good painting. When Artemisia was absorbed in a painting she could see ahead to the result and became ravenous to finish. She would not allow her subjects to budge but a few inches. She ignored the children's pleas for water or a moment to play.

As she was applying a muted rose to their skin tones, she saw Simone suddenly straighten up and stare over her shoulder. He turned to his mother, waiting for her reaction.

Artemisia whirled around and saw Agostino Tassi standing behind her.

"Painting!" he said in a belligerent tone, his breath reeking of alcohol. "You paint too much, Artemisia! You need to relax more."

He took a step closer and peered at the painting. She could feel the heat of his body. Little hairs on her skin prickled, standing on end.

"It's quite good," he whispered. "But you need a break from painting."

He took the palette from her hand and tossed it to the center of the room.

"My paints!" she cried. "Are you mad?"

He plucked the brush from her hand and threw it over his shoulder. "Too much painting!" he growled. "It makes you dull."

He turned on Tuzia and her children. "Leave us!" he thundered.

The family tableau broke up, the three subjects scattering like frightened birds.

"Tuzia!" Artemisia said. "Tuzia! Don't leave!"

The children's footsteps were already knocking a steady gallop down the stairs.

Tuzia's eyes had widened like a frightened deer's. Her hand stifled a scream.

"Get out of here, Signora!" snarled Tassi. "This minute! And close the door!"

"Tuzia! Don't leave!"

Tuzia threw a worried look at her.

"Get out!" Tassi roared.

The chaperone turned at the door. "Forgive me, Signorina."

Tuzia, the survivor. Tuzia, the traitor.

The door clicked behind her.

"Alone!" Tassi said. "At last!"

Artemisia stood up to run for the door. He caught her wrist, yanking her back. She winced in pain, cradling her hand.

"Slow down, sweet Artemisia." He pulled her close.

"Get away from me!"

"Shh!" he said, bending his head down to her breast, listening.

She knew he could hear her heart thudding madly. She looked toward the door. How many steps would it take to reach it?

"Let us walk around," he said. He kicked away the stool.

"You've been drinking, Maestro Tassi," she said. "A lot. Let me go."

"I haven't had much more than a few cups of wine," he said. "To cool my fever." He darted a look at her. Dark and wolfish.

"Let me go," she said again. "I won't mention this to Papa if you'll just let me go."

"Your papa," he snarled. "Your papa isn't here. Let's just walk, the two of us." He draped an arm around her shoulders and steered her by her left elbow. "Just a walk around the room."

Her eyes darted to the open door of her bedroom.

Artemisia stopped in her tracks.

"I am feeling ill," she said.

"Ill?"

"I have a fever," she lied.

"Fever!" he said, growling. "It is I who have the fever, Artemisia! And only you can rid me of it."

His gaze was lupine with hunger, dark brown flecks shimmering in his light brown eyes. As if to make a mockery of her fever, he pulled a lace-embroidered handkerchief from the sleeve of his tunic and mopped his head as he scanned her face, her throat, her body. He held her closer and she could feel a stiff protrusion in the folds of his velvet trousers.

The maestro dragged her forward, walking again. This time as they approached the threshold of her bedroom door, he pushed her in and followed behind, locking the door.

"What are you doing?" she screamed, fighting to reach for the door handle. "Tuzia! Tuzia!"

"Quiet," he ordered, pushing her onto the edge of the bed with one hand over her breast. She felt his fingers groping her bosom, kneading it like bread dough.

"Tuzia!" she screamed.

He pushed her down, threw up her skirts, and jammed his thigh between her legs. She wrestled madly with him, scratching and flailing, but he rode on top of her, gripping her wrists and flattening her against the mattress. The boards creaked under them.

"Tuzia! Come here at once!"

Tassi pressed his handkerchief over her screaming mouth, laying his forearm against her face. When she inhaled to scream, she sucked the handkerchief into her mouth and began choking. She pushed the cloth out with her tongue and pressed her lips tight together. Deep in her throat a gurgle of rage rose, trapped and barely audible.

She saw him fumble with his trousers with one hand. She felt that hardness, freed now, poking between her thighs, then a deep burning sensation in her *fica*.

"This is what you need, Artemisia! What I need," he gasped. "Take it, you whore. You dirty *puttana*!"

185

She scratched at his face and pulled at his hair. He jumped back in pain and before he could put his member back in her again she grabbed it, her nails sinking into the skin, pulling away a piece of flesh.

None of this deterred him. He was a rutting bull. He reentered her savagely, ripping, making her bleed. She bucked and flailed. He scratched her neck while pinning her arms down. His elbow struck her hard in the face. He thrust over and over until he finished with a shout.

Then he rolled off her, exhausted. A steady stream of blood colored the linen sheets, his flaccid penis, his hands.

"You really were a virgin," he said, staring at the blood in disbelief.

Never had she hated anyone more in her life.

She jumped up and ran to her table drawer and pulled out a knife. "You! You have dishonored me! I shall kill you, you animal!"

Seeing the knife in her hand, Tassi stood up. He made a show of opening the neck of his tunic, exposing his bare chest.

"Here I am," he said, playacting. "Kill me if you must."

Lo smargiasso, she thought. *The braggart. You underestimate me, you demon!*

Artemisia lunged at him, intent on plunging the blade into his heart. Panic flashed in his eyes. He deflected the knife by striking up at her forearm, sending the knife clattering to the floor. A thin ribbon of red soaked his shirtsleeve.

"You were going to *kill* me!" he said, incredulous.

"*Sì,* you monster! You have ruined me!" she cried. "I shall never marry, never leave this prison unless I am cast out in the streets as a whore!"

Her virginity was the only currency she had to bargain for freedom from her father. A suitable marriage rather than a nunnery. Without her virginity, Orazio was right: she was no more than a *puttana.*

She fell to her knees and wept, beating her fists on the floorboards.

For a long time she felt him standing over her.

At last he said, gently, "Stop crying, Artemisia. I thought you had lain with men before me. How was I to know?"

"I told you! You had no right to assume otherwise, you beast!"

"That's not what other men told me," he said defensively. "Cosimo and Niccolo told me you had lovers all over Rome. Cosimo told me he had you here on this same bed."

"Liar!" she screamed. "Dirty, filthy liar! I've known no man . . . until now."

He stared down at her. "Give me your hand."

"Go away!"

She could not look at him. She stared at the floorboards, the grains of sand and dirt on the wood. His boots made a scuffing sound as he bent down next to her.

She felt his hand caress her own, and then his fingertips sweeping strands of hair out of her eyes and mouth.

"Artemisia. Forgive me. I promise I will marry you as soon as I am out of the labyrinth I am in. I need to have Cosimo Quorli's blessing first."

"What?"

"He is my patron. Let me procure his permission and then we will wed."

"Cosimo Quorli!" she said. "You dare speak his name? He propositioned me! He lied that he lay with me! He is a worm."

Those words had a dangerous effect. Tassi drew back on his haunches, a cold stare dissolving his recent warmth. Artemisia recognized a rabid jealousy, a hard glint in his eye.

"But if it were true . . . I warn you, Artemisia." His voice was as cold as his glare. "I will not stand for any foolishness when you are my wife! I would kill you if I found out you had lain with another man."

"Foolishness?" Her voice cracked into a madwoman's laugh. She pointed to her bloody garments. "How dare you? There has been no foolishness on my part! *You did this to me!* You!"

He looked at her again as if he saw her ravaged condition for the first time. The raging jealousy faded from his eyes.

"*Cara mia!*" he whispered. "What have I done?"

Artemisia pulled the shreds of her bodice over her breasts. She felt a sticky trickle down her legs. She bit her lip hard to keep from crying.

"Hush now," he said, pulling her close. "Forgive me, my darling. We will think of our future. Together."

Future? Her world had exploded, her soul torn like a threadbare rag. *There is a future?*

She looked up at him. He lifted her from the floor, embracing her, his lips covering her face in warm, tender kisses.

"Florence," he said. "Artemisia! You've always wanted to see Florence." He cupped her chin in his hand as if she were a child. "*Cara mia!* We will go to Firenze together."

And with that one word—Florence—she stopped weeping. Despite her horror, her throbbing pain, her humiliation, her tears ceased. She looked up at her assailant, this monster who had raped her.

He spoke of a future.

Like Tuzia, Artemisia would become a survivor.

Chapter 23
ROME, 1611

She heard the muffled words through the door. Agostino and Tuzia.

"She needs attending," said he.

"What will her father say?" said she. "He will cast me from the house! I have nowhere to go—"

"Woman! Stop thinking of yourself! She needs a bath, her clothes washed and mended."

"Oh!" wailed Tuzia.

"Listen to me, Signora. Her father need never hear of this. Why should he, unless you tell? You care for her and keep your mouth shut. Nothing—*nulla!*—ever happened. Do you hear me?"

Tuzia moaned.

"I will take care of her in my own way," he said. "Signor Gentileschi shall never learn what happened today."

Why does he not tell her we are to marry? Artemisia thought.

She heard his boots thudding down the stairs and then an almost-silent tapping on the bedroom door.

"May I come in, Signorina Artemisia?" She heard the door open, then close. "Oh, you are a mess! He had his way with you, did he not?"

Artemisia leapt from her bed and pounced on Tuzia. She slapped her over and over again with her open palm, then pounded her head with her fists.

"Leave me be!" Tuzia shrieked. "Get off me!"

Artemisia stepped back and Tuzia bent over, gasping, her soap-cracked hands sheltering her graying head, her face contorted with anguish.

"You left him here to rape me!" Artemisia said. "You! My chaperone!"

"Forgive me! You saw how he was. How could I stay in the room? He would have beaten me—"

"I needed you here! You deserted me!"

Artemisia fled out of the bedroom into the bottega. She bent down and righted the stool from where Agostino had kicked it. She sat down and sobbed.

Tuzia followed her. "Let me heat up some water and draw you a bath." She shook her head. "Did he not propose marriage?"

Artemisia stared at her.

"*Sì,*" she said.

"*Sì!*" Tuzia exclaimed, her hand flying to her mouth in excitement. "You are to marry the great maestro?"

How can she be so happy? I have just been raped!

"He said he had to procure permission from Cosimo Quorli."

Tuzia's nostrils pinched as if there were a bad stench. "Why him?"

"He is Agostino's accursed patron. He does nothing without his permission."

"Nothing good will come of that man," said Tuzia. "*Niente!*" Then she ventured a smile. "But the maestro proposed marriage! See, Artemisia? It will all turn out well. To be married to such a handsome man, so accomplished . . . a great artist!"

Artemisia turned away. She could not abide Tuzia's eager smile. It was worse than the pathetic sight of her raw, chapped hands protecting her graying head.

"Fetch me a bath," she said. "Wash and mend my clothes." She wished that she could burn them. She began stripping off her garments, one by one.

Tuzia gasped at the quantity of blood as she gathered Artemisia's clothes.

"If Papa sees me like this," Artemisia said, "it will be me who is cast out on the street."

"Poverina!" Tuzia said. *You poor thing.*

Artemisia ignored her, feeling as if she was about to vomit.

Tuzia closed the door, Artemisia's soiled and tattered clothes bundled in her arms. The artist walked about the studio naked, ignoring the cold draft. By her easel was the small looking glass her father had given her as a birthday present. She inspected her face, swollen but not badly bruised, at least not yet. Her lower neck was scratched, but she could wear a shawl to conceal her wounds.

She looked down at her torso. She could still see Agostino's handprints on her hips and shoulders where he had gripped her tight. They were already turning purple. She could hide them under her garments. If Orazio noticed her face, should she say she tripped on a tool the masons left lying about?

With her looking glass she inspected her private parts. Her nether lips were torn, bleeding like raw meat. Her upper thighs were badly bruised. She ached for a bath.

Sticky juices still trickled out, dribbling down her legs. She wiped with her bare hand at the stinking dampness in disgust. The smell of old fish left in the sun.

She sat on her painting stool and inspected her eyes. They were red and swollen from crying. But she felt a wave of shame washing over her. As an artist, she knew her eyes well.

They will never recover the innocence I knew only moments ago.

She blinked back tears, and in refocusing, she caught a glimpse of blond hair, a painting reflected behind her. In the looking glass she saw her portrait of Susanna, naked and horrified, just as Artemisia sat now.

She spun around on the stool, feeling the varnished wood under her naked buttocks and genitals. She winced in pain and stared.

I have never painted the second elder's face.

Now that black hole, shiny gesso, stared back, accusing her.

She knew who it was now.

She began to paint.

∞

Orazio staggered in late that night. Artemisia stayed in her bedroom. She knew that she could easily avoid him for several days. His work at the Casino delle Muse kept him away from the house for long hours.

The next morning, Orazio left for the Quirinale before the sun rose.

Artemisia woke to the sounds of Tuzia banging pots and pans in the kitchen, then the smell of salt pork frying. When she smelled cinnamon and detected a fragile lemon scent, she knew for sure—Tuzia was making her special *carbonata*.

"*Strega,*" Artemisia murmured. *Witch.* But her nose and stomach led her, shamefaced, down to the kitchen.

"Ah! There you are, Signorina!" chirped Tuzia, a wooden spoon in her hand. She turned a rasher of bacon and then mixed parsley, sugar, cinnamon, and lemon with a pestle and mortar, mashing them together with bright enthusiasm. "Did you sleep well, *ragazza*?"

Artemisia cocked her head at Tuzia. "Sleep? I had nightmares all night long. I ache all over—I can barely walk."

"My *carbonata* will fix you up," said Tuzia merrily. She spooned the parsley, sugar, and lemon mixture onto the rashers, making the fat spit in the pan. "You need to look your best, *cara mia*—a wedding is in your future! What a beautiful bride you will be."

A bride?

Artemisia sat down at the table, which was set with a garish table-cloth embroidered with red and yellow ducks. She knew it was Tuzia's—her father would never bring such a monstrosity into the Gentileschi house.

"Now, *cara*. You eat up. *Buon appetito!*" Tuzia placed the plate on the table with a flourish.

Artemisia dug into the meal, closing her eyes as she savored every morsel.

There was a knock on the door, even though the masons were still working on the entrance and anyone could walk in.

Artemisia froze.

"That must be Maestro Tassi," Tuzia said.

"What? Here? Today?"

"He is scheduled for today as always. Nothing has changed."

"Everything has changed!" Artemisia pushed away her plate. The bacon rose in her throat, tasting heavy and foul.

Tuzia opened the door and Agostino marched in, wearing his brown velvet cap, a thick wool scarf wrapped several times around his neck.

"Ah! *Che freddo!*" he said. "How cold it is! For the month of May, it is freezing."

"It's that icy wind from the north," said Tuzia. "Come in where it is warm. I'll prepare some mulled wine for you."

Artemisia stood up abruptly, nearly upsetting her unfinished plate of *carbonata*.

Agostino doffed his cap. *"Buongiorno, Signorina."*

Buongiorno? Is that all he can say to me?

She was mortified to look at him, but she did. She scanned his face for any trace of sarcasm. Had he kept his word? Had he told anyone what had happened between them?

As though answering her question, he gave an almost imperceptible shake of his head.

"I will grind the cinnamon stick and cloves for the wine—you two can start on your lesson," said Tuzia. "Unless you'd like me to escort you, Artemisia."

"What difference does it make now?" she snapped. "The horse has escaped the barn, Tuzia!"

"I'd like to talk with you, Signorina," said Agostino. "Alone."

He approached her and she flinched.

"Keep away!"

"I will keep my distance," he whispered. "I swear it."

Climbing the stairs was painful with her injuries. When Agostino tried to take her arm to help, she shook it off furiously.

She lowered herself with a groan onto her stool. "Well," she said. "What did you want to say?"

"I intend to marry you," he said. "I haven't approached Signor Quorli yet, but I will. I thought it best to wait . . . a few days."

"Why did you . . . do that to me?" she said, her voice uneven. She had promised herself she wouldn't break down again in front of him. She would never—ever!—show him weakness again.

She hated him for making her vulnerable.

For that sin alone I will despise you forever!

"Oh, Artemisia! If you could understand how you have possessed me! Never have I had a passion—a fever!—for another woman as I do for you." He started to approach her, his hand reaching to caress her. She reared back, overturning the stool.

"You promised not to touch me!"

He took a step back. "How can I win your confidence, your trust, your love? I propose marriage, a new life in Florence. Or here in Rome—"

"Florence!" Artemisia demanded. "I want to leave my father's world. I want to get out!"

"Florence then!" he said. "*Tranquilla*, Artemisia—" *Calm down.*

"When?"

He looked away and then lowered his eyes.

I don't like this.

"Soon," he said. "I have business I must sort out."

"What kind of business? You work with my father—"

"Other affairs that don't concern . . . us," he said. "But then we will be husband and wife."

There came the *woot-woot-woot* of a pigeon's wings as the bird landed on the sill beyond the waxed canvas of the window. Agostino banged on the canvas with his knuckles, shooing the bird away.

"By May we should have opened the windows and be basking in sunshine," he said. "And yet there is still snow on the mountain peaks."

"I don't care about the weather," she said with a vicious slice of her hand in the air.

"Be pleasant, Artemisia. We might as well already be married, you and I. I've known you now. You are mine."

"No, I am not!" she said bitterly. "I belong to no one! Let us begin our lesson. That's what you are here for."

Tuzia came up a few minutes later and Artemisia was already drawing.

"Here we are," she said, carrying a tray with two cups of mulled wine. "It is terribly cold. Why in the world are we suffering such cold on a spring day?"

Tuzia chattered on, oblivious.

Agostino sat by the window where the morning sun diffused through the waxed canvas, giving his profile a soft light.

"*Scusa,*" Tuzia said, setting the wine on the little table by Artemisia. Then she gasped, having seen that Artemisia was drawing Agostino. She had made him pose. That way he could not touch her.

Artemisia knew Agostino did it to appease her. He did not know that this sketch would be a study for the second elder in her *Susanna and the Elders*. Artemisia found him to be a preening, arrogant model.

"It's very, very good," whispered Tuzia. "But so serious! Here, Signorina, drink some wine."

Artemisia waved her away. "Don't distract me when I'm working."

"Signorina," said the reluctant model. "Surely you are done."

"Not nearly. I want to sketch you in some different positions. Turn your head to one side, as if you are whispering into someone's ear."

"What?" he said, annoyed.

"Tuzia. Stand next to Maestro Tassi. I want him to whisper into your ear."

"Basta!" he fumed. "I've indulged you enough, Signorina!"

"Stay there! I need this."

Tuzia sat next to him. He awkwardly turned his mouth near her ear. Artemisia was certain Tuzia reeked of bacon grease from the *carbonata*.

"Closer, Maestro. Closer."

Agostino twisted his lips up in disgust, his nostrils flaring. It was a savage, arrogant gesture, just the way she needed him to be.

"Perfetto! Don't move!"

She managed to keep Agostino posed for only another quarter hour. Then he wiped his nose in disgust with his handkerchief as Tuzia walked to stand on the other side of the room.

Artemisia felt a shiver of terror.

Is it the same one he held over my mouth?

For the rest of the morning she worked on one of her father's paintings under Agostino's guidance. Orazio had many commissions that were overdue. Today she had chosen to work on the drapery and background of his portrait of Cleopatra.

Her work with drapery had improved significantly under Agostino's eye. She incorporated shadows and ridges, making the folds of the linen sheets look uncannily real.

"My God, you are good," he breathed behind her.

"I know it," she said, tapping her paintbrush. She frowned, realizing that while she was engaged in painting she did not think of him . . . or anything else. Painting was a blessed oblivion. Now his voice pulled her from her reverie, reminding her of her shame.

"Cleopatra's body. It is magnificent," breathed Agostino in her ear. "Did you paint her?"

"No, this is my father's painting. I am only assigned the details. You see? He has it wrong here. Look at her left shoulder. It's all wrong."

"Forgivable," he said, moving closer. He put his eyes only inches from the canvas. Then he turned to her, scanning her eyes as he had scanned the painting. "Did you model for him?"

The mean glint had returned to his eyes. Even Tuzia noticed and moved across the room toward the two of them.

"It's my father's work," Artemisia said, not answering his question.

"It is your body! Your breasts, your skin." He put his hand on her shoulder. She felt his fingers squeezing her, tense with aggression. "Your face!"

"That is not my face!" she spat. "Are you blind? There may be features of my face, but it is not me. And remove your hand. This instant!"

She hadn't considered that her father's Cleopatra would elicit such aggression.

She saw Tuzia studying Cleopatra, her face puckered with consternation, deep vertical lines around her lips. "I've never seen the likeness before," she muttered.

"Does he paint you, Artemisia?" Agostino demanded. "I cannot bear the thought of something so disgusting—"

"Disgusting?" she said. "A father painting his daughter?"

"Nude? Vile! Degenerate—"

"Vile? Disgusting? What about you raping me? Now that is *schifoso*."

"I'm sure Signor Gentileschi never painted the signorina nude," broke in Tuzia, waving the words away. "What a horrific thought!"

Artemisia and Agostino both turned to her.

"Leave us!" ordered Agostino. "Fetch me more wine, Signora."

"*Certo,*" said Tuzia, bowing and turning for the door. As soon as she left, he grabbed Artemisia's upper arm, squeezing it hard.

"As your lover, as your future husband, I forbid you to ever pose for him again. With clothes or without."

"Oh. So you are now ordering me?" she said, standing up from her stool, her hands on her hips. She scowled at her rapist. "No one will be telling me what to do in my life—ever again!"

He yanked her close to him. "I told you," he said, showing his teeth. "When you are my wife, I will abide no foolishness!"

With that he pulled Artemisia into her bedroom and raped her again.

∞

After he was finished and released her, Artemisia rolled over, turning away from him in her bed. She could hear the wind howl outside and rain lash the canvas coverings on the windows.

"Look at me, my love," said Agostino, playing with a strand of her hair.

She slapped his hand away. "Just because you are stronger than me doesn't make me love you. You violate my very existence. You are vile!"

She wiped her tears away with the heel of her hand. A pigeon lighted on the sill, puffing up its feathers.

Agostino sat up and caressed her cheek. "I am obsessed with you, Artemisia. I could not bear to think of your father seeing you nude."

"Why? My father wouldn't leap on me like a rutting goat."

"Rutting goat? Is that all you can say to your future husband?"

"If he behaves like a goat, *sì.*"

She could see this was a blow to his pride. He pulled a face akin to a child pouting.

She scoffed.

"How can I show my love to you, my treasure?" he said. "How can I prove my love?"

By not raping me?

"Let me take you to Florence. Tonight!" he said. "I'll arrange a carriage at once."

Artemisia struggled out of the bed, seeing a smudge of blood on the sheets. It disgusted her. "I'm going nowhere until we have wed. At least for now, no one knows of your treachery except Tuzia."

"Hush now, hush," he said, enveloping her in his arms. "You are mine. I will take care of you, my wife."

She said nothing but let him rock her in his arms. She had had no love since her mother died and Tuzia's abuse drove Maddalena away. To have someone hold her close, call her "my wife," was intoxicating. She let her soul drink from this well of affection, if only briefly.

"Still," he said, pulling away to look at her face. "When I am not here, you have only Tuzia to protect you. And what poor protection she is!"

She let you rape me!

"With only Tuzia here, who else might enter this house and defile you? The masons working below? A buyer of art? The knife sharpener, the cobbler? A nobleman who visits your father's gallery to consider a purchase?"

"Cosimo Quorli?" she said. She watched his face turn beastly.

He shook her by her shoulders. "Why mention him? Why?"

"Because he has tried to proposition me. I have told you this, over and over. He might yet try to rape me."

Agostino trembled with fury. He flung the door open to the studio.

"Get back to work," he said. "But choose another painting. I never want to see Cleopatra again."

Artemisia lay in bed that night thinking about a future with Agostino. It was true that he was handsome and gifted as an artist. He received patronage from the inner papal circle, especially Cardinal Scipione Borghese.

Agostino had proposed marriage—and the prospect of Florence.

But Artemisia and Agostino Tassi were already at each other's throats. Could they ever live under the same roof?

Would he try to direct her future paintings? Artemisia had buried Cleopatra deep behind other canvases. She had to work on it during the hours when Agostino was not there.

If a nude painting could inspire such an explosive response, what would he think when she moved on to more controversial works? For that was what her heart desired. Especially now that she was full of brutal ideas, tumultuous inspiration, even the darkness that Caravaggio expressed.

Especially the darkness.

Would Agostino quell that fire? Would he relegate her to painting the draperies and background details of his own paintings? Was he any different from her father, as a man and an artist?

Competition. She would mean competition for him. A woman. His wife!

She knew Agostino had earned the nickname *lo smargiasso*—the braggart—for good reason. Would he let her outshine him or would he smother her flame?

∽

Giulio worked harder than Francesco, but Artemisia could see he wasn't nearly as talented. At twelve the middle brother was still struggling with the human form. Orazio said his figures were blocks with no grace or movement.

And with that, Giulio was relegated to making frames and stretching and mounting canvases. After a year resenting his fall from behind the easel, he made his peace with his new position, as he found his hands could create objects other than paintings.

He adored wood, nails, and hardware. He built chests for art supplies, stools for every one of the Gentileschis, custom-designed easels of different heights. He even prepared exquisite paintbrushes using cat hair, horse mane, boar bristles, and squirrel fur, painstakingly wrapping resin-coated thread around the splayed tufts of animal hair.

Artemisia relied on him to create the perfect brush for her application of paint or a technique she wished to experiment with.

"I want to be able to highlight these borders the way Caravaggio did. But I can't get it right."

Giulio rubbed his chin, considering. "What if I make you a broader brush, close to the root of the hair where the clusters are tighter and don't absorb as much pigment? You could lightly paint in the highlights in a broader sweep."

Artemisia kissed her brother on both cheeks.

She loved Giulio more each day, even more because he accepted that his talents lay elsewhere than wielding a paintbrush. He was at peace. Unlike Francesco, he did not resent his sister's talent but did his best to help her flourish. He took special care with his preparation of canvas, ensuring that the gesso was set perfectly. And he had a keen eye for selection of pigments, seeing subtle shades of color and perfection in coarse nuggets, a talent that rivaled Artemisia's.

While painting and sketching talent had skipped Giulio, Artemisia could see it budding in Marco. He was the baby of the family and had no pressure on him. There were enough chores in the bottega to fill his day. But one day Artemisia stepped behind his easel to retrieve a prepared canvas and saw what her little brother had created.

"Me?" she said, startled.

"You can tell, Sister?"

Tears flooded her eyes when she saw the tenderness and accuracy in Marco's art. He had created a painting of her while she painted, her face a mask of serious absorption, engaged in her subject. Only a sibling or a lover would recognize and translate so accurately such an expression.

"It's magnificent. You must show it to Papa."

At this the boy balked. "I'm not ready yet."

Artemisia remembered how her father had treated her *Susanna and the Elders*.

"I understand, Marco. When you show it to him, it will be perfect."

The two brothers—Marco and Giulio—lingered in the bottega on evenings when Francesco was out taunting whores with his rough companions and their father was carousing in the taverns with his artist friends.

"Are you sure you don't want to go out?" Artemisia would ask.

They both shook their heads. Giulio was engaged with building frames, stretching canvases, or making paintbrushes, while Marco sat behind his easel painting his sister.

As they worked and talked, the boys created a picture of Rome for their sister, who rarely set foot outside the door without strict chaperoning.

"Papa plays dice with Guido Reni and Carlo Saraceni," said Giulio. "He loses the money we need to buy more paint and canvas. Then Agostino Tassi and Signor Quorli drag him off to the brothels."

"I hate the taverns," said Marco. "They're dark and they smell bad. I can smell it on Papa's skin in the morning. He sweats purple stains in his white shirt."

"He talks with other artists," added Giulio. "They argue about painting, about who's best, who's terrible. Who makes the most money."

Artemisia thought of Orazio biting into crispy sardines, carefully arranging their fried tails on the rim of his dish, the way he did at home. She could imagine him holding court around the plank tables of a dark tavern with sloshing jugs of cheap wine, fried artichokes, and small greasy fish.

She inhaled the bottega's smell of turpentine, resin, and walnut oil. She expelled her breath in a long sigh. She stood up from behind her easel and walked to the windows. The evening light slanted from the west, coloring the stone with warmth and striking definition. She saw a black-haired prostitute with a pockmarked face, soliciting men in the shadows.

Giulio stood next to his sister and looked out on the street. He stretched his arms over his head.

"Poor woman. She looks desperate," Artemisia said.

A signore pushed her away, sending her sprawling.

Giulio shrugged. "I think they all are."

"They're just trying to survive," she said. "And feed their families." Little Marco joined them at the window. He spotted the prostitute.

"Tuzia says they are bad women."

As if the woman could hear him, she looked up at their window.

Marco stuck out his paint-stained finger, pointing down at her.

"Don't!" said Artemisia, grabbing Marco's finger.

She nodded to the miserable woman below, feeling somehow complicit in the woman's suffering and shame. She herded her brothers away from the window.

"Don't ever point!"

"But Tuzia said—"

"Tuzia is a fool," said Artemisia. "She has no compassion for anyone. Think how that woman feels. You are fed and warm, a roof over your head. She has nothing."

The poor woman, reduced to begging men for sex. What else can she do? Perhaps the woman had no skill as a seamstress, no business as a washerwoman, no family opportunity to work at the market as a vendor. No prospects for marriage.

What is left?

Rome offered her no choice but to peddle her body, and then the city cursed her forever.

"A fallen woman!" muttered Artemisia.

"Fallen from grace," said Marco, clearly parroting something Tuzia had told him.

"Any worse than Cleopatra?" said Artemisia, gesturing to the easel where both she and her father were painting the Egyptian queen.

Giulio considered this, biting his lip.

"Cleopatra was a queen," he said at last. "She had a choice. I think the woman down there"—he gestured back toward the window—"doesn't have any choice. She's trapped."

Artemisia looked at her brother. In the soft light that flooded the bottega, his moss-green eyes softened with compassion. With understanding.

"What woman born in Rome is not trapped?" she said, turning back to the window.

Chapter 24
ROME, 1611

"Is Cleopatra finished?" said Orazio, entering the bottega the next morning. Tuzia was close on his heels.

"*Sì*, Papa. I have finished my work." Artemisia bit her lip but she couldn't help herself. "I suggest you revisit the outline of her shoulder."

Her father clenched his fists. "I do not need my own daughter to instruct me! That is enough. I will inspect your work this evening."

"How wonderful!" said Tuzia, attempting to distract him. "You will be home for supper this evening. I have a stew in the pot. Some wonderful marrow bones and—"

Orazio grunted. "Unless Cosimo Quorli asks me to attend a dinner elsewhere." He looked out the studio window. "Ah! There is his coach now."

Artemisia stepped over beside him to peer out. Sitting across from each other were Signor Quorli and Agostino Tassi. She saw another figure next to Tassi. A woman.

A lock of blond hair strayed beyond her black veil.

"Who is that woman?" she asked Orazio.

"Agostino's sister-in-law. His dead wife's sister."

The woman leaned forward in the carriage, looking up toward the window where Artemisia looked down at her. Agostino reached out his arm and drew her back into the carriage beside him.

∾

That Sunday, Orazio, Artemisia, Tuzia, and Francesco took a carriage to Mass. Tuzia had a charwoman look after her children.

The day was gray. The light that came through the stained glass window of the church was muted, intensifying the candlelight of the altar and the reflections off the gold chalice.

Shortly after the Gentileschis took their places, Agostino Tassi and Cosimo Quorli came in and sat just in front of them. As they all knelt in prayer, the sunlight broke through the saint-studded stained glass window, a fractured rainbow of color. Through her interlaced fingers Artemisia saw the soles of Agostino's scuffed shoes turned up facing her. A wet leaf, mottled-green and tattered, was plastered against one sole, the membrane transparent and the brown veins breaking the leaf into chambers of gold, red, and blue as the sun filtered through the colored panes of glass.

She gasped at the beauty of the instant. Agostino stole a look at her over his shoulder. His eyes smoldered with lust.

Artemisia didn't return the look. She remembered seeing him next to his sister-in-law, who had peered from the carriage at her, and how he had put his hand on the woman's shoulder, drawing her back in the seat.

The intimacy of that touch, how she had submitted to it, infuriated Artemisia. Surely there must be more to their relationship than being in-laws.

The priest began the benediction and the congregation rose to its feet.

Agostino stood, crushing the perfect leaf underfoot.

Artemisia nudged Tuzia. "Let's leave right after the benediction," she whispered.

"May the grace of our Lord Jesus Christ," intoned the priest, "and the love of God and fellowship of the Holy Spirit be with you all and remain forever."

"*Vai!*" Artemisia whispered to Tuzia. *Go!*

Her father had disappeared before communion. Her brother Francesco's head was still bent in prayer.

Tuzia and Artemisia hurried out the door.

The cool spring air of Rome was scented with woodsmoke and the first perfume of linden tree blossoms. The two women headed to the church vineyards for a walk. Artemisia drew in a deep breath of relief.

Tender leaves unfurled light green against the woody grapevines. Spring had finally arrived, capriciously late. Songbirds fluttered above the women's heads.

"*Grazie a Dio!*" she said. *Thank God.*

Tuzia took her arm to stroll.

"Why are Maestro Tassi and Signor Quorli here?" Artemisia asked.

"I did not invite them," Tuzia protested. "Your father did."

She let go of Tuzia's arm and strode ahead. Despite her anger at the presence of the two scoundrels, she rejoiced in the midmorning sunshine. How long it had been since she had walked in nature! She marveled at the flight of the little songbirds, her skirt's rustle sending them skyward. Wafts of scented air—the river's freshness, the smoke of wood fires from the taverns, the warming soil under their feet, releasing its earthy aroma—delighted her senses.

How can my father deny me these simple pleasures?

She walked quickly, knowing that she had left the two men far behind. She caught herself smiling for the first time in months.

Tuzia caught up to her, panting. "Ah, Artemisia!" she said, touching her cheek. "I knew the fresh air would release your spirit! You are naturally of a sanguine disposition, *cara.*"

Artemisia remembered it was Tuzia who had convinced her father to let her walk outside the house. "*Grazie*, Tuzia," she murmured. But then she saw them: Agostino and Quorli striding—almost running—after them. "They are here! Quickly, we must walk home. As fast as we can."

"We must find Francesco to escort us—"

"No! We cannot linger."

The two women wove their way through the vineyard toward Piazza San Giovanni. The square was full of the faithful and the carriages of the wealthy. Her father having abandoned them, they had no recourse but to walk home along Via Merulana. As they passed by the facade of the church, Artemisia caught sight of Francesco, frantically scanning the hordes of worshippers, looking for them.

He spotted his sister and ran toward the two women.

"Papa left me to escort you home!" he said. "I couldn't find you. Why did you leave so abruptly?"

"Do you see those two behind us?" Artemisia said, grabbing his elbow and steering him to see Agostino and Quorli. "They are pursuing us!"

"But they are only Maestro Tassi and Signor Quorli. What fear do you have of Papa's friends?"

Should I tell him? My reputation would be ruined . . .

"Escort us as you will," she said. "I'll be walking at a fast pace! Try to keep up." She picked up her skirts and strode quickly ahead, leaving a heavily panting Tuzia.

At the very least I can outwalk that fat Cosimo Quorli!

The gray paving stones near the church gave way to a muddy track. These were the outskirts of Rome, once inhabited by their Roman ancestors but now reduced to ochre- and sand-colored ruins. Hardy weeds grew between the strewn bricks, a tangle of greenery.

She felt sweat trickling down her back and under her armpits. Her blouse released odors of past wear.

She threw a look over her shoulder and saw that Agostino had caught up with Francesco. They laughed together, sharing a joke. The maestro tousled her brother's hair.

Agostino has charmed him.

As though feeling her stare, Agostino looked up. "Signorina Gentileschi!" he called. *"Aspetti!" Wait!*

She looked ahead, weaving now between an oxcart full of cabbages and three workmen carrying towering loads of hay on their backs. A flock of muddy sheep crossed the road ahead of her, nibbling on the green grass growing along its edges. The ground was pelleted with their excrement.

From lack of exercise, she panted. Her legs burned with exertion.

How weak I've become, a flightless canary caged by a negligent master.

Agostino advanced quickly, leaving Francesco with Tuzia. *"Aspetta, Artemisia!"* he said, using the familiar *tu* form. He reached her in a series of powerful strides and took her arm. She snatched it away.

"Don't you disrespect me!" she said. "Leave me in peace."

"But, Signorina," he protested. "It is such a beautiful day. The sunshine on your glorious hair leaves me breathless."

"You are breathless because you ran to catch up." Her quick stride—almost a run—had loosened her hair from its combs. She tucked errant locks under her rust-colored scarf. Her thick hair protested, spilling out down her back.

"I won't touch you," he whispered, drawing closer.

"You liar!"

"Only let me speak to you, Signorina."

"You pursue me like prey. Don't talk to me!"

"I am arranging things for our marriage," he said. "Soon we will be together as man and wife."

"Arranging things? What kind of things?"

He looked away. "These are affairs that do not concern you. The only thing that should command your focus is my love and devotion."

"Have you spoken to my father?"

"No," he said. "I—"

"Then there is no progress on marriage!" She felt the sting of bitter disappointment. She knew he couldn't be trusted. She had always known. Why would she ever believe that he really meant to marry her?

"You should not talk to me in this way," he said. "This is no way for a woman to speak to her future husband. It bodes ill."

"*You* bode ill, Maestro Tassi!" Now her voice dropped to a harsh whisper. "You have ruined me."

Francesco caught up with them, leaving Tuzia waddling behind alone.

"Why are you both in such a hurry?" he said, breathlessly.

He received no answer.

∽

For a week Artemisia feigned sickness to avoid seeing Agostino. She did not want to see him until he had approached Orazio for her hand in marriage.

Finally Orazio insisted that the lessons resume. Artemisia knew that Agostino had said nothing to her father.

Agostino continued to come to their house on Via del Corso. Tuzia's chaperoning was negligent at best. There were many times they were left alone.

One day Artemisia was working with a translucent veil that Agostino had strung in front of her paintbrush. As an exercise in perspective, she painted a bowl of fruit directly on the veil itself as Agostino stretched the material taut.

He stood close to her as she worked. She could smell his scent. While she did not find it repellent, it made her wary. It had been weeks since the last time they had had sex. A thought flitted across her mind.

Can he have decided I am not desirable as a wife?

She took a deep breath and shot a surreptitious glance his way.

If he does not ask for my hand . . . if we aren't to be married! What will become of me? Will my father beat me and cast me into the streets as a puttana?

A sudden dread gripped her heart.

I will be destroyed. I will never be a great artist.

"Signorina?" said Agostino. "Are you ill?"

Artemisia had frozen midstroke. The gauzy veil trembled in the early summer breeze entering the open window, despite Agostino's hand pulling it tight.

"Rest, Artemisia," he said. "I'll fetch you some water."

His scent retreated as he descended the steps to the kitchen. She heard the slosh as he filled a water jug from the cistern bucket.

She found her hand mirror and inspected her face, her lips, her hair. Since the rape she had neglected herself, forgetting to bathe, to brush her hair, polish her teeth with sage and salt. Her hair stood out like the gnarled snakes of Caravaggio's *Medusa*.

No wonder he had not touched her . . . she was abhorrent.

Agostino entered the bottega, a blue-and-white ceramic cup in his hand. "Drink this, Signorina," he said. "And lie down in your bed. I will tell Tuzia to attend you."

She tipped the cup to her mouth, her eyes closed. She felt the cool water sluice down her throat, comforting her. She thought of her choices.

She chose to survive.

She opened her eyes and met his worried look. The wolf was gone.

He stood to leave.

She caught his hand. "No, Agostino. *Aspetti.*" *Wait.*

"Signorina?" he said, staring down at her hand on his as though astonished at her touch.

She swallowed hard and nodded. "Come with me," she said, leading him toward her bedroom.

He embraced her, smothering her face, neck, and bosom in kisses. He lifted her from the floor and carried her through her door, shutting it with his foot.

From that point on, Artemisia considered herself Agostino's wife. She still had no ring on her finger. But she had looked at herself in the mirror and made a decision.

I will survive for my paintings. Nothing is more important than my art. Nothing, no one.

No one would come to her rescue. She knew this to be the truth.

Now she allowed him to pleasure himself in her bed, with her body, every moment they had together in private. He came to her at night, accessing her bedroom through the bottega.

They were lovers.

She dreamed of Florence, of their future studio, of her liberty from her father. Of the paintings she would create.

All she would give him—beyond her body, her heart and soul. She knew she was fooling herself when she dared to dream of love.

Artists are fierce dreamers.

∞

Weeks passed and Agostino Tassi became more and more tender toward her. His lovemaking was no longer rape, but long periods of kissing and caresses.

How could she let him touch her, this man who had raped her? She believed, as if in a dream, that they were already married. But sometimes that dream frayed and she saw through the sham.

How can I explain letting him come back to my bed, again and again?

She had nothing left. Her virginity had been a pearl that would buy entry into society by her marrying a respectable signore. Agostino Tassi had stolen that pearl. It was gone forever. And she was destitute. There was no one to turn to.

Her parched soul thirsted for his lingering touch. To be handled gently, even if it was by the hand that had stolen everything from her.

She was a caged bird who had no diversion except when the master opened the barred door for a few moments each day. Agostino told her of the blossoming of the linden trees, the flowers in the Campo de' Fiori, the first strawberries of spring. He told her of the first *agretti*—the delicate edible grass gathered from the marshes—served now in the taverns, along with chicory and fresh fava beans, nutty and sweet with a wisp of bitterness.

With his painter's appreciation of beauty she could see all Rome through his eyes, taste food and wines through his tongue.

He talked about the price of pigments, the quality of walnut and linseed oils, the new market for Caravaggio's paintings, and the flourishing new school of painters who emulated him.

He told her about Cecco.

"Cecco! Cecco del Caravaggio!" she said, smiling. "So he is quite successful now?"

Agostino's boyish face, animated with the gossip of Rome, suddenly turned stony, his eyes growing cold. "How do you know him?"

"I've met him several times, including at Caravaggio's studio."

Agostino clenched his jaw, making the tendons in his neck visible like tight cords.

"Oh, stop!" she said. "Cecco was Caravaggio's lover. He was my friend. I was a child."

"What in God's name were you doing in Caravaggio's bottega?"

"My father brought one of my first paintings there for the great master to see. Caravaggio encouraged me, beginning at age six."

"Michele Caravaggio was a villain and a murderer. A blasphemer! A lecher! Your father never should have let you near him!"

Let me near him?

She shook her head. "Caravaggio was Papa's best friend. He was the greatest artist I have ever known. No one compares to him!"

Agostino stood up, pushing her away from him. *"Buonasera, Signorina,"* he said. "I cannot abide your taste in artists."

He slammed the door behind him. *He can come and go,* she thought. *I remain forever locked in my cage.*

Chapter 25
ROME, 1611

The pleasant warmth of early June turned into the sultry days and sti-
fling, sticky nights of July. They made love, drenched in salty sweat,
linen sheets tangled between their legs and ankles. She traced the tuft
of hair that ran down his stomach, disappearing into his groin. He
shuddered under her fingertips, rolled her over, and made love to her
hour after hour.

Then Orazio announced that they were moving yet again. The rent
on Via del Corso was too high. He had to find a house closer to his
work on the other side of the Tiber, near both Agostino's apartment and
Cosimo Quorli's house. The Via di Santo Spirito in Sassia bordered the
Tiber River, close to Rome's ancient hospital. From Artemisia's bedroom
she could hear the church bell tolling, calling the faithful to Mass. The
Vatican was only a few blocks away.

Artemisia stood in her new bedroom and heard the swish of a skirt
approaching.

"The bells will wake us for a few nights until we become accustomed to them," said Tuzia, entering the room. "I don't know how I'll
manage to keep the children asleep."

Artemisia shrugged. Bells were not a major concern of hers at the
moment.

Tuzia. Tagging along with us one house after another.

"You know why that hospital is there?" said Tuzia. "The neighbor told me it was the legacy of Pope Innocent III. He had a dream that the fishermen were dragging nets along the Tiber. Instead of fish they drew up dead babies."

"Tuzia! Stop—"

"It was the pope's dream, not mine," she protested. "He decided then and there he was going to dedicate the ground to a hospital that would not only tend the sick but provide a maternity ward, an orphanage, and a center where fallen women could redeem their sins."

She looked pointedly at Artemisia.

"Have you had your monthly?"

Artemisia whirled around to face her. "It's none of your damned business!"

"I only meant if you had signs of a child coming, Maestro Tassi might hasten the wedding."

And if he never marries me?

Artemisia stared out her window at the hospital. There were groups of women coming in and out of the doors, their dirty hair shawled in coarse linen. Some had buckets, others carried reed brooms or mounds of dirty sheets. Every once in a while a nun in a black habit would give them orders, but Artemisia could not discern what was being said.

Is that where I might end my days? A home for fallen women?

"No," Artemisia said quietly. "No, Tuzia. I have had my monthly, regular as always. There is no sign of a baby."

What she did not tell Tuzia was that she continued to bleed every time she and Agostino made love. Bleed like a virgin.

"Pity," said Tuzia. She pulled an apple out of her apron pocket and took a bite. "It's been two months already." She crunched her apple. "I'd hoped to be making preparations for a wedding. Maybe you should tell him you feel queasy, to make him think there is a baby in the making."

"I have no intention of tricking Agostino into marrying me," Artemisia said, her hands on her hips. "He promised he would, and that's his word. I loathe playing to men's emotions, using womanly wiles to force their will. It is disgustingly weak."

Tuzia looked at her and then her apple. She decided her apple was more interesting. She took another bite and eyed Artemisia as if she were the stupidest fool she had ever encountered.

"Suit yourself," she said, through a mouthful of apple.

∞

Living only paces from Cosimo Quorli made Artemisia's life miserable. Now she was exposed to him several times a week. He constantly visited their house and asked about her, though she fled to her bedroom whenever she could.

What she most hated about his visits was that Agostino often came with him, though the maestro knew how much she detested Quorli.

"Come downstairs and visit," Agostino begged her. "Be nice, *cara*. It is important that Signor Quorli approves of my choice in a wife."

"Signor Quorli has known me since I was a child. If he does not approve of me now, he never will!" she protested. "What about whether I approve of him?"

"That doesn't matter," said Agostino. "But I must please my patron."

"Your patron propositioned me! He is a horrid man."

Agostino rubbed his forehead with both hands. He looked up, beseeching her.

"My treasure," he said. "Be reasonable. Powerful men determine the fate of all of us. And Signor Quorli is a most powerful man."

She shook her head, furiously. "He will not determine my fate, Agostino. You will see."

∞

"How are your lessons progressing?" said Orazio, spearing his mutton chop. "Are you becoming more adept at perspective?"

Tuzia shot Artemisia a look from across the table.

Artemisia pressed her napkin to her mouth. It came away with a greasy stain. "I think so. I'm applying some of Maestro Tassi's techniques on *Susanna and the Elders.*"

"Oh, that painting!" said Tuzia. She reached across the table for the bread loaf.

Francesco laughed. "Artemisia will be an old spinster and still painting that canvas!"

"Shut up!" Artemisia slapped her open palm against the table, making the crockery shake.

"Don't be an imbecile, Francesco," admonished his father. "That painting will be her calling card when she makes her debut."

"My debut? Will that be soon, Papa?"

He inclined his chin toward his gristly mutton. "There is too much salt on the meat again, Tuzia! I'm not made of money—salt is expensive and you ruin the taste of the food."

Tuzia bowed her head. "Forgive me. It won't happen again."

Giulio looked at his sister and then his father with his wide, innocent eyes. "Will Artemisia be showing her own art?" he said. "Like you, Papa?"

Papa grunted. "Someday. Not for a long while. I need her to work on my paintings until we can afford a second artist in the bottega."

"Papa," Artemisia said. "Why not? Why can't I devote myself to my own art? I'm nearly eighteen! I've been your apprentice for four years—"

"*Basta!*" he said, wiping his lips savagely. "You've got years to go before you can show your art. Satisfy yourself with working on mine."

Years to go?

She stood up from the table, making the wooden chair screech on the tiles, and threw down her napkin. "I am not waiting years to become an independent artist, Papa! I can't bear it!"

"Sit down, Artemisia," he shouted. "I've had enough of your temper!"

"No!" She turned on her heel and ran up the steps to her bedroom. She slammed the door and bolted it behind her.

∞

The new house in Sassia posed a problem for her trysts with Agostino. In the Via del Corso she had been able to unlatch the door at night. Now the main entrance connected through her father's and brothers' rooms. The only other entrance was through Tuzia's apartment upstairs and through the studio. Artemisia enlisted her help.

"I must see him," she begged Tuzia.

"Just wait until the days he comes for your lessons," Tuzia said.

"No! We must see each other at night."

"It's very dangerous," Tuzia said. "If your father found out—"

"*Per favore*, Tuzia," she begged. "I cannot bear to be without him."

Tuzia squinted. "Has he said anything more about marriage?"

"He wants me to go to Florence with him—"

"Without a marriage contract?"

"He promises—"

"Promises! Promises are for fools, Artemisia! He puts a ring on your finger first!"

Do I not recognize my own words in hers?

Artemisia felt as if she had swallowed a potion, an intoxicant. She could not sort out where her dreams ended and her life began. All she wanted was to be with her maestro, a desire that became an all-consuming hunger. She wondered if her common sense had been stolen along with her virginity.

If only I can love him enough, he will give me my freedom in marriage. And Florence!

She covered her face, pressing her fingers hard against her eyes to keep from crying. A bitter taste of desperation filled her mouth.

"There, there," Tuzia said. "*Poverina.* Your poor thing. Maestro Agostino has begged the same thing of me, to let him pass through my doorway to yours."

"Please!" she pleaded. "Please, Tuzia!"

"I can feel the heat you both share," Tuzia said. "But he must comply with his promises, Artemisia. If he does not marry you, you are ruined. Your father will cast you out without a penny to your name. And what shall become of me?"

That's all Tuzia cares about. What will happen to her.

Artemisia knew Tuzia was right. Even in the throes of passion, she could see the glimmer of the truth, of what would happen if Agostino would not marry her.

Rome had no compassion for a fallen woman. Especially a woman who was so bold as to claim she was an artist.

❧

Tuzia often left her apartment door ajar. Artemisia could hear the quarrels and tantrums of her younger children, the gossip of her two married daughters when they came to visit, and the squalling of their babies.

One day she overheard Agostino in Tuzia's kitchen.

"You must let me see her. I don't trust her father. Anyone who would speak so ill of his own daughter . . . he calls her a *puttana*, a dog in heat."

Artemisia sucked in her breath, the words punching her in the gut.

My father called me a puttana? *In front of Agostino?*

"Maestro Gentileschi is a passionate man," said Tuzia. "Do not take his flights of anger so much to heart—"

"You do not know how he speaks of her! I have almost struck him in the face when he insulted Artemisia. Let me drill a hole in the wall just here. Then I can see into the studio."

"Maestro!"

"Then I can spy on them. If I see him take a hand to her, I'll kill him!"

"Maestro! I can't allow you to drill holes in the walls! If the landlord sees, if Signor Gentileschi finds out—"

"You will, Tuzia!" said Agostino. "If you do not, I'll tell the world that it was you who left Artemisia unattended that day. You could have prevented me—"

"Don't threaten me, Maestro! It was your doing, not mine!"

There was a moment of silence. Then Tuzia spoke again.

"*Va!*" she said. "Go ahead. I cannot stop you. I curse the day I ever agreed to chaperone Artemisia. The two of you will be my undoing!"

Artemisia was enraged to learn how her father spoke of her—and now her anger spread to her lover for his eagerness to spy on her. Now that she knew, she could set up an easel or prop to block the view of any hole that was drilled.

But what terrified her were the wild lengths her lover would go to in his passion to control her.

Chapter 26
ROME, 1611

Weeks passed, the summer's heat leaving their skin wet with sweat, their bodies slipping and slapping against each other. Fitting together night after night.

He will marry me soon.

He must.

One night, well past midnight, as Artemisia lay in bed, she heard a tapping on her door. *Agostino!*

The moonlight slid through the window so brightly she could see the grain of the wood in the floor planks, the cracks in the plaster of the wall spread out like spiderwebs.

"Avanti," she whispered.

Agostino entered, closing the door silently behind him. "Artemisia! *Mio amore.*" His voice was husky. He lay next to her and covered her with kisses, pulling on the ribbon that held her nightdress closed. His hands reached under the linen, cupping her breasts, bringing them to his face.

"Take your clothes off," she said.

He didn't appear to hear her but nestled his head between her breasts. Then he reached up between her thighs, feeling the moist heat.

"Take your clothes off," Artemisia repeated.

"Quiet, my darling," he said, putting his fingers to her mouth. "You interrupt my lovemaking."

"Your lovemaking?" She pushed him away. "What about mine?"

He was panting with lust. "Shut up," he said. His penis was already sticking straight up from his trousers. He pulled at the tie to loosen his clothing just enough to free it. His hand sought her *fica*.

"Stop it!" she said, pulling away from him. She tried to wrestle him off her but he grabbed her hips tightly.

She felt the burning stab of his penis.

"I'll scream, Agostino!"

All she heard were his grunts, no different than a rutting beast's.

Of course she wouldn't scream. She had no choice. This was the man she was to marry. The alternative was too horrific to consider.

He finished with a wincing exhalation. She felt his penis wither inside her.

She looked down and saw she was bleeding again, staining her nightdress red.

"Look, Agostino!" she said. "You've made me bleed again!"

He hovered over her, the sweat from his chest dripping onto her face. "It is because you are weak."

She slapped his face. "I am not weak, you beast."

"All women are weak," he said, leaving the room.

She stared down at the blood sopping her nightdress and saw the streaks of dirt on her bed linens.

He hadn't even taken off his dusty boots.

∽

Two nights later he returned. She had locked her door.

"Let me in, Artemisia," he said. "I lust for you with all my soul."

"No," she said. "Last time I asked you to remove your clothes. You told me to shut up."

"You know I was in the throes of love. You drive me into a frenzy. *Cara*, how I hunger for you!"

"And what is there for me?"

"What do you mean?" he said. "Open the door, Artemisia."

"On one condition. Only if you remove your clothes," she said. "Every thread."

A snort of disgust. "All right. Open the door before I burst. You do not know the urge—the pain!—I bear."

The pain you *bear?*

She opened the door and he closed it hard—too hard for a midnight tryst.

"You must be quiet," she said. "What's wrong with you?"

"I must have you," he said, pulling her body to him. He guided her hand to his penis.

"Take off your clothes as you promised," she demanded, yanking her hand away from his grasp.

"Artemisia!"

"Do it!"

With a sigh of exasperation, he pulled off his tunic, his boots, his trousers. His penis was as straight and hard as Priapus's. He pushed her to the bed.

"No," she said, rolling out from under him. She scrambled to her feet, backing toward the door, her hand searching for the handle.

"I'm burning with desire—don't play games," he pleaded. "I must have you."

"Let me paint you."

His erection quivered. "*Pazza!* You are crazy. You can't paint me like this! Get back in bed, woman."

"No. I want to paint you. If you are going to have my body—I want yours. On canvas."

His penis was now at half-mast.

"That's wrong!" Outrage in his voice.

"And raping me was right?"

"I couldn't help myself, Artemisia. You know that. When a man's desire possesses him—"

"And my art possesses me! Lie down. In bed," she said, reaching for her sketchbook. "It won't take long. I want to get the muscles right, your *cazzo*—"

She frowned as she began to sketch, seeing his prick already shriveling.

He moved his hands to cover his manhood. She pulled his hands away.

"Don't be a child," she said.

She worked quickly, studying the dark bush of hair at his groin, the pendulous nature of his testicles—like a matron's sagging breasts. She sketched the thin sheath of fat at his hips, dimpling into hard muscles—an undulation as hard as marble that she had explored with her hands when he covered her.

"No more!" he said, rising from the bed. His penis was as flaccid and harmless as an earthworm.

He looked down in shame.

"You are not natural, Artemisia!" he said sourly. "You are—flawed, insane. *Pazza!*" He put on his clothes. He hopped a few steps, losing his balance, as he pulled on his boots.

He shook his finger at her. *"Peccato per te!"* he said, opening the door.

"Shame on me?" She laughed. "Really? You are the rapist."

He slammed the door, surely waking the house.

∽

A few days later Artemisia was drawing water from the cistern when she felt the hairs on the back of her neck stand up and a cold grip seize her spine. She turned and saw Cosimo Quorli standing only a few feet away by the stucco wall.

"Agostino is right. You are a beautiful muse," said Quorli. "But it is time you earned your keep." He came toward her, fumbling with the waist strings of his pants.

"Get away from me."

"Shut up, you wench," he said. "Agostino tells me sordid tales of you. The time has come for my turn! Give me what you so willingly give to those I employ."

She held the wooden bucket in front of her like a shield, the water sloshing over her, her dress clinging cold and wet. "Get away, I said!"

He struck at the bucket but she held fast.

"Give yourself to me willingly, you whore! Or—"

"Tuzia!" she screamed. "Tuzia! Tuzia!"

He lunged at her, but she shoved the bucket at him, smacking him in the mouth with its splintered wood. He roared in outrage.

"You bitch!"

"Leave the girl alone, Signor Quorli!" said Tuzia, running up behind her. "I'll call the *sbirri*, I will! I'll bear witness!"

At this point a couple of the neighbors had come to their windows to look down at the cistern.

"What's going on?" said a woman.

"Never mind," said her husband, panic lacing his words. "Come away from the window this minute, woman." He put his arm around his wife, shepherding her out of sight. "That's the pope's own steward! Don't interfere!"

A dog barked in the street. Other faces appeared in the windows looking down on the scene. Two boys playing climbed the stucco wall to see what was happening in the cistern yard.

Artemisia gripped her bucket tight in her hands, motioning to her aggressor.

"Leave, Signor Quorli," she said, spitting her words between her clenched teeth. "Leave before the *sbirri* arrive and everyone has a tale to tell. I certainly do!"

"If either of you two whisper a word of this to anyone," he said, "I'll see your father banished from Rome. And you! You, Artemisia! I'll have you working in the brothels where you belong."

He pushed Tuzia out of his way and hurried out the gate.

∞

The next morning Agostino stormed into the bottega. He grabbed Artemisia's bodice, ripping it down below her breasts. Then he shoved her to the floor.

"You whore!" he shouted above her, panting. "You swore you loved me. I was making arrangements for our marriage. You dirty whore!"

"What?" she said, still on the floor, her breasts bare. "You are mad!"

"You bedded down Cosimo Quorli! You gave yourself to him, my wife-to-be!"

"What do you mean, I gave myself to Cosimo Quorli?" she shouted, scrambling to her feet to face him. She pulled her bodice up over her breasts and stood heaving. "What makes you believe that man and not me?"

"He told me you had given yourself to him willingly!" screamed Agostino, his hands clenched in the air. He yanked at his hair, his eyes wild with jealousy. "How could you do this to me, Artemisia? I gave you my heart, my soul—"

And no wedding ring.

"Cosimo Quorli lies, you fool!" she said. "I have never lain with any man but you, Agostino. Why do you believe him over me?"

"Artemisia! He described your nipples perfectly. The pink color, the shape."

"You think he has never lain with a childless woman? Of course he could describe my nipples. Or he saw my father's nude paintings of me—"

She heard the silence, the cessation of his breathing.

Oh no. What have I said?

"Those paintings—your father's nudes?" said Agostino. "So they *are* of you!"

She stood like a cat with a bird in its mouth. There was no denying it.

"How disgusting! Your father . . . your own father!"

"So what?" she shouted back. "*Sì! Certo!* I helped my father correct his atrocious renderings of a woman's anatomy. They were abhorrent!"

"You posed for him naked! Santa Maria!" he cried, clasping his hands and looking up at what must have been heaven.

"Oh, stop your false piety!" she said. "It's nauseating. You! You rapist! Take that up with our Lord and Santa Maria!"

"How could you?" he sputtered, disgust contorting his face.

"How could I? How could I help my own father improve his work? How could I help the man who raised me from a baby to be an artist, who taught me how to hold a brush, choose my pigments, stretch a canvas, mix my paints—"

"I will never allow you to be alone with him again!"

"You will not allow? You will keep me from my own father? What jurisdiction do you think you possess?"

"You are mine!"

"By whose authority?" She laughed bitterly. "Certainly not by the law or God!" Her mouth was wet with spit. She rubbed her lips on her wrist. "Get out! And tell Signor Quorli to go to hell."

Agostino slammed the bottega door. Artemisia drew a deep breath. She pulled out her canvas *Susanna and the Elders*, set up her easel, and began to paint. She scraped away the younger man's right hand, reworking it so that his forefinger pointed down toward Susanna, condemning her.

Chapter 27
ROME, 1611

In the fall of that year, the Stiattesi family came to the Gentileschi house to live. Giovanni Stiattesi was a cousin of Cosimo Quorli, so Artemisia instinctively disliked him. It was months before she realized that he, too, harbored a deep hatred for the pope's steward, his own flesh and blood.

Orazio explained that the Stiattesis' presence was an arrangement that Cosimo Quorli made. The Gentileschi house in Sassia was large and there were rooms left vacant even with Tuzia and her two sons there. Quorli was helping with the rent—all money flowed through the pope's steward's hands. He told Orazio he needed privacy in his own home, so the Stiattesi family could not stay with him.

The truth was Cosimo Quorli hated his cousin as much as his cousin hated him.

"Signor Quorli invested all his cousin's money poorly. Now they are destitute," Agostino told Artemisia. "Quorli thinks Signor Stiattesi is a prude. He joins us at the taverns and brothels, laughs loud at lewd jokes just like the rest of us. When he is in his cups he beds down a whore, every now and then. The next day he goes to confession and atones for his sins like a schoolboy. He even tells his wife!"

At least he has a conscience, Artemisia thought.

Signor Stiattesi was tall and lean, completely unlike his cousin Signor Quorli. Artemisia first met him in the bottega while they were at work. He bowed his head in front of Orazio, who barely looked at him. Stiattesi raised his eyes, focusing on the nude Orazio was painting.

"I will expect you to oversee the costs of our household, the management of sales and purchases related to art," said Orazio, dabbing paint. "I keep tight purse strings. See that not a *baiocco* is wasted."

"*Sì, Maestro.* Not a penny will be lost under my scrutiny."

Stiattesi stared again at the nude on Orazio's easel. He darted his eyes at Artemisia. When he saw she was waiting calmly for a reaction, he dropped his glance to the floor, blushing deeply.

Yes, it is me.

"It will be my honor, Signor Gentileschi," Stiattesi said, his fingers kneading the velvet cap in his hands. "I am so very grateful to you for giving my family a place to live. You are an honorable gentleman."

"You shall earn your board, Signor Stiattesi," said Orazio, lifting his eyes from the painting at last. "I will also expect your wife to accompany Artemisia to evening affairs such as Cosimo Quorli's invitations . . . and to Mass when Signora Tuzia cannot."

Evening affairs? At Cosimo Quorli's? She shuddered.

"You may leave now, Signore," said Orazio.

The moment Signor Stiattesi closed the door, Artemisia launched an attack.

"Evenings in Cosimo Quorli's house? After what I told you? The man is a lecherous—"

Orazio raised his right hand. Artemisia put her forearm up to defend against a blow.

"You will attend the banquets at Cosimo Quorli's house," he said. "Or I will beat you, Artemisia!"

"I *detest* him, Papa."

"I don't care. He is the hand that feeds this family. More and more commissions come my way—through him and only through him! If you spoil this we are ruined!"

"But Papa! I've told you how he pursues me. Why do you turn a deaf ear to me?"

Orazio's eyes fixed on her, turning turbid gray. "Tuzia!" he shouted. "Tuzia, come here!"

Tuzia came running up the stairs.

"*Sì, Signore!*"

"Sometime before February, go through Artemisia's clothes and find her best gown. One that does not have paint stains. We are to attend a dinner at Cosimo Quorli's house for the Feast of Carnevale."

Tuzia shot Artemisia a look. She hated Cosimo Quorli almost as much as Artemisia did.

"I want my daughter turned out in good form. No paint stains, chipped nails, or threadbare gown. I want her to look the lady she is not."

"*Sì, Signore.* I believe the ochre satin you use in your paintings is her best dress."

Gentileschi gold. How many years ago did Papa coin those words? Happier times . . .

Orazio studied his daughter as if he could hear her thoughts. He took a deep breath. "Signora Stiattesi will accompany you," he said. "She is accustomed to these affairs. I'm sure she will have an idea of what to do with all your hair."

He made an exasperated gesture with his hands, like birds fashioning a nest.

"We have several months to prepare, Signore," said Tuzia.

"You will look stunning and be gracious, Artemisia," he said. "Or there will be a high price to pay."

Artemisia lingered in bed long after her father and brothers had left the house for work at Casino delle Muse. Her pillow was soggy with tears.

There was a gentle tap on the door. Signora Stiattesi entered, her skirt making a soft rustle.

"What is the matter, Signorina?" asked Signora Stiattesi. "You are always up at the first ray of sunrise, working on your paintings. Are you ill? Your eyes are quite swollen—"

"No," Artemisia said, turning her face toward the wall.

She heard soft footsteps approaching the bed. A cool hand touched her forehead.

No one had touched her like that since her mother died.

Not finding a fever, the signora's hand still lingered, combing back Artemisia's hair with her fingers. "Is something troubling you, Artemisia?"

"I can't tell you," she mumbled. As the signora pulled back her hand, Artemisia caught it, holding it against her cheek. She closed her eyes and thought of her mama. Her tears began to flow once more.

"If you cannot tell me," said Signora Stiattesi, "why don't you go to confession? You can tell what burdens your heart to a priest. God will give you comfort."

"God?"

Do I need God to give me forgiveness? I want God to strike down Agostino Tassi and Cosimo Quorli!

"*Certo,*" the signora said. "There are many times I have found solace in confession. Your secrets, your sins, your worries. Come, get dressed and I will accompany you."

Signora Stiattesi's simple faith moved her. Artemisia had confessed her pride, her vanity, peccadilloes of no importance throughout her life to priests.

Can I really share my sin—Agostino's sin—with a priest?

Artemisia allowed the signora to pull her to her feet, comb her hair, and help her dress. The Church of Santo Spirito in Sassia was only minutes away. At the very least she would escape the house.

The second she entered the church, she was certain she had made a mistake.

Cavernous and cold. The great gilded nave, lined with apses, lit with beeswax candles, an arched ceiling far above. The air smelled ancient and damp. The frescoed walls arched, majestic but heartless, from the floor, displaying no pity for the tribulations of mankind. Let alone a fallen woman.

The chilled air in the nave was an icy hand clutching her spine.

There was no solace here! No bosom of compassion. Why had Signora Stiattesi brought her?

"Come, Artemisia." Signora Stiattesi led her to a confessional box. "May God give you comfort. There is a kind priest I know personally who will listen to you and not judge. Trust me, *cara*."

Artemisia pushed back the curtain of the confessional. She knelt on the bench, hearing the ancient wood creak under her weight.

"Forgive me, Father, for I have sinned."

"How long has it been since your last confession?"

"Last Saturday eve."

"I'm listening, my child. God shall hear your confession."

Artemisia knew his voice. It was the round-faced priest who kept pigeons in cages in the bell tower. He would lock them up at night, away from hawks. Marco had discovered the priest and his pet birds when they first came to live in Sassia. Her little brother was always begging her to see them.

Come, sister! You will see. He is a nice signore.

He's a priest. A prete, *Marco. You must be careful he doesn't convince you to abandon art for the church.*

He's different than the other priests, Artemisia. Come see. The pigeons flock to him, climbing about his shoulders and arms. They give him baci!

Kisses from a pigeon?

Little pecks.

It was true. When she visited with Marco, she discovered this priest was a kind man who seemed more interested in pigeons and God's creatures than the sins of the world. He tousled Marco's curls and set a white dove on her brother's shoulder.

"Please go on, my child," he said, breaking in on her memory.

She cleared her throat. "I have had carnal relations with a man who is not my husband . . ."

And so Artemisia confessed her sins. To God and Father Giordano.

∞

Signora Stiattesi was kneeling in prayer at the altar when Artemisia approached her.

The signora genuflected and rose.

"Do you feel better?" she asked.

"Strangely so," Artemisia said. "I still have my troubles. But I am ready to paint again."

The women walked arm in arm out of the church. Artemisia felt a pair of eyes watching them. Without turning, she knew it was Father Giordano.

She envied the pigeons his gentle touch.

∞

The weather was cold again. The leaves on the vine that climbed the Gentileschi house had turned russet. The brothers fitted their bottega windows with waxed canvas to keep out the chilly wind while still allowing natural light for the artists to work.

Although the boys were still engaged in work at the Casino delle Muse, several days a month they all labored together to finish Orazio's commissions. Francesco was given more and more assignments, but his were limited to details that were not as crucial as the skilled execution of form and texture Artemisia was given. He and Giulio were assigned preparation: the stretching of the canvas, the gesso background, the grinding of pigment, the straining, and sometimes the mixing with walnut oil. Artemisia did the actual brushstrokes, carefully following her father's instructions on painting details such as fabrics, shoes, and backgrounds. Little Marco was charged with cleaning their brushes, bowls, and palettes and sweeping up.

It was Orazio's brush alone that did the main figures of the compositions and most of the dazzling textiles illuminated in the paintings. Artemisia's work was relegated to the shadows, secondary figures, and backgrounds. But as time went on, her brush overtook his. She painted features of the models and created the sumptuous garments they wore, under her father's supervision . . . and with his admiration.

While Orazio was in the bottega, his offspring labored only on his paintings. But there were days when he was busy at Cardinal Borghese's project, and on those days the Gentileschi children would relax. They worked on Orazio's paintings, but they also set up their easels to paint their own canvases.

Francesco was progressing as an artist in his own right, though Artemisia found his brushstrokes heavy, brutish. He was wrestling with painting a soldier's boot, daubing far too much paint at a time.

He felt his sister watching and without turning said, "*Sì? Cosa,* Artemisia? What?"

"I'm just watching you," she said. "I think you'd have better luck painting one thin coat at a time with a finer brush rather than dumping all that pigment on the canvas at once."

"*Vaffanculo,*" he said. *Go fuck yourself.*

Giulio giggled but Marco didn't. Ever since their mother's death he had clung to his big sister. "You shouldn't talk to Artemisia that way," he said. "She's a signorina and older than you."

She tousled Marco's blond hair, the sun glinting copper highlights in the childish curls.

"She's not a proper lady," sneered Francesco. "You've heard what Papa calls her. A slut."

Artemisia's hand reached out like a viper, striking him. His palette clattered to the floor, his easel toppling over.

He jumped to his feet, his hands balled into fists.

"Don't hurt her!" screamed Marco.

"Leave her alone, Francesco!" shouted Giulio.

Together the younger boys gripped Francesco's tunic as he lunged for her.

"You touch me," she said, "and Papa will throw you out of the house!" She grabbed a metal scraper from the table, holding it out like a weapon. Her hands searched frantically for her palette knife while she kept her eye on him.

She felt the wooden handle and gripped it tight. She raised both weapons up, threatening him.

Francesco was bigger than the other brothers and knocked them aside. He crouched as he approached her.

"You take another step and I'll cut your face," she said. "Papa will kill you."

"Leave her alone!" cried Giulio. "Marco, run and get Tuzia!"

Marco took off running.

"It's true, you know," Francesco said, almost close enough for her to slice him. "He says you are a bitch in heat. You sit in the window like a *puttana* begging men to fuck you."

Artemisia felt the blood drain from her face. "Papa never said that! You liar!"

"You should hear what he says in the taverns! And I've heard in the streets that fat old Cosimo Quorli has had you. Do you know how ashamed I was to hear this? My own sister—a *puttana*!"

She would have preferred a beating to the words he spat at her. "I despise Cosimo Quorli! Why didn't you defend me against such malicious gossip?"

"Defend you! You have ruined the Gentileschi name!"

"How could you believe what you heard? Francesco!" She fell to her knees, not caring anymore whether he attacked her physically or not. She sobbed, clutching her stomach.

"I've heard enough!" roared a masculine voice. *"Basta!"*

Francesco turned and Artemisia looked up. Agostino Tassi stood in the doorway.

Marco stood behind him, panting, Tuzia by his side.

"Make Francesco stop!" cried Marco. "He's ugly and mean to our sister. *Brutto!"*

Francesco turned to Agostino, his mouth twisted viciously. "You may have the little ones fooled, you and Tuzia," he snarled. "But I hear your footsteps on the stairs at night. You go through Tuzia's apartment, then to Artemisia's room. I hear the grunts and moans. I hear the—"

"Make him stop!" shouted Marco, covering his ears with his hands. "Make him stop!"

"My sister is a—"

Agostino struck Francesco hard across the mouth. He fell to the floor.

Marco screamed.

Artemisia went to Marco's side and hugged him against her breasts. "It's all right, little one," she said. "No one hurts me." She wasn't sure that he understood the sexual insults, but the savage tone of Francesco's words clearly terrified him.

"What were you doing in Tuzia's apartment?" Artemisia whispered to Agostino.

"Coming to see you," he said. "I heard the boys were in the bottega. Tuzia let me wait upstairs."

She didn't know if she believed him. She held Marco tighter. She knew he could hear her heart beating, feel the thuds in her rib cage.

Francesco picked himself up from the floor. He glared at them and then at his painting. He kicked the canvas across the floor, storming out of the bottega without another word.

Artemisia dried her little brother's tears but hers were still brimming.

Chapter 28
ROME, 1612

A storm blew through the narrow streets of Rome, lifting the dust and pelting the pedestrians with wet grit. Artemisia was alone in bed, the sheets damp from the mist creeping through the shutters. The plaster walls were studded with drops of moisture.

The boys were asleep, exhausted from their hard labor in the Casino delle Muse. Orazio, Agostino, and Cosimo Quorli entertained themselves in the taverns of Rome.

Artemisia's fingers stretched out on the bed, feeling the coarse weave of the linen sheets. This bed. So much had happened here. Humiliation had overwhelmed her here, the ravage of her body, her mind. The bed had moved with them from Via del Corso to Sassia, a four-legged phantom haunting her with memories.

Now she gave herself willingly to the man who had raped her, believing desperately she was to be his wife.

Don't be a fool, Artemisia. You are a used woman.

The wind blew hard, rattling against the wooden shutters. She wished she could run through the storm, the rain drenching her body, sluicing away the memories, the filth. Her sins.

She shivered under her blanket. The sultry nights of summer, the sexual abandon, were gone. She touched her finger where a wedding ring would be. The skin was uniformly white, no trace of the ghostly pale where a ring should rest.

Eight months had passed since the rape. She had not moved a step closer to marrying Agostino. Instead of his courting her and celebrating their nuptials, he was out drinking and probably visiting the brothels with her father.

Used woman. Fallen woman!

Her hands clenched until her nails bit into the soft flesh of her palms.

She had wanted freedom from her father, from this infernal cage. Her fighting nature had fashioned a fantasy: to flee to Florence and start her own studio, pursue passionate themes, like Caravaggio. Ah, Maestro Caravaggio, more than a year dead.

But fucking never let her paint something 'nice.'

His words haunted her. She thought of *Susanna*. She had not looked at it in months now. It was hidden under her bed, where Agostino would never see it.

She jumped up, leaving a depression in the wool-flocked mattress. Often there were two depressions. But not tonight.

She dropped to her knees, feeling the cold tile through her night-dress. She pulled out the canvas bundle and unwrapped it carefully.

Susanna had never looked more terrified.

There he is. My rapist. He has never been more than that.

Artemisia decided she would tell her father in the morning.

∞

But she could not tell her father the next morning. He was in a foul humor—and a dangerous one. He spat criticism at her painting.

"Artemisia! The scarlet of Judith's dress—the color is all wrong!"

"What do you mean?"

He plucked at her sleeve, drawing her toward the painting of Judith. Though it would be sold as his painting—his alone—at least half of it was Artemisia's work.

"Look! If the sun is entering the window at this angle here," he said, positioning his brush above the canvas at a steep angle, "the shadows would begin here—and here! The color is too dull. The sun would color it bright. Hasn't Maestro Tassi taught you anything?"

Oh, he's taught me plenty, Papa.

"And your fabric!" said Orazio. "There is no lyricism, no softness in your colors. It's flat. Tedious!"

"I'm sorry, Papa," she said, without emotion. "I'll try again."

"Brighten it up. Your work is too harsh. Brutish."

Al diavolo! To hell with you!

She thrust out her hand, her thumb pinching her fingers in a gesture of anger. "It's not a carnival. It is real, Papa. Caravaggio—"

"You are no Caravaggio!"

"Papa!"

"Your work is a waste of precious paint. We'll have to send the boys to the apothecary to buy more madder red."

"Send me! I need to get out. I'm going mad within these four walls."

"Punto e basta!" he roared. *Enough!* "Get to work scraping, daughter. Salvage what pigment you can."

Artemisia decided it was not the time to discuss Agostino.

But she knew she would have to find the right time. Soon. Very soon.

∽

The week of Carnevale brought dread. Artemisia and her father would attend Cosimo Quorli's theater party and banquet.

"A change of scenery will do you good," said Signora Stiattesi, brushing Artemisia's hair and sweeping it up into a loose chignon with two tortoiseshell combs. "Signor Quorli hosts a magnificent supper buffet following the theater."

Artemisia chewed her lip. "I detest that man."

Signora Stiattesi bowed her head and said nothing. He was her husband's cousin, after all. She was discreet.

The signora tucked a loose strand of Artemisia's hair into the chignon. She stepped back and observed her handiwork.

"Oh, my! Signorina Gentileschi, you look so . . ."

"So what?"

"So elegant . . . so dramatic!" said the signora, content with her choice of words. "You will shock the guests this evening with your beauty. Here, let me put a little beetroot on your lips."

With Artemisia's permission, she used one of the artist's horsehair paintbrushes to apply the stain. Her hand was steady and accurate.

"Oh, Santa Maria! You are *bella!*" she exclaimed, clasping her hands. "The signori will not be able to take their eyes off you."

Artemisia smiled, still gazing at the liquid drop of beet juice clinging to the paintbrush.

Such a magnificent red. Red is so powerful. The glory of the setting sun. The crimson spots on the sheets, my shame.

She had not seen Agostino in over two weeks. She had made excuses not to see him when he did try to sneak into her bedchamber. She asked Tuzia to bar her door to him, telling him that she was ill.

"What men will be there?" Artemisia asked, gazing at her reflection in her looking glass.

"Oh, I'm not certain. I should think several of Signor Quorli's associates from the Quirinale . . . and of course, Agostino Tassi."

Artemisia tilted the mirror, catching the reflection of the signora's face, who stood behind her. She could detect no complicity in her face.

Could she possibly know about Agostino and me?

"Oh," Artemisia said. "Maestro Tassi always attends soirees at Signor Quorli's house, I should imagine. Quorli is his patron."

Signora Stiattesi gave a nod but said nothing.

"Will he bring his sister-in-law and her husband?" Artemisia asked, putting down the mirror.

"He often does, it seems," said Signora Stiattesi. "Honestly I don't think they merit the invitation. The man is only his assistant—he's completely lost in conversation. I think he has no formal education."

"What about her?"

"The *cognata*? Maestro Tassi's sister-in-law?"

"*Sì*. What do you know about her?"

"She's a pretty thing. That flaxen hair always turns men's heads."

"I wonder if she looks like Maestro Tassi's late wife. Her sister," Artemisia said.

"I suppose so. The women of the northern states more often have that blond hair and cornflower eyes."

Artemisia touched her beet-stained lips, again studying her reflection in the mirror. "Do she and her husband have children?"

"*Sì*. Two. I see her at Mass sometimes with them."

She drew in a breath, this time returning Artemisia's look in the handheld mirror.

"It is a strange coincidence," she said, holding Artemisia's eyes. "The children look uncannily like Maestro Tassi."

~∞~

At his home, Cosimo Quorli presented theater and a late supper as a culmination of Carnevale's festivities. The music from string instruments filled the hall. The aroma of roasting fowl and meat wafted from the kitchens, even though Signora Quorli had strategically positioned rows of ceramic-potted orange trees, pungent and sweet with flowers, to line the entrance and corridor to the ballroom.

The guests wore masks and fancy dress—as fancy as they could muster. Artemisia was dressed in a red gown, the one Papa had her pose in for the Casino delle Muse fresco. With her stained lips and cheeks and her powdered and scented skin, she knew she looked far better than she ever had managed to before. She touched her hair where the combs were fastened, making sure they were secure as she descended from the coach.

Her father took Artemisia's hand as her foot grazed the ground. "You look magnificent, Artemisia," he said. "So much like your mother."

He turned away, brushing a tear from his eye. "Keep a watchful eye on her, Signora Stiattesi," he whispered. "I entrust my daughter to you." He walked ahead, preparing to greet his hosts.

"Ah! You forgot to put on your mask, Signorina," said Signora Stiattesi. They stood by the steps of the carriage as the signora tied the red ribbon on a silver-painted half mask. She gave the bow a soft pat.

Artemisia immediately looked for Agostino. She tried to be furtive in her glances, even though with a mask it was difficult for anyone to discern where she was looking.

Artemisia curtsied to Cosimo Quorli and his wife, engaging her eyes, not his. She could feel Quorli's salacious look devouring her, but she stood tall and chatted pleasantly with his wife, a woman with a puckered, mean mouth and haughty, arched eyebrows.

She could sense Quorli seething. The ultimate offense she could give was to offer all her attention to another woman and not him.

Artemisia smiled in satisfaction, never looking once at her host. She picked up her skirts to walk up the few steps to the entrance, knowing full well Quorli was lusting after her exposed ankles. She felt the sting of his eyes.

Does his wife know what a lecher he is? How can she bear it?

The sweet, heady scent of orange blossoms enveloped her. She relaxed and took a deep breath, relishing it.

"Deliziosa!" sighed Signora Stiattesi at her side.

Artemisia broke off a small cluster of orange flowers and tucked them into her hair combs. Signora Stiattesi gave her a nod of approval.

They walked arm in arm into the ballroom where the play was to be staged.

The first person the women saw as they entered the room was Costanza, Agostino's sister-in-law.

"Buonasera, Signora," said Signora Stiattesi, graciously. "Have you met *la signorina* Artemisia Gentileschi?"

Costanza lifted her chin, her nostrils pinched ever so slightly. "We may have met briefly, perhaps," she said, eyeing the artist like a suspicious cat. "I cannot remember. I certainly have heard of you, Signorina."

"Piacere," Artemisia said. "A pleasure to meet you."

Costanza gave her a cold eye. "You must excuse me," she said. "I told Maestro Tassi I would not leave his side this evening. I see him over there by the stage. We are to sit in the front row." She gave a curt nod and moved away.

"And what about her husband?" Artemisia whispered.

"I don't see him here tonight," said Signora Stiattesi.

Artemisia watched Costanza approach Agostino. Her hands flew about like a whirl of birds taking flight, and he put out a hand to calm her. As he looked about the room searching for Artemisia, Signora Stiattesi took Artemisia's arm and turned away.

"Let us take our seats," the signora said, guiding her. "Here, in the back rows, so we are not splattered by the sweat of the actors."

Artemisia silently blessed her for her kindness.

She is protecting me the way my mother would.

Artemisia squeezed her protector's hand. *"Grazie,"* she whispered.

The play was stodgy and dull. But to Artemisia it was a host of colors and light—she didn't care a fig about the dialogue or story. The light from torches and lanterns striking the moist skin of the actors, makeup beaded with sweat, rouge melting in irregular puddles on their faces. The passionate gestures, the dramatic sweep of hands across the face, the exaggerated emotion of their bodies on stage. Ah, here was spectacle!

The sumptuous feast following the play more than made up for the abysmal acting. It was rare that Artemisia had had such fine cookery. Tuzia prepared simple lentils and stews, making the most of cheap cuts of meat and scraps, with little or no seasoning except wild oregano and garlic, and precious little salt. Orazio gave her only a small amount of money to manage the household budget.

Artemisia's plate was soon stained with the grease and red juice of wild boar, seasoned with ground cumin and oregano. She picked an errant bristle out of the charred skin, the pig hair frizzled from the fire. There was a salad of fresh herbs, wild rocket, and tender watercress, garnished with pulverized mint and salty cheese. Fried balls of mozzarella cheese and egg, dusted with nutmeg and cinnamon, made their rounds balanced carefully on silver platters. Along with these were zucchini slices, sautéed and marinated in white wine vinegar and mint, served on focaccia.

Wine goblets were filled magically by an army of servants carrying silver pitchers. Voices rang out, tongues loosened by the fruit of the vine. Artemisia heard the shrill laugh of Agostino's sister-in-law, who had imbibed too much.

She looked over Signora Stiattesi's shoulder to see Costanza simper at some outrageous compliment Signor Quorli had paid her.

"È vero!" he said. *It's true!*

She laughed again, covering her mouth with girlish fingers.

Agostino's face tightened, tense with anger either at the remark Signor Quorli had made or at his sister-in-law's gullibility.

He knows she is a simpleton.

His face darkened like the sky seconds before a thunderstorm. He looked up and caught Artemisia's eye.

She tried to look away but his eyes burned with lust, with urgency. As his sister-in-law continued to giggle, he turned to Signora Quorli, whispering in her ear. She looked up and glanced at Artemisia.

And then nodded.

Agostino rose to his feet and without so much as a farewell he left the room.

A few minutes later Signora Quorli excused herself to visit her guests. Her husband carried on, flirting outrageously with Costanza, who suddenly seemed distracted. Her eyes flitted from her host to the door where Agostino had exited.

Signora Quorli made her way to Artemisia's place at the table.

"Serve Signorina Gentileschi a *maritozzo*," she told the servant in an unnaturally loud voice.

He bowed and offered Artemisia the platter with the puff pastry filled with sweet cream. *Maritozzo* . . . an "almost married."

Artemisia's face burned. The hostess gave her a knowing look, arching an eyebrow. Even Signora Stiattesi froze.

Does everyone know?

Artemisia stared at the dessert. "No, *grazie*," she said, looking up at her hostess. "I'm afraid I have no more appetite."

"Pity," Signora Quorli said. "In that case, I would like to take you to see other rooms in the house."

"*Certo.*" She rose to accompany her hostess.

A horrified look crossed Signora Stiattesi's face. She gathered her skirts to follow her charge.

"Oh, no, cousin," said the hostess, placing her hand on Signora Stiattesi's shoulder, directing her back down into her chair. "I will chaperone our guest. I will bring her back in a few moments. I'd like to have a word with her in private."

Signora Stiattesi bowed but Artemisia could see anxiety lining her forehead.

"Don't worry!" said Signora Quorli. "I will take very good care of our Artemisia. Will you please follow me, Signorina Gentileschi?"

Artemisia instinctively disliked this woman. She had married that ogre, Cosimo Quorli. She sensed the malevolence that had formed the haughty contours of her face, the icy contempt in her eyes.

Signora Quorli led her out of the banquet hall and into the red-wallpapered corridors of the Quorli art collection. Her voice murmured names above the rustle of her skirts.

"Guido Reni, Annibale Carracci, Jacopo Tintoretto—a minor work."

Artemisia looked to the painting next to the Tintoretto. "This is a Giorgione!"

"Sì," said the signora. She gave the artist a patronizing smile, as cold as her eyes. "I see that you have been educated."

Artemisia turned to study her hostess's face. She wanted to remember what a woman looked like when she stuck out her claws at a member of her own sex.

Va' al diavolo, lurida troia! Go to hell, you miserable bitch!

As she opened her mouth to speak, a figure approached them, his bootheels clicking against tiles.

"Ah. What a coincidence," purred Signora Quorli. "Signor Tassi. I believe the two of you have met."

"Artemisia!" he said. "Come with me."

He grasped her hand and pulled her into a room beyond the Tintoretto.

"My love!" he whispered as the door shut behind him. "At last!"

His lips covered her mouth, her throat, her breasts, a frenzy of passion.

She heard the click of a lock.

"Aspetta!" Artemisia said. *Wait!* She rattled the brass door handle. "We've been locked in!"

She heard the low chuckle of a male voice, one she recognized easily.

Cosimo Quorli, you pig!

"Let me out!" she demanded, beating the door with her fists. "Let me out!"

"Come away from the door, *tesoro*," whispered Agostino. "My treasure. It's only so that we will not be disturbed. Every time I've come lately to your house you are ill or not disposed to see me. I cannot bear it!"

"Let. Me. *Out!*"

"I cannot. *Guarda!* Look! He jiggled the handle. "The door is locked from the outside." He shrugged, lifting his open palms in the air in a gesture of futility. "There is nothing we can do for now." He gave her his wolfish smile. "We are alone at last."

Agostino grabbed her. Not like he would a lover but a whore.

"This red dress—the red dress of Casino delle Muse. I knew at once you wore it for me!" He yanked at her bodice, exposing her breasts.

"Don't! This dress cost my father a fortune!"

His mouth was already sucking her nipples. She heard him grunt a rude laugh. "Your dear papa," he said, his voice garbled between licks and slurps. "Perhaps he suggested you wear it."

He did. Tuzia wanted me to wear the ochre one.

She gathered the velvet fabric in one hand and pushed him away hard with the other. "Why did you say that? About Papa?"

"Come here, Artemisia, my darling," he said, wiping his slobber off on the back of his wrist. "I am not in the mood to discuss your father."

"Get your hands off me! Why did you say he picked out the dress?"

"Is it not the dress you wore for his fresco at Casino delle Muse?"

"Of course it is," she snapped. "It is one of my finest dresses. That's why I'm wearing it tonight."

"And you look ravishing," he said, closing in on her again. "But even more so naked."

"No!"

"Take off the dress, Artemisia," he said, a mean look crossing his face. "Now. Or I will rip it off."

"No, you won't!" she said, her eyes locked on his. "I will scream, Agostino. I will scream so loud it will bring all the guests rushing down here. My papa included."

She felt his muscles freeze, his grip loosen. "You wouldn't dare. They will accuse you of being a whore."

"A whore?"

"You, alone with me, unchaperoned."

"I was chaperoned! Signora Quorli—"

"Led you here. Cosimo Quorli locked the door."

"Get away from me," Artemisia said, backing up. She stumbled on a chair behind her but quickly regained her balance. "I talked to your sister-in-law, Costanza. She was curt with me, sour. Is she in love with you?"

"What difference would it make?" said Agostino. "She may know I love you. I do love you, Artemisia."

"You love me? Then marry me, as you promised!"

He gave an exasperated sigh. "When things are sorted out, Artemisia. There are problems—I've told you."

"What kind of problems? What kind of problems that take so many months to sort out?"

Agostino sucked in his breath, momentarily quelling his desire. "Cosimo says you are not worthy of me," he said. "That you are too high-spirited, capricious. That you will bring me nothing but trouble."

"To hell with Cosimo Quorli! What about us? What about our studio in Florence?"

Agostino threw his hands into the air in exasperation. "Are you too thick-headed to understand my predicament? My very future is in Cosimo Quorli's hands. He is the pope's own steward! The commissions I have received and will receive in the future flow from him. Without him I have no future."

"Then . . . you won't marry me?"

"Artemisia—do you want my destruction?"

"Your destruction! *Your* destruction? What about me? I am ruined!"

"Not to me you are not. You are my woman."

Your woman? Your whore?

She slapped him with all her might, making his head snap back. "I am no one's woman!" she screamed. "I am my own woman. Get your filthy hands off me!"

"Artemisia. Be reasonable. Your virginity is gone. I can take you as my mistress."

"Your mistress? I do not take you as my master!"

Agostino looked shocked, his eyes like a bewildered child's.

"No man is my master. Ever!" she spat. "No man shall own me."

Agostino composed himself. He lifted his lip in a nasty sneer. "Your father is your master, is he not?"

"Papa?"

"Your darling papa," he scoffed. "He keeps you locked in the house. And how innocent is he? Painting you naked—he is as culpable as anyone in your predicament."

My predicament? Not our predicament?

"Have you forgotten he brought me under your roof?"

"To tutor me!"

"Ah. Is that what it was? Tutoring."

She stared at him. *What is he intimating?*

"I've heard he was trying to arrange a marriage for you, to another artist," he said. "Probably only to make me jealous and force me to take you as my wife. Do you think he's innocent?"

Does my father have any inkling of my relationship with Agostino? Did he want this to happen?

"Any marriage your father contracts now will be annulled once your husband learns you have been deflowered. But we can live—"

"Live as master and whore?" she spat. "You have misjudged me, Agostino. As long as I live I shall have control over my being. I shall tell

Papa everything! He will know—how you raped me, how you promised marriage, how you lied!"

Agostino's face lost all bravado. "No, Artemisia. That would be a dangerous thing to do. You have no idea how dangerous."

"He'll kill you!"

"Don't bring your father into this, Artemisia. Don't rub his face in it. He is a proud man with a dangerous temper."

"Rub his face?" she said, bewildered. "He'll know the truth for the first time. Oh, you'll see his wrath!"

"What makes you think he does not already know the truth? Eight months you have been my woman." He was staring at her, his eyes hostile and steady. "Do you really think Orazio Gentileschi is that stupid?"

"He . . . he knows nothing! He'll kill you when he learns!"

"Ha!" said Agostino. "He has called you a whore since the day I met him. How was I to know you were a virgin? I blame him!"

She sucked in her breath.

They heard steps—more than just one person outside. Then the clicking of a key in the lock.

The door opened just enough for Cosimo Quorli to stick his face in the crack. "Agostino, you rake! If you haven't finished your business after this long while," he said, "then it is your bad luck."

He flung open the door. Beyond the leer of Cosimo Quorli, Artemisia saw the heads of several other guests, including the Stiattesis and their children.

She pushed past the Quorlis into Signora Stiattesi's embrace. Her husband put an arm on Artemisia's shoulder. "Shall we take you home, Artemisia?" he said.

"*Sì,*" she whispered. She closed her eyes in anguish. "I never want to see any of these people again."

◦◦◦

Later that night, Orazio slammed open the downstairs door. Artemisia heard him mounting the stairs, unsteadily but quickly. His steps stumbled into his room and she heard an anguished roar.

Artemisia tightened her grip on the paintbrush but continued her work on *Susanna*, working on the gray-bearded elder's face.

How many times have I painted and repainted this damned canvas!

"You!" he said, storming into the studio. He thrust his finger in her face. "Where is my painting of Judith?"

Judith?

"What do you mean, Papa?"

"I was just in my room . . . it's missing off the wall!"

Artemisia stared at him in astonishment. "I have no idea. Did someone enter the house while we were out and steal it?"

Orazio staggered a step, his fingers rubbing his beard. "How dare you get up and leave the Quorlis' so abruptly!" he said, forgetting *Judith*. "Uncouth, uneducated. Without my permission, you left without a whisper of gratitude to your hosts!"

"Hosts!" she said, her hands clutching her brush. "Hosts! Do hosts lure you into a chamber and lock it so you can be raped?"

Her father stared at her, his eyes bleary from drink. "What did you say?"

"Signor Quorli locked me in a room with Agostino Tassi."

"You are lying!" he said. But as he said it, he staggered once more, losing equilibrium.

"Am I, Papa?" she said. "I have witnesses. Ask the Stiattesis. Signor Quorli told Agostino he had plenty enough time to 'do his business,' when he finally unlocked the door. He said it in front of a whole party of guests, seeing Agostino and me alone."

"You were seen? Others witnessed this?"

"*Sì.* I am sure the tongues are wagging all across Rome at this very minute."

Again he faltered. His hand searched for the nearby stool. He sat down, putting his head in his hands.

"He raped me, Papa! Agostino Tassi raped me!" she screamed, trembling with rage. "Look at me! I am innocent. You brought him into our house and he raped me!"

"*La gente* . . . the people know?" he mumbled through his hands.

"Look at me!" she cried. "I am your daughter. *Sì!* People know. To hell with them! What about me, Papa? Damn the people, what about *me?*"

He looked up, his face ugly and raw. His eyes were bloodshot from too much wine. "There is no hope," he cried, clasping his hands. "He took your virginity. He must marry you! Of course he will marry you!"

"He will not. Oh, *sì*, he promised," she said, shaking her head, eyes wet with tears from a rage that matched her father's. "But he lied, Papa. Cosimo Quorli will not let him."

"Cosimo? What do you mean, not let him?"

"Signor Quorli says I would not be suitable as a wife."

"*Cosa?* What? How could Cosimo betray me?"

"Betray you? *You?* What about me! Are you deaf and blind? Cosimo says I am his child, Papa!" she said. "That he and Mama had . . . sexual relations."

"Stop it!" screamed Orazio, clapping his hands over his ears. "You are my daughter! You are my flesh and blood."

He fell from the stool onto his knees, sobbing.

Artemisia had never hated him—or loved him—more. All in the same heartbeat.

"Of course I am, Papa!" she said, taking his hand. She squeezed it tight, tighter than she should do with any artist. "Do you think this talent, my most glorious gift, ever flowed through that man's filthy veins? Mama knew. She told me I was your child."

Orazio's mouth contorted in agony. He looked wounded, ancient.

"I have your gift, Papa," she said. "Is there any more proof than this?" She gestured toward the easel and her *Susanna*.

It is perfection, and I know it.

They both stared at *Susanna* in silence. She felt him squeeze her hand in return, strength returning. He struggled to stand, taking support from her.

"No, daughter," he said, finally. "We will fight. I will take Agostino and Quorli to court. I will expose their evil. And I shall find you a husband."

"I don't want a husband, Papa! I want to paint."

"You have too much talent to squander. Rome will not allow a whore and a painter to prosper."

"I'm no whore!"

Papa waved away her words. "In the eyes of Rome, you have no honor. I cannot present you to my patrons or to the Medici Court as we planned. Not unmarried and without your maidenhood intact. Rumors will travel—"

"My maidenhood? A piece of useless flesh erases my talent? A few moments of a man's violence destroys my life?"

Orazio gave an exasperated gesture, throwing his hands in the air. "I do not control society's rules! You are a fallen woman, Artemisia. We will restore your honor."

"To hell with my honor! To hell with Rome! I only want to paint."

"Listen, daughter!" he said, clenching his fist. "We will beat them at their game. We will prove, once and for all, that you are my daughter! You will be the finest painter in Italy. The name Gentileschi will be revered!"

Is he defending my honor or his?

"I will sue them both, the filthy bastards! They stole my *Judith*!"

Is the theft of Judith *really the equal of my rape? Papa!*

"I will write the pope tomorrow morning," he raged. "I'll have Signor Stiattesi draw up the legal papers immediately. I'll drag them both into court."

"Court?" Artemisia said. "That would mean I will have to testify."

"*Sì,*" he said. "*Certo.* You will tell them the truth, how Agostino wronged us."

Us? I am the one who was raped.

"But Papa! Then all Rome will know."

"*Sì,*" he said grimly.

"Papa! I will be an outcast."

He drew a deep breath. He sighed noisily and then held his hands out in supplication. "You already are, Artemisia. All great artists are outcasts."

He smiled ruefully, his eyes still wet with tears.

She thought of Caravaggio. She saw again his *Judith Beheading Holofernes*, the shocked look in the dying man's eyes, the sword severing his neck. The deep red of his blood. But his Judith looked meek and confused as she hacked through the man's neck.

My Judith will know just how to sever his head from his body. There will be no hesitation. That is the way it must be.

"*Sì,*" she said. "I will testify."

"*Mia figlia,*" he said, kissing her head. *My daughter.*

She turned back to her easel, regarding Susanna and her menacing rapists. She picked up her paintbrush, dabbing on a minute drop of dark paint, a touch of filth on the younger villain's finger, pointing down toward the white, pristine body of Susanna.

"I remember something you told me when I was a little girl, Papa. You told me boys would hate me for my talent. Now men will hate me not only for my talent but because I stand up and tell the truth."

Orazio nodded. "I remember that day. We were coming home from Caravaggio's bottega. You were hurt because his boy Cecco turned mean on you. You remember what else I said?"

"The best revenge is to thrive."

"*Sì.* I've taught you well, daughter." He gazed at her *Susanna.* "And your *Susanna* is exquisite. Better than mine."

He silently closed the door.

Chapter 29
ROME, 1612

If there was any question as to whether Signor Stiattesi—an attorney and a notary—would support Orazio in a case against Stiattesi's own first cousin, it was quickly answered.

"I have never hated a man more than Cosimo Quorli," said Stiattesi as he sat in the Gentileschi bottega. "His business dealings and bad counsel in investments have caused my ruin." He took a deep breath. "Cosimo Quorli is the most evil soul who walks among us. His wife is no better. I will gladly scribe your petition to the pope and present it myself."

Artemisia clasped her hands in gratitude. "Bravo, Signor Stiattesi. You recognize the devil when you see him! You are a brave man."

"*Grazie*, Signor Stiattesi," said Orazio, looking at him and then at his own daughter. "Both Artemisia and I are grateful."

"We shall have that witch Tuzia arrested as well," said Stiattesi. "None of this would have happened if she had been a proper chaperone."

Orazio's face fell. "Oh, no!" he said. "Leave Tuzia out of this."

"Why should we? It is her fault!"

"Just leave her be."

Papa! She failed me. She failed you!

"Signor Gentileschi, with all due respect, the court will demand that she testify and will issue a warrant for her arrest. She was the chaperone!"

Orazio turned away, looking out the window. His gaze rested on the line of laundry Tuzia had strung out earlier that morning. "Could we . . . suggest that Agostino Tassi broke into our house and raped Artemisia?"

"Papa!" said Artemisia, tears of anger stinging her eyes. "She left me alone with him!"

"With all due respect," repeated Stiattesi, bowing, "we must present a truthful—and believable—case. Forgive me, Signorina, as I speak bluntly."

"Honesty is appreciated," Artemisia said, wiping the tears from her eyes.

"As I understand it, Signorina Gentileschi and Signor Tassi had carnal relations for eight months."

Artemisia tightened her lips. "*Sì.* That is correct. I believed he was to be my husband."

She saw her father's fists clench.

"And in this time, Tuzia was complicit?"

"*Sì,*" she said. "She let him in. Night after night."

Artemisia studied her papa's face. She saw rage—and sorrow. Tuzia had betrayed them both.

Or did she? How much did Papa know?

Artemisia wondered for the first time whether her father had told Tuzia to be less than vigilant in her chaperoning. Perhaps he had hoped that with a taste of Artemisia's charms, Agostino would fall passionately in love and ask for her hand in marriage.

She looked at his profile, the bunched cords of his neck betraying his rage.

No, Tuzia betrayed us both. She wanted me married and gone from the house, leaving her to be mistress.

"If this case is to move forward, the court will most certainly require Tuzia's testimony," Stiattesi said.

"All right," said Orazio, hunching his shoulders in defeat. "All right."

◯◎

Tuzia was arrested two days later.

The guards raised a commotion, pounding on the door late in the evening. Artemisia ran to the stairwell, hiding in the shadows while Giulio opened the door. The guards' torchlights spewed black smoke, flames leaping with the draft from the open entrance. Their shadows grew, towering on the plastered wall behind them, menacing giants.

"No, no!" Tuzia protested as the guards dragged her from her apartment door into the stairwell. "I'm innocent! The signore—"

Signor Stiattesi arrived with his wife and interrupted her screams, cutting through with a stern voice. "Do not protest, Signora Medaglia! And keep your mouth closed. What you say will go on the record in the court!"

"Where are you taking me?" she screamed. "What of my children?"

Of course! Her children will be alone now.

Artemisia stepped from the shadows to answer, but Signora Stiattesi replied, standing stricken by her husband's side. "I shall see they are taken care of properly. I promise, Tuzia."

"Send for my older daughter!" said Tuzia, twisting her head around as the guards dragged her off. "Where are you taking me?"

"Tor di Nona," said a guard. "The tower prison. Stop your screaming, woman! It's making me deaf."

The torch flames leapt as the street door opened. Artemisia could see neighbors had gathered, hearing Tuzia's protests.

Another figure was silhouetted against the ochre wall. His face was ugly with rage.

"It's your doing, Artemisia," said Francesco as he emerged from the shadows. "You are a dirty curse to all of us." He pushed past her to watch Tuzia get loaded into the wood-barred wagon to be imprisoned.

Now Stiattesi told them that Agostino Tassi had already been apprehended in the Via della Lungara. He, too, was imprisoned in the Tor di Nona.

"Tassi is imprisoned?" Artemisia said. She fought the emotions the news brought. Her rage momentarily quelled, her mouth curved into a smile of revenge.

He can't touch me now! I can sleep through the night.

⁓

Artemisia stepped into the coach with her father, pulling up the hem of her skirt against a gust. The cold March wind was blowing through the streets of Rome, lifting the grit from the streets and flinging it into their eyes.

"*Puttana!*" rang out a voice. "The whore Gentileschi!"

She looked up to see a beggar dressed in filthy rags, cupping his genitals.

Orazio's head had snapped around. "*Vattene, pezzente!*" he roared. *Get out of here, you beggar!* He seized the coach driver's whip and ran after the man.

"Leave him alone, Papa!" Artemisia shouted. "He's nothing but an addled tramp."

The man disappeared into the growing crowd watching them depart.

Orazio's eyes searched the mob. He still clutched the whip in his hand, his yellow teeth clenched, his lips drawn back in rage.

"Get in the coach!" Artemisia hissed. "You are providing drama for them, Papa."

He turned back, his eyes blazing. He gave the whip to the driver.

"*Vai!*" he called. *Go!*

"*Puttana! Puttana!*" rang out the voices. But among them Artemisia heard one woman call, her voice defiant above them all.

"*Brava*, Artemisia! *Brava!*"

Then several more women's voices joined the first woman's.

"*Brava*, Artemisia! *Brava!*"

Chapter 30
ROME, 1612

Three magistrates—one bald, one with a port-wine stain across his left eye and cheek, and one enormously obese—were seated on a raised dais, their high-backed chairs perched behind a table covered with an ivory cloth. Below them sat a scribe and two notaries.

Crimson drapes embroidered with entwined laurel leaves lined the wall behind the judicial panel. The terra-cotta floor shone with beeswax polish. Oil paintings of past popes hung on the walls. Artemisia drank in the smell of wealth and authority.

There were chairs for the defendants and plaintiffs; the witnesses were made to wait behind a red silken cord. Each group was separated from the others by guards.

It was meant to be an impressive setting, representing the power of justice and the papal laws of Rome. But for Artemisia it became no more—or less—than the setting for the most painful, most difficult seven months of her life.

The scribe read the complaint prepared by Signor Stiattesi and Orazio.

Most Holy Father,
Orazio Gentileschi, painter, most humble servant of
Your Holiness, respectfully reports to you how, through
Donna Tuzia di Stefano Medaglia, his tenant, and as
result of her complicity, a daughter of the plaintiff has
been deflowered . . .

"*Sverginata*" was the word the court used to describe what had happened. From virgin to not virgin.

Such a colossal change this fragile speck of flesh has made in my life, she thought.

The complaint continued:

> *. . . by force and carnally known many, many times*
> *by Agostino Tassi, painter and close friend and colleague*
> *of the plaintiff. Also taking a role in this obscene affair*
> *was Cosimo Quorli, your* furiere.
>
> *This act was injurious, and more so to Orazio*
> *Gentileschi. As it was done under the trust of friendship,*
> *it is like a murder. I implore you in the name of Christ to*
> *take action against this ugly intemperance by bringing to*
> *justice those who deserve it. Besides granting a very great*
> *favor, your action will keep the wronged plaintiff and his*
> *other children from disgrace. And he will always pray to*
> *God for your most just reward.*

This was the first reading Artemisia heard of the case against Agostino and Cosimo Quorli. The magistrates' questions asked in Latin bewildered her. She waited anxiously for the translation in Italian. "And he will always pray to God for your most just reward"? She tried to imagine her father on his knees, pleading with God to reward the pope.

. . . Signor Orazio Gentileschi accuses Agostino Tassi of third degree rape—stupro violento—of his daughter Artemisia Gentileschi. According to the charges stipulated in writing by Signor Gentileschi, the rape took place in his residence on Via del Corso on May 6, 1611.

Agostino was brought from behind the cord to stand in front of the judges. He looked directly at the magistrates and at no one else.

"What says the defendant, Agostino Tassi?"

"Not guilty, Your Honor."

The scribe's quill scratched at the parchment.

"First we ask Signora Tuzia di Stefano Medaglia to speak," said a magistrate. "Produce the deposition taken at the Tor di Nona March 2 and March 23, 1612."

Artemisia looked around the room. As usual, Tuzia's husband was nowhere to be seen.

Tuzia approached the dais, her head bowed low. Bits of straw clung to her hair from where she had slept on a pallet in the tower prison.

"Signora Medaglia, you state that Agostino Tassi gained access to the Gentileschi house through the front door. That said door was left open by masons making repairs?"

"*Sì*, the principal door to the street was left open," said Tuzia, wringing her hands. "We were seated in the bottega, where Signorina Gentileschi was painting a portrait of my boys and me."

"You were the chaperone, *è vero?*" said the port-stained magistrate.

"*Sì*, Your Honor," she said meekly.

"And yet you left the room."

Tuzia's mouth formed an O of fear. Artemisia saw her head tremble, her hands clasped tight against her side. "The signore ordered me from the room."

"You left your charge, the Signorina Gentileschi, alone with Signor Tassi?" said the bald judge.

"The passion—the rage!—that was in Signor Tassi's eyes when he ordered me from the room—I was not in a position to argue, Your Honor!"

The magistrate glared and pointed his finger at her. "That was very much your position, Signora Medaglia. And your responsibility."

Artemisia searched Tuzia's face for remorse. The judge had said exactly what she had thought all along.

It was your responsibility, Tuzia. You let him rape me!

"He convinced me he had honorable intentions," she protested.

"You thought Signor Tassi intended to marry the signorina?"

"*Sì!* He told me he did. I believed him."

I believed him too. We were both fools. But Tuzia was supposed to protect my honor. Instead she played the ruffiana. *The pimp. Was she really that foolish or did she purposely leave me to him? Would she dare to disobey my father or . . . did he know?*

Her eyes darted to her father. All she could see was rage in his eyes. At whom—Tuzia or just Agostino—she wasn't sure.

∞

Signor Giovanni Battista Stiattesi appeared rumpled, his eyes swollen to slits. He had worked long, late hours to prepare himself and his case for this moment. Now he was ready.

"Signor Agostino Tassi is a dishonorable man. I bring proof from the Duchy of Tuscany in form of charges and former imprisonment. He raped his wife and was forced to marry her. Then he raped his sister-in-law and still carries on sexual relations with her."

Artemisia sucked in her breath, fury emanating from her very core. She turned and stared at Agostino across the room.

Disgusting worm! He was returning to her bed after mine!

Stiattesi paused for a moment, took a deep breath, and plunged ahead.

"After Tassi's rape of her sister, his wife left him in Florence for a lover. Tassi then sent letters, which I have obtained from Tuscany, that amount to nothing less than a contract"—another pause—"hiring two assassins to murder his wife."

Artemisia gasped along with much of the room.

Agostino is a murderer?

There was a long silence in the room. Then the bald magistrate moved the questioning ahead.

"His wife resided in Florence?"

"*Sì, Signore.* But she then fled to Lucca. That is where he sent the assassins to kill her. You can see from the documents I provided from Florence—"

"Only answer the questions asked, Signor Stiattesi," warned the magistrate. "To confirm your *interrogatorio* taken in the Curia. You state that Agostino boasted several times to have had carnal relations with Signorina Artemisia Gentileschi."

"*Sì,*" said Signor Stiattesi. "He also stated he had promised to marry her."

The sounds of scratching quills and clinking inkpots rose in the silent room.

"Please speak of Cosimo Quorli. You stated that Signor Quorli defamed Signorina Gentileschi."

"*Sì.* Signor Quorli spread lies about Artemisia Gentileschi throughout Rome. He claimed to have fathered her. He also said he had carnal relations with her. He bragged to Agostino Tassi that it was . . . 'a way to make families larger.'"

Again the scratch of quills on parchment. The magistrates frowned as they murmured together. The fat one looked at Artemisia in disgust, his upper lip curling.

Why does he look at me this way? I am the victim.

Artemisia realized that the fat judge held her to blame. If he believed Cosimo Quorli, then she was a sordid woman, fathered illegitimately with a cheating slut of a mother. And worse, if Quorli lusted after the woman he considered his daughter, that, too, was her own fault. If they believed Cosimo Quorli, everything was the result of Artemisia's own wanton behavior. And of course they believed him. These were papal magistrates and Cosimo Quorli was the pope's purveyor and steward. They would know each other, laugh and share stories at fine dinners held in honor of the pope.

Cazzo! Fuck! Why am I judged by men? Men who are cut of the same cloth?

"Do you know of Orazio Gentileschi's painting of Judith, Signor Stiattesi?"

"*Sì.* Signor Quorli coveted the painting of Judith and convinced Signor Tassi that he should obtain it for him."

Artemisia glared again at Tassi, standing on the opposite side of the room behind the silken cord. He was wan and pale now, his customary brightness as tarnished as an old coin found in the street. Incarceration in the Tor di Nona did nothing to aid his polish.

Where is your cocky look and beautiful plumage now, Agostino?

Artemisia remembered Tassi's questions about *Judith*. She remembered how she had heard him in Orazio's bedroom that day with Tuzia.

You bastard! You said you wanted me near you always, even when you slept. That you would hang Judith *over your bed, my brushstrokes near you, as if they were my hand caressing your skin.*

Agostino did not look at her. He focused his eyes on the magistrates. She saw a weak spasm strike his cheek, a muscle twitching uncontrollably.

Good. You are miserable.

∞

The next week when she entered the courtroom, she saw a small bed on the dais. A high, four-post iron frame was placed around it. Two workmen were busy hanging white linen drapery from the rods at the top, creating a curtain around the bed.

"What is that?" she asked her father.

He pressed his fingers to his eyelids. "I had hoped it would not come to this."

Her voice caught in her throat. "Papa! What are they going to do?"

Orazio shook his head, looking at the terra-cotta floor. "Be strong, my daughter. Remember what I've taught you."

Two women entered from a side room, their hands folded as if in prayer.

The bald magistrate called the session to order. "Signorina Artemisia. Will you please approach?"

She walked toward him, glancing again at the strange women.

"The court has called for these two midwives to examine you. We must establish that you are indeed not a virgin."

"I am not. I was raped by Agosti—"

"Please. Signoras, approach. You must be examined, Signorina, for the court record."

The two women, dressed in dark serge dresses, came near her. One smelled strongly of onions and the other gave off a faint waft of medicinal herbs.

"State your names and profession for the court."

"I am Signora Caterina di Collo," said the foul-smelling one. "My profession is midwife."

"I am also a midwife," said the second. "My name is Signora Diambra di Fiori."

"You will help Signorina Gentileschi disrobe and examine her," said the fat magistrate. "For the record . . . the court wishes to know if her maidenhead is intact."

"*Sì, Signore,*" they answered, nodding. The woman who smelled of herbs walked to the curtained bed, holding open the fabric and beckoning to Artemisia.

The onion-reeking woman took Artemisia's elbow, steering her toward the bed. *"Venga, Signorina,"* she said, briskly. *Come along.*

Artemisia pulled her arm away. "I can manage." *Without your help.*

She sat on the bed, the two women standing beside her, and heard the clang of the metal rings closing the flimsy curtain that separated them from the public.

"Per favore, please stand up now," said the other, gentler midwife, extending her hand to help Artemisia.

Onion Woman began to untie Artemisia's skirt.

"I can take off my own damn clothes," Artemisia hissed.

The woman leapt back into the curtain, rattling it on its rings. Artemisia heard a cough and a stifled laugh beyond.

"Silence!" ordered the birthmarked magistrate.

When Artemisia had removed her skirt and underclothes, Onion Woman bent Artemisia's legs, placing her soles on the cold, rough sheets and her knees in the air. "Now open your legs, Signorina," she commanded.

Artemisia looked at the woman's hands. They were as grubby as a charwoman's.

"Do as she says," whispered the other woman, holding Artemisia's hand. She gave a reassuring squeeze. Artemisia breathed in her herbal scent, deciding she liked it. "It will go easier on you, Signorina. We will try to finish the examination as quickly as possible."

Again a murmur from the courtroom.

Artemisia shut her eyes tight. She felt the prying of bony fingers as the foul-smelling midwife worked her way up Artemisia's *fica.* The midwife fished about, poking Artemisia's insides. As she lifted her arm, a rank odor of body sweat soured the air even more.

Artemisia fought the urge to kick the woman in the head.

Why is she taking so long?

The midwife's touch made Artemisia harden her body to her. The examiner's rough hands twisted and her fingernail scraped Artemisia's tender flesh. She felt as if she were being raped all over again.

The midwife finally shook her head and withdrew her finger.

Next the second woman took her turn. Her hands were scrubbed clean, though green and saffron-colored stains clung to her cuticles.

"Do you paint?" Artemisia asked, staring at the woman's hands.

The midwife's face broke open in a smile. "Oh! No, Signorina," she whispered. "The thought! I make tinctures and grind plants and seeds for my medicines."

Artemisia nodded. That was the scent she had detected.

This woman's touch was much more gentle. There was no rooting around, only a gentle probing that took but a few seconds.

"No," she pronounced, withdrawing her finger. She shook her head adamantly.

"You may put on your clothes, Signorina," pronounced Onion Woman.

When Artemisia was dressed, the curtain was drawn. They approached the magistrates.

"The hymen is broken," pronounced Onion Woman.

"Do you concur, Signora di Fiori?"

"*Sì,*" she said. "I felt nothing intact. The veil and virginal cloth are broken."

"Signorina Gentileschi is not a virgin," said Onion Woman.

Of course I'm not! That is the point.

"Furthermore," Onion Woman pronounced, her lips drawn tight and prim, "Signorina Gentileschi has not been a virgin for quite some time."

◦◦◦

The trial became an endless torment, as if punishment for a woman daring to demand justice.

Her only escape was to paint. The rasp, the drag of bristle against canvas. The images emerging against a rusty-iron background saved her. When she began painting she was in another world. One where Agostino Tassi had never existed. Images beckoned to her, the form and texture of passionate women—and men—who begged to live on her canvas.

Day bled into day. The suffering in court, the escape into her painting.

She stared hard into the gesso, seeing their stories, these suffering women. The injustices of their torture came to life on her canvas. What rights did women have in Rome? What recourse for crimes against them?

All of Rome was shocked that Orazio and Artemisia testified against the powerful Cosimo Quorli—the pope's own steward!—and the talented artist Agostino Tassi.

"What a spectacle the girl is making of herself! To confess to such a sordid deed . . . for what end? She will most certainly lose," people said.

"Rape? A man can't be expected to control his natural urges. That's all. The father should never have let Signor Tassi into his house with such an attractive daughter.

"Of course he raped her!"

But there were women who took her side. Women who had endured groping hands on the street, who were harassed in the marketplace doing their shopping, whose daughters caught leering men's attention. They knew too well how it was to be tormented by men who took liberties with their bodies.

Men took what they wanted from women and then discarded them like an empty nutshell after the soft meat has been eaten. Rome was littered with discarded women, many of them forced to make their living as prostitutes once their virtue was plundered.

They knew she was right—and they knew she could never win. No woman ever won against a man, especially one of power like Cosimo Quorli! She took on the Church and men.

I must survive. I shall lose my mind if I succumb, Artemisia thought.

At night she heard the jeers in the streets from drunken louts who stopped outside the house and shouted to make themselves heard.

"Whore!" they chanted. "Artemisia, *la puttana!*"

But in the still of night after the drunks had stumbled home, she heard the women who crept out into the night, not to shout, but to whisper, knowing, woman to woman, that she would hear their voices like the soft birdsong before the break of dawn.

"*Brava*, Artemisia. *Brava.*"

Artemisia rose from her bed, trying to see the women in the dark, but they vanished like ghosts, their footsteps echoing on the cobblestones.

In the course of the drawn-out trial, there were only a few days a week when Artemisia was required to appear in court. Many days were spent gathering witnesses and their depositions, and on those days she lost herself in her painting.

One afternoon at the easel, she felt a tap on her left arm, tugging her away from the world she had created.

"Come eat, Sister," pleaded Marco. "You've had nothing all day."

"Oh, little one," Artemisia said, so absorbed she didn't embrace him. "Run along and eat. Put some food for me on a plate under a linen towel."

"You haven't eaten what we left for you yesterday."

She looked at him. "I haven't?"

Francesco came up the stairs, wiping grease and crumbs from his face. "Let her starve," he said, taking his place behind his easel.

"Leave her alone, Francesco," shouted Marco. "Sister. Please come."

Artemisia turned back to her canvas, women screaming at her to be liberated by her brush.

"Put the plate under a cloth," she repeated to Marco. "I will eat later. I promise, *cara*."

∞

It was at about this time in the trial that Artemisia began receiving letters from Signora Quorli, who sent an acne-pocked adolescent to deliver her correspondence to the Gentileschi house in Sassia. The boy smirked as he handed Artemisia the folded letter, sealed with crimson wax and the seal of the House of Quorli.

The signora's cursive handwriting vexed Artemisia. She had learned to read from print in a prayer book and from her father's correspondence in his own hand, hiding her rudimentary literacy from everyone. The savage flow and arched flick of Signora Quorli's cursive writing were nearly indecipherable.

She rushed up the steps to the bottega to show the letter to her father. The parchment trembled along with her body, which was shaking with rage.

How dare she address me!

"*La cagna!*" Artemisia said. *The she-dog!*

Orazio took the missive and scanned the words. "Her handwriting should be more elegant for a woman of her social station."

"Papa! I don't give a fig about her handwriting! Tell me what she says."

Orazio pinched his nose and read aloud.

> *Signorina Gentileschi:*
> *Your sordid behavior worthy only of the basest* puttana
> *has resulted in the unmerited dishonor of my husband*
> *and family. I knew you were an artist—among the filthi-*
> *est caliber of Roman society. Was it not enough to let all*
> *Rome partake in your body without tempting Signor Tassi*

and then my husband—a married man? You sully our
pope's great servant with your travesties.
    You shall be condemned by the court, the pope, and
all of Rome.
    Signora di Cosimo Quorli

Artemisia pressed her hand to her heart. She felt a stab of pain. Then a roiling rage overtook her again.

"The sordid bitch!" She hurled a pigment jar against the wall, shattering it. Streaks of madder root stained the plaster red.

Orazio said nothing. He stood up and walked to the corner where his sons stored the prepared canvases. He selected a large one and set it down on her easel.

"Paint your rage," he commanded. "Here on the canvas, Artemisia. Not on our bottega walls!"

She sat down on the stool and stared at the canvas, blank and beckoning. She remembered the previous day's testimony, Stiattesi telling the magistrates how Agostino had bragged about raping her. All Rome knew!

She closed her eyes, remembering the bloody sheets.

She stood up and walked out of the bottega, heading toward her room.

"Come back and paint!" roared Orazio. "You are a Gentileschi, not a sulking coward!"

She returned with her white bed linens in her arms. She walked to the wall and swiped the sheets across the madder red streaks, then set the bloodred bedclothes in front of her.

"I am no coward, Papa. I will paint!" she said. "Don't ever doubt it! I will paint or die."

That night, she saw only bloody sheets emerge on the canvas.

But it is a beginning.

◯◎

"Silence in the court!" demanded the grossly fat magistrate. "The court orders the youth Niccolo Bedino to approach."

Niccolo Bedino? The surly apprentice who shattered my mother's chamber pot?

The boy's filthy hair hung in his eyes. He dared not look at Artemisia. His shoulders hunched, driving his chin into his chest.

Agostino Tassi put him up to this!

"State your name and occupation for the court."

"I am Niccolo Bedino. I am an apprentice painter."

"Where are you employed?"

Niccolo hesitated. He darted a look toward Agostino. "I currently work at Maestro Tassi's behest."

"Scribe. Please read Niccolo Bedino's original deposition in regard to the Gentileschis' bottega."

"'Apprentice to Orazio Gentileschi, I worked for nearly two years in the bottega and home of the master,'" read the scribe.

What? He lasted only a week or two with us, the lying bastard!

"'I ate at their table and had a room adjacent to Signorina Gentileschi. Such filth and low morality! I've seen everything. Signorina Gentileschi had me scurrying all around Rome, delivering hundreds of love letters to her many lovers in the city.'"

Artemisia exchanged looks with Orazio. She saw the borders of his jaw tighten with rage.

"Impossible!" Orazio shouted from his cordoned area. "Liar! My daughter can neither read nor write!"

"Silence!" ordered the bald magistrate, his pate glistening with sweat. "Signor Gentileschi. You will remain silent or be ordered *fuori*!"

Orazio pinched his lips together, his nostrils flaring.

"Approach the table, Signorina Gentileschi," the magistrate said.

Artemisia's heart pounded. This testimony—untrue!—could brand her as a woman of loose morals. And her father had said she could neither read nor write. She had never shared the secret of her poor literacy skills, gained by studying the offensive poem she had learned by heart at such a tender age. It was quite useful now in testimony to deny literacy.

"Did you write these said letters?"

She shook her head adamantly. "I left the convent school at an early age in order to devote myself to painting. I am unlettered, Your Honor. This is a lie."

Thank God I never told anyone I had the rudiments of literacy.

"Bailiff. Take Niccolo Bedino to the *strappado*."

"I speak the truth, Your Honor!" Niccolo wailed as two guards hauled him off to the torture room below.

The *strappado*! Artemisia took a deep breath and closed her eyes, imagining Niccolo's hands tied behind his back with a rope. The rope would tighten and he would be hauled up in the air, suspended. His arms would rip out of their sockets as he was pulled higher.

I will be vindicated! Truth will prevail.

After a half an hour, Niccolo was brought back into court, howling with pain. His shoulders were both dislocated. His tunic was twisted as the mismatched bones strained against the cloth.

"Do you confirm your testimony, Niccolo Bedino?"

"*Si!*" said the boy. "Artemisia Gentileschi sent me delivering her dirty missives. I tell the truth!"

There was a stirring in the court. Eyes sought her out, eyes casting disgust.

The testimony was damning. Artemisia had not counted on an apprentice's devotion to his master to perpetuate such a lie.

But men would cover other men's sins.

Chapter 31
ROME, 1612

The letters kept coming. Orazio read them aloud one by one.

> *Signorina Gentileschi:*
> *Not only do you display your whorish behavior before all*
> *Rome in this trial but my honorable husband, servant of*
> *God and Serenissimo Pope Paul V, has fallen ill under the*
> *duress of the court proceedings.*
> *You Scrofulous Whore! You are to blame for my hus-*
> *band's ill fortune. May God punish your wickedness.*
> *Signora di Cosimo Quorli*

Orazio handed Artemisia the letter and went on dabbing paint on the musical score of his *The Lute Player*. Artemisia had posed for the study a few months before, though the face was not hers but that of a girl who sold bread in Campo de' Fiori.

Despite the torment of the trial, Orazio had never painted so well.

"I hope Agostino Tassi dies in the Tor di Nona," Artemisia muttered. "And descends into the blazing inferno!"

Orazio answered, never lifting his eyes from the canvas. "The demons of hell can fight over his wretched soul. Like rabid dogs in a frenzy over a rotting carcass."

He smiled broadly at his daughter for the first time in years. Artemisia knew it was because his painting was going well.

And his painting was all that ever mattered.

Even if Niccolo Bedino's lies were about to threaten his daughter's reputation, her life!

By God, the art was marvelous.

∞

"The witness is Signorina Artemisia Gentileschi, daughter of the painter Orazio Gentileschi," said the port-stained magistrate in Latin.

Artemisia approached the magistrates' dais. She felt her hands sweat, sticky and hot. She knew every eye in the courtroom was riveted on her.

She lifted her chin and looked the magistrate in the eye.

"Where do you abide?" he asked her.

"Near the Santo Spirito hospital in Sassia, Your Honor."

"At the time of the alleged rape, where were you living?"

"We lived on the Via del Corso."

The birthmarked magistrate spoke again. "So you currently live quite close to Signor Quorli . . . and Maestro Tassi."

"*Sì.*"

"We have your deposition, Signorina Gentileschi. Now we must confirm the veracity of your statements and accusations against the defendant, Maestro Agostino Tassi."

The magistrate nodded to the table. "Please sit, Signorina. You will be administered a test to ensure you are telling the truth."

I will be tested? What kind of test? Test that bastard Tassi! Why me?

A man dressed in a loden tunic approached her. Artemisia studied his face. His eyes were slits, hooded and ringed with blue circles. He betrayed not a trace of emotion. He opened a crimson box on the table and took out two thin wooden boards, not much larger than her hand, perforated with holes.

The sibille! she realized. *They think I'm not telling the truth.*

The man wove a cord through her fingers over one, under one, over one, under one, threading the cord through the perforations in the wood and around her flesh just under the knuckle bones.

He gave a tug on the ends of the cord in opposite directions. They tightened around her fingers. She felt the cord bite into her skin.

She could hear her heartbeat, thudding in her chest, ringing in her ears. There was nothing—except her eyesight—that she treasured more than her hands. Hands that created paintings, fingers that had held a paintbrush since she was a baby in a cradle.

She held her two hands, laced with fine rope, against her breast.

"No," she whispered. "Not this."

She shot a terrified look at her father. He, too, was horrified, rubbing his own fingers.

Then he nodded to his daughter, closing his eyes.

Only a few paces beyond him was Agostino Tassi. Artemisia's eyes met his. Then he looked away.

The torturer shook his head, admonishing her.

"Please focus your attention to us, Signorina," said the red-splotched magistrate. "We will review your deposition and ask you to confirm its veracity. At appropriate times, the administrator will tighten the cord to encourage truth telling."

"I told the truth. I—"

"Where were you at the time of the assault?"

"I was at our home on the Corso. I was painting a portrait of Tuzia and her sons."

"You said that Agostino Tassi entered the room unbidden?"

"*Sì.*"

The magistrate nodded to the torturer. He pulled on the ends of the cord.

She winced.

"How did Signor Tassi enter your house?"

"The masons were working on the front entry. He walked in freely."

The magistrates consulted their papers and her earlier deposition.

"Entering your father's bottega?"

"*Sì.*"

"What was his mood, his salutation?"

"Agitated. He burst into the bottega saying, 'Don't paint so much!'"

"Don't paint so much?"

"Tighten," said the fat magistrate.

She sucked in her breath against the pain and saw Agostino flinch. *You piece of shit! You don't have the torturer's cord cutting into your flesh. You flinch at the truth as if it burns you.*

"*Sì.* He snatched the paintbrush from my hand and grabbed the easel, throwing them both across the room. Then he ordered Tuzia to go."

"Go where?" asked the magistrate.

"Out of the room. *Fuori!*"

"Did Signor Tassi say why he wanted Tuzia to leave?"

"He told her he had matters he wanted to discuss with me in private."

The magistrate flicked his eyes at Tassi.

"And Tuzia obeyed him?"

"She left. She left me alone with him."

"What happened when Agostino Tassi and you were alone?"

She looked directly at Agostino. "He put his head on my breast."

All the magistrates nodded to the torturer. The cord cut. Blood seeped around the borders, thin bright rings of red where the cord cut into her flesh.

She stared, horrified, at the blood on her fingers.

No! This cannot be happening!

"Then what transpired?"

"He said he wanted to go on a walk."

"A walk?"

"Around the room. He pulled me to my feet and we walked in small circles. On the third time around we reached the threshold of my bedroom. He pushed me in and locked the door after us."

"What did you do?"

"I begged him to unlock the door. I began screaming as loud as I could for Tuzia."

"What happened then?"

"He took out his handkerchief and placed it over my mouth to muffle my screams. He shoved his two knees between my thighs and threw up my skirts. He loosened his pants and took out his *pene*."

"Did you resist?"

Her fingers were burning now, the pain enveloping her.

How far will they cut? To the bone?

Will I ever be able to paint again?

"*Sì!*" she gasped. "I fought. I scratched his face, tore at his hair. I grabbed his *pene*, digging my nails into it. I came away with a piece of his skin. But he would not stop."

"Tighten the cord," said the bald magistrate.

She thought she might cry but she did not. She sent her mind back to that dark moment in time as if she were recalling a painting in vivid detail. She closed her eyes, remembering.

"He shoved his penis up my *natura*. He kept thrusting. When he had finished his business, I saw blood on the sheets, on his penis."

"What did you do then?"

"I jumped up and ran to the table where I kept a knife. I said, 'I am going to kill you.'"

You bastards! Unloose my hand! If I cannot paint I will die.

"How did the defendant react?"

"He pulled down his tunic, showing me his breast. He said, 'Here I am.'"

"And then?"

"I charged him with the knife."

"Tighten!"

"Aaah!" The cord had cut into her tendons.

Surely I will never hold a paintbrush again!

"Continue, Signorina Gentileschi," said the magistrate with the wine-stained face. "The sooner we finish the interrogation, the sooner the cord will be removed."

Artemisia gagged. She could not stand to look at her fingers, dripping now with blood, coagulating in rivulets down her forearm.

"You!" she shouted, lifting her imprisoned fingers toward Agostino. "This is the pretty wedding ring you give me, and these are your promises!"

"Signorina Gentileschi," admonished the bald magistrate. "You will confine your testimony to our questions and not address the defendant!"

She hung her head in anguish.

"What happened with the knife?" said the bald magistrate. He withdrew a handkerchief and blew his nose, wiping it several times.

"Agostino was surprised I attacked him in earnest. He dodged my blow, so just the tip of the knife nicked him. He bled a little."

Not as much as I am now!

"He . . . Aaah! He said, 'I'm sorry.'"

"I'm sorry?"

"*Sì.* 'I'm sorry. Here, give me your hand. I promise I will marry you as soon as I get out of this labyrinth.'"

"Labyrinth? What did he mean 'labyrinth'?"

"I didn't know. I think he meant getting permission from Cosimo Quorli. I don't know."

The judges' heads were bowed, as they furiously scribbled notes.

"Did he say anything else?"

"He said he would not brag about it. That he had deflowered me. He expressed surprise I was a virgin. He said he had no idea—that the stories he had heard were that I was a woman of loose morals."

"How would he have that impression?"

She shook her head, gasping for breath through the pain. "Cosimo Quorli made up vicious lies about me. He's hounded me since I was a child. I was shut up in our house on the Corso. I never left the building without a chaperone. No male visitors were allowed in our bottega without my father being present . . . except for his two friends, Cosimo Quorli and Agostino Tassi. But only with Tuzia in the room."

The obese magistrate looked down at her. She was curled, hunched over her tortured hands.

"Signorina Gentileschi. You said you bled. But you also stated in your deposition that it was your menses. How could you tell the difference in the blood?"

"It was redder. The blood was different."

"You could tell the difference?"

"I'm a painter! I notice color. The red was different."

She didn't recognize her own voice. It was nearly a scream. A screech.

The bald magistrate made a quick chop of his hand, looking disgusted. He gathered his sheets of parchment.

"*Grazie*, Signorina Gentileschi. Release her hands. That is enough."

"No!" shouted Agostino. "Don't let her go. I want her to answer my questions!"

There was a murmur in the room as Agostino waved a sheet of parchment.

"Maestro Tassi," said the port-stained magistrate. "You may submit your questions to us. But she will be released from the *sibille*." The magistrate nodded to the torturer to loose the cords from Artemisia's hands. She brought her fingers to her mouth, sucking on the bright red wounds.

The magistrates passed the sheet of parchment among themselves.

As they read, the bald magistrate motioned to a kerchiefed servant woman who waited in the corner with a jug of wine. She bowed and silently poured red wine into cut crystal goblets for the three judges. After she had finished she stole a glance at Artemisia, bobbing her head almost imperceptibly, her hand cradling the belly of the jug.

The fat magistrate made a peevish gesture for the servant to leave.

"Signorina," he began, "these are questions submitted by the accused. You are to answer truthfully."

"Sì," said Artemisia, wincing with pain.

The magistrate began reading Tassi's questions aloud.

"'Who made you testify against me, where did he approach you, and with what words?'"

She shook her head, incredulous. Despite the pain in her hands, she drew herself up like an angry swan, staring at Agostino.

"It is truth that has induced me to testify against you. Truth alone and no one else."

The magistrate waited for the scribe to record the testimony and then continued reading.

"'Tell the truth: many men, including a cleric called Artigenio and unknown others, frequented your house, and you are warned that if you deny this, it will be proven with evidence.'"

Artemisia's face wrinkled with disgust. She shot back her answer.

"Artigenio was a friend of Tuzia and frequented her house, but did not frequent mine."

Agostino broke in. "Ask her whether she has ever done a portrait for Artigenio."

"I hear the question!" interrupted Artemisia. "Yes, I was asked to paint a portrait of him for his beloved, and I did it. I was paid well for it. What do you have to say about that?" Her eyes blazed into Agostino's.

The same magistrate resumed. "'Did your father know and did he see the said men and me when we came to your house?'"

"Artists and other men were constantly in our bottega, as we frequented theirs. I was certainly never left alone with them. My father would never have allowed it."

"'Were you left alone with any man?'"

"Only with Agostino Tassi."

The three magistrates whispered together. The port-stained magistrate nodded and took up the reading of Agostino's questions.

"'Who found out that you had been deflowered?'"

Artemisia dropped her mouth open in rage. "You, Agostino Tassi! You deflowered me! Then you told Stiattesi about it. You told him after you promised you'd never tell a soul!"

"'Were you hoping to have me as a husband?'" read the magistrate.

"I was hoping to have you as a husband, but now I don't because I know you have a wife!"

The scribe scribbled away, his quill bobbing up and down with the furious pace of the testimony.

The magistrate waited until the scribe had changed to the third sharpened quill, dipping it in the pot of ink.

"'You say you were forced to submit to sexual advances. Why didn't you make any noise? Why didn't you shout for help?'"

Artemisia looked from Tassi to the three magistrates. "Because, sirs, he gagged my mouth and I could not shout."

The fat magistrate frowned and looked back at the questions. "'With what end, with what hopes did you give this testimony?'"

"I testified with the hope that you"—Artemisia spat back, her eyes blazing into Agostino's—"that you would be punished for the wrong you did!"

The magistrate put down the parchment. "That is the end of the defendant's questions."

As Artemisia was dismissed and court was adjourned, Signora Stiattesi took her arm. "You did well, *cara*," she whispered. *"Brava."*

The two women stepped outside the Quirinale into the evening and to the waiting coach. An ill-kept woman, haggard lines on her face, approached them.

What hardship has this woman suffered to give her such a wretched look? She is either a beggar or a prostitute. But look how her eyes burn with joy.

The woman gave Artemisia a grateful curtsy before a guard shooed her off.

"We hear your words, Signorina," she called. "You speak for all of us."

Chapter 32
ROME, 1612

After the news of her rape, Orazio no longer cared whether Artemisia left the house or not. She was already spoiled goods, so what did it matter?

She stayed home for many days, nursing her wounded fingers, crying with pain and rage. But she was young and healing is a miraculous gift bestowed upon youth. The flesh of her fingers knit back together, though severely scarred. She was able to envision painting again. Her spirits began to recover, too, and eventually she felt ready to venture out into the streets of Rome.

She pulled her brown woolen shawl over her face to disguise herself as well as she could, but it was impossible to stay hidden in the market as she spoke and bartered with merchants. She heard the gasps and whispers, gossip rippling across the piazza. Artemisia lifted her head higher and moved forward through the torrent of whispers, finger-pointing, and insults.

When she reached the *funghi* stall, she breathed in the deep, earthy aroma of mushrooms, a refuge for her senses. She touched a pale morel, the puckered flesh melding into a phallic tip.

"Them's what you want to touch, a whore-woman like you!"

She spun around and saw a squint-eyed man with brown teeth. His putrid breath made her cover her nose.

"*Fuori*, you addle-brained lecher!" shouted an ancient woman's voice.

The old grandmother Chiara, the one-eyed mushroom witch, chased him off with a hard slap of a rag. "Don't pay him no mind, Signorina," she said. "He's the idiot of Campo de' Fiori."

"*Grazie,*" Artemisia said. "For chasing him off."

A shrug. "*Niente.*" Then a smile. "*Buongiorno*, Signorina Gentileschi. It has been so long since I've seen you."

"You remember me?"

"Of course I remember you. The artist!"

Artemisia hung her head and took a deep breath. "And you know of the trial?"

"Oh, *cara*! All Rome knows of the trial." She lifted Artemisia's chin with her finger and caressed her cheek with her soiled hand. Artemisia closed her eyes in bitter shame.

"Ah, Signorina. Do not mourn!"

"How can I not? Little boys call me lewd names, women shun me. Men leer."

"They are fools, cruel and ignorant. Signorina! *Ascolti.*" *Listen to me.* She stepped back a pace, tilting her head from left to right to left again, taking a good, long look with her one eye.

"I see you have a power now you did not possess before. The loss of innocence has given you a gift of strength your maiden self was lacking. I see fire and wind in you, a growing force. Ah! That I could live to see you reach the pinnacle of your gifts."

"Gifts?" Artemisia said. "My virginity was stolen!"

"And replaced with rage. Much more useful than virginity, *tesoro*!" She chuckled.

Her words were strangely comforting. Artemisia laughed in spite of herself.

"I feel a fire burning inside you," the old woman whispered, holding out her dirt-crusted palm as if testing the heat of wood embers. "It will leap through your fingers and set your canvas aflame!" Her lips tugged the wrinkles into a smile. "Let it burn, *ragazza*. Let it burn!"

Artemisia wondered if the woman wasn't as daft as the idiot of Campo de' Fiori. But her joy was contagious, a potent antidote to the lonely chasm that was her life.

"You have no idea what a vast sea you will join someday," Chiara said, picking up the discarded *funghi* that Artemisia had touched. She pinched the tip of the morel, the fleshy top breaking off between her fingers, then shook the decapitated mushroom in Artemisia's face.

Both women laughed, an uproar that rang through Campo de' Fiori. The market was bewildered by their raucous behavior—a fallen woman and an old witch, laughing at a mangled mushroom.

∞

Niccolo Bedino's testimony was on everyone's lips.

"He says she's a whore! A *puttana*—"

Artemisia walked to the window and looked down to the street.

"I don't remember the boy," said the washerwoman, shaking her head. "I took wash in for the Gentileschis on Via del Corso. No, I never saw him."

"He was there two years, they say," said Ruby, the prostitute who lived with her mother down the block. "Delivering love letters from her, all over the city."

"I don't believe it," said the washerwoman. "And I never washed no bloody sheets. No pecker tracks. The boy is lying. I'm going to say so in court, in front of the magistrates."

"She could have washed her own sheets, you know," said Ruby.

"That signorina? Ha! She's too busy painting!"

But for all the talk in the streets, all the raging opinions—those who scorned Artemisia and those who defended her—the only opinions that mattered were those of the judges at her trial.

And they seemed prepared to believe the lies.

The trial was nearing its end and Agostino Tassi was about to be released.

Niccolo Bedino's adamant testimony had condemned her. Under the assault of his vicious lies, Artemisia would be forever marked a woman of loose morals. She could never be presented at court or be commissioned by a noble family. She couldn't even earn her living painting still lifes. No one wanted the taint of a fallen woman.

Lying men had condemned her. But then, at the last minute, it was another woman who gave her a glimmer of hope. A blood relative of Agostino Tassi himself. His sister, Signora Olimpia Bagellis. Agostino had made bitter enemies of his sister and her husband by suing his brother-in-law for an unpaid debt.

Agostino Tassi's sister had his coloring—dark brown hair pulled up in a chignon, brown eyes that sparkled. In this case her eyes glittered with vengeance. She lifted her head as she walked by her brother in the courtroom, her nostrils pinched as if there were a foul odor that emanated from him.

"Do you know the witness Niccolo Bedino, Signora?" asked the bald magistrate.

"*Sì.* It was I who placed Niccolo Bedino in my brother's bottega. Signor Tassi needed another set of hands to work in the studio, to clean his house. Niccolo is devoted to my brother. I can tell you that Niccolo never worked at the Gentileschis' during the long period of time he stated. Well, he may have worked briefly for the Gentileschis—I cannot attest to that."

"Did you know your brother's home situation? Did he employ Niccolo Bedino?"

"During that time, Lent 1611, my brother was cohabitating with his sister-in-law, Costanza." Olimpia sniffed with disdain. "I remember Niccolo sleeping in the kitchen."

She shot her brother a sharp look.

Artemisia watched the exchange of venom between the two siblings. She thought about Costanza's coolness toward her.

Did Costanza have any idea that Agostino was making love to me? Did she smell me on his body?

The testimony—from his own sister—contradicted the strongest evidence in favor of Agostino. The *colpo di grazia* came from the painter Valerio Ursino, a former friend whom Agostino had double-crossed.

"Agostino Tassi is my friend," he began. "I went to visit him in the Tor di Nona. This boy, Niccolo Bedino, was there in the prison as well. I asked Agostino why he had gotten the boy to lie when everyone—artists, I mean—knew that Niccolo worked for Tassi for years."

"And what did Maestro Tassi reply?"

"He answered he had told Niccolo to tell the truth. But it was all a lie."

"How do you know?"

"We artists constantly visited each other's bottegas. I even lived briefly with Agostino during the time Niccolo was supposedly working for the Gentileschis. He was like a dog at Tassi's heels, underfoot in Tassi's studio.

"I left Maestro Tassi's cell and encountered Niccolo hanging about, as doglike as ever. I asked him why he had lied in testimony. He replied, 'If I hadn't lied, Maestro Tassi would have cast me out. He has promised me a large reward.'"

The scribe scratched madly at his parchment.

Niccolo Bedino was called back to testify.

"Lector! Please read the deposition from the youth, Niccolo Bedino."

"'I saw men—artists, models—on a number of occasions kissing and caressing Signorina Gentileschi,'" read the lector. "'Their names are as follows: Geronimo Modense, Artigenio, Francesco Scarpellino.'"

"Artigenio? Are you mad? The wart-faced priest?" said Artemisia.

"You will refrain from speaking, Signorina Gentileschi," said a magistrate. "Strike that from the record, scribe."

"'The daring and lack of morality was astonishing,'" continued the lector. "'Geronimo Modense and Artigenio touched Artemisia intimately in front of her own brothers. They said nothing.'"

I should have let my brothers beat up this liar long ago!

The bald magistrate addressed Niccolo. "Niccolo Bedino. Do you have more to add to your testimony?"

"*Sì*, your honor. Signor Tassi has told me worse things, how Signorina Gentileschi would disappear into the vineyards with strange men after church services. Signor Orazio himself asked Signor Tassi to accompany his daughter to Mass. He was distraught with her whoring."

"That's enough," said the port-stained magistrate. "Signorina Gentileschi, will you please approach."

She gathered up her skirts and walked toward the dais.

"Do you know these men mentioned? First: Signor Geronimo Modense?"

"I have heard of him. He may have been to our bottega accompanied by my father. I've never exchanged a word with him."

"Artigenio?"

"I have already testified to this. I was never alone with him."

"Francesco Scarpellino?"

"He studied briefly with my father. I was never alone with him or any of the artists who frequented our bottega. Other than Agostino Tassi."

"And the other men reputed to be your lovers?"

"I have answered these questions already! I lost my virginity to one man. Agostino Tassi. There have been none after him."

"Then you disagree with the testimony of Niccolo Bedino."

"He is a liar!"

"That is all."

But despite all the testimony condemning Niccolo Bedino's lies, his damning deposition struck hard at Artemisia's reputation. If she had acted in lascivious ways, the court wouldn't care whether she was raped or not. Rome was not in the business of protecting women.

"Tassi has paid him off!" Orazio whispered hoarsely in Artemisia's ear. "The bastard has bribed him to speak against us."

Us?

"If he did, you know where he got the money," she countered.

He shook his head.

"You know where, Papa. Cosimo Quorli!"

Orazio met her eyes. "I am a fool, daughter. Of course you are right . . . may he burn in hell!"

∽

Artemisia tossed in her bed that night, unable to sleep. She had visions of Cosimo Quorli ladling gold coins into greedy hands.

The swine! These men think nothing of accusing me. Quorli has convinced all Rome I am a whore.

A shaft of moonlight spilled from the window shutters, pooling on the tiles in striations of light.

Lead white. The color of death.

The illumination beckoned her to the window. She lifted the latch on the shutter, opening it to the night air. The moon had risen high enough to cast a milky glow over the Church of Santo Spirito. In the distance, she could make out the rim of the bell, the stones of the tower steeped in moonbeams.

Her eyes searched the rooftops, from palazzo to palazzo, stopping on Cosimo Quorli's, its tiles still dark at the cusp of the moonlight.

You haunted my mother to her grave. You won't have me, you bastard! I swear before God! I—

She jumped as the bell of Santo Spirito tolled once. Bats flew out of the tower, making errant undulations in the pale light as the single tone of the bell dissipated into the still night air.

Hours later, there was a commotion in the street. Artemisia was still in her nightclothes, washing her face over a ceramic bowl. She set down the jug and went to the window.

A bloodred sunrise colored the rooftops.

"He's dead!" shouted a boy to the night guard walking the streets.

"Who?" said the laundrywoman, poking her head out her doorway. She rested her reed-bristled broom against the stucco wall.

"Signor Quorli! He died in the night."

Artemisia clasped her wounded hands in prayer and kissed her knuckles. She made the sign of the cross and whispered, *"Grazie, Dio! O grazie!"*

At least now if she lost in court she had had a taste of revenge. Her mother's soul could rest in peace.

But if her mother's soul gained perhaps some peace from Quorli's death, Artemisia could find little peace for herself.

All of Rome knew her as a fallen woman. Every day, she could listen from the window as their neighbors and passersby reacted below.

"They are a whorish lot, those artists," said a baker's runner, his young cheeks dusted white with flour. He stuck out his lip in righteous indignation.

"They say she poses naked for her father," hissed a bearded man. "That's her you see—and her nakedness—in his paintings."

"Che schifo!" said a piss collector, overhearing the conversation. He put down his bucket half-full, the contents sloshing. *How disgusting!* Flies buzzed around a stinking open barrel in his donkey cart. He collected the contents of Sassia's chamber pots, the fetid curing agent bound for the local tanner.

"They should lock up the father and the girl both for indecency," said a laundrywoman, burdened with a basket of dirty clothes on her back. She reached up to stuff an errant sheet into the basket. "Everyone knows artists are mad and vulgar creatures."

"God's eyes are upon them," said a priest, standing nearby. "May justice be served in his holy name."

When Artemisia stepped out to go to Mass on Sunday, flanked by her brothers, her father, and the Stiattesi family, the jeering started.

"There's the whore herself," called a grizzled old woman, covered with a gray shawl. "Showing her brazen face among decent folk."

"Puttana! Puttana!" shouted two young boys, not more than ten years old.

Her brothers Giulio and Marco started to chase after them, but Orazio shouted to them, "We are going to church as a family. Stay together."

"But Papa!" wailed Giulio. "Did you hear what they said?"

"They are ignorant, snot-nosed brats," said Orazio. "Wretched urchins. Stupid as stones. Stand tall and walk on."

At Mass Artemisia felt the searing looks on her back as she knelt in prayer.

She knew Orazio was right. She could not pursue her career as an artist without marrying. In Rome's eyes she was a whore without a husband at her side.

But branded as a fallen woman—rightly or wrongly—she couldn't imagine that there was any way she could find that salvation. She had been raped by a man and he had not married her. His brutal sin was hers to bear, forever.

She could feel her life as an artist slipping away, further and further out of reach.

As she rose to her feet at the end of Mass, she felt a gentle pressure on her hand. She looked up to see a young nun, her aquamarine eyes meeting Artemisia's.

"May God bless you," she whispered, looking up under her black veil. "There are so many who walk in your footsteps, Signorina. Have courage for all of us."

The nun disappeared into the crowd filing out of the church. Artemisia did not know why, but she thought of Giovanna Garzoni. She felt a pang of shame, wondering what the young artist thought of her now.

❦

And then, as the trial was about to end, one last witness was called to testify.

She recognized him at once and gasped. The kind priest who kept pigeons. The *prete* who had heard her confession.

"State your name and occupation."

"My name is Pietro Giordano. I serve at God's will, a priest in Santo Spirito."

"We will ask you to corroborate your own deposition, *Prete*."

The round-faced priest nodded, his flaming cheeks making him look like a child.

My God! Is he about to divulge my confession? The Church will excommunicate him!

But it was not Artemisia's confession Father Pietro was about to share.

"According to the testimony you gave April 12, 1612, you stated that Signor Tassi came to you in confession a Sunday of last year, 1611."

"*Sì,*" said the priest, clasping his hands in front of him.

The room buzzed. Would this priest actually forsake his vows and divulge holy confession in front of the papal magistrates?

"And you stated that he was agitated."

"*Sì.* Signor Tassi's heart was burdened. He shared with me that he had mortal sins to confess. He had raped a young woman, deflowered a maiden against her will."

The gathered witnesses gasped. Several made the sign of the cross. Artemisia stared at the priest, dumbfounded.

This priest has shared holy confession as testimony! He has forsaken his vows.

"Could this have coincided with the date of May 6, 1611?"

"It could have been. I know it was a cold day, unusual for a Roman spring. Signor Tassi was wrapped in a long woolen scarf. He complained that his fingers were numb in prayers and wrapped them in his scarf."

"What else did he say?"

"He said that he wanted to rectify his sin. He wanted to marry the girl, but he was not sure whether his wife was still alive. He wanted absolution."

"I see," said the bald magistrate. "Absolution. That is your business, of course, *Prete*. Ours is justice."

"Did you see Signor Tassi again?" asked the port-stained magistrate.

"*Sì,*" said the priest. "He is a parishioner. I see him frequently at Mass."

"Did he ever speak to you again about his relationship with the girl?"

"No," said the priest. "But I went to see him, imprisoned in the Tor di Nona, to give him confession."

The priest closed his eyes as if balancing on a precipice and gathering courage.

"Without compromising anyone else's sacred rite of confession, I will say that I know that Agostino Tassi bribed several men to lie to this court about their relationships with Signorina Gentileschi."

The crowd in the room drew a collective gasp. Artemisia shot a look at Agostino, whose face had gone white.

Prete Pietro looked at Artemisia in sorrow, the corners of his eyes and mouth bent down in anguish. He had broken his vows, divulging the secrets of confession. He knew he would be excommunicated.

He has sacrificed himself for me. And the truth.

Prete Pietro's testimony as a priest was more damning than any other.

Artemisia drew the largest breath she'd ever taken in her life. She closed her eyes, thanking God and this lonely, magnificent priest.

Agostino—you are finished. A holy Roman Catholic priest has condemned you before the holy papal magistrates!

Chapter 33
ROME, 1612

She woke the next morning with a scorching fever to paint. Though she hadn't eaten anything to break her fast, she had no hunger—only the feel of a brush in her hand, animal hair on canvas, would satiate her.

She knew what she had to paint: *her* Judith and Holofernes. Not anything like her father's. She closed her eyes, recalling Caravaggio's composition. Her mind painted the image on the dark canvas of her eyelids. The bloody sheets, the rich fabric of the murderess's garments. To the right, the tentative Judith trying to work out the angle of the sword, her brow buckled with concentration. There in the foreground . . . the wizened Abra, Judith's servant. She looked like an ugly troll, not participating in the murder but standing ready with the sack like some beggar.

That was Caravaggio. Her composition would have the work of two strong women, united in their labor. It could not be easy to sever a neck. She remembered the Beatrice Cenci execution. Her Judith would be confident, the pressure she exerted on the hilt of the knife—a sword?—engaging every muscle. Nothing tentative about her. Abra would be young and capable, too, a partner in the bloody act. Two women knowing exactly what they were doing.

She pulled out the canvas with the bloody sheets, the one she had started the night she was so enraged. She knew exactly what she would paint without sketching or preliminary drawings. Her hand ached to create her vision.

She had to paint. She'd steal, fight, even kill if anyone got in her way.

～⊙

She didn't know how many hours had passed. The frozen moment of her painting was the only time she knew.

But her concentration was broken by the sound of voices coming up to the bottega. She recognized the voice of Signor Stiattesi.

"Pierantonio is an honorable man," he said. "He's a painter."

She heard a grumble that could only be her father's.

She quickly covered the canvas so no one could see her work and stood ready to meet them as the two men came through the door of the bottega.

Signor Stiattesi looked at her father. Orazio shrugged. Stiattesi took a deep breath and said, "Signorina, if you would consent to marriage with my brother, Pierantonio, I believe we could make arrangements for such a union to take place. If you do, you will be offered a chance to pursue your career. You could share his studio."

A studio. Not my father's bottega.

"Signor Stiattesi and I have discussed this proposal," said Orazio, folding his arms across his chest. "But there is no use in pursuing it any further unless you are in favor."

"What if I refuse?"

Orazio's eyes flashed open with joy. "You stay and work in our bottega," he said. "I have many commissions. You'll work harder than you ever have, but together we will prosper together!"

"And my work, Papa?"

Orazio stared at her, the happiness fading from his face. "Of course I will allow you some time to work on your canvases, Artemisia. But you'll have to devote the lion's share of your talent to my commissions. You have to know that Rome has a low opinion of you. I don't know how we would sell your paintings now, after the trial."

"But I was vindicated!"

Her brother Francesco had slipped in the door and now stood beside the two men, glowering at her. "You're not a virgin!" he said. "All Rome knows of your sin. Romans won't touch your work."

So my choice is to stay and work in the Gentileschi bottega to do the background and detail work for Papa? With a brother who hates me? With Rome's streets filled with gossip, leers, and dirty insults?

"Where does this brother live?" she said.

"In Firenze, Signorina."

Florence!

It wasn't her entire dream, only a broken piece of it. She felt the jagged shard, turning it over in her mind, touching its rough edges. The man would be different from her dreams—but what matter? She was an artist, an artist who would make her debut in Florence!

I've changed color and composition on a canvas many a time, scraped away original paint to create something different, something better. Why not do the same with my life?

"I should like to meet him."

Orazio drew a great breath in, making his nostrils flare.

Signor Stiattesi shuffled his feet, darting a look at him. "My brother is not a rich man," he said. "The costs of travel from Florence—"

"Artemisia!" said Papa. "There is no time for introductions, damn it. *Cazzo! Sì o no?*"

"I won't have an opportunity to meet him?"

"No! Listen, daughter—you are in a bad spot. You have been dishonored publicly. There are very few good men—perhaps none—who would consider taking you as a wife, knowing you are not a virgin."

"Papa—I have other virtues! My painting—"

"He's right," said Francesco. "You are a *disgrazia*, sister. A disgrace . . . *Vai!* Go to Florence! Leave us in peace."

"You shut up," snapped Orazio. "You aren't half the artist she is!"

Francesco's face turned scarlet, a fleck of white spittle forming at the corner of his mouth. He turned on his heel and left the room, banging the door behind him.

"He's a good man, my brother," said Signor Stiattesi, turning to Artemisia. "An artist who will understand . . . your passion! He will show you love, give you freedom to work."

"I'm guaranteed a place to paint?"

"In his studio, Signorina. At his side. He will make a place for you to paint your own art."

She half closed her eyes, imagining this.

"He will shelter you," said Signor Stiattesi. "Give you children—"

Her father grunted, shaking his head.

Artemisia had not become pregnant during the eight months of lovemaking with Agostino. She wondered if she was damaged. The bleeding.

Better not mention that now. We are bargaining.

"A painter," she said. "Is he quite good? Pierantonio Stiattesi? I've never heard of him."

"I am no judge of art," said Signor Stiattesi. He looked vaguely at his shoes.

"Hmm . . . ," she said.

"*Basta!* You act as if you are a queen, Artemisia. He is a painter," said Orazio, his face turning crimson. "Not of the caliber of a Gentileschi, but a man who is willing to take you as his wife."

Then Orazio's voice turned softer, almost pleading.

"Or you can stay in our bottega and work on my paintings, help me with my commissions. What do you say, daughter?"

All she could think of was Florence. Michelangelo, Donatello. Leonardo. Or being condemned as a fallen woman in Rome.

"*Sì,*" she said, turning back to her canvas. "I will marry this man. Now let me go back to my work in peace."

∞

For days Artemisia hardly left the bottega. Her father and brothers were still working on the Casino delle Muse, desperate to finish it under a flurry of threats from the wrathful, impatient Cardinal Scipione Borghese. She scarcely saw them at all.

One afternoon, they came home just in time to catch the last hour of sun. When they walked into the bottega, she was painting Holofernes's head.

Her father and brothers stood stunned behind her, their eyes riveted on the canvas.

"You know Rome will recognize him," said Orazio. "Even how you've disguised him, with the heavy beard."

"I won't debut this in Rome," she said, taking aching comfort in each stroke of the brush. "It is a wedding gift to myself." She laughed ruefully. "I will unveil it in Florence."

"It's brutal," said Francesco. "*Brutto!* It's ugly!"

"It's truth," she said, dabbing more red paint from her palette.

"The lighting is harsh," said Orazio. "It is not lyrical."

"Death is not a lyrical subject, Papa. Neither is rape."

He nodded. He looked at his daughter and then again at the canvas. "It . . . it reminds me of Caravaggio."

Artemisia said nothing.

Orazio approached the canvas, pointing to the bright blood on the bed linens.

"Too much?" she asked him, her brush still moving.

"Just right," he said. "For you, Artemisia. Just right. It will be a masterpiece."

Francesco said nothing, trembling with rage.

She nodded. Her gaze moved to the rendering of her victim's torso. She remembered—felt—the undulations of his muscles. She knew that body so intimately she could feel it under her fingertips. She closed her eyes and drew a breath and consulted the image on the black screen of her eyelids, reliving the moment she first saw his body naked. How the muscles and skin she had learned to caress might constrict in horror and in death, under the bloody sheets.

Ah! Sì. Like this.

Her hand reached out with power. Artemisia's power in art was telling truth.

"Caravaggio was right," murmured her father, laying a hand on her shoulder. "I should never let you paint something 'nice.'"

He studied the painting for a minute longer.

"I shall write to my friend Michelangelo Buonarroti, the Maestro Michelangelo's grandnephew in Florence."

"Oh! Papa!"

Still her father could not look away from the painting. He stroked his beard, his thumb running across the salt-and-pepper hairs on his chin. "He should know of you," he said. "All Europe should know of you, Artemisia."

She was too moved to speak. She savored the resonance of his praise, the words still echoing in her ears.

"Signor Buonarroti could introduce you to the Medici Court and Granduca Cosimo the Second," said Orazio, finally looking at her. "You deserve success, Artemisia. You will find it in Florence. I know you will succeed."

Chapter 34
ROME, 1612

She was alone, painting. There was a tap at the bottega door.

"Signorina Giovanna Garzoni is here to see you," said Signora Stiattesi. "She insists it is quite imperative she visits you. The signorina is escorted by her older brother, who will remain below in the street until after your *reunione*."

Giovanna Garzoni, the young artist whose talent Artemisia had admired—and maybe felt challenged by—so many years ago.

We were both so young and innocent then. Perhaps she still is.

"Please ask Signor Garzoni into the kitchen for a cup of wine. I shall be pleased to welcome Giovanna here."

Artemisia had received no visitors—none since the beginning of the trial eight months before. No one wanted to be in the company of a woman of ill repute.

As Signora Stiattesi descended the stairs, Artemisia looked down in the street and saw a black-haired man with a pale complexion, his long, tapered fingers wrapped around his sister Giovanna's shoulder.

So protective yet so tender.

A pang of envy seized Artemisia's heart. Except for her little brother Marco, she had never experienced such affection and chivalry.

She heard them enter at the street level, their shoes scuffing the travertine steps toward the *piano nobile.*

"Artemisia is just up the stairs in the bottega, Signorina," said Signora Stiattesi. "I shall send up some refreshments. Your brother will wait with me down here."

Artemisia heard the light step of Giovanna mounting the stairs. Her tread was as delicate as her art.

Artemisia threw open the door and embraced her.

"Oh! How you've grown, Giovanna!" she said, holding her at arm's length to see her in full. "Look at your beautiful hair, tied up like a woman's now. How glorious you are!"

Giovanna looked into her eyes, politely dismissing Artemisia's compliments.

How silly I am, gushing over her. She is an artist and has no time for pleasantries.

"I begged my uncle to let me visit you," Giovanna said. "It took some time to persuade him."

Artemisia drew in a deep breath, feeling the shame burst hot over her face. Even artists of Rome disdained her. She directed her guest to a stool by her own.

Giovanna scanned Artemisia's face, her body. She was in no rush to talk. Her eye was taking in every detail.

"I haven't changed, Giovanna," Artemisia said.

"No, you are wrong," she said, shaking her head and unloosing a tendril of blond hair.

Suddenly, Artemisia was somehow nervous, somehow afraid of the changes this young girl, this brilliant young artist, might be able to see in her face. Laughing to break the moment, she said, "Next week I will be married."

"*Cosa?* Who are you to marry?"

"Another artist. From Florence. Here, come with me. Let me show you the painting I am finishing now."

They walked over to the painting of Judith beheading Holofernes, set on an easel.

Knowing Giovanna's sensibilities as a miniaturist and a painter of still life, Artemisia expected her to recoil at the bloody scene. Instead, she bent down and inspected every inch of the canvas, every brushstroke. She walked several feet away and sat on the ground, looking like the twelve-year-old prodigy she was. She was fascinated and terrified. Artemisia loved how she let her horror show, but her artistic hunger overcame any fear.

I remember how I studied Caravaggio's The Calling of St. Matthew *with the same insatiable thirst. I was younger then than she is now.*

Giovanna sat for a long time, her legs crossed under her skirt, staring. "It is the expression I love the most," she murmured. "Judith knows just what she is doing. There is no regret—not a trace! She is as powerful as any goddess."

She nodded, as if something was settled in her mind.

"It is a masterpiece, Artemisia. *Brava!*"

After a long moment to let that statement ring, Giovanna looked up, her clear blue eyes searching Artemisia's. "I've followed every detail of the trial, Artemisia. I have suffered along with you."

No one had said that to her before. Artemisia took a deep breath, savoring Giovanna's kindness. "I thank you for your sympathy, Giovanna."

"Not sympathy, Artemisia. Empathy!" she said fiercely. "Your suffering, the injustice! How could he do—*that*—to you?" Her face contorted in anguish.

"You mean rape me?"

Giovanna covered her mouth, the whites of her eyes prominent.

The word—stupro—*tears into her breast like it did mine so many years ago.*

"I cannot rinse the images from my mind. I suffered as you suffered, Artemisia."

Artemisia knelt down beside Giovanna, hugging her, feeling the little-girl bones in her arms. "Oh, Giovanna!"

Giovanna's voice was muffled by the fierce embrace. "You've gained power through your turmoil. I see it in your face. I see it in this painting. But . . . I do not think I have the same constitution as you, Artemisia. I know I don't."

Artemisia tightened her arms for another quick hug and then sat back.

"The image of that man forcing himself on you. It—it sickens me! I've had nightmares, night after night."

"Giovanna—you are young. These things—"

"Artemisia. I—I have taken a vow of chastity."

Artemisia dropped open her mouth, astonished. "Giovanna! You aren't going to enter the convent! Not with your talent, you can't—"

"No. I have no intention of vowing chastity to the Church," she said with disgust. "I am vowing chastity—and devotion, forever—to Art."

Santa Maria!

Artemisia pulled up her skirt and crossed her legs, sitting on the cool terra-cotta floor.

"I have passion—but not like you, Artemisia." Giovanna gestured toward *Judith Slaying Holofernes.* "An ordeal like yours would extinguish that flame in me forever. I must shelter it so that I may paint. Nothing is more important to me than my art."

"Never to marry? Ever?"

"Only if my husband consents not to touch me," she said, looking at her so seriously Artemisia laughed.

"Not to touch you? But *cara,* that's what men do in marriage, what women do—"

"No!" she said, defiantly. "I have already vowed to the Holy Virgin. I cannot break my promise. I will keep myself pure for my art."

Artemisia bit her lip. *Don't argue with her! She is baring her soul. And who is to say she is not right?*

How could Artemisia confess she had learned the sublime pleasure of intimacy—the touch of flesh, the sounds, the mounting urge and crescendo? Between episodes of brutality, there were tender moments Agostino and she had shared. He made her desire other men naked and hungry for her flesh, her caresses.

Men who would love her. Men who would give her pleasure.

But not all women could survive the wounds and shame as she could.

"Giovanna—"

There was a discreet knock on the door. Signora Stiattesi peeked in.

"Forgive me for disturbing you. Signorina Garzoni. Your brother has asked me to tell you it is time to leave."

"Grazie," said Giovanna. "I will be down immediately."

The two artists picked up their skirts and stood.

"I haven't had enough time with you today, Artemisia," said Giovanna. "And I admire you more than anyone I know."

"I feel the same about you, Giovanna. I don't know what the future holds, but I feel our paths are destined to cross again."

Giovanna smiled, her soft blue eyes wise beyond her years. She cast one more look at *Judith Slaying Holofernes.*

"I am certain of it, Artemisia. Godspeed."

Chapter 35
ROME, 1612

At last, on November 28, 1612, Agostino Tassi was sentenced for the crime of rape, putting an end to the horror of Artemisia's trial. He was banished from Rome for a period of five years.

He was not sentenced to the galleys—someone powerful, perhaps Scipione Borghese, must have intervened. Being an already married man—his wife had escaped his attempt to have her assassinated—Agostino was not forced to marry Artemisia.

The punishment was issued the day before Artemisia's wedding day. A fine gift indeed.

She had yet to meet her husband-to-be. Pierantonio arrived in the coach from Florence at the northern gates, Porta del Popolo, just in front of the church of Santa Maria del Popolo, where Artemisia's mother lay buried. Pierantonio's brother, Giovanni Stiattesi, and Artemisia's father, Orazio, were waiting in the piazza to meet the coach as it arrived.

Artemisia stayed in the house, sitting on a stool in the bottega. Her hair was coiled in braids and pinned up off her neck with tortoiseshell combs. Signora Stiattesi applied a fine talc powder to make her skin even paler than it already was.

"I look dreadful!" Artemisia said, looking at her unnatural color in her mirror. "Give me a towel and let me remove the powder. It's ghastly."

"I think you look pale and beautiful," Signora Stiattesi said, biting her lip.

"Well, I don't," Artemisia said, wiping hard at her skin. "Color is my business—you've made me look like I'm dead. I certainly am not!"

When she saw the color in her cheeks emerge, she heaved a sigh. "Better," she said. "There is life in me yet!"

"*Sì,*" the signora said. "Perhaps it is better. You are a natural beauty."

"And your brother-in-law," Artemisia said. "Is he attractive?"

The signora stepped to the window to peer out. "They should be arriving any moment."

"You didn't answer my question, Signora," Artemisia said, still dabbing at her face with a towel while looking in the little mirror.

"*Sì,*" the signora murmured. "He's very attractive. He—"

"He what?"

"Perhaps he is too attractive," she blurted out. "He has quite a reputation in Florence—more for his conquests than for his art."

Artemisia put down the mirror and stared at her. "And your husband thinks his brother will be a good husband for me?"

Signora Stiattesi wrung her hands and her face flushed crimson. "*Sì.* He thinks it is the only way out for you. Otherwise, your father will swallow you up like a shark does a little fish. He has witnessed your fights and seen how Signor Gentileschi works you like a slave, finishing his own paintings. You have little time for your own. He believes you are a great artist . . . I believe my husband is a little in love with you himself," she said, turning away.

"Nonsense!" Artemisia said, seeking the signora's hand and grasping it.

"It is true, Signorina." The signora's voice was thick with emotion. "I cannot blame him. Your vitality and courage have made me love you too. I shall miss you, Signorina Gentileschi."

Artemisia thought about Signor Stiattesi's testimony and his vituperative letter to the pope accusing his cousin Cosimo Quorli.

"My husband thinks that Pierantonio will allow you to thrive," said Signora Stiattesi. "He believes that you will flourish in Florence, given his brother's connections and those of your uncle, Aurelio Lomi. You must leave Rome."

"But . . . his brother is a philanderer," Artemisia said.

The signora shrugged and looked her in the eyes. "Whose husband isn't?" she said, turning back to the window.

Artemisia thought of her father, Cosimo Quorli, Agostino Tassi, and Giovanni Stiattesi's evenings carousing and visiting the brothels.

She's right.

"Ah! There they come!" Signora Stiattesi said, looking through a crack in the canvas window covering. Artemisia leapt to her feet and craned her neck to see this man who was to become her husband.

Orazio ushered him through the principal door, and Artemisia heard their steps as they mounted the stairs up to the bottega. She heard the voice of Giovanni Stiattesi.

"He will introduce you to his brother," said the signora hurriedly, giving Artemisia an embrace. "When you are married, we will be sisters."

The door flew open and the three men entered.

Pierantonio was indeed attractive. He wore a jaunty velvet cap over his black hair. He had the sharp eyes of an artist, taking in the details of the studio before he even looked at his wife-to-be.

"May I present my daughter, Artemisia," said Orazio.

"Piacere, Signorina," Pierantonio said, bending down to kiss her hand. She liked the warmth of his hand and how his eyes lingered on the flecks of paint that still adhered to her cuticles. He smiled up at her, his hazel eyes sparkling. "Yellow ochre," he said, studying her fingertips.

"An excellent color, Signorina Gentileschi. It looks even more refined on you."

Gentileschi gold.

"Such a flatterer, *fratello*," said his brother. "You've always had a silver tongue."

Pierantonio flashed him a look. It was not necessarily fraternal love. Then he turned back to Artemisia. "I understand you are a most remarkable artist," he said. "My brother has written of your accomplishments. While he is no artist, he certainly is an excellent judge of art."

"You will have to decide for yourself," she answered.

She looked at her father, who gave a curt nod.

"Pierantonio, would you not like a glass of wine first?" offered his sister-in-law. "After your long journey you must be parched."

"Bring the wine jug upstairs, *per favore*, Signora," said Orazio. "Along with a tray of biscotti."

While Orazio addressed Signora Stiattesi, Pierantonio caught Artemisia's eye. His look smoldered with desire.

Let's see what you think of my art first.

∞

"Favoloso!" exclaimed Pierantonio as he looked through her work. "Such power!"

When he reached *Susanna* he stood motionless.

"You did this?" he said.

"I did."

He knelt and studied the details, the brushstrokes, the anguish on the face of Susanna. Artemisia saw his jaw tighten as he scanned the two lechers.

His eyes lingered on the scene.

"I want to bloody the elders' noses," he said. "Look how she suffers!"

Artemisia sensed his emotion.

"She did. She does."

He turned to her. Artemisia held her chin high. He nodded.

Perhaps he is a good painter, perhaps he isn't. But he has the sensibilities of an artist.

She felt her father's eyes boring into her, into him. She glanced away from Pierantonio and toward Orazio. His face had hardened.

Why is he angry? He brought this man—no! He bought this man to be my husband. Every penny he has or can borrow will go into my dowry to give the Gentileschi family honor. He will count out the scudi and pay this man to take me away, like an injured cow.

"Let me show you Artemisia's latest painting," said Orazio, guiding Pierantonio toward the other corner of the room. She watched how he aggressively plucked at Pierantonio's sleeve.

He whipped off the green linen draping her canvas of Judith and Holofernes.

Pierantonio gasped. His chin drew back in repugnance, his mouth puckered at the bloody sword slashing its way through Holofernes's neck.

"Emotion? *There* is emotion, Signor Stiattesi!" thundered Orazio. "That is my daughter's power!"

"Judith shows no more remorse than a butcher," said Artemisia's husband-to-be, inspecting the heroine's face.

"What remorse should she feel?" Artemisia said, moving toward them. "Holofernes was a murderer of her people. Judith had a job to do. She answered violence with violence."

"*Sì,*" said Pierantonio. "But a woman!"

"*Sì,*" she said. "A woman."

He turned back to the painting, staring. "Such power is rare." He drew a deep breath and sought her eyes. "You will meet great success in Florence, Signorina Gentileschi. They will worship you!"

Orazio glared at him.

Papa realizes he's losing me.

"Call me Artemisia," she said, extending her hand so that he might kiss it.

As she felt his warm lips on her skin, she breathed a sigh.

Yes. He will do.

⌒◎⌒

"Strap that trunk tighter, coachman! It will jostle and break the pigment jars inside."

The driver turned away from Artemisia's trunk, looking down at her. *"Scusa, Signora,"* he said, gesturing with a jab of his hand. "This is my job. I know what I'm doing."

"It doesn't look like it to me," she said, hands on her hips. "You have no idea how dear those colors are. Strap the trunk tighter, I say!"

"Do what she says," said Orazio.

The coachman muttered under his breath. He ordered his son to fetch him more rope.

"Have you heard back from Uncle Aurelio?" she asked Orazio.

"Not yet. But *Judith Slaying Holofernes* should have arrived by now. He'll waste no time in delivering the painting to the Medici Court."

She pressed her lips tight together. Orazio had decided that *Susanna and the Elders* cut too close to the truth of her rape. Instead he had sent the powerful painting of Judith severing the head of the Assyrian general Holofernes.

"Will the *granduchessa* like it?" she said, her brow puckering. "It's rather strong."

"Of course it is. It's your work, Artemisia. It makes no difference whether Cristina di Lorena likes it or not. It will be your introduction to her son, the Granduca Cosimo. He has an eye for great art, like his grandfather."

"And Maestro Michelangelo Buonarroti?"

"He is expecting you to visit his palazzo. Remember—Via Ghibellina in Santa Croce. Write him as soon as you arrive."

Artemisia looked past her father's shoulder. A knot of women of all ages had gathered silently a few dozen paces from the coach. She recognized the herb-stained hands of the midwife, the sweet but sad face of the nun, the beggar woman who had approached her carriage one night as she left the trial.

There were others she did not recognize. They watched wordlessly as Artemisia prepared for the journey to Florence.

The coach driver approached them. "Will the signora do us the honor of climbing into the coach," he said, wiping the sweat from his brow. He gave an exaggerated bow as if she were royalty.

Artemisia raised her eyebrow, sensing sarcasm, but saw he had tied another rope crisscrossing taut over her trunk. She nodded in satisfaction. *"Piacere,"* she said.

Pierantonio took her arm and helped her into the coach.

"You take good care of her, Signor Stiattesi," said Orazio.

"I shall, Maestro. I know she is a treasure."

"That signora can take care of herself," the coach driver said. *"Molto brava!"*

Orazio's eyes shimmered. He pulled out a white kerchief Prudenzia had embroidered for him years ago. He wiped his nose.

Two children, a boy and a girl, whisked by him, chasing pigeons like Artemisia used to do as a child on this very piazza. Orazio stared at them and back to his daughter.

His face buckled with emotion.

He walked up to the side of the coach, where she had settled into her seat. He climbed up onto the carriage step, his fingers clutching the rim of the window inches from her face. His nails were chipped and curled, yellowed with turpentine.

"Artemisia. This isn't how I had planned it," he said, his voice a hoarse whisper.

"But this is what it is," she said. She put her hand on his. "Like a powerful painting that forces your hand. Life has its own destiny."

"My daughter! What talent you possess—"

"You live in my blood, Papa. You'll see. I'll make you proud."

"Forgive me. If only your mother were still alive, I wouldn't have made the mistakes—"

"Perhaps neither of us would have. Be well, Papa. I love you."

"Thrive, Artemisia," he said. "Show them—"

"Signor Gentileschi. We are ready to depart."

Orazio let himself down from the coach. He hunched his head, sobbing into his handkerchief. The two children stopped their play and looked silently up at him. The pigeons fluttered back down to the ground in their eternal search for food.

The women raised their hands, bidding farewell. Some hands high, some low and timid. A few folded in prayer.

Still the women said nothing but watched in respectful silence.

The driver clucked to the horses and the wheels jolted forward. Pierantonio reached out his arm, protecting Artemisia from tumbling out of the seat.

She patted his hand. "*Grazie*, Pierantonio," she said. "But it is not necessary, *cara*. I'll be all right."

They pulled away from the Piazza del Popolo, from her mother's grave, from her desolate father, out through the northern gates.

Toward Florence. Toward her future. Toward the dreams that she had forged long ago and never surrendered.

As long as I live I will have control over my being. No man will determine my destiny.

The coach's wheels churned up powdery dust, coloring the wilted grasses along the road.

Gentileschi gold.

Author's Note

Artemisia Gentileschi went on to paint masterpieces for the Medici Court in Florence, making her name known throughout Europe. Her technique, reminiscent of Caravaggio's, was greatly admired, as was her passion as an artist. She was the first woman to be admitted to the distinguished Accademia delle Arti del Disegno in Florence.

Her work was sought after by royalty. She painted commissions for Cosimo de' Medici, Philip IV of Spain, the Duke of Alcalá, and Michelangelo Buonarroti the Younger (grandnephew of the great Michelangelo). In 1638 Artemisia joined her father, Orazio, in England at the court of Charles I.

She met her friend Giovanna Garzoni in Venice in 1628 and helped her to secure a position in the Duke of Alcalá's court in Naples in 1630. (The Duke of Alcalá may have been Artemisia's lover.)

Artemisia had at least four children but only one daughter survived to adulthood, joining her mother's studio as an artist herself. Pierantonio Stiattesi proved to be an unfaithful husband but Artemisia appeared to flourish despite his infidelities. She took several noble lovers of her own over her lifetime, though she never divorced or remarried. She continued to have enormous success with her painting.

Her literacy improved over the years. She was a prolific letter writer but committed grammatical and spelling errors, betraying her lack of formal education.

Her final stage in life was spent in Naples, where she ran a thriving studio. Her death was sometime around 1656. There is some speculation that she died in the plague that swept through Naples at that time.

Artemisia Gentileschi was an extraordinary woman, not only for her own time but for all time.

Historical Note

Record keeping was often spotty in the seventeenth century, a compilation of baptisms, taxes, and court records. As a result, I have had to make some decisions based on the best information available.

The various buildings the Gentileschis lived in are long gone, and their exact locations are virtually impossible to nail down. Street numbers were not commonly used for addresses and some street names have changed over the past five hundred years. (For example, Via Paolina is now called Via del Babuino.)

I have relied on R. Ward Bissell's excellent work *Artemisia Gentileschi and the Authority of Art: Critical Reading and Catalogue Raisonné* to provide general guidance as I described where the family lived in Rome.

In addition, I have made some slight changes in dates (paintings, for example) in order to maintain the narrative flow of the novel.

The often brutal trial of Maestro Tassi on Artemisia's charge of rape was conducted in a number of different locations, according to Bissell's research. For the sake of continuity and clarity for the reader, I have condensed my trial scenes to a single location.

For readers interested in the life and accomplishments of Artemisia Gentileschi, I recommend exploring the fine historical documents, books, and museum catalogs that I mention in my acknowledgments.

Also, London's National Gallery will feature a special exhibit of the work of Artemisia beginning April 4, 2020 and running through July 26, 2020.

Acknowledgments

In writing this novel I researched voraciously, hungry for any detail I could find about the life of Artemisia and also about her father, mother, brothers, and fellow artists. Having read dozens of books and articles on Caravaggio before dipping into Artemisia's world, I was well acquainted with seventeenth-century Rome via fine books such as *A Life Sacred and Profane* by Andrew Dixon and so many others in my research for *Light in the Shadows*.

Artemisia Gentileschi: The Image of the Female Hero in Italian Baroque Art by Mary D. Garrard, Princeton University Press, was of great value, especially for its inclusion of the English translation of the trial proceedings. (I compared this to the Italian original.)

Also the Metropolitan Museum's and Yale University's publication *Orazio and Artemisia Gentileschi* by Keith Christiansen and Judith W. Mann helped me enormously, particularly in comparing the father's and daughter's styles of art and development.

Roberto Longhi's book *Gentileschi Padre e Figlia*, published by Abscondita, was also helpful, as was *Artemisia Gentileschi: The Language of Painting* by Jesse Locker.

The story of Artemisia's friendship with fellow artist Giovanna Garzoni came from reading R. Ward Bissell's suggestion of the connection between the two painters. His book *Artemisia Gentileschi and the Authority of Art: Critical Reading and Catalogue Raisonné* helped me understand their relationship.

A special note of thanks to Dr. Sheila Barker of the Medici Project in Florence. I appreciated her scholarship both in articles and as editor of *Artemisia Gentileschi in a Changing Light*.

Another extremely useful publication by Abscondita was the combined verbatim record of the trial, *Precedute da Atti Di Un Processo per Stupro* combined with *Lettere (Letters) of Gentileschi*. These writings were curated by Eva Menzio.

The two works of fiction I most admire on the subject of Artemisia Gentileschi are of course Alexandra Lapierre's *Artemisia*, a grand historical study and novel rolled into one, and *The Passion of Artemisia* by Susan Vreeland, a slim, beautiful book. I think it is interesting to note the differences and similarities in how we authors brought Artemisia to life in our respective novels. Each of us employs a distinctive palette in painting our hero. I owe much to these two women authors who have gone before me.

In Colorado: Thanks to the usual suspects, including my sister, Nancy Lafferty Elisha, who has always believed in me, despite many rejections and failures. Others who have helped along the way are Sarah Kennedy Flug, Natasha Riviera, Emily Longfellow, Sandy MacKay, Dave Mortell, Bridget Strang and the Strang Ranch, and Maree McAteer, among others.

Special gratitude to Italian native Lucia Caretto, who helped me many days on translating documents, Italian text, and trial proceedings. She is a dear friend and gives her time generously.

Thanks to the city of Rome and its exquisite 2016–2017 exhibition of Artemisia's paintings. I spent many hours and several visits studying Gentileschi's masterpieces at the Palazzo Braschi at the Museo di Roma. An opportunity of a lifetime!

In Florence I was able to see a combined show of Caravaggio's followers, including works by both Orazio and Artemisia Gentileschi. Also

I saw firsthand some of Cecco's work in the Uffizi. Walking the streets of the Santa Croce neighborhood, I dreamed of Artemisia's footsteps approaching Michelangelo Buonarroti the Younger's palazzo, where she painted the glorious *Allegory of Inclination* installed in the ceiling of Casa Buonarroti.

Special gratitude to my perspicacious developmental editor, David Downing. Thanks, David, for your partnership. Your guidance served me well.

In editing a historical novel I believe copyeditors have to work overtime. They must question all the facts and dates for historical accuracy. Then they must be able to bend the rules when a novelist has intentionally compressed time, moved scenes, and shuffled ages or chronological order to make a story flow. My thanks to Kelley Frodel and Ramona Gault, who have ticked all those boxes with aplomb. Appreciation to Emma Reh, who coordinated the editing process.

Proofreading is laborious and meticulous work. My profound gratitude to Nick Allison.

Thank you, Senior Editor Erin Calligan Mooney at Lake Union, who orchestrated the publication of this book.

A cover design synthesizes the essence of the novel to give readers a clue about mood, tone, and contents. It is a delicate art when practiced well. Thank you, Jeff Miller at Faceout Studio.

As always, thanks to my agent, Deborah Schneider, who has believed in me and supported my work for such a very long time.

Special gratitude to my champion at Lake Union, editor and publisher Danielle Marshall.

And to all the Lake Union team!

About the Author

Photo © 2017 Andy Stone

Linda Lafferty is the author of *The Bloodletter's Daughter, House of Bathory, Light in the Shadows* (with Andy Stone), *The Girl Who Fought Napoleon*, and the Colorado Book Award winners *The Drowning Guard* and *The Shepherdess of Siena*. Her books have been translated into ten languages. She holds a doctorate in bilingual special education and taught in Spain for three years. Lafferty is also an avid equestrian and horse lover.